The Little Theatre on the Seafront

KATIE GINGER

HQ
An imprint of HarperCollins*Publishers* Ltd
1 London Bridge Street
London SE1 9GF

This paperback edition 2018

First published in Great Britain by
HQ, an imprint of HarperCollins*Publishers* Ltd 2018

Copyright © Katie Ginger 2018

Katie Ginger asserts the moral right to be
identified as the author of this work.
A catalogue record for this book is
available from the British Library.

ISBN: 9780008310141

MIX
Paper from
responsible sources
FSC™ C007454

This book is produced from independently certified FSC™ paper
to ensure responsible forest management.

For more information visit: **www.harpercollins.co.uk/green**

Typeset by Palimpsest Book Production Ltd, Falkirk, Stirlingshire
Printed and bound in Great Britain by
CPI Group (UK) Ltd, Melksham, SN12 6TR

Prologue

To my dearest girl,

What a wonderful life we've had together, my darling Lottie. I'm so sorry that I'll miss so many things, such as seeing you get married and have children, but my time has come and I'm off to see your granddad. It's been a long time since we last saw each other so we should have a lot to talk about, which will be a pleasant change from our married life together.

With all this death business I've been thinking about you and what you'll do after I'm gone, and I've decided something – you need a shake up, my girl!

I love you, dear, but all you do is go to work, come home again, and that's it. You're thirty years old and you should be doing more with your life than spending your evenings with a little old lady like me.

If you remember, I have tried to get you enjoying life a bit more, but to no avail. Last year I set you up with that lovely handsome window cleaner, but you didn't bat an eyelid. In fact, I'm not entirely sure you even knew what was happening. And then there was that time at Christmas, when I tried to get you to go to your school reunion ... but you stubbornly refuse to enjoy anything that takes you out of yourself and out into the world. To be frank, dear, it's no way to live.

So, I've decided that a bit of emotional blackmail is in order. And

1

as spending your evenings fussing over me won't be an option anymore, you're going to take over my place as chairman of Greenley Theatre and carry on my, dare I say it, good work, on the 'Save Greenley Theatre' campaign.

Think of it as one of those New Year, New You, type things!

Good luck, my dear. I know you'll make me proud.

Lots of love,

Nan

P.S. I haven't actually arranged this with the committee yet so that will be your first job. Have fun!

Chapter 1

Lottie waited outside her house for Sid, her colleague and best friend, to pick her up. She checked her watch and rolled her eyes. He was late, as usual. In all the years she'd known him he'd never been able to get anywhere on time – even primary school. After five more minutes of shuffling to stay warm she saw his battered old car round the corner and hid the box behind her back.

'Here you go,' she said as she climbed in.

'You got me an Easter egg,' Sid replied, smiling. It was an *Incredible Hulk* one.

'I couldn't resist.'

'Me neither.' He handed over a large posh box.

Lottie giggled and had a quick look at the huge milk chocolate egg covered in a white chocolate drizzle. Her mouth began to water. 'You're the best.' Sid's grin grew wider. Lottie tucked the egg down by her feet while Sid tossed his onto the backseat where it was cushioned by a mound of rubbish and they headed to the first job of the day.

Lottie leaned forward and peeked at the picture on his top. 'Don't you think that T-shirt's a bit off for meeting an old lady?'

Sid pulled it to his nose and sniffed 'What's wrong with it?'

'I don't mean it's skanky. It's the picture.'

'What's wrong with the picture? Dragon Slaying Vampires are a great band.'

She raised her eyebrows. 'I'm not sure a half-naked woman with enormous breasticles, standing on top of a dragon's severed head in a giant pool of blood, is really appropriate for an octogenarian. Do you?'

'Oh,' said Sid. 'I suppose not.' He shrugged. 'I'll keep my jacket on.'

'Yeah, good luck with that.'

Sid was the reporter on the *Greenley Gazette* and Lottie was his photographer. Over the years they had covered every sort of local issue from the first day at school to hardcore crime and had learnt that old ladies over the age of seventy love to have the heating on. And it was already turning into a surprisingly sunny February day.

Lottie peered up at the clear blue sky and soft white clouds overhead. She loved living in Greenley-On-Sea, especially on days like this. The sun shone brightly, and the air was crisp and clean carrying a hint of salt from the sea. The streets were full of children on their way to school, laughing and giggling at what the day might hold in store.

'You were late again,' she said, teasingly.

Sid pointed to two takeaway cups in the cup holders. 'I stopped to get coffee.'

'Aww, thanks.' She sipped the skinny mocha savouring the tang of coffee and sweet hit of chocolate, then removed the lid to swipe up some of the whipped cream.

'I have no idea why you have it made with skimmed milk and then put cream on top.'

'Because,' said Lottie, popping the lid back on, 'I can convince my brain that whipped cream is mostly air and therefore has no calories and skinny milk is mostly water, so really, it's not that bad for me. In fact, on a day like this it's actually good for me. I'm hydrating.'

Sid's deep set hazel eyes under slightly too bushy eyebrows looked at her sceptically. She'd known him all her life and he knew her better than anyone else in the entire world, especially since Elsie, her nan, had passed away just after Christmas. She felt a familiar stab of grief tighten her throat but pushed it down. 'Do you want to have lunch at mine today?'

'Have you got any decent grub?'

'Sidney Evans, you only ever think about your stomach.' Lottie smiled and considered the sparse remains in the fridge. 'Beans on toast?'

'Yeah, alright.'

They were now in the posh part of town where old white Georgian houses with large sash windows lined the roads, but before long they would be out the other side back to the normal houses. 'So who's this old dear we're seeing this morning?'

He bobbed up and down in excitement. 'Mrs Harker and her opera-singing parrot.'

Lottie stared. 'Opera?'

'Yep.'

She blinked. 'Oh.'

'I know. I love my job,' Sid replied, beaming as if it was Christmas.

Sid parked the car in front of an ordinary mid-terrace house. A neat front garden with a small path led them to a plain white front door. Lottie climbed out first. 'I think I'll get a photo of Mrs Harker outside holding the parrot. It'll be a nice juxtaposition of the ordinary and the extraordinary.'

Sid tutted. 'You take this all far too seriously sometimes.'

They walked to the door and Sid gave a cheerful knock. A petite woman in her eighties wearing a floral dress and long beige cardigan opened the door. 'Good morning.'

'Good morning, Mrs Harker. I'm Sid Evans, from the *Greenley Gazette*, and this is my photographer, Lottie Webster.'

'Come in, won't you?' asked Mrs Harker, leading the way.

5

Lottie followed Sid into the porch and was immediately struck by the heat. It was like having a boiling hot flannel shoved on her face. She looked at Sid and grinned as a redness crept over his cheeks. It was going to be fun watching him cook, a little bit of payback for last week when they'd done the weekly shop together and he'd kept secretly adding things to other people's baskets. She'd giggled at the time but it was quite embarrassing when he got caught. Of course, he'd come clean and charmed his way out of it while Lottie hid at the end of the aisle, peering round from the pick 'n' mix.

As they entered the living room, Lottie slipped her coat from her shoulders and spotted a cage with a bright red parrot perched inside. The bird didn't move and for a moment, Lottie worried it was stuffed. It wouldn't be the first time they'd interviewed a crazy person.

'I understand,' said Sid, 'that you have a very unusual parrot, Mrs Harker?'

'Oh, yes, Mr Neville is very talented.'

'Mr Neville?' repeated Sid. Lottie recognised from the twitch in his cheek a grin was pulling at his mouth.

'Yes, Mr Neville's my parrot. He sings Tosca.'

Sid nodded. 'And can we see this talent in action?'

Lottie readied her camera as Mrs Harker approached the CD player and switched it on. The music started and Mr Neville, as if by magic, came to life. He opened his wings and rocked on his feet as he screeched in unison with the music. Lottie lifted her camera and took some shots. Calling it singing was going a bit far, but it was certainly entertaining. A moment later, Mrs Harker switched off the music and Sid conducted the interview.

'Well, thank you very much, Mrs Harker,' he said when he'd finished. 'That's quite a parrot you've got there.'

'He's great, isn't he?' she replied, opening his cage to take him out. 'Did you want to take your coat off, young man? You look a little bit hot.'

'No, thanks. I'm fine,' said Sid, wiping his top lip.

Lottie repressed a laugh.

'I was so sorry to hear about your grandmother passing, Miss Webster,' said Mrs Harker.

Lottie paused as a shiver ran down her spine. 'You knew my nan?'

'Yes, dear, I went to school with her and we played bingo together for years. She was a lovely woman.'

'Yes, she was.'

'It was wonderful what she was trying to do for the town, she was always working hard to make a difference. Such a shame she never quite got the theatre going again.'

Lottie opened her mouth, but nothing came out. Grabbing the bottle of water Sid offered, she took a big drink.

'Did Mrs Webster talk much about the theatre?' Sid asked. He must have seen her impression of a goldfish and stepped in.

'Oh yes, she had grand plans. Elsie was going to make it like it was when we were young. Get the community involved again. I think that was where she met your granddad, Miss Webster.'

Lottie's eyes darted to Mrs Harker's face. She had no idea that was why the theatre meant so much to her nan. From the depths of her mind she remembered Elsie telling her the story. How she spotted him from across the aisle and that was that. Love at first sight. Lottie had responded by saying how lovely and picking up her book, burying herself in another time, another place. She bit her lip feeling ashamed.

'All the bingo club were behind her, you know. Johnnie, the caller – the guy who calls out legs eleven and two fat ladies, and all that – he said that we could move back there when Elsie finished renovating it.'

Lottie tightened her grip on the water bottle and swallowed. She needed to get outside into the fresh air. 'I think, Mrs Harker, it would be a lovely idea to get a picture of you and Mr Neville in front of your house, if you don't mind?'

'Not at all, dear,' she replied, admiring Mr Neville and stroking his feathers. 'Are you sure you're alright? You look quite pale.'

'Yes, I'm fine, thank you.' Lottie's voice was high and squeaky. Her hand shook as she clicked the camera, but finally, after a few attempts, she had the shot.

Sid escorted Mrs Harker back to her door and said goodbye as Lottie climbed into the car and pulled another bottle of water from her camera bag. She watched Sid remove his jacket and move round to the driver's side to get in.

'Okay, you were right,' he said, wiping his forehead with the back of his hand. 'I was absolutely roasting in there. Why do old dears always have the heating on? I mean, I know it's still chilly, but come on.' He looked at Lottie, his furrowed brow accentuating his crooked nose. 'Are you alright?'

'I am now I'm out of there.'

'Was it the bit about your nan?'

Lottie stared at him in disbelief. 'Of course it was! I wasn't so impressed by an opera-singing parrot I nearly fainted.'

'Alright,' he said sarcastically. 'I was just checking.'

Lottie pushed a stray lock of hair behind her ear. If Sid wasn't so genuinely clueless when it came to women she would have been cross with him. 'Sorry. I know I'm being unbearable at the moment.'

His cheeky grin returned. 'That's okay.'

'It's just that, I knew the theatre meant a lot to Nan, but I ...'

'What?' asked Sid, softly.

She shook her head, unable to steer her brain into forming a sentence. A familiar wave of grief and sadness washed over her, tinged with panic and fear at what she was being asked to do.

'Listen, Lots. I know you don't want to deal with your nan's letter but I think we have to. You can't keep ignoring it.'

Elsie's final gift to her hadn't been at all what Lottie had expected and she had no idea how to deal with it. 'There's nothing to talk about, Sid. I'm not doing it and that's final.'

8

'But, Lottie, your nan must have thought this was what you needed. You can't keep shoving your head in the sand and pretending it never happened.'

She crossed her arms over her chest. 'Yes, I can.'

'No, you can't.' Sid ran his hand through dark curls that maintained a stubborn unruliness no matter how short they were cut. If Sid was her type – which he wasn't – she might have thought him handsome in a geeky way. 'I'm not trying to annoy you.'

'I know you're not. You don't need to try.' She gave a weak smile.

Sid started the engine and began to drive off. 'But why leave you a letter? Why not just ask?'

Lottie shrugged. 'Nan knew full well that if she asked me face to face I'd tell her to bog off.'

'And stomp off out of the room,' he said teasingly.

She turned to him and widened her eyes in fake surprise. 'I don't do that.'

'Yes, you do.' He smiled. 'But it's fine, I don't mind. I just don't understand what you're afraid of.'

Lottie opened her Easter egg and broke off a piece of chocolate, waving it in the air as she spoke. 'Oh, I don't know, making a fool of myself in front of the entire town, letting Nan down, everyone laughing at me.'

'No one would laugh at you, Lottie.'

'Despite what Nan thinks—' Lottie felt her heart twinge, the words catching in her throat. 'What Nan thought, I quite like my life.'

Sid looked at her sceptically. 'You like being safe, Lottie, that's not the same thing.'

'But what if I take over the theatre and make things worse?'

'How can you?' Sid glanced at her quickly before turning his eyes back to the road. 'What could you possibly do to make it worse? Burn the place down? Blow it up? You're not planning on blowing it up, are you?'

Lottie scowled.

'Oh, I know,' he continued in a mocking tone. 'You're going to run National Front rallies, or host puppy kicking competitions?'

'No, but—'

'It's a small local theatre for a small quiet town. Not a top notch, swanky London showbiz place.'

Lottie cocked her head and broke off another piece of chocolate. 'But I don't know how to do this.' Her voice was rising and she pulled it back. It wasn't Sid's fault. 'I'm not a project manager, I have no idea how to be a chairman and do chairman-type things. And, I know absolutely nothing about theatres.'

'But you are ridiculously bossy.'

'No I'm not, I'm just … organised.'

Sid's face broke into a wide grin and he grabbed her hand, giving it a squeeze. 'You can do this, Lottie, I know you can. Just give it a chance.'

Lottie ate another piece of chocolate.

'The thing is, Lottie,' he continued, 'your nan was right. You do need to get out more. I mean, when was the last time you had a boyfriend?'

'When was the last time you had a girlfriend?' she countered.

'It was 2003, but this isn't about me.'

Lottie repressed a smile. 'You were twelve in 2003.'

'Yep, but I'm perfectly happy with my life; you're not and you haven't been for ages.'

Lottie folded her arms over her chest. It was true. She had been feeling restless for a long time now. But when her nan became ill, she'd retreated even further into her safe, quiet life. It wasn't that she didn't like people, she did. She'd just never quite got around to getting a social life, that was all. 'What's your point?'

'I think if you stopped looking at everything so negatively you'd see this could be good fun.' Sid was always trying to chivvy her up.

Lottie toyed with her camera, opening and closing the lens, her mind racing. 'I've got to do this, haven't I?'

'We have,' said Sid, smiling at her. 'I'll be there for you.' He stopped at a junction. 'Shall we head to yours now? We can have lunch and start coming up with a plan to get you on the committee.'

Lottie checked her watch. 'It's only half eleven.'

'I know, but I'm starving. Please?' He stuck his lower lip out just as her stomach rumbled.

'Alright then. Just for you.'

Chapter 2

Lottie had lived in the same house all her life. As a diplomat, her father worked all over the world and in the beginning, when he was posted to the back of beyond, her mother had stayed at home with Lottie. But when Lottie's father was posted to Vienna, a city her mother longed to visit, she declared herself allergic to parenthood and departed with him for health reasons. Lottie's nan had stepped in and it had, for the most part, been a happy and harmonious relationship.

The house sat on the brow of a hill with views of the sea and steep steps leading up to the front door. There was no front garden to speak of, just a tiny square of grass with soil too chalky to grow anything pretty. Blue paint peeled from the front door, stripped off by the salty sea air, leaving patches faded to grey and exposed bare wood. Lottie thought it was beautiful, like a piece of art.

They mounted the steps and Lottie found her keys to let them in. Sid, who was as familiar with the house as she was, marched through the dark hallway into the living room, slung his jacket onto the back of the sofa, then sat down and put his feet up on the coffee table.

'Oi! Get your hooves off,' ordered Lottie, following him in. 'Nan never let you do that, so don't start now.'

He huffed and removed his long gangly legs. 'So, what's the plan, Stan? How are you going to get on the committee?'

Lottie dumped her bag on the sofa and flopped down too. 'I guess I'll have to tell the committee the truth. Maybe show them the letter?'

Sid nodded.

'But that isn't going to guarantee anything, is it?' Lottie thought out loud. 'I think the mayor is acting chairman at the moment. He stepped up when Nan got sick and he didn't like her anyway so he could easily say no. I think her constant campaigning over one thing or another got under his skin.'

Sid shook his head. 'Nah, it would look too bad. How could he say no to a lovely old lady's final request? But you still need to show you're up to the job. I think you should give them an action plan or something. At the very least give them some ideas for what you could do to make it popular again, or get more funding.'

'A presentation?' asked Lottie, her voice shrinking. She hated speaking in front of people. Public speaking was as scary to her as wearing a bikini.

'What else are you going to do?'

Lottie thought for a moment but couldn't come up with a better idea. 'Okay then. But I've got no qualifications, or experience that'll help in any way.'

'That doesn't matter,' said Sid, cheerfully. 'Just talk about how you're going to make it successful. Be positive.'

'And how am I going to do that?'

Sid scratched the back of his head. 'I don't know. What plans did your nan have for the theatre?'

'I don't know actually. I guess I could read through Nan's stuff and see if there's anything in there?'

Sid stretched out his long arms then rested them behind his head. 'When's the next committee meeting?'

Lottie went to the dresser, pausing as her eyes scanned the photos of her and her nan together, and searched through the pile of letters. She found the boring black and white newsletter and read the dates. Her face froze. 'Oh, shit, it's next Thursday.'

'Oh dear,' replied Sid. 'We'd better get cracking if we've only got a week.'

Lottie groaned and trudged over to a stack of boxes at the back of the living room. The house remained untouched since Elsie's death and her possessions were everywhere. Though Lottie had tried several times to get rid of things, each time her sorrow had taken over and she'd stopped.

'Aren't we eating first?' asked Sid, concerned. 'I'm starving.'

'Can we get started with this lot and then eat, please?' Lottie's new diet only allowed twelve hundred calories a day and if she ate lunch too early she'd be an angry maniac by dinner time, raiding the fridge, or eating cornflakes straight from the box. And she'd already eaten half an Easter egg in the car.

'Okay,' he conceded, pretending to be huffy. 'Got any biscuits to tide me over?'

'In the tin.' Lottie grabbed a large cardboard box with 'Save Greenley Theatre' written on the side. Sid moved the coffee table so Lottie could drag it between them, then she sat on the floor, cross-legged, and removed the lid. A mass of papers slid out and Lottie groaned in response.

'I'll make tea, shall I?' said Sid and headed off to the kitchen. When he returned a few minutes later with two steaming mugs, Lottie was surrounded by mounting piles of paper, the box not even half empty.

'Look at this,' said Lottie, handing a theatre programme to Sid. 'It's really professional. I thought it would all be black and white photocopies or printouts that someone did at home with crappy clip art.'

'And look at the list of names for the am dram group,' he replied, nodding in agreement. 'They had quite a big cast. Sometimes you get people playing loads of parts, but it must have been quite popular.'

Lottie picked up a dozen more and waved them at Sid. '*A Midsummer Night's Dream, Hamlet, King Lear* ...'

'Who knew Greenley loved Shakespeare?'

'Here are the Christmas ones. Oh look, this one is so pretty.' She shoved a programme for *Aladdin* into Sid's face. Lottie gazed at the window seat, her favourite spot in the house, and the light pouring in chased a memory in her mind. 'Do you know, I think I remember Nan taking me to a panto when I was little.'

'So do I, actually. And we went in Mrs Thompson's class in primary school, do you remember?'

Lottie tried to picture the day Sid was talking about. 'Just about.'

'You must do,' said Sid, smiling at the memory. 'Ben Humphreys wet himself because we wouldn't stop for the toilet and that horrible Reece called him Potty Poo Pants for the rest of the trip.'

'Oh yes, now I do.' Lottie laughed and then, picking up another bundle of papers, groaned again.

Sid scowled. 'Can you stop making that noise, please? It's like a cross between a stroppy teenager and a dying cat.'

'Sorry.' She cupped the mug of tea in her hands hoping the warmth would make her feel better. 'It's just that I always assumed the theatre was just another one of Nan's causes. She was always on one crusade or another.'

'She did love this town. What's that lot?' asked Sid, pointing to a different bundle of papers before taking another sip of tea.

Lottie rifled through. 'It's the minutes from the committee meetings.' She skimmed a couple. 'There's loads of good ideas in here from Nan and they're all vetoed.'

'Like what?'

'Like starting a youth theatre, or asking local businesses to fund some of the renovations in exchange for their names on the brochures.'

'Not bad,' replied Sid, leaning forwards. 'Who vetoed them?'

'The rest of the committee.'

'And who's that?'

'Umm …' Lottie flicked through the pages. 'There's Mayor Cunningham, but it just has him down as a committee member. It doesn't look like he's there in his official capacity, just a normal person.'

'A normal person in Greenley?' asked Sid.

'Well, relatively normal.' It was true that Greenley had more than its fair share of eccentrics. 'The secretary's Sarah Powell, and the treasurer's Trevor Ryman. There's some spare seats too.'

'Well,' said Sid, sitting back. 'Mayor Cunningham probably wants to be chairman to sell the land to a developer. He did that with the hospital, didn't he?'

'Oh yes. Everyone was campaigning to save it and he and his council cronies pushed through the sale before anyone could do anything about it.' Lottie tutted. The whole town had felt hood-winked and her nan had been apoplectic with rage.

'And Sarah Powell works in my doctor's surgery,' Sid carried on. 'She's fancied Cunningham for years so she's always going to vote the same way he does.'

Lottie's eyebrows knitted together. 'In this day and age? What a wimp. Who's Trevor Ryman? Does he own the solicitor's in town?'

'Ryman, Wayman and Galbraith? Yeah, his dad set it up and he took it over when the old man retired. I remember covering it. They gave him a carriage clock.'

Lottie laughed. 'A carriage clock?'

'I know, shocking, isn't it? The poor man built the business up from scratch, worked there for fifty years and his idiot son gives him a carriage clock as a retirement gift.' He shook his head. 'Terrible.'

Lottie took a swig of her tea and held up the papers. 'Listen to this: "Proposal by Elsie Webster to bring back amateur dramatics group to get the community involved and raise much needed funds, vetoed by committee due to lack of funds for marketing.'"

Sid sat quietly squinting which normally meant he was thinking. 'Now, there's an idea.'

'What?' asked Lottie. Sid's ideas could be either fantastically clever or completely bonkers. You were never quite sure what you were going to get.

'Marketing. We could run an ad in the paper.'

'For the am dram group?'

'Yeah. Why not?' Sid was full of excitement, talking quickly. 'That takes care of the marketing costs so they won't be able to say no. And it'd be a huge step to bring back the Greenley Players. We'll do an article and include a picture of you.'

'Me?' Lottie asked, her eyes wide with worry.

'Yes, you. You're going to be the new chairman. We need a picture of you and one of Elsie, giving her a really lovely tribute. That'll get everyone going.'

'No way,' Lottie said, re-fastening her long blonde hair into a ponytail, even though it was already perfect.

Sid shook his head in disapproval. 'Come on, Lots. I don't know why you think you're some ugly troll that should live under a bridge somewhere.'

'Fat, ugly troll to be precise,' she said, tidying the papers on the floor.

'You're impossible, you really are. You're not bad looking at all, you're …'

Lottie started at the compliment and looked up to see Sid had turned a violent shade of red.

'I'll make some more tea,' he said and, grabbing up the mugs, hurried from the room.

Lottie heard the kettle boiling in the kitchen and considered what Sid had said. Not the compliment, that was just too odd to think about, but the idea of free marketing was a good one.

The pictures on the dresser caught her eye again as if Elsie

17

was watching her. If she was going to try and do this, she wasn't going to fail at the first step. Lottie went to the hall and pulled her laptop from her bag, came back to the sofa and sat with it on her knees. When Sid returned, his face fell. 'What? We need to get started on my presentation straight away.'

'But can't we have lunch first?'

Chapter 3

Sid walked through the town heading for his favourite record shop. LPs, it seemed, were making a comeback. There'd been a time when his nerdy hobbies had been laughed at, but now it was cool. The collection he'd inherited from his parents – a weird mix of Motown and prog rock – must be worth a fortune now. Not that he'd ever sell.

A smile spread across his face as he thought of Lottie. He'd asked her to come into town as it was the weekend and they weren't working, but she'd refused saying she was busy practising her presentation for the board. At last there had been a break-through. If only he'd been able to break through to her heart, but he knew deep down he'd missed his chance.

After two previous attempts in their early twenties – one at a New Year's Eve party when he'd tried to kiss her and ended up kissing the top of her ear, and another when they'd had a few too many watching a movie and after an odd surge of adrenalin, Sid had decided he'd declare his feelings, then bottled it – he'd realised he was well and truly in the friendship zone.

Neither episode had ended well. He'd been left red-faced and embarrassed, making jokes and laughing it off and Lottie had gone into hiding for days. Then when they'd finally seen each other again both pretended nothing had happened and the awkwardness had eventually faded, leaving them back where they'd started.

If he was honest with himself, which up until lately he'd avoided as much as possible, he'd always thought that somehow, at some point, he and Lottie would end up together. One day something would happen to force them both into realising they loved each other. Because he did love Lottie. For him it had always been more than friendship but she just never seemed interested in anything else.

Sid blamed his love of movies for all his years of being single. He'd always hoped that one day UFOs might land in Greenley or the Zombie-Apocalypse would descend and after he'd beat off a horde of flesh-eating zombies with nothing but a severed leg, Lottie would fall into his arms, kiss him and cry, 'Oh, Sid, you saved me!' If that had happened everything would have been alright, but strangely it hadn't, and he'd missed his chance.

Sid shoved his hands in his pockets. No, the window of opportunity had closed and now he was destined to be Lottie's friend for the rest of their lives. He lifted his head; had someone just called his name?

'Sid?'

Looking over his shoulder, he saw a woman of startling gorgeousness running towards him. Her long brown hair bounced behind her and her smile was warm and friendly. He vaguely recognised her but couldn't place her. Surely he wouldn't have forgotten a girl who looked like that?

'It is Sid Evans, isn't it?' she asked, a broad smile on her face.

He knew he was staring and made an effort to close his mouth. 'Yeah, it is. Umm, hi.'

'It's Selena. Selena Fleming. We went to uni together. Do you remember? We were in the same halls in first year and then I was constantly at your house because you guys had a garden?'

Sid reached back into the depths of his mind. He could

remember a sullen goth emo girl with large boobs and chubby cheeks called Selena. He'd seen her a lot as she was dating one of his friends, but this couldn't be her. Could it? She looked like a personal trainer or something. 'Did you date Hayden Lukas?'

'Yeah! I'm surprised you recognised me. I've changed a bit since then.' She flicked her hair back behind her shoulder.

You're telling me, thought Sid. The Selena who stood in front of him now was tall and slim. Or at least she appeared taller. She wasn't hunched over with long hair falling into her face, being angsty and deep.

'I used to dye my hair black and wear that awful heavy eyeliner.' Her eyes dipped down, embarrassed. 'It does nothing for me.'

'I remember you now,' Sid said with a grin. 'You were one of the grammar school girls from here, weren't you? You and – oh, what's her name ...' He shook his head, he'd forgotten her as well. 'You both ended up at Greenwich.'

'Shelly Spicer.'

'Yeah. She was horrid. She always thought she was better than everyone else.'

Selena smiled and leaned to one side, jutting out her hip. 'She was a bit mean. Do you remember you played me The Cure that night at Hayden's birthday? I'd never heard them before but I thought that song was brilliant.'

'Do you still like them?' he asked, hopefully.

'Only that one song, but ever since you played me Pink Floyd I've been a huge fan of theirs.'

Sid beamed. 'Really?'

'Yeah.'

It was better than nothing. Sid rocked on his heels searching for something to say. He was normally very good at conversation and if she'd been a little old lady with an opera-singing parrot he would have been fine, but Selena had the biggest brown eyes he'd ever seen and they were staring at him so intently he'd almost forgotten his own name. 'So what are you doing back here?'

She tucked her hair behind her ear. 'I've moved down here for good. I was living with a boyfriend up north but we split up and so I've come home.'

'Oh. Sorry to hear that.' He pushed his hands deeper into his pockets unsure what else he could do with them.

A faint redness had come into the apples of Selena's cheeks during their awkward silence. 'So what are you doing now?'

'I'm the reporter on the local paper.'

'Oh my God! Really?'

'Yeah. It's not as exciting as it sounds though, Greenley's not really a hotbed of crime and passion.' Sid felt his cheeks burning. Why did he say passion? 'Umm, what about you?'

'I work at the beauty salon over there.' She pointed to a shop with a large pink sign over the door that read *Indulgence Spa and Boutique*. 'I sort of flunked my communications degree. I was too busy partying with Hayden, so I retrained in nails and beauty and I love it. I love making people feel good about themselves. Seeing the smile on someone's face when they've had their nails or brows done and they feel a million dollars, it's really nice.'

It was a nice sentiment and Sid found his respect for her growing. Who'd have thought the sullen, sulky student he'd known would have turned out like this? 'I'm glad you've found something you like doing.'

'Do you like being a reporter?'

'I do actually. I like Greenley too.' He peered around at the old-fashioned High Street dotted here and there with trendy bars and posh cafés. Normal run of the mill chain stores mixed with strange, quirky independent shops and they even had a little seaside museum.

Sid knew he should say something else – ask her a question or start a new conversation – but his mind was too busy shouting 'GIRL!' at him and he couldn't think straight.

Selena glanced away as the conversation lulled again, then looked back up at him. 'You haven't changed much.'

'Haven't I?' He ran a hand over his chin, wishing he'd shaved. Was that a good or a bad thing? 'Neither have you. I mean, less make-up, obviously, but you know … you don't look older.'

Selena giggled at his fumbled compliment. In James Bond movies he always said things like, 'You're a beautiful woman,' but Sid worried he'd sound like a weirdo stalker if he said anything like that. Or that he was taking the piss.

'Well, I'd better go,' Selena said, checking her watch. 'I've got my first client at ten. You didn't mind me saying hi, did you? It's just that I saw you and I couldn't believe it was you. I couldn't let you go without saying something.'

Sid shuffled, trying not to smile too much. 'No, I didn't mind. It was nice to see you too.'

'I'll probably see you around then?' She stared up at him from under long thick eyelashes.

'Umm, yeah. Probably.'

'Okay.' She edged away still staring at him and Sid couldn't figure out why. 'Bye.'

Sid gave an awkward wave then shoved his hand back in his pockets. 'Yeah. Bye.'

Selena swung around and headed back to the shop and Sid looked down to find what she'd been staring at. His *Star Wars* T-shirt was clean on this morning and his flies were done up. Weird.

He walked on to the record shop. Selena Fleming had looked a lot different without all that weird make-up and she and Hayden clearly hadn't lasted. It was strange how people always ended up coming home to Greenley. Sid quickened his step and thought no more of it. Nick at the record shop had put aside a rare album for him so he'd better hurry. He was due to open at any minute.

Chapter 4

In her living room, an hour before the committee meeting, Lottie paced back and forth, forcing her nerves down until finally, she lost the battle altogether. Unable to bear the ticking of the clock and its agonising countdown any longer, she grabbed her coat and car keys and headed off. Now here she was, twenty minutes early, sitting in the main meeting room clutching her laptop, waiting for the rest of the committee to arrive.

The grand, grey stone columns of the town hall belied its rather dull interior. When the mayor was appointed, he'd refurbished it to make it a modern conference space, and as such it had lost all character and historical importance. No one used it for conferences. The only people who used it were the camera club and they hated it – and him. They never failed to tell Lottie when she covered their exhibitions or the annual general meeting that took about ten million hours and made her long for death.

Earlier that week, Sarah Powell, the committee secretary, had been less than helpful when Lottie tried to have her presentation added to the agenda, telling her that, 'Only the chairman can approve last minute additions and Mayor Cunningham is a very busy man.'

After much negotiation, Ms Powell said she'd do her best to

contact Mayor Cunningham and would let Lottie know the result. When she called back, she said with evident disdain that Mayor Cunningham had graciously made room for her on the agenda. Yippee.

In the harsh fluorescent light, Lottie took her nan's letter from her handbag. Seeing the fragile spidery handwriting, it felt like she was there speaking to her. 'I hope you know what you're doing,' Lottie said to the letter before refolding it and putting it back.

'Miss Webster?' asked Mayor Cunningham as he marched into the room. He was a tall man in his late forties. His balding hair had been cut close to his head, but the remains of a small island on the front of his forehead bobbed in a sea of pink flesh. It was slightly triangular shaped as if it stayed there pointing to where the rest of his hair could be found, hiding at the back. His suit was a good fit, but the cheap fabric shone in the unforgiving light, like he'd been sprinkled with glitter. An evil Liberace. Ms Powell followed close behind, a puppy at his heels.

'You only needed to come for your agenda item, Miss Webster. You didn't need to attend the whole meeting.'

'Oh, sorry,' said Lottie. She felt her neck and cheeks get hot. This wasn't a good start.

'I'm surprised that Ms Powell didn't tell you that.' Mayor Cunningham walked to the head of the table and placed his black briefcase down, unclipping the shiny brass clasps. It popped open and he pulled out some papers organised with various coloured Post-it notes.

'I did,' Ms Powell replied quickly.

'I don't think you did,' said Lottie.

Ms Powell's eyes shot to Mayor Cunningham, fearful of disapproval.

Lottie felt her nerves rise up and she cleared her throat. 'I have a presentation on my laptop. Is there a projector?' Presuming one would be all set up she began to panic at its absence. Lottie wasn't technically minded and the prospect that should one be found she'd have to set it up herself caused her stomach to churn.

'Ms Powell will set it up for you, if you really require it.'

'I do,' Lottie answered, trying to sound confident. Mayor Cunningham turned to Ms Powell and without speaking pointed to a cupboard in the corner of the room and she hurried to follow his unsaid instructions.

There was something quite unlikeable about Ms Powell, Lottie decided. She had the walk of someone who was perpetually neat and tidy and very, very efficient. Her face, which could look kindly if relaxed, was pinched and her eyes looked out at the world suspiciously. She appeared to have no sense of humour whatsoever. A perfectly smooth chin-length bob framed her face accentuating her small features.

As Lottie struggled to connect the relevant wires to her laptop, Trevor Ryman ambled in. He placed his own briefcase on the floor, brown this time, and battered, and pulled out his bundle of papers, bereft of even a single Post-it note.

'Shall we begin?' asked Mayor Cunningham, just as Lottie finished fiddling. She sat listening to the other agenda items with more interest than she'd expected. The theatre had a small fund that wasn't nearly big enough to do all the work required. The building was structurally sound but needed the roof patched up and the inside needed general refurbishment before any productions could be put on. It wasn't looking good.

'As I've said before, it's more work than a small committee and our town council can handle,' said Mayor Cunningham. 'I do believe the land would be better sold to provide more affordable housing. We may have to cut other services if we don't make our budget this year and we don't want to be the ones responsible for that.'

'I agree,' said Ms Powell, nodding.

'I see what you mean,' said Mr Ryman. 'But I do feel we need to explore all options before we throw in the towel.'

'I don't see why. No one in this town would bother coming to a production, even if we could put one on,' Mayor Cunningham replied.

Lottie, who was busy making notes in her pretty notebook, raised her head. 'I disagree. I think people would come—'

'Miss Webster, with all due respect this has nothing to do with you.'

But it might, thought Lottie, and carried on. 'But look at these.' She pulled out the programmes her nan had kept over the years and laid them on the table.

'May I remind you, Miss Webster, that you are not a member of this committee and are here for one item only.'

Lottie simmered with annoyance but continued on regardless. 'I realise that, Mayor Cunningham, but I think we need to acknowledge that the nearest theatre is over an hour away. I think people would come to local productions if we had decent facilities and a good programme. That's why my nan never stopped working towards re-opening the theatre, she believed it too.'

Ms Powell stared at Lottie as if she had just walked up to Mayor Cunningham and punched him in the face. Mayor Cunningham stared at her too, unspeaking. Mr Ryman picked up the programmes and flicked through them. 'There does seem to have been an appetite for the theatre at one point.'

'But that was years ago,' said the mayor, throwing the leaflet he'd picked up back into the pile. 'Before on-demand TV and Netflix.'

'Still, there might be an interest now.'

Lottie couldn't help but nod. 'The Christmas pantomimes were particularly well attended, and the summer Shakespeare. I thought we could look at doing something more modern. Something easier to understand that would appeal to even more people—'

'Moving on,' said the mayor, looking down at his agenda. Then his face fell. 'Oh, Miss Webster, I see it's your turn, anyway. And you'd like to address the committee in Mrs Elsie Webster's place?'

'Yes, I would,' she said. The moment had finally arrived. Lottie stood and clicked on her presentation. It projected onto a pull-down screen at the end of the table and she slid her notes out of her folder. A surge of nerves threatened to loosen her fingers but she held firm and began.

'As you all know, my nan passed away about two months ago.' She swallowed down the lump in her throat and took a deep breath. 'On the day of her funeral, I was given a letter she wrote to me a few days before she died asking me to take over her place as chairman of the committee. I know you've been acting as chairman since her death, Mayor Cunningham, and I'm sure Nan would say you've done a wonderful job,' she lied. 'But she's asked me to take over now and try to continue her work.'

Ms Powell and Mr Ryman shuffled in their seats, glancing at Mayor Cunningham. Deep wrinkles showed on his forehead as he scowled and a muscle twitched in his jaw. 'I don't think protocol allows for someone to just take over another's seat, Miss Webster. Particularly that of chairman, which is an elected position. I'm sorry, but it can't be done.'

Despite Sid's reassurances, Lottie had worried Mayor Cunningham would say no. As all her fears threatened to be realised she dug deeper, unwilling to let her nan down.

'How do we even know you can cope with the responsibility?' asked Ms Powell, snidely.

Lottie's fingers tightened around her notes. She could put up with a lot of things, but being patronised by a woman who made puppy dog eyes to a man like Roger Cunningham wasn't one of them.

'I didn't think you would let me take over, just like that,' said Lottie. 'Which is why I've prepared a presentation of some ideas I've had. I think they could really get things moving again.'

The smug smile disappeared from Ms Powell's face, the mayor twisted his cufflinks, and Trevor turned over a sheet of paper and readied his pen. 'Please go on.'

Lottie stood a little taller and opened the first slide on her presentation. 'The first thing I was going to suggest is bringing back the amateur dramatics group.'

Ms Powell's head popped up at the mention of the amateur dramatics group and she watched Lottie with eager eyes. The ends of her razor-sharp bob swished around her chin until the mayor glared at her and she looked back down at her notes. Lottie knew she had her own faults but at least she didn't have a crush on a complete douchebag like Mayor Cunningham.

'As you can see from the programmes in front of you and the images on the screen from the *Gazette* archives, the group was very popular and had lots of members. It put on at least two productions a year.' She looked up to see all eyes focused on her and swallowed, feeling the butterflies jiggling in her stomach. 'From my research and the old accounts books I found, events were very well attended.'

'And how to do you propose to do all this, Miss Webster, as we have such limited funds?' asked the mayor.

'And no money for advertising,' added Ms Powell.

Lottie imagined how wonderful it would be to smack Sarah Powell in the face with her folder but instead smiled sweetly at them both. 'I work for the *Greenley Gazette* and they've kindly agreed to run an advert for members of the amateur dramatics group. Free of charge, of course. It'll start this week if you agree.

'This will raise much needed publicity for the theatre, which I understand has been a problem for some time.' Lottie congratulated herself on sounding like a grown-up professional type of person.

A blotchy redness crept up the mayor's neck.

'I like this idea,' said Mr Ryman. 'Free of charge advertising can't be turned down.'

Mayor Cunningham steepled his fingers like a Bond villain. 'And what happens if no one is interested?'

'Then I guess we'll know how the community feels about the

theatre,' answered Lottie, feeling her shoulders sag. But then she remembered Sid's words to be positive and lifted her head. 'But if it is successful, we can work with the group to bring the theatre back to life and plan a production.'

Mayor Cunningham scratched the small triangle of stubbly hair on his forehead. 'Are you aware of how much work is needed on the theatre, Miss Webster?'

'Only what's been covered in the minutes. I haven't visited the theatre myself yet, but, of course, I've seen the outside.'

'Well, I can tell you it's a lot.'

'And there are mice,' said Ms Powell.

'Mice?' Lottie imagined them putting on their own production, all lined up on the stage wearing top hats and waving canes in perfect choreographed unison. She bit her lip, trying not to laugh.

'Yes, but,' said Mr Ryman, shifting in his seat to lean over the table, 'if this is successful, we could then look at community funding. Maybe a bid to the Heritage Lottery Fund? I know the council can't afford to run the place anymore and I've said before there are avenues we haven't explored. We could follow the marketing campaign with an appeal.'

Lottie smiled at him, thankful for a possible ally.

Mayor Cunningham eyed Mr Ryman as if he wanted to stab him with his pencil but Trevor didn't notice, or at least, didn't care. The mayor said, 'Perhaps we should put your taking over as chairman to the vote. It is an elected position after all.'

Lottie's stomach lurched. Mr Ryman seemed like he would vote for her but if Ms Powell did vote the same way as Mayor Cunningham, the numbers were against her. Lottie decided on a last-minute attempt to convert Sarah Powell to her side. 'Can I just say that the *Greenley Gazette* will be happy to follow the story with regular articles and advertising space. Free of charge, of course.'

David, her editor, hadn't actually said that but there was little else to print these days and she was surprised at how much she wanted this now. She met the mayor's steely gaze and carried on. 'If your objections are lack of funds for advertising, then that's already covered, and there's a guarantee of more to come.'

Ms Powell looked up and Lottie was sure there was a flicker of agreement in her small eyes.

'Miss Webster—' began the mayor.

'Hang on,' said Mr Ryman, cutting him off. He turned to Mayor Cunningham. 'I don't think a vote is required. Whilst seats on committees aren't usually hereditary, I do think the request from the late Mrs Webster makes this an unusual circumstance.' He leaned in and with a lowered voice said, 'We wouldn't want the *Greenley Gazette* reporting anything negative, would we?'

Lottie opened her mouth to tell him that she'd never be so underhanded when he turned to her and gave her an almost imperceptible wink.

'I suppose you're right, Mr Ryman,' said the mayor. He turned to Lottie. 'It would only be right to honour the wishes of our dear Elsie. May I suggest, though, that we reassess the situation once the auditions have taken place and we're aware of the community's response?' He glowered at Ms Powell.

'Agreed,' Ms Powell answered and Lottie wondered if there had been a note of uncertainty in her voice.

Mr Ryman nodded.

'Your title will therefore be Acting Chairman, Miss Webster, until this trial period is over.'

Lottie nodded in agreement. It was as good as she was going to get.

'Meeting adjourned then.' The mayor stood up, shoving his seat back. He pushed the papers into his briefcase and luminous Post-it notes flew onto the floor. Ms Powell followed him to the door chattering in his ear.

Mr Ryman lingered behind the others as Lottie switched off her laptop and began to unwrap the mass of cables that had somehow twisted themselves around each other. 'I'm very sorry that your nan passed away, Miss Webster. My condolences.'

'Oh. Thank you.' Lottie kept her eyes down, worried they would fill with tears as her body relaxed with relief.

'She was a very energetic and likeable woman,' Mr Ryman continued, trying to catch her eye. Lottie hoped he would get the hint that she didn't want to talk about this right now.

'Yes, she was.'

'I attended the funeral you know?'

At this Lottie looked up. She hadn't recalled seeing him there. 'Did you?'

Mr Ryman gave her a warm and friendly smile. 'I thought it was a lovely service. I guess I'll see you at the next committee meeting then.' He held out his hand, and she gave it her strongest shake.

Lottie remembered Sid telling her about the carriage clock and she felt like she'd misjudged Mr Ryman. Perhaps he was just rubbish at buying presents.

'Can I just ask,' said Lottie, releasing his hand, 'why has the theatre sat empty for the last few years? Why couldn't my nan make any progress?'

Mr Ryman studied the clasps on his briefcase before looking up. 'Your nan tried everything she could to get things going again. To begin with, the committee kept changing and no one could agree on a way forward and then, when the mayor joined the committee, people started leaving and it dwindled to just us. He can be quite … negative sometimes. And forthright.'

Lottie nodded as a smile crept over her face. 'I did get that impression.'

Mr Ryman tucked his briefcase under his arm. 'Well, goodnight then. See you next time.'

'Yes, goodbye.'

Lottie sat down in the empty room and exhaled a long, deep breath. For the first time all day she could breathe properly. Her nan had brought her luck tonight, Lottie could feel it – she was definitely watching. The tension in Lottie's neck and shoulders had given her a headache, but at least now she could go home, have a glass of cold white wine and relax in the bath. There was just one thing she needed to do first. She grabbed her phone and dialled Sid's number.

'So, how'd it go?' he asked with a mouthful of food, probably peanuts if she knew him at all.

Lottie slumped backwards and laughed with relief. 'I only went and pulled it off, didn't I?'

Chapter 5

Sid watched the credits roll – everyone else was leaving but he knew to hang on. He'd seen enough of the Marvel films to know there was a secret scene after the final credits, a bit of a teaser for the next movie and all those other people were going to miss it. Ha! Idiots.

He sat back eating the last of his popcorn as he watched, excitement building in his stomach. It didn't disappoint. But then he realised it was actually quite depressing, he was going to have to wait ages for the movie to be released. Still there was the new *Batman* film coming out soon and he and Lottie were going to see it.

Once the lights had come up he brushed the popcorn from his chest and peered down at the piles scattered around his feet. Using his foot, he pushed some in front of the chairs next to him. He wasn't trying to make more mess for the nice guys who worked there, he just didn't want them knowing that all of it was down to him. In his defence though, hand to mouth motor skills were quite difficult in the dark.

Sid grabbed his coat and made his way out into the foyer, giving a double take when he saw Selena standing with a group of friends. They were all as glamorous as she was with perfectly coiffed hair and matching outfits. One girl even wore a miniskirt even though the weather was cold and damp. He didn't know people dressed up for the cinema. What was the point? It was dark and everyone's eyes were on the screen.

Selena glanced over. She wasn't wearing a miniskirt like her weird friend, just normal jeans and a T-shirt. It was a bit tighter than Lottie wore hers but still nice. Her hair was tied up in a strange, sprouty bun thing on the top of her head but it suited her, and her dark eyes were studying him. All the roundness her face had carried in their youth had gone and she now had delicate cheekbones. Selena smiled, said something to her friends and made her way over to Sid. 'Hi again.'

Sid nodded and shoved his hands in his pockets. 'Hi.'

'Did you enjoy the movie?'

Sid's expression grew serious as he considered. 'Yeah, it was good. A bit slow in the beginning but once it got going it was fun. Did you?'

'Yeah.' Selena bit her bottom lip. 'But we only came for Chris Hemsworth. Well, they did.' She pointed to her friends.

'Oh, right.'

She chuckled. 'I did enjoy it though. Like you said, a bit slow at the start but it got better. Did you watch the secret scene?'

Sid's eyes widened, surprised that she knew. 'Yeah. Did – did you?'

'Always!' She gave a big grin and something happened to Sid's heart. 'So many people don't know about it. It makes me laugh when they get up to leave as soon as the credits start and look at me like a weirdo for staying put.'

'Me too! Do you come to the movies a lot?'

She nodded making the sprouty bun thing wobble. 'When I can. I like a good action film. I'm not keen on all those depressing artsy type things designed to make you bawl your eyes out.'

'Me neither,' he said and could feel the silly grin on his face pulling at his cheeks. Sid scratched his head, urging himself to

35

think of something to say. He loved movies, she loved movies, surely he could think of something.

'Where are you off to now?' Selena asked inching forwards. Sid was grateful he hadn't had to think of something. He'd have probably sounded stupid or said something pointless.

'Just home.'

'Oh, and where's that?' She edged closer.

'One of the flats on the seafront.'

Her eyes opened wider. 'In one of those nice old houses?'

'Yeah.' He registered the surprise on her face. 'I came into some money and bought one when housing prices were still low.' God, he was talking about housing prices. He sounded like an old man. He'd be talking about pensions next, or rheumatic joint pain. A wave of heat ran up the back of his neck and he placed his hand there, hoping to stop it.

'Does it still have all those fancy period features?'

He pictured his flat. Underneath the piles of clothes he dumped on the floor and the mass of rubbish he hadn't cleared up yet, there was probably something there. There was definitely an old Victorian fireplace in the living room, though at the moment it was full of video games. 'Yeah, it's got a few things like that.'

'I'm impressed.' Then her face clouded over. 'I've had to move back in with my mum and dad at the moment. But hopefully it won't be for long.'

'I'm sure you'll be fine once you get back on your feet.'

'Thanks.' She smiled at him and Sid felt a burning in his lungs. One of the girls Selena had come with called her name. She spun back to Sid and though he wasn't sure, her expression seemed like she wanted to stay. 'Sorry. I have to go.'

'Oh, alright.'

'Did you want to come with us?' she asked, looking him straight in the eye. 'We're going to that nice bar on the High Street. The girls want to dance.'

Sid couldn't think of anything he'd like to do less except for maybe clean his flat. He wasn't a dancer. His signature move was more of a lunge. And he'd be the only guy amongst a load of fashionable, glamorous girls. Some blokes liked that sort of thing but to him it was like asking if he wanted to swim naked with sharks with a T-bone steak tied to his neck. 'Umm, no thanks,' he said, hoping she wouldn't take offence. 'But you have a nice time.'

'Okay.' She went to walk away then turned back rifling in her bag to pull out a pen and a tiny notebook. 'Look, here's my number. We could meet for a coffee or something some time and chat about the old days.' She wrote it down then tore out the piece of paper and handed it to him.

'Yeah. Sure, that'd be nice.' His stomach wriggled in a weird way that was both pleasant and unpleasant at the same time.

Selena left, glancing over her shoulder as she went, and Sid walked out unsure if his legs were actually moving or if he was being wheeled along by some supernatural force. His heart gave a pang and the fleeting thought of, 'If only it was Lottie,' ran through his head. No. That ship had sailed long, long ago. The thought of trying again with Lottie and it being another awkward and embarrassing moment that could potentially ruin their friendship forever made him squirm. No way. It wasn't worth the risk. But he wouldn't tell Lottie about Selena. Not just yet. She had enough on her plate and besides there wasn't anything to tell.

The grin on his face returned and hurt his cheeks. He examined the number in his hand. A girl as gorgeous as Selena had given him her number. And she remembered the music he'd played her at uni, and she even knew about the secret scene. He was the luckiest man in the world. But then his elation fell away to be replaced with panic as he contemplated the number again. What the hell was he supposed to do now?

Chapter 6

The wind blew stronger on Greenley seafront than Lottie expected even though it was spring and sunlight pierced through the gathering clouds, bouncing off the sea. She wrapped her coat around her. She liked spring weather, it was easier to dress for than summer when clothes revealed so much flesh. Big jumpers and coats hid her flabby upper arms and were far more comfortable.

Lottie's nan could never understand her self-consciousness, believing Lottie was just big boned. She'd always had puppy fat but unlike most of the girls in her class at school, Lottie's had stayed stubbornly in place past adolescence and long into adulthood.

Sid waved as he drove past, then parked down the street and climbed out. 'Morning,' he said, crossing over to join Lottie opposite the theatre where she stood gazing at it.

The Victorian building had a square front of grey stone, with two tall oblong windows either side of a majestic revolving door. The boarded-up windows were decorated with scrawls, spray painted swirls, and a useful list of expletives. The revolving glass doors, most of which were broken, were sheltered by a faded blue domed canopy, and at either end of the building, a rotting wooden frame encased an old, tattered, water-stained poster. The once bright colours paled to a sad, washed out hue.

Sid pointed to the wall. 'Donna's well liked, isn't she? Very popular with the boys.'

Lottie followed his gaze and laughed. 'It is beautiful, isn't it? Even in this sorry state.'

'It is, actually. Do you know, I never really appreciated it until now. It's been closed up for so long, I've just got used to walking past it.'

'It's such a shame.' Lottie was beginning to see why it had meant so much to her nan and could imagine it in its heyday all those years ago. She snapped another couple of pictures. She'd always had a fascination with old abandoned buildings and had taken quite a few photographs of the various ones around town over the years. There was something about how the light played on them creating shadows and stark contrasts, emphasising the desolation and loneliness of these old places. She'd always planned to turn them into an exhibition but had never quite been brave enough. Maybe she should start an Instagram account or something?

'"Jez woz ere",' Sid read. 'Clever.'

'Bloody idiots. Haven't they got something better to do than write all over lovely old buildings?'

'Obviously not.' Sid took out a packet of crisps from his backpack and opened them. Before he could say anything more an enormous seagull swooped down and snatched the bag, making him scream. It flew to a nearby roof and bashed the packet down until it gave way and the contents spilled out.

'Did you see the size of that thing?' asked Sid, breathlessly, his face frozen in panic. 'It's a monster.'

Lottie burst out laughing, doubled over.

'It's not funny. I could have died.'

'Oh, Sid. You should have seen your face.' She screeched, giving a quick impression, then descended into hysterics once more.

Sid bent forwards with his hands on his knees still trying to calm down. 'But look at it. It looks like it's been drinking protein shakes from the sports centre bins. That's not normal. Seagulls shouldn't be the size of small aeroplanes.'

'Sid, stop it.' Lottie wiped the tears from her face but continued laughing as she spoke. 'Right, now I've calmed down a bit I'll get the outside shot as the weather's nice. I don't like the look of that rain cloud.' She nodded to the sky over the sea where a band of dark grey cloud threatened to envelop the town.

'Okay, I'll wait for you.' Sid finally stood up and adopted his usual stance of hands in pockets, leaning against the back of a bench.

After taking the pictures, Lottie and Sid crossed the road and walked to the door. The clouds had quickly blown in and spots of rain began to fall. The rain gathered pace and Lottie pulled a heavy set of keys out of her bag and tried to find the one for the front door.

'Come on, Lots, we're getting soaked.'

'I'm trying. There's like a million keys on here.' She examined them individually and found the right one. Pushing the glass door with her fingertips in case it smashed to pieces in her hand, they edged inside as it revolved to the sounds of rusty gears and grinding metal.

'Wow,' said Sid, walking in and placing Lottie's camera bag down on the floor. Lottie brushed the rain from the sleeves of her cardigan and inspected the interior.

Inside was a small square balcony higher than the theatre floor. On either side, a few steps led down to where row upon row of seats lined up in front of the stage. A deep crimson carpet, discoloured and threadbare in places, echoed the faded grandeur of the exterior. It was an unusual layout which Lottie felt gave the place even more character.

Without realising where her feet were taking her, Lottie drifted towards the stage. In her mind she could see actors performing to a full house and wondered which seats her grandparents had sat in that fateful night. She turned to tell Sid, but he was too busy staring at the ceiling.

'Did you ever think there'd be a place like this in Greenley?' he asked, gazing upwards. Lottie followed his eyes and gasped.

The ceiling was covered in intricate plaster cornicing framing painted murals of Greco-Roman myths. It wasn't quite the Sistine Chapel, but it wasn't too shabby either.

'What's that one supposed to be?' asked Sid, pointing.

Lottie tried to make out what the figures and cherubs were doing. It looked quite rude actually. 'I think it's supposed to be Dionysus. That is not appropriate for children though.' She turned to him, her eyes wide with excitement. 'I had no idea this was here. Did you?'

'Nope.' Sid scrunched up his nose. 'What's that smell?'

'Damp. There's black mould all over the walls. Look.' She ran her hand down and bits of paper fell off and stuck to her fingers.

Each wall had four ceiling-height columns evenly spaced along them and, in between, a once gold wallpaper peeled off, now cold and wet to the touch. She took some more photos. The town needed to see how bad things were.

'Maybe knocking it down isn't such a bad idea after all,' said Sid, finding a clean page in his notebook.

'Don't say that. It just needs airing out and cleaning up. Strip the walls and replace the carpet and it'll be fine.'

Sid grinned. 'When did you become Miss Enthusiastic?'

'I'm just trying to be a bit more positive, like you told me.' Lottie stuck out her tongue and Sid mirrored her. She circled around and smiled. 'Sid, just look at the stage.' Lottie ran up a set of stairs at the front edge, brushing the curtain with her shoulder causing dust motes to dance in the light. Lottie tucked the camera strap over her head and rubbed her cardigan clean. 'Can you imagine standing up here performing to everyone?'

Sid sat down in the last row and put his feet up. 'Go on, do a dance or something.'

'No!'

'Please? For me? Or tell me a joke.'

Lottie tucked her hair behind her ear. 'Umm ... what's brown and sticky?'

Sid smiled. 'I don't know. What is brown and sticky?'

'A stick.'

He gave one of those embarrassing half laughs. 'That is the worst joke I've ever heard.'

Lottie giggled. 'Yeah, sorry.' She stared out at the desolate and dejected theatre and her smile faded. She climbed down off the stage and joined Sid.

He must have seen her face fall, as he lowered his legs and leaned forwards before asking, 'What's the matter?'

'How am I going to make this work, Sid?' She raised her hand to start biting her fingernails. 'There's so much to do. Sarah Powell said there might be mice.'

'Mice?'

Lottie cocked her head. 'Are you imagining them all dancing on stage?'

'Something like that.'

The corners of Lottie's mouth lifted for a second then fell back down. 'I haven't seen any yet though, so that's one good thing. Do you think people will turn up to the auditions?'

'I guess we'll find out soon. And don't forget another advert runs this week.'

The first advert had looked amazing. Two actors in Shakespearean dress were silhouetted on a bright green background. One held out a skull and the other, on his knees, despaired with his head in his hands. Bold black type read, 'Greenley Theatre needs you!' and underneath was the information about the auditions.

'And we've got a load of flyers to give out too.' Sid pulled out his notebook. 'When we run this article with all your pictures, I was thinking we could say something along the lines of, "Many of us knew Elsie Webster and the wonderful service she performed to the theatre and the town. Now her granddaughter, Charlotte Webster, will be carrying on her good work, and the theatre couldn't be in better hands."'

Lottie pressed her hand to her chest. 'Oh, Sid, thank you. It's beautiful.'

'I'm glad you like it,' he replied, blushing. For someone so good with words Sid was like an awkward teenager face to face.

'You've helped me so much with all this,' she said, taking off her camera and placing it on the seat next to her. 'How can I say thank you?'

Sid scratched his head, ruffling his fluffy hair. 'You don't have to thank me, Lottie. I liked your nan. She was a like a mum to me too sometimes, wasn't she?'

'I suppose she was.' Lottie bit her lip. 'Do you miss her too?'

'Yeah, I do. A lot. Elsie looked after me when Mum and Dad died.' He cleared his throat and Lottie saw a stab of pain cross his features. Though Sid tried to be cheerful Lottie knew he still felt their loss deeply. He never spoke about his parents so Lottie never asked but he knew she was here if he ever needed to talk.

It was almost seven years since they'd been involved in a terrible car crash, and with the money they left him he'd bought his lovely flat on the seafront. He hadn't been able to bear being in the family home all alone whereas Lottie couldn't imagine being anywhere else. Up until then Sid had been full of ambition but after the accident those thoughts had faded. He'd eventually regained his cheerfulness but never ventured further than London when they'd had days out together. He was now perfectly content to just take each day as it came and stay put and Lottie had never felt the need to challenge him.

'Thanks again for doing this,' said Lottie, giving his hand a squeeze.

He gave her a smile that didn't reach his eyes and she knew that flash of pain was lingering somewhere in his mind, but his voice was, as usual, cheerful when he said, 'That's alright, I like it. It's fun. Who's going to judge the auditions? Can I?'

'No. Firstly you have terrible taste.'

'I do not.'

She pointed to his Megadeath T-shirt and raised an eyebrow.

'Fair enough.'

'Anyway, you're writing the articles. You need to be impartial. A bit anyway.'

'Oh,' Sid moaned. 'I thought I could have a big buzzer to press if they were rubbish.'

Lottie gave him her 'Don't be silly,' look. 'I guess the mayor will want to be on the panel.'

'And how about David? As the boss of the newspaper, we should probably ask him.'

'Great idea.' Lottie surveyed the dilapidation and she gave a sigh as her face crumpled.

Sid rested a hand on her shoulder. 'Don't worry, Lots. Everything will be okay.'

'I hope so,' she replied. 'I really, really hope so.'

Chapter 7

Just over three weeks later, the day of the auditions dawned and Lottie awoke to the melodic sound of birds singing, and the sun shining through the window. For once she was excited about life again, and sprang out of bed, dancing as she dressed. It was the first time she'd woken up in the house and not felt the sudden dread of reality approaching or a heaviness in her heart as she realised she was alone.

Grabbing her jeans and slipping them on over her thighs, she didn't care about the cellulite on the backs of her legs or her rounded stomach as she zipped them up. Most of the time Lottie was reasonably content with herself, or if not content, then not quite so preoccupied. The little extra weight she carried was nothing a couple of weeks of healthy eating and few trips to the gym wouldn't cure, if she could be bothered. But when she was upset she focused on the bits she didn't like as a way of not thinking about everything else. That today she didn't care quite as much meant the darkness was lifting. She tied her long hair up in a ponytail and was just spraying some perfume when she heard the front door open and a voice call her name.

'Lots, are you there?'

'I'm just getting dressed, Sid,' she yelled back down the stairs. 'Be down in a minute.'

She opened the curtains and stared out over the town. Being on top of the hill allowed her a view of the skyline of Greenley. It wasn't London, Miami, or New York, but it was home and the higgledy-piggledy rooftops, leading out to a calm, grey-blue sea, were a familiar and comforting sight. The kettle whistled and she knew Sid was making them tea.

'Morning,' said Lottie as she met him in the living room. He'd made himself comfortable on the sofa.

He blinked as he watched her. 'Morning. You look nice.'

'Do I?' She stared down at her usual jeans, noticing they were slightly grubby in places and rubbed at the spots with a wet finger.

'Yeah, you do.' His forehead wrinkled slightly. 'What's different?'

'Nothing.' Sid stared at her, one eyebrow raised, and she held out her hands. 'Honestly, nothing.'

'Really?'

'Yes.' Lottie laughed. 'I promise, I'm not trying to catch you out.'

He narrowed his eyes. 'You look very chipper this morning, though.'

'I'm excited! Aren't you? It's am dram day,' she sang, making jazz hands.

'Have you been drinking?'

'Ha ha.' Lottie grabbed her bag and coat. 'Oh, I asked a guy called Conner to come and play people's music. He said he has some device on his laptop that'll take the vocal track off for the singers. He emailed to say he's studying film and media at university and thinks it'd be good for him and his budding career. I told him he's in.'

'What, into the Greenley Players?' Sid sat forwards.

'Yes,' Lottie said slowly. 'He wants to direct and do behind the scenes type stuff.'

'Does the mayor know?'

46

Lottie shook her head. 'No. Not yet.'

Sid sat back again, an incredulous look on his face.

'What?' asked Lottie. 'I'm the chairman. I can do that if I want.'

'It's nice to see you taking charge,' he said, smiling. 'Have you got the list of auditionees? Or should I call them victims?'

'I've got everything together already. Ta da!' Lottie picked up a folder and waved it in the air. 'But we need to get going. I've got some setting up to do before the rest of the panel get there.'

'Right-o.' Sid swallowed his tea and grabbed his leather jacket.

Lottie took a few quick mouthfuls of hers, leaving her cup half empty. She drew level with Sid at the end of the sofa, gave him a mischievous look. He read her mind, and they both raced to the front door. Lottie won.

'Are you sure you're alright?' Sid asked, as he drove them to the theatre. 'You seem a bit … odd.'

'Odd?' Lottie faked offence. 'That's charming. I'm fine, honestly, I'm just in a good mood.'

The outside of the theatre looked a mess. They'd need to come up with a way of fixing it at some point, but for now she had to concentrate on today. Lottie pushed the revolving door and they went inside. The musty damp air hit her nostrils and she grimaced.

Sid turned on the main lights then headed off to a small box at the side of the room that held the lighting and sound equipment. 'Let there be light,' he shouted and with the flick of a switch, the stage was illuminated. The lights flickered for a few seconds before fully committing to staying on and Lottie gave a silent prayer they'd last the whole day. She dropped her folder onto one of the seats before climbing up onto the stage to grab a broom and begin sweeping.

Sid came down and sat on the front row then checked his watch. 'It's eight-thirty, what time are the rest of the panel getting here?'

'Nine o'clock,' answered Lottie, sweeping with vigour. 'The first audition is at nine-thirty.'

'Anyone we know on the list?'

'A few. You'll have to wait and see.' She'd kept the list top secret because she wanted to see his reaction when some of them turned up.

'Spoilsport.'

Lottie stuck out her tongue, feeling playful. 'Don't just sit there, lazy bum, come and grab another broom. This place is filthy.' She watched him open his mouth to moan. 'No moans and groans. You're my best friend, you have to help. I reckon if this place had a good airing it would make a big difference.'

'You sound like your nan.' Sid huffed and stood up to join Lottie. He found another broom and began sweeping at the back of the stage.

'Thank you,' Lottie replied, then stifled a laugh. 'What are you doing now, you idiot?'

'Dancing, of course,' said Sid, wiggling his hips before leaping over the handle. 'Come on.'

A grin grew on Lottie's face and she began dancing too as they swept the stage. They were both giving a vague interpretation of a tango with their respective broomstick partners when the rest of the panel walked in.

Mayor Cunningham arrived first and coughed as his lungs filled with the damp air. 'Goodness me. Are we going to be in here all day? It stinks.'

Lottie stopped herself from rolling her eyes and walked down to meet him. 'I know it's not ideal, but we need the acoustics of a proper stage and there wasn't anywhere else. It's probably worse because we just swept.'

'Very well,' replied Mayor Cunningham. 'I don't suppose there's any tea or coffee is there?'

'Damn, I didn't think of that,' replied Lottie.

'Really, Miss Webster, if you're to be our chairman, you must plan these things more thoroughly.'

'No worries,' said Sid, jumping down off the stage, moving to

48

Lottie's side. 'I'll nip out and get us all coffees and some bottles of water for the auditions.'

'Oh, Sid, thank you,' said Lottie, touching his arm. She'd always loved the feel of his old leather jacket. He'd worn it for as long as she could remember and it was part of him.

'I'll have a black filter coffee,' ordered the mayor.

Lottie flashed her eyes, knowing Sid would be thinking the same as her. 'Sid, can I have a—'

'I know what you have, Lots,' he replied and gave her a cheeky wink.

The revolving door squeaked and David, their editor, walked in. He was a great boss and a really nice man, but since his divorce seemed to be having some sort of midlife crisis. He'd recently acquired a tattoo in a language he didn't speak and had turned up today in a suit jacket and open-necked shirt revealing the greying hairs on his chest. Lottie wanted to go and do the buttons up but resisted. Hopefully, it wouldn't be noticeable when he was sitting down. 'Morning, everyone,' called David. 'I found this young man outside. Does he belong to you, Lottie?'

A young man with dyed black hair gelled forward over his face and a piercing through his bottom lip shuffled in. He gave Lottie a quick smile then kept his eyes on the floor.

Lottie took a few steps towards him. 'Hi, you must be Conner. Thank you so much for coming.'

'S'alright,' he replied, removing his laptop and a small portable amp from his backpack. 'Shall I set up over there?'

'Yes please,' said Lottie. 'There must be a power point some-where.'

'I can find one.' Conner wandered off with his laptop under his arm.

'I'm just getting coffees,' said Sid to David. 'One for you?'

'Oh, yes please. That'll go down a treat.' He smoothed down his thinning hair.

Sid looked over to Conner. 'How about you, Conner? Do you want anything, mate?'

Conner looked up from under his long fringe. He seemed surprised at being included. Lottie wondered how he could ever see where he was going with his fringe all over his face then chastised herself for sounding like her nan again. She was getting old. 'Umm, can I have a Coke, please? I can give you the money.'

'That's alright, mate. I can spare it. Be back soon.'

Lottie smiled at Sid. Conner was relaxing already and she was sure some of it was because of Sid. A hint of a smile had passed over Conner's face when he talked to him. She turned her attention to David and the mayor. 'I thought we should sit a couple of rows back from the front. We don't want to end up with sore necks at the end of the day.'

'Good idea,' replied David. 'Lead the way.'

Lottie indicated the third row back. 'Here we are then. Sid will be back soon with the coffees. Conner, is there anything I can help with?'

He shook his head and Lottie noticed his fringe was gelled so firmly it didn't move. 'I'm pretty much done. I've found all the music on the list you gave me.'

'Great, thanks.'

'Who's that boy?' asked Mayor Cunningham.

'He's the first member of the Greenley Players,' announced Lottie.

The mayor eyed her, his face growing redder. 'You've appointed someone without speaking to anyone first?'

Lottie felt a shiver of nerves at his tone then pulled her shoulders back. 'Yes. Yes, I did. He doesn't need to audition as he wants to direct and do more on that side of things.'

'But don't you think you should have spoken to us all first?'

'Well, no,' said Lottie. 'We're going to need people on both sides of the stage, so to speak. So I didn't see the point.'

'Well I disagree,' Mayor Cunningham replied huffily before

plopping down on his seat. 'It's almost nine-fifteen. Your young man better hurry up.'

Lottie rolled her eyes and hoped he would keep his temper under control for the auditions. She had a feeling they'd need all the help they could get today.

Twenty minutes later Sid returned with a dozen bottles of water, plastic cups, a Coke and four coffees precariously balanced in a cardboard holder not quite up to the task. He handed out the drinks, placed the water and cups by the stage and took his place behind the mayor and David.

The first auditionee arrived looking terrified and Lottie went to meet them with a beaming smile. The young man with shoulder-length blond hair looked like a surfer, and climbed up onto the stage carrying a guitar case.

Lottie returned to her seat but couldn't stop jiggling her legs.

He opened the case and readied himself to play. After clearing his throat, he began to sing. At least, that's what he was supposed to be doing. Lottie's face froze as he played the guitar badly and shouted out the lyrics to a song he'd clearly written himself about his dead dog. She waited for him to finish and cleared her throat. 'Thank you, we'll let you know.'

The mayor gave Lottie a smug smile. 'Let's hope the next one's better,' she said, giving a cheery one in return. But the rest of the auditions followed suit. The acting was on a par with the worst primary school nativity play and the singing would have made Simon Cowell's eardrums run out of his head screaming and stab themselves on the first sharp object they could find. Someone even did some interpretive dance, though what they were inter-preting, Lottie couldn't quite figure out.

At about eleven o'clock and twenty people in, Deborah McCray arrived in a flamboyant red dress with a green scarf draped across her shoulders. Sid leaned in to Lottie and whispered, 'Isn't she the mad artist from Primrose Cottage? The one who paints those awful watercolours?'

Lottie gave a single nod, not wanting to draw Mrs McCray's attention, and whispered, 'Yeah. Do you remember that picture of someone's kid in her gallery window? It was the creepiest thing I've ever seen.'

'It still haunts my dreams,' Sid replied and they both chuckled as Lottie stood up to meet her.

'Hello, Mrs McCray.'

'Hullo there.'

'If you'd like to make your way to the stage and introduce yourself to the panel, then tell us what you'll be doing.'

Mrs McCray climbed the steps, hooking her dress up as she went. The light surrounded her and shone through her rusty coloured hair as her harsh Scottish accent announced, 'I'm Mrs McCray, a local artist, and I'll be singing "Casta Diva", from the opera *Norma*, by Bellini.'

'Is this going to be like Mr Neville the opera-singing parrot?' whispered Sid and Lottie chewed her lip trying not to laugh.

Everyone waited. Conner pressed some buttons on his laptop and the song started playing. Lottie took a deep breath preparing herself for a horrendous screeching to fill the room, but, to her surprise, gentle, tuneful notes emerged. A soft and beautiful sound, rising and falling then building to a crescendo, held them all captivated. Conner turned to Lottie and his eyes were so wide in amazement she could actually see them.

When Mrs McCray finished Lottie stood up to applaud. She looked to her left where Mayor Cunningham sat with his mouth open.

'That was amazing,' said Lottie. 'Bravo.'

Mrs McCray's weather-beaten face wrinkled as she smiled. 'Och, well, thank you very much, darlin'.'

'Yes, thank you,' said the mayor. 'We'll let you know.'

When Mrs McCray had left, Lottie turned to him. 'I don't see why we can't tell people now whether they're in, or not. It's not like we can have too many people.' Feeling emboldened by the last few minutes she said, 'Mrs McCray was exceptional, so, as acting chairman, I'd like to proceed on the idea that we'll take whoever has any talent. Okay?'

The mayor raised an eyebrow then sat back and Lottie felt a teasing nudge from Sid.

Gregory Oliver was the next to arrive with his partner, Cecil Bates. 'Darling,' Gregory said to Lottie, taking her in both hands and kissing her on the cheeks, even though they'd never really met before. He was tall and handsome with salt and pepper hair. 'We've come for the auditions. Have we much competition?'

'We can't tell you that,' said Mayor Cunningham. In the muggy atmosphere of the theatre his bald spot was beginning to shine.

'You'll be fine, Mr O.,' offered Sid with a wink.

'Off you go, Mr Oliver,' said Lottie, directing him to the stage. 'Just give us a quick intro before you start.'

Gregory climbed the steps and said, 'Well, I'm Gregory Oliver and I run the bookshop on the seafront and today I'm going to give a reading from Shakespeare.' He then closed his eyes and stood in silence for a moment before his voice boomed out. '"O' reason not the need! Our basest beggars are in the poorest thing superfluous."'

'Well, he's certainly projecting,' whispered Sid into Lottie's ear.

'Shhh,' she said, playfully.

'"Allow not nature more than nature needs, Man's life is cheap as beast's."' He cast out his hands and with one did an Eighties' air grab. '"No, I'll not weep. I have full cause of weeping, but this heart shall break into a hundred thousand flaws or ere I'll weep. O fool, I shall go mad!"' Gregory fell to the floor with his head in his hands.

It seemed a little melodramatic, but it was Shakespeare, it was always melodramatic. Even in khaki chinos Lottie could picture him on the stage, under the spotlights, and hear the crowd applauding, though she worried about his knees.

'Bravo,' shouted Cecil, clapping enthusiastically.

Lottie stood. 'Yes, bravo.'

'Well done, Mr O.,' said Sid, as Gregory came down off the stage. 'That was brilliant.'

'Are you actually on the audition panel, Mr Evans, or are you here to report on them?' the mayor called out.

Sid glanced at Lottie for a moment, a playful smile on his face, before turning to the mayor and saying, 'Just being friendly, Mayor Cunningham. Never hurts, does it?'

'Cecil's also auditioning,' said Gregory.

'Oh, of course,' replied Lottie. 'Sorry, Cecil. Please?' She gestured for him to move onto the stage and sat down again. Her legs were beginning to ache from all this upping and downing but it was better than doing squats in the gym.

Cecil smiled at the panel. 'I'm Cecil Bates and I also run the bookshop on the seafront. I love soy chai lattes and long dog walks on the beach, and today I'll be singing.' Cecil was shorter than Gregory and a little younger by the look of it. He had kind bright blue eyes in a smooth perma-tanned face. Conner began playing the song and without visible signs of fear or nerves, Cecil sang 'Memories' from *Cats*. It was an unusual choice, and though not as good a performer as his partner, it was still very respectable. He even managed to stay in tune, most of the time.

'I think he's good,' said Lottie, quietly. 'It must be difficult to dance and sing at the same time.' She turned back to the stage and not caring if it annoyed Mayor Cunningham said, 'Well done, both of you. You're both in.'

'Marvellous,' shouted Gregory, giving her another kiss on the cheek. Cecil did the same and hand in hand they left the theatre.

The mayor huffed at her and fiddled with his cufflinks. 'I really don't think we should be telling them straight away, Miss Webster.'

Lottie bit her lip then swivelled to face the mayor. She was getting cross with his negativity now. Things were going so well he just needed to be more positive. 'I know what you said, Mayor Cunningham—' He opened his mouth to continue arguing but

54

Lottie carried on. 'If there's someone who we're on the fence about, I won't tell them straight away, but for someone who is so clearly good I don't see the point in keeping them waiting. It's mean. So like I said, I'd like to carry on as we have been.'

The mayor scanned the ceiling and Lottie spied Sid staring at her agog. 'What?' she mouthed, and he gave her a big thumbs-up.

After Cecil's audition they broke for lunch. Lottie had hoped to sit with Sid but just as she sat down Sid got up and went to chat with Conner who stayed where he was, alone in the corner. That was just like Sid, thought Lottie with a smile. For all his silly jokes he was one of the kindest people she knew. They reconvened at one o'clock and two women walked in just as they re-took their seats.

'Is this the auditions?' asked the taller one with long platinum blonde hair.

Lottie got up to the meet them. 'Yes. Yes, it is. Please come in.' The women stepped forward, giggling nervously.

'So how does this work then?' the smaller, dark-haired one asked. 'Do we just get up there and sing?'

'That's right,' said Lottie, and they climbed the steps to the stage giggling and pushing each other in encouragement.

'I'm Tiffany,' said the taller one with the bright white hair similar to wire wool.

'And I'm Claire,' said the small one whose thick mask of foundation formed a ring under her chin. They tittered once more and the music began.

As they sang Lottie tried to keep her face from screwing up in pain. The terrible high-pitched squeaking and their inability to sing in any sort of harmony was like having hot needles shoved in her brain and her eardrums tortured. Sid grabbed his notebook and pen and bent over so they couldn't see his giggling.

'Thank you, we'll let you know,' Lottie said, as the girls climbed down from the stage and left the building.

David blew the air out of his cheeks. 'They were awful, weren't they? It was like two cats mating while someone played an out of tune violin.'

Mrs Andrews arrived early for her audition just as the last person was finishing. Lottie asked her to sit at the back where she made loud scoffing noises. The several hard stares Lottie gave did little to stop her. At last she was able to say, 'Your turn, Mrs Andrews, if you'd like to take the stage.'

Lottie and Sid had met Mrs Andrews several times before. Her husband was a local MP and as such Mrs Andrews had a lot of influence, and money. She very much enjoyed her public role and was often called upon to attend posh events. After the advert had gone out, she'd emailed Lottie saying she didn't think she should have to audition as she already had 'considerable experience', but Lottie had replied politely insisting.

Mrs Andrews walked up rolling her hips and wiggling her bottom like Marilyn Monroe in white jeans so tight you could see the outline of her knickers. David bent towards Sid and whispered, 'She'll put her hip out doing that at her age.' Lottie hid behind her folder, laughing.

On the stage Mrs Andrews' confident eyes scanned the panel. Her face was a seamless sheet of beige tan, slightly pinched at the eyes. Only her hands gave away any real signs of age from the wrinkles and gathering age spots. She flung her arms out wide. '"No shame but mine: I must, forsooth, be forced to give my hand opposed against my heart."'

She clasped both hands against her surgically enhanced chest. '"Unto a mad-brain rudesby full of spleen; Who woo'd in haste and means to wed at leisure."'

Although the mad flailing of arms was quite off-putting, her delivery of the monologue was reasonably good, better than a lot of the others they'd seen and reluctantly Lottie put her on the list. 'That was good, Mrs Andrews,' she said, unwilling to give her too much praise. She was already too big for her boots. 'I'm sure we'd love to have you on board.'

'Hear, hear,' said the mayor and Lottie scowled at his simpering.

As the end of the day neared, the weary judges tucked into supplies of biscuits Sid had brought with him. 'Oh, custard creams,' said Lottie, taking three. 'My favourite. Conner, would you like some?'

From the edge of the stage where Conner sat playing on his phone, he lifted his head and crept over, keeping his eyes on Mayor Cunningham. Poor boy, the mayor was quite intimidating.

'Thank you so much for coming and helping us out on a Saturday,' said Lottie. 'I hope your mates didn't tease you about being busy with some oldies like us?'

'Nah, they didn't.' He took a couple of biscuits and shuffled away back to the steps. Lottie frowned. She couldn't work out if he was shy or lonely. She hoped it was the former.

'Who's next?' asked Mayor Cunningham.

'Lee Carter,' Lottie replied. 'He's the last one.'

Mayor Cunningham's small pig-like eyes screwed up in disgust. 'He's a criminal. And he's late.'

'I'm sure he'll be here any minute,' said Lottie, ignoring the other remark.

'Alright?' called a voice from the back of the room. Thankful that Mayor Cunningham hadn't said anything ruder, Lottie went to meet Lee at the door.

Lee Carter was one of the mechanics at the local garage. He was known for getting into the odd scuffle and had been fancied by all the girls in Lottie's year at school, including her. He had a strong square jaw and short gelled hair, and had they been planning a production of *Lady Chatterley's Lover*, it was clear what part he would play.

'What will you be performing for us today?' asked Lottie, by now feeling like a pro.

As he climbed the steps to the stage two at a time, Lee said, 'I thought I'd do a bit of acting. S'alright, innit?'

'Lovely,' said Lottie. 'Whenever you're ready.'

Lee nodded and without pausing began to recite Marlon Brando in *The Godfather*. It was entertaining and not comical in the slightest. He had stage presence and charisma by the bucket full and Lottie couldn't pull her eyes away. If she had anything to do with it, he was definitely in.

When Lee left, the mayor turned to Lottie. 'Definitely not.'

'Oh, for heaven's sake,' Lottie replied, unable to hide the exasperation from her voice. 'Why not? I thought he was great.'

'He's a criminal.'

'He is not,' said Lottie, matching his determined expression. 'He's a perfectly nice man.'

Sid sat forward. 'He got a warning for drunk and disorderly once, that's all. And it was New Year's Eve. Everyone's drunk on New Year's Eve.'

Not me, thought Lottie, sadly. And not Sid. She was normally asleep by nine-thirty. 'I think you're overreacting, Mayor Cunningham. All he did was try and steal a bollard.'

'He looks like a thug.'

'I disagree,' Lottie said, remaining calm. After all, she was the acting chairman and she could pull that card out again if she needed to. 'And I vote yes.'

The mayor eyed her disapprovingly then turned to David for his casting vote. 'David?'

'I vote yes, too,' said David. 'He's a very good mechanic.'

It wasn't quite the reason Lottie was hoping for but never mind. Lee was still in.

The mayor looked back at the empty stage, his lips a thin pink line.

Just as they were beginning to pack up, the door squeaked again and Lottie spun around to see Sarah Powell creeping in. She grabbed her clipboard and checked the list. Sarah wasn't due to be here. Perhaps she'd come to speak to the mayor.

'Excuse me,' said Sarah in a small voice. 'I was wondering if I could still audition.'

'What the devil?' exclaimed Mayor Cunningham edging out into the aisle and Lottie shot him a glance that said, 'Shut up or I'll stab you.' Thankfully, he did, but she followed him with her eyes until he sat back down, just to make sure. At first Lottie thought Sarah was ill. Her face was pale and her top lip clammy. Then, from the way she was wringing her hands in front of her, Lottie realised she was nervous. No, not nervous, terrified.

Although she'd been pretty hateful at the committee meeting, the Sarah that stood in front of her was almost childlike. Lottie felt sorry for her and said, 'No, it's not too late. What are you going to do for us?'

'I ... I was going to sing. If that's okay?'

'Yes, it's fine. I won't have your music though. Will you be okay without it?'

Sarah nodded and Lottie worried she might throw up at any minute.

'This way,' said Lottie, gently holding her elbow and leading her forwards. She could feel her trembling beneath her fingers. Sarah climbed the stairs and gazed around as if searching for the exits, 'Take your time, Sarah,' said Lottie, softly. She'd never seen anyone so terrified. Lottie angled her head and smiled, hoping to put her at ease.

Even from the third row they could see Sarah was shaking and her hands were clasped in front of her, the knuckles white. 'What are you going to sing for us, Sarah?' asked Lottie, keeping her tone light and friendly. She hoped it would prompt her to begin.

Sarah opened her mouth to speak, but nothing came out. She was paralysed with fear. Lottie felt the heavy silence of the room weigh on her shoulders. The poor woman. This must be so embarrassing and awful for her. Unsure what to do Lottie turned to Sid. He winked with his usual easy confidence, then walked onto the stage and whispered something into Sarah's ear. Some of the fear disappeared from her face and she gave a nervous laugh. Sid returned to his seat and Sarah closed her eyes.

After a pause she began singing 'Nothing Compares 2 U', in a soft but powerful voice. The song was one of Lottie's favourites and always gave her goose bumps but as Sarah sang even her goose bumps got goose bumps. Every nerve in Lottie's body tingled with emotion. Sarah's hands moved in time, even without the music, clenching and releasing her fists.

There was something so pure and heartfelt in Sarah's voice, it was like it enveloped Lottie's soul. Sarah's face registered terror when she finished and opened her eyes to the stunned silence. Lottie immediately stood and clapped and Sid and David joined her.

'Thank you,' said Sarah, in a hushed voice, her face reddening and tears forming in her eyes.

'You were marvellous,' said Lottie. 'You're definitely in.'

Mayor Cunningham slowly stood to join them and once Sarah had left said, 'If that's all of them, Miss Webster, I'll be off.'

'Yes, that's everyone,' Lottie confirmed, an enormous smile on her face. 'Quite a good turnout, don't you think, Mayor Cunningham? I think it's been a pretty successful day.' She didn't care if he couldn't wait to be out of there, or if she was just rubbing it in – she'd had the best day ever and Greenley-On-Sea had proved to be a hotbed of talent.

Mayor Cunningham strode past her then paused at the door. 'I concede, Miss Webster, it was a better turnout than I expected.'

Lottie and Sid high-fived. The Greenley Players were officially reinstated.

Chapter 8

Sid wandered aimlessly along the seafront and took a deep breath of the salty sea air. The bright gold afternoon sun reflected off the sea in a glorious haze of light and strangely shaped clouds drifted across the sky. The seashore was littered with clumps of dark green seaweed and the regular dog walkers chased their mischievous dogs away from it.

Sid was bored. Lottie was busy again. She had another committee meeting coming up and wanted to go through all her nan's papers to make sure she knew everything inside and out. As the auditions had gone so well and the troupe was now all go, she'd decided to catalogue all the different plays the old Greenley Players had done and do something called 'brainstorming', which sounded incredibly painful. Sid had offered to help but she wanted to be alone. Perhaps he could nip round later with her favourite pizza. She'd like that.

Sid sighed. He was happy for her, of course he was, it was just that all this suddenly being alone took some getting used to. They'd spent mostly every weekend together for years. Not all day every day, but they'd nip into town together, go to Nick's record shop, look at the tat in the Saturday market, have Sunday lunch in their favourite old-fashioned pub, that sort of thing. He kicked a stray pebble back onto the beach. Anyway, she was too busy to meet him and as it was a Sunday he found himself at a loose end with no one to play with.

The piece of paper with Selena's number on rustled in his pocket. She'd given it to him weeks ago and he still hadn't had the courage to do anything with it. Every time he looked at the note and thought about calling he'd see the carnage in his flat and decide she was still way out of his league. But it wasn't too late, was it? Not like with Lottie. He could always call Selena and see if she wanted to meet for a drink. He wouldn't say dinner, he didn't want to sound pushy. But they could have a drink as old uni mates catching up, just like Selena suggested.

Sid found himself nodding along to the voice in his head and before he lost his nerve, grabbed his phone and called. She sounded happy he'd rung and they agreed to meet at the Hare and Hounds at seven. Sid hung up and decided he would break the habit of a lifetime and wear a shirt, as long as he could find where he'd left one.

The pub was in the next village along from Greenley and had bare wooden tables, chalkboard walls and a menu that boasted things like spinach foam and hazelnut jus. Sid entered and creased up his nose at the strange smell.

Selena spotted him from over her shoulder and waved. She was already sat at the bar in a short black dress that displayed her amazing figure. Her long hair was tied back in a simple ponytail, but still reached down past her shoulders. Sid wondered how a woman who looked like that could ever be interested in him. As the fear mounted he pushed it down and ran a hand through his combed hair. Glad he'd checked for signs of a monobrow before leaving, he walked forward to meet her. 'Hello.'

'Hello,' she replied, smiling. 'I was worried you weren't going to show.'

She'd been worried? Really? 'Why?' he asked. He wasn't late.

'I don't know. I thought at first maybe you were ignoring me.'

Selena giggled nervously and turned back to her nearly empty drink.

Sid felt the knot in his stomach loosen a little. He wasn't sure if it was a surge of self-confidence or his normal just-not-giving-much-of-a-fuck attitude returning, but he began to relax. 'Yeah, sorry about that. It's been pretty mad these last few weeks with all the am dram stuff.'

'That sounds fun.'

Sid perched on the barstool next to Selena and his leg brushed hers as he climbed up, sending a shiver through him. 'It was okay.'

'Anyone I know in the group?' Selena finished her drink.

'Maybe. I can't really say yet. We're going to print a list in the paper this week. Would you like another drink?' Sid asked. He needed one. The nerves in his tummy were biting again making him feel sick.

'Yes, please.' Selena turned to the barman who stood waiting to take their order. 'I'll have a glass of champagne, please.' She turned back. 'If that's okay?'

'Of course.' Sid ordered a beer for himself and drank half of it. 'Shall we find a table?'

Selena nodded and smiled before slipping elegantly from her stool and grabbing her coat. For a guy with no experience it seemed to be going pretty well so far. He hoped the rest of the night would too.

Selena led them to a table by the window and sat down. 'Thanks for the champagne. Wine's a bit of a killer for me and I don't really like beer or spirits. Too many shots when I was at uni.'

'On those one pound a shot nights?' He laughed. 'Yeah, me too. The Student Union's got a lot to answer for.'

Selena angled in towards him. 'Do you remember when that guy's shoe ended up on the roof of Cooper Building and was there for the whole term?'

'Oh, yeah.' Sid smiled at the memory. Most of his uni days were a faded blur now, barely recalled. It was nice to talk about them with someone again. He'd been so happy then. 'They never did find out who it was, did they?'

Selena laughed and shook her head. 'I always imagined him hopping home that night all drunk and wobbly.'

Sid chuckled too.

'I like your shirt,' Selena offered and Sid blushed. He wasn't used to receiving compliments on his clothes.

'Thanks. Are you glad to be back in Greenley?' he asked. Selena's olive skin glowed in the sunlight shining through the window and her long dark hair reminded him of a chocolate waterfall.

'Sort of. Obviously I wish it had worked out with my ex-boyfriend. I thought at one point we were going to get married, but it just wasn't to be. I'm happy to be back for a while though.' She ran a hand over her ponytail and pulled it around over her shoulder the ends resting on her cleavage.

Sid pictured her ex and in his mind, he looked like Harrison Ford playing Han Solo. Someone rugged and handsome. In short, nothing like him.

'So what about you?' Selena asked before taking a sip of her drink. She sounded genuinely interested and Sid's nerves rose up once more, wanting to give her the right answers. 'Did you come back straight from university?'

'Yeah.' Sid thought about mentioning his parents but didn't. He didn't want to ruin the mood. 'I got a job on the paper then decided to stay. I've been with the *Gazette* ever since.'

'Didn't you ever want to work for a big paper or the BBC or something?'

'No. Not really. I'd have to wear a suit then.' Sid joked but it had taken all his self-control to wear one for the entirety of Elsie's funeral. Thoughts of Lottie threatened to push in but he buried them. He hated the way his brain did that. 'And I'd have to sit in a hot stuffy office. I think I'd miss the sea.'

Selena ran her fingers over the stem of her glass and her voice was all soft and dreamy. 'That's one of the things I missed most when I was up north. I love being by the sea and hearing the waves. Even though I could do without the seagulls waking me up at stupid o'clock in the morning.'

'Definitely,' agreed Sid, and he told her about the enormo-gull that had attacked him the other week. Hearing Selena laugh was like listening to his favourite record. A feeling of warmth flooded through him, and pride at having been the one to make her smile.

'I'm surprised you survived,' she replied, a hint of a laugh still in her voice. 'There was one in town harassing pedestrians the other day. Some poor old man who was sat on the bench opposite the museum had to fight it off with his walking stick. I couldn't stop laughing. You should have heard the names he was calling it.'

Sid grinned. 'You'd be surprised at the wide vocabulary of the older generation.'

Selena laughed again and Sid watched her face as it filled with joy. 'So what about you?' he asked, unwilling to let the conversation fall into silence. 'Any plans for a big career somewhere?'

'No, not really.' Selena kept her eyes on the glass as she shrugged. 'I like what I do. It makes people happy. Do you live on your own?'

Sid tensed up. Did he look like one of those guys who had always lived on their own, all scruffy and untidy? Or worse, smell like it? He resisted the urge to try a surreptitious sniff of his shirt. 'Umm, yeah. Yeah, I do.'

'That's nice. I'd kill for some space at the moment.'

He could understand but felt a tinge of sadness for something he'd never have again. He'd got on well with his parents and he missed them.

'But I'm saving up,' Selena continued, cheerfully. 'So I should be able to rent somewhere within a few months.' She looked up at him from under her impossibly long eyelashes and her dark brown eyes held him captivated. 'Anyway, are you seeing anyone at the moment?'

Sid frowned. 'Umm, no. No, I'm not.' He thought about mentioning Lottie but what would he say? She wasn't his girlfriend so what was the point of saying anything? He didn't know much about girls but he knew they could get jealous. He'd read it in a copy of *GQ* at the doctor's once. Sid swallowed the other half of his beer.

'Thirsty?' Selena joked.

He felt his cheeks burn. 'It is quite hot today.'

Her face lightened. 'We have been talking nonstop.'

They had, hadn't they? He chanced at a look at his watch. They'd already been there for forty-five minutes. Wow. It only felt like five. In his mind he applauded himself at how well things were going and watched Selena smile back. He noticed her cheeks plumped up when she did and he wanted to stroke the smooth pink tinged skin. 'Did you want another one?'

'Yes, please, but I'll need something to eat before I drink too much more or I'll get tipsy. Even on this, I'm still a bit of a lightweight.'

Before Sid could worry about rejection he said, 'We could eat here if you like?' He glanced at the menu. He had no idea what a compote was but the odd smell he'd first encountered had gone away and he was sure he'd be able to find something suitable to eat. Every pub had a variation on a good old burger after all.

'That'd be lovely,' Selena replied, edging closer so her leg rested against his. Sid admired her full pink lips and wondered what it'd be like to kiss them.

Sid switched to Coke as he was driving but they drank and chatted, and he found that Selena was surprisingly funny. She made jokes at her own expense, which he liked, and they talked about the music they used to listen to. They chatted about uni friends and speculated on where they were now, wondering if any of them had ended up doing the jobs they'd actually studied for. As Selena pointed out when she'd touched his arm, he seemed

66

to be the only one doing that, which was a win as far as she was concerned.

But the moment that blew Sid away was when, during dinner, the conversation turned to Eighties movies and Selena said one of her favourite movies of all time was *The Goonies*. Sid had a mad passion for Eighties movies and *The Goonies* was one his favourites too. Selena even knew the names of all the Brat Pack.

'You fancied Andrew McCarthy?' Sid asked, unable to hide the surprise from his voice. Andrew McCarthy had always played the shy, geeky characters. Characters like Sid, and the flicker of hope he'd been harbouring suddenly flared up.

'I know,' she replied, smiling. Her eyes dipped in embarrassment as she tucked her hair behind her ear. 'But I bet you always fancied Molly Ringwald,' she teased.

Sit sat back holding his empty glass of Coke, shaking his head. He had. There weren't many people who even remembered those movies, let alone still watched them. He'd thought he and Lottie were the only ones. 'Maybe a little,' he replied, pretending to scratch his cheek to see if the heat he felt inside was noticeable. When Selena sipped the last of her drink he found himself saying, 'One for the road?'

When Sid drove them home that night and parked in front of Selena's parents' house, he didn't know if he should give her a kiss or not. The date had gone well. Better than well, actually. He didn't have anything to compare it to but it had been fun.

He pulled on the handbrake and turned to Selena. 'I had a really good time. Thanks.'

'Me too.' There was a glint in her eye but he didn't know if it was just the moon reflecting down.

Sid waited for a second but she didn't get out. He could smell her perfume and the hairs on the back of his neck raised with anticipation. Was she really waiting for a kiss? From him? Of course from him, he thought, there was no one else there. He was just about to lean in and see if she would welcome a peck on the cheek when a wave of nerves so strong they nearly pushed his dinner out of his stomach rolled over and without thinking he sat back.

Selena looked away and her voice was quiet. 'Goodnight then.'

He felt so jittery all he could say was, 'Umm, goodnight.' And she glanced at him one last time then opened the car door and climbed out.

Fuck it.

Chapter 9

Lottie strolled down to the theatre about a week after the auditions. The first meeting of the amateur dramatics group was about to begin and they were waiting outside for her to unlock the door. The evening air had cooled and some of the players did little dances on the spot to keep warm. Thankfully, work had been slow and David had let her go early to have time to grab something to eat before the meeting.

Some of the successful auditionees had already dropped out but there was still a decent number and a bolt of sickness shot through Lottie at the thought of speaking in front of everyone. But Lottie knew she had no choice. Her nan really was a scheming old so-and-so. She was having to face every conceivable fear doing this, and even some she didn't know she'd had.

Lottie opened the theatre door and led them inside. As they entered everyone peered around as surprised as she'd been the first time she saw it.

'Gosh, it really needs some work doesn't it?' said Gregory.

'I had no idea it was this bad,' Cecil replied.

Sarah caught up with Lottie as she walked down towards the stage. 'I'm not sure our budget will even make a dent on all this.'

'No, it won't,' Lottie replied with a sigh. She'd have to deal with that sooner or later but right now she wanted everyone to be cheerful and enjoy this first meeting. 'But it's okay, we'll think of something.' Sarah smiled and took a seat.

'Yuck, what's that stink?' called Mrs Andrews, tottering in wearing silver high heels.

'It's just a bit of damp, Mrs Andrews,' replied Lottie. 'It'll get better as we clean up.'

'Is that what we're doing today?' she asked, panicked.

'No, Mrs Andrews, don't worry. If everyone could take a seat, please?' The players filled the front row, watching her and her voice wavered until she hit her stride. 'Welcome, everyone, to the first meeting of the Greenley Players. I thought today, as it's our first meeting, I could introduce myself and we could discuss some plans for the group. I want everyone to be involved in the decisions that are made about where we go from here. This is a community theatre so we should all get a say. I thought we could start by going around and introducing ourselves?'

There were murmurs of agreement and nervous glances.

'I'll begin,' said Lottie, shakily but hoping to chivvy them up. 'My name's Lottie Webster and my nan, Elsie, was chairman of the committee – she asked me to take over her place before she died. So here I am.' Inwardly, Lottie congratulated herself. She'd never said this sentence before without pausing to keep back tears, even when she'd been practising at home. This time she'd actually sounded confident.

Lottie looked to her left, to where Deborah McCray sat and smiled, encouraging her to begin. Mrs McCray raked a hand through her un-brushed red hair. It wasn't Titian red, or Scottish Highland red. It was red from a bottle and had faded to a rusty, orangey-brown.

'Well, hullo there, my name is Debbie McCray,' she shouted in a strong, almost indecipherable Scottish accent. 'I'm an artist and I've lived here in Greenley for almost ten years now.'

'Thank you, Mrs McCray,' said Lottie, trying to hide her confusion. She hadn't understood a word.

'Call me Debbie.'

'Debbie it is then.' At least she'd understood that. Lottie turned next to Mrs Andrews.

'My turn?' Mrs Andrews stood up to face the room. 'Well, I probably don't need an introduction. I'm sure you all know me.'

'I don't,' replied Conner. Gregory either hiccupped or laughed, Lottie wasn't sure as she was too busy trying to suppress her own giggle. Gregory then leaned into Cecil and whispered, 'Half the men in Greenley know Mrs Andrews.'

'Intimately,' said Cecil and they snickered like school boys.

Lottie cleared her throat and eyed them disapprovingly. They stopped and kept their eyes down.

Mrs Andrews glared at Conner. 'My name is Adelaide Andrews. My husband is an MP, sitting in the House of Commons as we speak, and because of that I have a certain measure of influence and position within our lovely little community. Of course, I also have a lot of experience of West End theatre.'

Gregory stopped nursing the can of gin and tonic he'd brought with him.

'Oh, really?' asked Lottie, wondering why Mrs Andrews hadn't mentioned it before. 'In what capacity?'

'Well ...' Mrs Andrews paused. 'Well, I'm rather a connoisseur, I suppose.'

'Oh, I see. Thank you, Mrs Andrews.' Lottie was beginning to regret having added her to the group. She had a feeling Mrs Andrews was going to be trouble. She was clearly used to getting her own way and being the centre of attention. Lottie made a mental note to read a self-help book on team building or managing difficult people.

'Hello, everyone,' came a cheerful baritone voice. 'My name's Gregory Oliver, I used to be an actor in the West End before retiring down here to Greenley. Cecil and I run the bookshop on the seafront.'

His teeth were dazzlingly white and his lined face creased as he smiled. Lottie tried to pinpoint his age and could only place him somewhere between forty and fifty-five. The murmuring voices were now replaced with those of surprise and excitement. 'I had a few supporting roles, not exactly leading, but—'

Mrs Andrews coughed and Lottie was sure she said 'liar' while doing it.

'Are you alright, Mrs Andrews?' asked Gregory. 'Fur ball in your throat?'

'I'm fine, thank you,' she replied, narrowing her eyes. 'Just a tickle.'

'As I was saying, I had a few small supporting roles, probably more than my fair share, if I'm honest, but also chorus line and understudy work. I'm quite familiar with the theatre world and how it all works, so I hope I can be of some help.' He sat back and crossed his legs, his shiny white loafers catching the light.

Lottie had heard rumours about Gregory having been an actor but as she'd never seen anything with him in she just thought everyone was over-exaggerating. She'd imagined him playing roles like 'extra number 341', or 'man in background who walks past with a paper'. Possibly even 'dead body in morgue', but nothing quite like this.

'I was always a jobbing actor,' Gregory continued. 'But I had some decent parts. Despite my best efforts to decapitate the leads I never got to actually be the star, but hey-ho, such is life. I have a decent baritone voice—'

Mrs Andrews scoffed again. Cecil glared this time but she tossed her hair and studied her nails. What on earth had happened between these two to warrant behaviour like this? Lottie would have to find out.

'It may be a little rusty, but I do love to sing – though Cecil here is far better than me.'

'Stop it!' replied Cecil, tapping his arm. He turned to the group. 'Hello, everyone, I'm Cecil and I run the bookshop too. I love, love, love a good musical number! Give me a top hat and cane and I'm away.'

'It's true,' said Gregory, looking at everyone. 'You should see him at parties.'

Everyone giggled. Lottie didn't go to parties, but if Gregory and Cecil ever held one she definitely would. She could imagine them being amazing fun. 'Thank you very much,' she said. 'I'm sure you'll both be invaluable.'

'And may I say, dear,' continued Gregory, 'how much we all miss dear, dear Elsie. She was a lovely woman. Very fond of a murder mystery. Always in when we'd had a delivery.'

Lottie smiled at him. She was getting used to people saying nice things about her nan and it made all this theatre stuff seem worthwhile. 'That's very kind of you to say, thank you. I think she was lovely too.' Lottie looked to Conner. The poor boy had sunk as low in his chair as possible without actually being underneath it.

'Well, umm, I'm Conner Shaw. I go to uni at Strawley and I'm doing Media and Film and … well, I just thought it'd be cool to do something like this.'

'Aww, what a wee sweetie,' said Debbie at which Conner went an impressive shade of pink.

'What about you, Lee?' Lottie asked.

Lee's eyes moved to her, a hint of fear in them. He sat up in his chair and clasped his hands in his lap. A faint redness appeared on his neck, rising up to his cheeks. 'Well, I suppose I'm mainly known for having got into a few fights on Saturday nights, but, actually, I've always wanted to act. You know those big dramatic scenes in movies? I've always wanted to be the one doing that. And I've been trying to change my ways since I turned thirty. You know, be more mature.'

Lottie was glad she'd defended Lee against Mayor Cunningham's accusations. He wasn't nearly as full of himself as everyone thought he was and something like this might help him show everyone how much he'd changed.

'I can't wait to see it,' said Gregory. 'I'm sure you'll be fantastic.' Lee visibly relaxed and Lottie decided she wanted Gregory to adopt her.

'I've, umm, I've never done anything proper, like Shakespeare.' The colour on Lee's chiselled cheekbones became more pronounced as he spoke. 'I don't even remember reading it at school. I was always at the back of the class messing around. Lottie can tell you that.'

He raised his eyes and Lottie was surprised he even remembered her. She'd fancied him back then, just like all the other girls in her year, but he'd hung out with the cool kids and she and Sid had bumbled around together at the opposite end of the playground, him reading his comics while she stuck to her favourite books. 'It's true,' Lottie replied, giving him a warm smile, glad she didn't fancy him anymore. 'You were always the one getting into trouble. But we're all starting from square one here. And you, Sarah?'

Sitting in the more relaxed atmosphere of the group Sarah no longer appeared snooty or stuck up. She was wearing jeans and a T-shirt and had pulled the sleeves of her cardigan down into her hands, just as Lottie did. When all eyes turned to her, Lottie saw Sarah swallow and nervous fingers started fiddling.

'My name's Sarah Powell. I work at the doctor's surgery on Hope Road and I'm also the secretary on the theatre board.' She smiled at Lottie. 'I've never done any acting but I like to sing and …'

'And?' asked Lottie, gently.

Sarah gave an embarrassed laugh and kept her eyes down. 'And it took all my nerve to turn up to the auditions. That's why I was last. I kept telling myself to go then getting scared. I've always got such terrible stage fright.'

74

Lottie felt her eyebrows raise. Sarah had seemed so together at the committee meeting, unlikeably so, and so immune to things like stage fright. Lottie was definitely having to rethink her attitudes towards people at the moment. She hadn't realised that everyone had insecurities, like her. They just didn't always let them get the better of them.

'I can help you with that, darling,' said Gregory.

Sarah's eyes brightened. 'Really?'

'Yes. You'd be surprised how many stars get it. I've got some good breathing exercises I can teach you.'

As the introductions continued Lottie was amazed to see how people encouraged each other and shook their heads at the self-deprecating comments. In an hour they had begun to bond and a good-natured camaraderie was developing. When the conversation died down, Lottie gathered their attention. 'I thought we should begin by having a chat about what you all thought the next steps were for the theatre. What do you guys want to do first?'

'I think we need to look into how much it'll cost to refurbish the theatre,' said Mrs Andrews gazing around. 'Unless the committee are doing that.'

'I'm beginning to,' Lottie said, confidently. 'And I can tell you that, at the moment, the theatre needs the roof fixing and the outside needs a clean-up. Inside, it's all cosmetic but still fairly costly and time consuming.'

'Do we have to wait for the next committee meeting?' asked Debbie. 'Or can we make decisions ourselves?'

'Maybe we should decide on a production?' replied Gregory.

'Yes,' said Cecil. 'We could do a musical.'

'I think we should organise a fun day to clean up the outside of the theatre,' mumbled Conner.

'Wait,' said Lottie. 'Quiet, everyone. What did you say, Conner?'

Conner sunk down again. 'Umm, I said, I thought we should organise something like a community fun day to clean up the outside of the theatre.' He sat forward and brushed the mop of gelled hair to one side so Lottie could see his eyes. 'It'll get lots of people involved too and shouldn't cost much either.'

'How will it work?' asked Mrs Andrews, obviously unaware how cleaning *anything* actually worked.

'Well,' Conner continued his voice a little louder this time. 'We could pick a date and buy a load of mops and buckets, and brooms and stuff, and then have them lined up outside the theatre. Everyone can come along and just grab one and clean a bit.'

Mrs Andrews scoffed. 'You have great faith in mankind, or no knowledge of it at all if you think people are going to come along and clean for free.'

'I disagree,' said Lottie, seeing the blush on Conner's cheeks. 'I know lots of people who'd come.'

'We can have some music playing too,' Conner continued. 'Make it a party. We can call it the "Big Clean".'

'We could have a collections box,' said Gregory, sitting forward. 'People might donate something. Even if it's only coppers, it all helps.'

'It's agreed then,' said Lottie. 'What a great idea, Conner.'

'Wait a moment,' replied Mrs Andrews. 'I'm not cleaning anything.'

Lottie wondered again how best to deal with Mrs Andrews and decided she needed to assert some authority. 'Mrs Andrews, being part of this group means us all working together. Sometimes we'll get to do exactly what we want and other times we won't. If anyone isn't willing to compromise like that then they might as well leave now.' Lottie felt a flush on her neck and cheeks as everyone looked at her. Cecil and Gregory were smirking at Mrs Andrews who stared at Lottie. If Mrs Andrews was blushing, Lottie couldn't tell from the screen of make-up, but she hoped it had worked.

'Very well,' Mrs Andrews replied and she sat back down, twisting the large diamond ring on her finger.

Enthusiastic voices began to all talk at once but Lottie left them to it. She moved to the side of the room and stood back leaning against the stage. Without thinking, she opened her mouth to speak to Sid, forgetting he wasn't there. He was mysteriously busy with something today. Lottie pulled her sleeves into her hands. It was a shame. He'd have been proud of her tonight, just as her nan would. She was even a little bit proud of herself.

Chapter 10

Three weeks later and the Big Clean was starting. Sid took the handle and placed the brand new mop back in line with the others. Giving Lottie a warm smile he said, 'Lottie, you've moved those mops and buckets around three times. Will you just calm down?'

'I'm sorry. I'm just nervous.' Lottie pulled her cardigan tighter around her.

Sid moved around in front of her and placed his hands on her shoulders. 'It'll be fine. People will arrive soon. Just be patient.'

Lottie smiled and gave a resigned nod.

'And we've got a great day for it.'

Lottie followed his gaze upwards. A clear cerulean sky stood over a barely moving sea, and on the pier, fishermen cast their lines, then relaxed back to wait for a catch. As Lottie drew her gaze down her eyes met Sid's. He looked exactly the same but different somehow. She hadn't seen him as much lately and Lottie realised she'd become so used to seeing his face she'd forgotten how deep and dark his eyes were. Like a rich coffee colour.

Sid kept his hands on Lottie's shoulders but his grin faded and he looked at her more seriously. More ... grown up. She waited for him to speak but he didn't. Mrs Andrews bustled over and

Sid let go and shuffled a little further away. She pointed to a group of youths arriving with musical instruments and amps.

'Who are that lot?' she demanded to know.

'It's the band,' said Lottie, standing on tiptoe and waving at them.

Although terrifying to look at, with slick black hair and piercings, the band were made up of quite sweet lads. Lottie had expected them to be called things like 'Punk' or 'Spit' but was happy to find that Lewis, Jordan, Isaac and Rupert were very polite boys, and very thankful to Lottie for the opportunity to play at the Big Clean. It wasn't long before they were doing a good job entertaining the blossoming crowd with some of classic rock's greatest hits.

Lottie eyed Mrs Andrews' cream tight-fitting dress. 'Do you want an apron, Mrs Andrews?'

Mrs Andrews looked at Lottie like she'd asked her to ride a unicycle or something else completely absurd. 'What for, Miss Webster?'

Lottie hid her confusion and tried to answer seriously. 'For cleaning.'

'I'm not cleaning anything. This is Chanel. I'm supervising.' Mrs Andrews stalked off and Lottie, with a resigned huff, followed.

She had already prepared for this scenario and rehearsed what she was going to say, even though she had hoped it wouldn't be necessary. 'Mrs Andrews, can I have a quick word?' Mrs Andrews slowed down and Lottie led her away from the others. Despite her concern, Lottie mustered her courage and kept her tone strong. 'I know you don't particularly enjoy cleaning, Mrs Andrews, and that you weren't exactly in favour of this but you will have to do your bit with everyone else and keep the buckets topped up. If you don't, people won't help, they'll just leave.'

Mrs Andrews rolled her eyes and turned away from Lottie, as Lottie suspected she would. She pulled out the ace up her sleeve.

'We're in the public eye today, Mrs Andrews. I'll be taking photographs and Sid will be going around getting quotes from everyone. It's important we're all doing our bit. I'm not asking you to scrub the walls yourself, just keep the buckets topped up with clean water. That's all. We all need to pitch in.'

Pursing her lips and tossing her hair back over her shoulder Mrs Andrews reluctantly nodded and Lottie went to the rest of the players to give them a pep talk.

'Everyone ready?' she asked. Smiling faces turned and nodded at her. 'We've already assigned tasks so if you're on donations duty this morning you should be going round with the buckets asking people to be generous and the rest of you are on cleaning, then we'll swap around this afternoon. Okay?'

Gregory and Cecil and a number of other players picked up their clean buckets with donations written on the side. Everyone else headed off to the mops and buckets welcoming those already there.

There was a buzz in the air as more and more people arrived. Though it was only May it was still warm and children dressed in shorts and summer dresses were grabbing up mops and buckets and splashing water all over the place while their parents stood behind, directing their efforts. The Greenley Players kept the buckets filled with water or wandered around with collection boxes.

'It's going very well, isn't it? Lottie said to Sid when she caught up with him later.

'Yes. Better than I expected.' He took his pen from behind his ear. 'Now, if you'll excuse me, I need to go and get some quotes for the article and you need to take some pictures.'

Lottie picked up her camera and saluted. 'Yes, sir.' She began roaming through the crowd, taking photos of the kids cleaning while the adults smiled fondly and scrubbed the higher parts of the walls.

A warmth rushed through her as she realised what she'd done.

Lottie never before thought she could achieve anything like this. She had made this happen and seeing the town coming together filled her heart.

Mayor Cunningham strolled around mingling with the crowd, a smug smile plastered on his face, shaking hands and probably, thought Lottie, taking all the credit. Which was fine, she was too busy enjoying the day to care. She looked to see if Sarah was close by but she wasn't near him. She was over with a large group of children smiling and handing out brooms.

Lottie was just about to take a breather when a smooth, deep, voice came over her shoulder. 'You must be Charlotte Webster. I've heard an awful lot about you.'

Lottie turned to see a tall man smiling down at her. He wore a tailored shirt that clung to his arms and stomach, and jeans. When Lottie lifted her head, piercing green eyes sprinkled with flecks of gold stared quizzically back at her.

'It is Charlotte Webster, isn't it?' His voice swirled and echoed around her head and his gleaming white smile shone like a spotlight on her face. Realising her mouth was hanging unattractively open she closed it and tried to smile.

'Yes, it is. I'm umm … hello.' Be confident, she told herself. You're acting chairman 'How do you do?' She held out her hand hoping it wasn't sweaty.

'Hi, I'm Jeremy Bell.' His stance was confident and he rested his hands lightly in his pockets. 'You've done a great job here today. It's not often you see a community coming together like this and certainly not to clean. It's amazing.'

'Thanks. It's been a great result.' Some hairs had escaped from her ponytail and Lottie brushed them behind her ear. 'Do you live in Greenley too?'

'Sometimes. I have a second home here, on the marina. I work in London during the week and come down at weekends.'

'Right,' said Lottie. Despite the warmth of the midday sun, she fidgeted with her cardigan, pulling it around her. 'Do you know

Mrs Andrews then? You're neighbours.' Lottie indicated where Mrs Andrews was. Unfortunately, at the time Mrs Andrews' face was screwed up in disdain as a smiling girl in a sun hat handed her a mop.

Jeremy followed her eye line and smiled. 'I do, a bit. I don't see my neighbours very much, though. I often don't arrive till late on Fridays and leave Sunday evenings to be back in London.'

Lottie searched for something to say. 'Sounds busy,' she managed then felt herself melting under the sight of his incredible eyes.

'Well, it was nice meeting you. I'll see you around.' Lottie watched him walk away to stand at the mayor's side.

'Who was that?' asked Gregory who had wandered over.

Lottie was too busy studying Jeremy's left hand for a wedding ring, so she didn't respond at first. She came to and saw Gregory staring at her, one eyebrow raised. 'Oh, his name's Jeremy Bell.'

'He's gorgeous, isn't he?'

'Yes, he is,' said Lottie, then realising she was speaking out loud, added, 'if you like that sort of thing.'

'You mean a tall dark handsome man with impeccable taste? What's not to like, darling?'

Lottie glanced over again at Jeremy. He had a confident, easy manner and a tall muscular frame but his smile was so warm and genuine. His eyes caught hers and Lottie turned quickly away.

'What did he want?' asked Gregory.

'Nothing,' Lottie said, confused. She wondered if she'd missed part of the conversation when she was staring at him or letting her mind wonder what his chest looked like.

'Nothing?' Gregory asked, smirking.

'He just came over and introduced himself.'

'Oh, sweetie, he was chatting you up, obviously.'

'I don't think so.' But her heart gave a flutter at the thought.

Gregory tutted. 'Of course, he was. I saw the way he smiled at you. That was a come-hither smile if ever I saw one.'

'Thanks for the vote of confidence,' said Lottie. 'But I really don't think he was.' She peeked back over her shoulder to catch one more glimpse of Jeremy's face. He was chatting to the mayor but his eyes still flicked to hers. Feeling scruffy, she brushed the dirt from her jeans and pulled her T-shirt down to hide her tummy.

Towards the end of the day, as the evening light paled, Lottie stood back and surveyed the gleaming theatre. It looked totally different and she lifted her chin and smiled. The graffiti had vanished, the paintwork was clean and the canopy glistened as the remaining drops of water dried in the sun. She lifted her camera and took a shot just as Mayor Cunningham approached with Jeremy a few steps behind.

'Ah, Miss Webster, I've been looking for you. I wanted to speak to you about Mr Bell here.'

Lottie quickly retied her ponytail, trying to look less like a Victorian street urchin.

'Mr Bell is a property developer, interested in the theatre.'

'What?' Lottie said sharply, taken by surprise. She hadn't expected him to say that. Her body tensed and she looked at Jeremy, whose eyes widened too. What was going on? Was Mayor Cunningham lining up prospective buyers already? She hadn't even had a chance to succeed yet. How could he? Anger spilled out of her voice as she spoke. 'What do you mean, a property developer?'

'Now calm down, Miss Webster,' said the mayor, nervously glancing to Jeremy. 'There's nothing to get worked up about. He just wants to—'

Calm down? Calm down? God, he was patronising. She wasn't a child. They couldn't take all this away from her already. She wouldn't let them.

'It isn't what you think,' said Jeremy edging out from behind him.

'No?' Lottie's lip quivered as she tried to control her anger.

She glared at the mayor, then at Jeremy. 'A property developer interested in the theatre? At the moment, it seems to be exactly what I think.' Lottie pivoted round and stomped off to the mops and buckets.

After all the effort she had put in, that scheming dick of a mayor had a property developer on speed dial. He must have been planning this all along. No wonder he was happy for her to take over as chairman, he knew it wouldn't be long before they sold it off. Bastard. And she was just beginning to enjoy herself.

Lottie looked around for Sid and as she turned saw Mayor Cunningham placating Jeremy in his usual slimy way. Well, ha! Hopefully he'd change his mind now. Jeremy glanced up then came walking towards her. 'It really isn't what you think, Miss Webster.' He ran a hand through his short, light brown hair. 'Please let me just —'

Lottie put her hands on her hips, the anger pushing the words out of her. 'Let me guess, you want to buy the land to chuck up about a million houses no local person can afford to buy so more second homers just like you can move in?'

'No,' he said, calmly.

Her breathing paused as she took in what he'd said. 'No?'

'No,' he replied, the most charming smile she'd ever seen forming on his lips. 'Firstly, that's not the type of property I develop. I deal with other types of commercial premises – offices and things like that. And secondly, I'd like to talk to you about your plans for the theatre and see if I can help. I'd like to get involved, if I can.'

'Oh.' Lottie felt her face grow hot. She'd made a complete fool of herself. A complete fool. She looked like a total arse now and cleared her throat. 'Really?'

'Really,' Jeremy laughed. 'Perhaps we could talk about it more over coffee sometime. I'd love to help if you're still looking for volunteers.'

His openness combined with the fact that he wasn't actually

the devil incarnate had thrown her and she was utterly lost for words. 'Umm ... right ... okay.'

'I thought that as I've refurbished a lot of buildings before I could help with the more technical side of things. I know all about building regs and planning permission – all the exciting stuff.' He bowed his head and kept his eyes down, embarrassed.

Lottie felt herself smile and he lifted his eyes to meet hers. They were as green as fresh spring leaves.

'And I could give you an idea of how much things should cost. It's boring, but it might be useful.'

'I'm sure it'll be really helpful,' Lottie said quickly. She fiddled with her cardigan sleeves. She was going to have to apologise for her behaviour now. She felt stupid and mumbled the words out. 'Sorry about before. I – I've just been working really hard on this and—'

Jeremy held up his hands. 'No need to apologise. Passion's a wonderful quality.'

From the burning at the tops of her ears she knew she was blushing.

'Listen, can I take your number or email? Then we can talk some more another time. I can see you're really busy today.'

Lottie's heart flipped over and she told it to calm down. It was only a business meeting. Not a date. She took her phone from the back pocket of her jeans and fumbled around trying to find her own number.

'Here's my card,' Jeremy said, giving her a business card from a small silver holder. Lottie took it just as Sid approached.

'Alright, Lots?' he asked, standing beside her to face Jeremy.

'Yes, I'm fine, thanks.' Sid stared at her expectantly. 'Oh, sorry, I should introduce you, shouldn't I? Sid, this is Jeremy Bell. Jeremy, this is Sid Evans.'

'Nice to meet you, Sid,' said Jeremy, offering his hand.

Sid took it and gave it a good shake but he didn't give his usual cheerful grin. 'You too.'

Silence descended and Lottie frowned at Sid. He was normally so friendly and chatty. What had come over him? 'Sid and I have known each other forever,' she said to Jeremy filling the void.

'Are you involved in the theatre as well, Mr Evans?'

Lottie felt Sid's shoulder against hers he was standing so close. 'Sort of. I'm the reporter with the local paper and we're covering the renovation of the theatre.'

Jeremy nodded then smiled at Lottie. 'I see. You're doing such a fantastic job, Miss Webster. It really is remarkable.'

'Lottie and I work together, don't we, Lots?'

She gave a quick smile at Sid, then turned back to Jeremy. 'Yes, I'm the photographer.'

'That sounds exciting.'

'It's not,' said Lottie, giving a little laugh.

'But it is fun, isn't it?' replied Sid, nudging her.

'Jeremy wants to be involved in the theatre campaign too.'

'I definitely do,' replied Jeremy. 'Tell me, Miss Webster, what's your next step?'

Lottie began to relax and her shoulders dropped to their normal position below her neck, rather than hiding up near her ears. 'I really need to start looking into how much it'll cost to sort out all the repairs.'

'Fantastic,' said Jeremy, his eyes brightening. 'That sounds like something I could help with. When do you think we could—'

'Lottie?' shouted Mrs Andrews angrily from across the way. She was stood by the theatre door holding a broken mop, her dress was covered in dirty water and she was glaring murderously at a small child. 'Lottie!'

'Oh no. Sid, could you just go and sort that out, please?' Sid didn't move. 'Sid?' she asked again and reluctantly he nodded. She didn't blame him. No one wanted to deal with Mrs Andrews in a mood.

'Nice to meet you, Mr Evans,' Jeremy called.

'Yeah, you too,' replied Sid as he grumpily shuffled off.

Lottie turned back to see Jeremy smiling down at her and her stomach jumped up and tried to strangle her lungs. He had a crooked but sexy smile and perfect teeth.

'So, how about we meet for a coffee some time to talk about the theatre?' said Jeremy. 'I could give you an estimate for the repairs and take you through what needs to happen first?' Lottie swallowed and nodded. 'Great. How about next Saturday? I can't really do much before that I'm afraid.'

The smile on her lips lifted her cheeks so high she could almost see them in her peripheral vision. 'Umm … yes, that'd be lovely. Thank you.' Inside, Lottie groaned. Should she have said thank you?

Jeremy smiled and held out his hand. 'It's been lovely to meet you, Miss Webster. See you then.'

Lottie smiled to herself as Jeremy walked back into the crowd. Sid had finished with Mrs Andrews and was now over in the corner talking to a leggy brunette swishing her hair around. She seemed to think she was in a shampoo commercial but it was still another person she'd never seen in the town before. Her nan was right. The theatre really was bringing everyone together, and she, Lottie Webster had made it happen.

Chapter 11

Mrs Andrews responded to Sid's help by caressing his arm and shooting lascivious glances that made his skin want to climb off and hide behind a bush. He glanced back over his shoulder. Lottie was still talking to that bloke and what was worse, she was smiling. She couldn't be flirting, could she? Lottie didn't know how to flirt.

Something about this made Sid anxious. Jeremy was too suave, too sophisticated, too perfect, too … smug. His teeth were straight and not tombstone-y, his hair was shiny and behaving itself and it was clear he was one of those gym-type blokes. He probably drank protein shakes, like the seagulls. Sid hadn't thought Lottie would go in for that sort of thing. But maybe she was just being polite as he wanted to help with the theatre.

There was no denying the day had gone well, better than anyone expected. And even Lottie with all her stressed out worrying and pessimism couldn't deny it. He'd got some lovely quotes for the next article and the town really seemed to be behind the theatre. Even the mayor, when he'd given his quote, conceded how well things were going.

Sid peeked over his shoulder again. Lottie was still talking. He scowled and went to get a drink from the ice cream van. 'Hello, Rob. Can I have a can of Coke, please?'

'Here you go, mate, it's on me, I've made a killing today.' He took one from the chiller behind him. 'Thanks for inviting me along. I'll make a donation over the next few days when I know where I am.'

'Brilliant. Thanks. Every little helps.'

As Rob passed him his can, a long lithe arm reached out holding a five-pound note.

'Can I have the same, please?'

On hearing Selena's voice, Sid turned and his heart stopped for a second. The way Selena was dressed took his breath away. She was wearing a tight Captain America T-shirt and tiny shorts over her long, toned legs. Her hair was down and curling about her shoulders. She looked like a model. Selena smiled. 'Hey, stranger.'

Sid's mouth had suddenly gone dry and his tongue felt like a husk. 'Selena. Hi.'

'Hey.' She looked down and shuffled her feet. 'How have you been? I haven't seen you for a few weeks.'

'No, sorry. I've been really busy with this.' He motioned around him. They'd texted a few times but, unsure how he'd come across and not wanting to risk one of his awful jokes being taken the wrong way, he'd kept them short and sweet.

Selena tossed her hair back over her shoulder. 'I was worried you were avoiding me.'

Sid quickly shook his head. 'No, no, I haven't. I wasn't. I've just, you know—'

'Been busy?'

'Yeah.' Sid scratched the back of his head.

A small smile appeared on Selena's plump lips. 'So, you haven't been avoiding me then?' She seemed so insecure and shy. Like him.

'No,' he replied a little too quickly. 'Definitely not.'

Sid remembered the awkwardness of sitting in his car at the end of their first date and swallowed as his body jittered with embarrassment. He lowered his head. It unnerved him to stare at such a perfectly beautiful woman and he was so completely inept when it came to flirting. 'I, umm … I—'

'Listen,' said Selena, opening her can of Coke. 'It's okay. If you don't want to see me again that's fine. I'm not offended.' She gave an odd laugh that Sid couldn't understand. 'It doesn't have to be weird or anything—'

'No, it's not that.' He reached out and his fingertips brushed her skin sending a tingle through his hand. She looked at him kindly. 'I'm just not very good at dates and things like that.'

Selena pouted. 'Maybe you need a bit more practice.'

'Maybe I do.' Sid smiled and congratulated himself on some good flirting.

Selena took a sip of her drink and Sid watched her long elegant neck as she tipped her head back. 'So what have you been doing today?' she asked. 'Are you writing another article?'

'Yeah.' Sid pulled his notebook from his pocket. 'People really enjoyed it and I've got some good quotes.'

'Can I give a quote?' she asked, brushing her hair back.

'Of course.' Sid grabbed the pencil from behind his ear and opened his notebook. Back on safer ground, he was feeling more confident.

'I was going to say that I think it's amazing we might get the theatre back. I think it'll be brilliant.' Selena blushed. 'That's not very clever is it?'

'It's still a good quote,' he reassured her. A dimple appeared in her left cheek. Selena really was the prettiest girl he'd ever seen, apart from Lottie. From the corner of his eye he could see Jeremy and Lottie laughing and smiling. And they'd already swapped numbers. His heart squeezed and he knew he had to be brave again. 'Listen, I think we're all heading to the pub after this, did you want to come?'

A moment of hesitation flickered across her features. 'I'd love to, but I'm actually here with my friend. It's her birthday.'

'Oh, right. I see.' Sid chastised himself for being overconfident and dropped his eyes. He didn't want to see a pitying look on her face.

'But we might swing by later. If I come will you buy me a drink?'

Sid smiled and the way she looked at him flooded his body with a feeling he hadn't had since 2003. 'I might do.'

Her eyes flashed. 'If you do, I might lend you my *St Elmo's Fire* soundtrack.'

Sid smiled and a chuckle forced its way out of his mouth. He really had thought it was only Lottie who liked cheesy Eighties movies. With a carefree shrug he said, 'How can I say no, then?'

Selena looked over her shoulder at her friends, then back to Sid and her hair wrapped around her neck like one of those slow-motion TV shots. 'Okay, see you later.'

A little while later Sid went with Lottie and the rest of the Greenley Players to the pub but kept his eyes on the door. When he thought of seeing Selena again, his stomach squirmed and he found himself shuffling in his seat.

'So, Charlotte Webster has a date,' said Gregory, cradling his gin and tonic. They were jammed into a corner of one of the oldest traditional pubs on Greenley seafront. It was tiny, dark, and always packed, but it was an institution in the town and Sid and Lottie had been drinking there for years. The owner was cricketing mad and every wall was covered with photos and souvenirs.

Sid looked up from his pint.

'That Jeremy Bell is rather lovely.' Gregory nudged Cecil's arm. 'Come on then, tell us all about him.'

Sid didn't want to hear about Jeremy Bell and tapped the corner of the beer mat on the table.

'It's not a date,' said Lottie, slowly turning her wine glass in her fingertips. 'We're just meeting for a coffee to discuss the theatre and how he can get involved. He said that as a property developer he—'

'A property developer?' replied Sid, sitting up. 'You didn't tell me he's a property developer. He's probably after the land, Lottie.'

Gregory and Cecil caught the severe note in his voice and scanned his face.

'He isn't,' she said, turning a little pink. 'He said he develops commercial property, like offices. He doesn't build homes.'

Sid's forehead creased with deep lines of concern. 'What sort of commercial property? It's not anything like, oh, I don't know, theatres, maybe?' He told himself it wasn't jealousy, he'd let those old feelings go. It was just that they'd worked so hard on the theatre and he couldn't understand how she'd risk it.

Lottie paused. 'He definitely said offices.'

'He could be lying, Lottie. You only met him today.' Okay, that sounded a bit ridiculous even to him, but still. 'Or he could be planning to put up an office block where the theatre is.'

Gregory and Cecil swung back around but Sid saw them raise their eyebrows at each other.

Lottie looked back down into her glass and Sid felt a twinge of guilt. He'd embarrassed her in front of everyone. 'I didn't get that impression. He said he wants to help.'

An uneasy hush fell between them and Gregory and Cecil turned back round, their nosiness obviously getting the better of them.

'So, what else do you know about him?' asked Gregory, glancing between the two of them. Sid chewed the inside of his cheek. He really didn't want to know any more about Jeremy sodding Bell right now.

Lottie's voice carried a happiness he hadn't heard in a long time and it was crushing to think he'd never made her sound like that. 'He lives in London during the week and he has a second home here on the ...' She trailed away but Sid had to know how the sentence ended, even though he already suspected the answer.

'A second home where?' he asked.

Lottie's eyes flicked up from under her eyelashes. 'On the marina.'

Sid knew he was being weird. He just couldn't shake this feeling that she had let him down. He wouldn't be like this if it was some nice normal bloke. It was just that Jeremy was the type of person they'd always disliked. A posh, put together toff. He grabbed his empty pint glass and headed up to the bar just as the door opened and Selena walked in. She came straight up to him while her friends went and found a table.

'Hello again,' she said, standing close. Sid couldn't help but notice her large breasts jutting out from the top of Captain America's shield.

His annoyance at Lottie turned to confidence in Selena's presence. 'Hello. I was just ordering a drink. Did you want one?'

'Yes, please. Can I have a glass of Prosecco? I'd love some bubbles.'

Sid leaned his lanky frame over the counter and ordered. When he turned to watch the room he deliberately avoided Lottie's gaze even though he knew she was watching him.

'I can't stay long,' Selena said. 'Like I said, it's my friend's birthday so I'll have to get back to them soon, but I wanted to say hi, as I promised.'

'That's okay,' said Sid, hiding his disappointment. He'd hoped she'd be staying a while. He heard Gregory and Cecil laugh loudly and noted Lottie was still watching him. 'Listen, I was wondering if you fancied going out again sometime?'

'I'd love to,' Selena replied with a wide smile and stood a little closer to him. 'I can lend you that CD then.'

He had to watch his big bony elbows or he was going to knock into her boobs. Suddenly feeling the need to impress, Sid turned to the bar and said, 'Actually, mate, can I make it a bottle of Prosecco, please?'

Selena stared wide eyed. 'You don't need to do that. I've already said yes.'

'I know,' Sid replied, his self-assurance returning. He spied Lottie still staring. 'I just thought you and your friends might like it. You said it was a birthday.'

'Thank you.' Selena lifted her head and kissed him on the cheek. The touch of her lips on his skin sent his heart into spasm and an adrenalin rush through his body. 'You're just the sweetest. Call me tomorrow, okay?'

'Okay,' he replied, trying to stop himself imagining kissing her properly, and while Selena took the bottle to the table and her friends screamed in delight, he picked up his pint and headed back to the Greenley Players. Lottie could see whoever she wanted. He was moving on. And who could be more perfect than Selena?

Chapter 12

'Can I have a skinny mocha, please?' said Lottie as the barista took her and Jeremy's drinks order. They were sat on the patio at one of her favourite cafés on the seafront. A couple of chain places had opened up in town which meant before long all the cafés, even the small independent ones Lottie preferred, were serving different types of coffee made any which way you chose. It was a good thing as far as she was concerned.

'Did you want whipped cream on that?' asked the barista.

'Yes, please.' What was the point if you didn't have cream? Lottie watched the frothy waves roll back and forth on the shore and the gentle breeze blew stray strands of hair into her face. She loved the taste of the briny air and the way the smell mixed with the scent from the little vase of flowers on the table.

'I'll have a black filter coffee, please,' said Jeremy. He was looking more relaxed this morning in a T-shirt, jeans and trainers. His plain T|-shirt looked weirdly desolate. She'd obviously grown far to accustomed to Sid's dubious taste.

Once the barista had gone Lottie asked, 'So how were you hoping to get involved in the theatre, Jeremy?'

He raked his hand through his short hair. 'Well, you mentioned before about the place needing fixing up. As a property developer

I thought maybe I could take a look and give you some pointers. Let you know how much it might cost.'

'That'd be great,' Lottie replied, fiddling with her cardigan sleeves. 'What sort of property is it you develop again? You said commercial, but I'm afraid I wasn't sure what that meant.' She just wanted to double check.

Jeremy smiled. His teeth were lovely and straight. 'I do lots of different things. Laboratories, offices, supermarkets. But it's really my project management skills I thought could help. Especially once you start on any building work.'

Lottie nodded. 'I think that'd be fantastic. We don't have anyone with that sort of expertise.' He really could fill the gap for them.

Jeremy paused while the barista brought over their drinks. The thing Lottie loved about this café was the mismatched china plates and dainty crockery. They also did wonderful muffins but as Lottie didn't really know Jeremy properly yet she didn't want to be scoffing one while he sat there talking.

'So, tell me,' he said, smiling at her. Lottie felt her insides do a little dance. 'How did you come to be involved with the theatre in the first place?'

Having talked about her nan's letter so many times now, Lottie felt confident replying without tears springing to her eyes or tightness strangling her throat. 'It's been abandoned for a couple of years. My nan died recently and she was chairman of the theatre committee. She was always campaigning to get it back up and running and she left me a letter asking me to take over, so I did.'

'Wow, that's quite something.' His eyes widened and Lottie hoped he was impressed rather than just surprised.

Lottie's voice lost some of its confidence. 'It's a bit odd, I know.'

'It's certainly a lot to deal with. How do you feel about it?'

That was a good question. She'd been so busy organising everything she hadn't had a chance to actually think about it. She was definitely busier than ever and while she wouldn't call the

Greenley Players friends, there were a few she could see herself getting along with. It had also stopped her living in her own little world. She'd been out most nights at various things or if she was at home she didn't just read and imagine another life, she was busy with plans and ideas of her own.

'I'm really enjoying it actually.' Her voice grew stronger again. 'A lot more than I thought I would. It keeps me very busy and we haven't even started with any productions yet. I'm sure once we do it's going to be a full-time job.'

'But you're having fun?' His tone was so caring Lottie was taken aback.

'Yes. Yes, I am.' She took a sip of her mocha and Jeremy drank his coffee.

He leaned back in his chair and savoured the taste. 'That's good coffee. Better than most of the places I know.'

'This is my favourite café,' said Lottie, eyeing up the muffins through the open door.

'I can see why. Greenley really is a lovely town. I'm surprised it's not more touristy.'

The conversation lulled and as small white clouds scurried across the bright blue sky, and the sound of hungry, eager gulls chatting to one and other rang in her ears, Lottie searched for something to say. 'Did you move down recently to Greenley?'

Jeremy's green eyes settled on Lottie and she felt a flutter in her chest. 'I hadn't heard of Greenley until about eighteen months ago. I was searching for a holiday place, somewhere I could relax and unwind after my manic week in the city and that's when a friend recommended this part of Kent. I came down and had a look around and fell in love straight away. It was love at first sight.'

Lottie looked across to the sea. The way he'd said 'love' echoed in her ears and she thought of her grandparents and the theatre, and how everything had changed, leading her to this moment. Seagulls danced in the sky and a few fishing boats returned to the harbour. 'It is a wonderful place. I love it here. I'm surprised I haven't seen you around town before.'

Jeremy lifted his cup but didn't drink. 'I've kept myself to myself since I moved down. I love the peace and quiet and go for walks just as the sun's rising. I'm up so early during the week that I tend to get up early at weekends too and I'm back in before the rest of the world really wakes up. I've had friends down and been out for dinner a few times.'

Lottie could imagine him walking along the beach haloed by a glorious rising sun and her breathing went a bit funny.

Jeremy took another sip of his coffee. 'When I saw the Big Clean in the paper I knew I had to stop by and see what was going on. It seemed such a great idea and for such a good cause.' He looked straight at Lottie. 'And what I saw was really mind blowing.'

Lottie felt so at ease with Jeremy she admitted, 'I'm really proud of what we achieved that day.'

'You should be. And your friend on the paper, what does he think of it all?'

'Sid? He really encouraged me to do this.' Not wanting him to get the wrong idea she added, 'He's my best friend. We've known each other for years. He knew my nan too.'

'Encouraged you? Weren't you sure at first?' When Jeremy sat back in his chair, Lottie could see toned, muscular shoulders beneath his T-shirt and averted her eyes to study her cup, unnerved by the stirring in her body. She brought her mind back to their conversation. 'Not really. It seemed like too big a job for me.'

Jeremy leaned in towards her. She could smell his aftershave, scents of something earthy mixed with spice. 'I really admire what you're doing here, Charlotte. The thing that drew me to Greenley was that it still had a remnant of community spirit, like you see in old movies where everyone knows everyone else. You don't get that in London. What I saw last week at the Big Clean was amazing, you brought everyone together. The whole place came alive and there was such a buzz.' He gave an embarrassed shake of the head. 'Sorry, I'm gabbling.'

'Not at all.' Under the table Lottie pulled her cardigan sleeves into her hands. 'And umm, everyone calls me Lottie.'

'Lottie it is then,' he said, taking another sip of his coffee but watching her over the rim.

She gave a smile and, stunned by the way the gold flecks in his eyes caught the light, she turned her cup on its saucer. 'It'll be great to get an expert opinion on the theatre before I start asking for quotes. I always worry about getting overcharged.'

'That's very wise. How about I take a look tomorrow? I won't be going back until the evening. We could have a look around and then maybe we can grab a drink afterwards?'

Two meetings with a handsome man in two days was pretty much unheard of for Lottie. Things like that didn't happen to her and yet, here she was with this dark-haired, golden-eyed Adonis and he was smiling. She found herself wanting to know him better. 'That sounds great.'

Sid was due to meet her for Sunday lunch tomorrow but she'd have to cancel. This was much more important and he'd understand. He hadn't minded the last time. 'Shall we say eleven then? At the theatre?'

'Perfect,' said Jeremy. 'It's a date.'

Chapter 13

Lottie and Jeremy were sat at an outside table of one of the new trendy bars. 'Here you are,' said Jeremy, sliding Lottie's wine glass in front of her. He took a large mouthful of his beer. 'That's better.'

Lottie had followed him around the theatre while he nodded and measured and wrote notes on his phone. Now they were sat, ready for her to hear how much it would cost to fix, and she was more than a little anxious.

'Roger told me what a challenge the theatre is,' Jeremy said. 'And now I've been in I can see why.'

'Roger Cunningham?' she asked warily.

'Yes.'

'How well do you know him exactly?' She hadn't meant to sound suspicious and she took a breath in, hoping Jeremy hadn't noticed.

Jeremy cradled his pint. 'A little. In a personal capacity. He's not a bad sort, you know. He can be a bit brusque sometimes, but he really thinks he's doing the best for the town. I disagree with him that the land would be better for housing. I'm more along your lines that we should keep it as a theatre.'

'Really?' Lottie's head lifted.

'Definitely. There's so many other places around here houses could be built. A building like this needs to be preserved. I think there's a lot of potential there.'

Lottie nodded, surprised he agreed. 'It was very popular before and I think it could be again.'

'So do I,' Jeremy said with a smile, then took another sip of his beer. On the beach near them the seagulls squawked with delight at the remnants of food they found.

Lottie sipped her wine. The use of Mayor Cunningham's first name had made her nervous. She'd have been more comfortable if Jeremy had called him Lucifer or Spawn of Satan and Sid's warning rang in her ears. She'd covered enough events with the mayor to know he was smarmy and snobbish at the best of times but if Jeremy disagreed with him that was a good sign. Lottie's mind wandered to Sid and what he was doing now. He'd sounded a bit fed up when she'd called to cancel lunch.

'So,' said Jeremy pulling out his phone and reading through, 'do you want to know how much I think repairs will be?'

Lottie nodded and readied herself for bad news.

'Well …' He took a deep breath.

'Oh no,' Lottie moaned.

'Don't be so scared, it's not actually that bad. The roof does need some repairs, that's why the place is so damp. Once you get the roof fixed it'll help a lot, but you'll need a lot of decorating inside. I think the seats can be salvaged. A good clean and they'll be fine. Structurally you're okay, it just needs sprucing up. The roof is definitely your worst problem. Get that sorted and everything else can follow after.'

'It sounds very expensive,' said Lottie, realising she'd been biting her fingernails. That wasn't very attractive.

'You've been very lucky actually. If the roof was worse you'd be looking at a lot more money.'

'Can you give me an actual figure?'

Jeremy nodded. 'I think you're looking at about ten thousand

101

pounds for a patch-up job. More if you choose to re-do the whole roof or change the seats and update the lighting.'

Lottie's eyes widened. 'But we haven't got that sort of money. I don't know how we'd even get it. I mean, the Big Clean raised about three hundred quid, but that's not nearly enough.'

Jeremy took a sip of his beer. 'Basically, there are two ways to get funding. You can either raise the money or be given it. Raising it will probably involve investors, I don't think you'll be able to make enough through community donations or sponsorship. There just aren't enough local businesses or individuals around here who could give that sort of money. You could try and get some grants, but that's much harder work. They involve a lot of paperwork.'

'How do you know all this?' asked Lottie, her mind struggling to take in everything he was saying. And his shirt fitted so well over his biceps, she was having to pull her eyes away.

Jeremy sat back and cocked his head to one side. 'I've worked with the Heritage Lottery Fund and things like that before. They won't give you any money until they've seen a ton of paperwork and detailed plans.'

Lottie didn't have time for all that. She had a full-time job to do on top of this.

'I think your best bet,' Jeremy carried on, 'is to find some big, national companies and approach them directly, or talk to the council. They might have some links already.'

Lottie nodded. 'Okay. I'll have a think about it. We need to find a more permanent solution in terms of funding. We can't just keep hoping for handouts from the council.'

'That's a great business mindset,' said Jeremy and Lottie glowed at the compliment. 'If there's any way I can help, let me know. You've got my number. We could always meet again to discuss it if you'd like.' Jeremy reached for his glass and his hand brushed Lottie's.

Lottie felt her breath catch as his smooth skin touched hers.

Then her mind began whirling around trying to figure out what she needed to do now.

Jeremy leaned towards her over the table. 'We could have dinner or something?'

'Hmm?' said Lottie looking up and meeting his gaze. She could hear her heartbeat getting faster.

Jeremy chuckled. 'I'm trying to ask you out on a date but I'm clearly making a bad job of it. I'm sorry. I wanted to ask you to dinner before but I thought you and that chap from the paper were an item.'

'Sid? God, no.' Lottie knew she'd screwed up her face unattractively and made an effort to unwind it.

'So … dinner next week?'

Lottie smiled and felt it light up her face. She resisted the urge to clap. 'I'd love to.'

'Great. I'll book us a table for Saturday night. Where would you like to go?'

Lottie didn't care if they only went to Nando's. It was still a date. Lottie Webster had a date! She took a sip of her wine trying to hide the grin tugging at the corners of her mouth. She had to at least try to play it cool. 'I don't mind.'

'To next week,' said Jeremy, raising his glass in toast.

Lottie lifted hers. 'To next week.' She couldn't bloody wait.

Chapter 14

The Greenley Players chatted excitedly and gathered in a line on the front row of seats while Lottie prepared to begin. She searched frantically in her camera bag for her notes, having stuffed them in just as she was leaving work. She'd been running late after spending the entire afternoon trying to get a shot of Greenley's cutest pet – an unpleasant Pekinese who Lottie and Sid thought bared an uncanny resemblance to Mrs Andrews. Finally, she found them, crumpled and dog-eared, and turned around.

'First of all, I wanted to say thank you all so much for your efforts in making the Big Clean such a big success. It was amazing and the theatre looks brilliant now. What we need to decide today is, what do we do next?'

'What about actually putting on a production?' asked Gregory.

'I don't think the theatre's quite up to that yet,' said Lottie. 'I know the outside has been cleaned up, but it's still a bit of a state inside.'

'I know that,' said Gregory, kindly. 'I was thinking more about something like "Shakespeare in the Park".'

'Shakespeare?' said Lee in mild panic.

'Yes.' Gregory's tanned face wrinkled as he smiled.

'Are you sure that won't be a little too much for our first

performance?' asked Lottie. 'Couldn't we start with something easier? Something modern? And shouldn't you all get to know each other a bit more first?'

Gregory cleared his throat. 'When I was on the stage—'

'Here we go,' muttered Mrs Andrews, rolling her eyes.

'When I was on the stage,' Gregory continued, 'there would be a small amount of time getting to know each other before rehearsals and the read-through began. I really think we should capitalise on the level of interest we've had and put on a summer production. We can bond and learn as we're rehearsing.'

'I agree about capitalising on the interest but that doesn't give us much time,' said Lottie. 'It won't be enough time to decide on a play, assign parts and rehearse. We'd need to sort out costumes, stage settings … everything.' Lottie couldn't hide the panic in her voice no matter how hard she tried.

'Not if we have it on the bandstand in the park,' said Gregory. 'We'd only need costumes and we could probably borrow them from somewhere else. The theatre in Strawley maybe? Oh, come on, Lottie. Let's give it a try.'

Lottie looked around the room at the hopeful faces staring back at her. Was she just being pessimistic? Jeremy's advice about finding investors had been weighing on her mind. Even though he'd said to go to the council she didn't want to ask Roger, he'd be completely unhelpful – but she had no idea who else to ask. Everyone was looking at her expectantly. She knew sod all about the inner workings of theatre companies and Gregory did have more experience than her. And, she had to learn to start trusting other people more. 'Okay,' said Lottie to sighs of relief. 'What play shall we do?'

'I was thinking *Much Ado About Nothing*,' said Gregory, pulling a copy out of his bag. 'And I've already had some ideas about casting.'

Lottie chewed the inside of her cheek biting back a mixture of annoyance and amusement. The cheeky sod had been planning this all along.

Gregory was leaning so far forward trying to see everyone he was about to fall out of his seat. 'It's such a perfect play for this time of year.'

'Will the park give permission for us to perform?' asked Mrs Andrews.

Lottie shrugged. 'I suppose if there's nothing else booked.'

'There's nothing booked,' said Gregory. 'I checked. In fact, I made a provisional booking.'

Of course he had, naughty man. Lottie raised her eyebrows. She'd expected to be reining in bossy Mrs Andrews but hadn't thought she'd have to do the same for Gregory. She liked him, which made it ten times harder, but she couldn't let him take over either. With a stern voice she said, 'Gregory, you really should have spoken to all of us first.' Beneath his bronze tan she saw a hint of red on his cheeks and felt a pang of guilt. 'How many performances were you thinking of?'

'We need a Saturday evening performance,' said Debbie. 'And then a matinee and an evening one on Sunday.'

'That's what I was thinking,' said Gregory, barely able to contain his excitement.

'I'm not sure about a matinee,' replied Lottie, trying to be diplomatic. 'We don't want to push our luck with the public.' There were mumbles of disappointment but the majority agreed. 'What do you think, Conner?' asked Lottie, keen to get everyone's input.

'Sounds cool. I'll need to read it though.'

'Never heard of Shakespeare?' asked Mrs Andrews.

Without stopping the tapping on his phone, Conner replied, 'I've read *Hamlet*, *King Lear*, *Macbeth*, and *The Tempest*, but not that one.'

Lottie smiled. *Well done, Conner.* She looked at them all. 'Are we all agreed then?'

Everyone cheered but Lottie couldn't shake the feeling of dread lurking in the pit of her stomach. It was all happening too soon.

Too fast. She tried to remember which one *Much Ado* was and if there'd been a film adaptation she might have seen, but so far she was coming up blank.

'So, for casting,' said Gregory, pulling a list from his book and lifting his finger to start pointing.

'Hang on—' Lottie interrupted, holding up her hands. She really didn't want to embarrass him but her annoyance was rising. He could have spoken to her before the meeting. They all had her number. 'I'm happy to listen to your ideas, Gregory, but I'd really like to have the final say on the casting once I've discussed it with Conner. Especially as he'll be directing.'

'Me?' Conner asked, looking up from under his fringe with bright eyes.

'Yes,' Lottie said. 'You said you wanted to do the directing and behind the scenes work rather than act. You don't have to though, if you don't want to do it just yet.'

'No, no. I do. That'd be great.' Conner rested his phone in his lap.

'Great,' said Lottie, excited by his response. 'Then Gregory, you tell us your ideas and once Conner and I have had a chat about it, we'll confirm parts.'

To Gregory's credit he didn't sulk or moan. He gave Conner a reassuring grin and nodded to Lottie that he'd understood. 'I was thinking lovely young Sarah could be Hero, Mrs Andrews I suppose will have to be Beatrice and—'

'I don't see why she gets to be Hero, and I have to be Beatrice,' said Mrs Andrews, standing up and pointing an accusatory finger at Sarah. 'She's a singer, not an actor, like me.'

Sarah stared like a rabbit in headlights under Mrs Andrews' glare.

'Because,' interrupted Gregory, 'Hero is supposed to be young and beautiful, and you're, well …' He waved his copy of *Much Ado* up and down the length of her body.

Lottie took a deep breath. 'Now, now, everyone, if you're—'

'In the old group,' Gregory interrupted, 'your nan was always happy to listen to my ideas and—'

'I appreciate that,' said Lottie, cutting him off in return. 'But this is a new group now.' Lottie's heart fluttered unpleasantly as she spoke but she had to press on. 'As I was saying, if you're all going to be like that we might as well not bother. With any luck we'll be doing lots more plays and everyone will get a chance to be in the spotlight.' She looked at them all the same way her nan did before saying, 'I'm not cross, I'm just disappointed.' Mrs Andrews crossed her arms over her chest. 'Carry on, Gregory.'

'And I thought Lee could make love to Sarah and be Claudio—' Lottie bit her lip as Sarah blushed furiously at Gregory's choice of words. 'I'll be the evil Don John and poor Cecil will have to be Benedick.'

Lottie remembered now that Benedick was in love with Beatrice. Oh yes, poor Cecil. Mrs Andrews was not amused and her angry eyes focused on Gregory who continued to name cast members. When he'd finished Lottie said, 'Thanks, Gregory. I'll email you all tomorrow to confirm your parts once Conner and I have discussed it, but next time, we'll hold auditions so everything's fair, okay?'

On hearing the door squeak, Lottie turned and her mouth dropped open. Sid held out his hand to a beautiful woman who was smiling and laughing at something he'd said. She had perfectly pruned eyebrows and her hair was long, silky and dark. As Sid walked her down the aisle towards the stage he placed a hand in the small of her back. It was the woman he'd been talking to in the pub after the Big Clean. Lottie hadn't realised they knew each other so well.

Some women looked glamorous no matter what they did, and for others, like Lottie, it was a promised land. The girl wore tight skinny jeans, a white T-shirt and trainers that, unlike Lottie's, were not coated in mud and assorted debris. Her stomach was flat and smooth, and her breasts high and perky. Lottie wrapped her cardigan around her and the players went back to chatting.

'Afternoon,' said Sid. 'This is Selena. I brought her in to see the theatre. You don't mind, do you?'

'Hello,' Selena said, wrapping her arm through Sid's. 'You're Lottie, aren't you? Sid's told me so much about you.' She gave Lottie a dazzling smile.

'Hi, yes I am.' In shock she looked to Sid then back to Selena. 'Nice to meet you. So how do you two know each other?'

'Oh, I'm his girlfriend,' Selena said, then turned to Sid and smiled up at him. 'Aren't I?'

Sid looked down at her and said, 'Yes,' then gave the soppiest smile Lottie had ever seen. Her stomach fell to the soles of her shoes. Girlfriend? When did all this happen? How? How did this happen?

'What are you guys up to?' asked Sid.

'Umm, we were talking about putting on our first production and how it should be directed,' replied Lottie, happy that she sounded lofty and theatre-ish. Feeling small and dumpy next to Selena, her insecurities were making her defensive. Plus, Sid had a girlfriend and he hadn't even told her he'd had one single date.

'Wow, that's exciting. I nearly auditioned,' Selena replied.

'Really?' Lottie always thought girls who looked like Selena did exactly what they wanted, having a self-confidence Lottie could only dream of.

'Yeah, but then I thought, you're probably not going to want someone who only dances, are you? Although I could probably act if I put my mind to it. I've never tried.'

Lottie nodded along with what she was saying, still taken aback by the idea of this gorgeous woman being with her Sid. 'We've got all sorts of talents in the players. Maybe you can audition next time?'

'Yes, maybe.' Selena shrugged a shoulder.

Sid wandered off to talk to the players and was immediately grabbed by Mrs Andrews, leaving Lottie alone to chat to his new girlfriend. She still couldn't believe he'd got one. She'd always thought she'd feel happy for him when the day came, so why didn't she? 'So, what do you do?' asked Lottie.

'I work in the beautician's in town.'

'Do you like it there?'

'Yeah, it's nice. I get a free mani every week.' She waved her fingers at Lottie to show off perfectly shaped and painted nails. 'You should get your nails done. I could give you a discount, you know, mates' rates.'

'Oh, right, thanks.' Lottie glanced down at her hands to see chewed, uneven nails at the end of her short stubby fingers. She glanced at Selena's nails. They were more like almond-shaped talons. Selena was being so friendly, Lottie felt even more intimidated. 'So how did you and Sid meet?'

'We were at university together. I moved away afterwards but now I'm back. You've known Sid for ages, haven't you? He told me you're basically like his sister. That's why I was so excited to meet you.'

Sister? Sister? They weren't like brother and sister, they were best friends. How on earth could he say sister? Their relationship was so much more than that. It was indefinable. It transcended so simple a label.

Lottie nodded but it felt like a siren was going off in her head. 'How long have you and Sid been seeing each other?' she managed to ask. Lottie knew she sounded like a mum or nosy great-aunt at a wedding but she couldn't help it. Seeing as Sid had never said a word she had to find out somehow. Why hadn't he told her?

'We've been out on a few dates. We're going for dinner tonight as well.' She flicked her hair back over her shoulder and Lottie nearly had to duck as the long soft tendrils flew through the air. 'And he said he'd tell the waiter what I want. I'm not very good at saying things in French or Italian, or whatever language it is.'

Lottie smiled. That was so like Sid, even though he couldn't speak French or Italian either. From the corner of her eye she studied Selena's perfectly made-up face. For some reason Lottie had always thought Sid would end up with someone more relaxed and low maintenance, like she was. But not her, obviously, because she'd never felt that way about him. Selena just didn't seem his type. What on earth could they have in common?

'What do you think of my best friend here then?' asked Sid, joining them. The use of that term stung Lottie.

'She's lovely,' replied Selena, giving a dazzling smile.

'And what do you think of my girlfriend? Aren't I the luckiest man in the world?' He stared down at Selena. Sid had never looked at anyone like that and it made his face seem different.

'You certainly are,' Lottie replied. She wished they would go away and soon. She needed to process this new, world-shattering news. It was like Greenley was in a snow globe and someone had just picked it up and shaken it around. 'Where are you off to now then?' she asked, hopeful they would take the hint.

'I've got to be back at the salon in twenty minutes,' said Selena. 'Just enough time for me and Sid to get a bite to eat. Have you been to the new salad bar in town? It's awesome.'

'But Sid hates salads,' announced Lottie, before she could help herself. He did though. He was always moaning whenever anything resembling a vegetable landed on his plate. It was shocking that he didn't have rickets.

Selena gave her a smile and put her arm through Sid's again. 'I bet you don't have time for lunch at the moment, do you? You must be so busy. I think you're doing amazing by the way.'

'Th—thanks,' mumbled Lottie. Selena was talking so quickly and Lottie had no idea what to make of this whole situation let alone the fact that Sid now seemed to enjoy eating lettuce.

After another one of those soppy grins, Sid looked at Lottie. 'Isn't she the best? Come on, honey, we'd better get moving.'

'Don't forget about mates' rates,' Selena called over her shoulder as Sid led her away. 'You should treat yourself!'

Lottie folded her arms over her chest and scowled as the door revolved slowly behind them. Sid had a girlfriend. She uncrossed her arms to pull her cardigan tighter and stared at the fading murals on the ceiling. How could that have happened without him saying anything? They saw each other all the time, he could have said something whenever he wanted! But they weren't seeing each other that much now, were they? Most nights after work she had to dash off to committee meetings or work on the theatre plans, or research this and that, and at work all she did was talk about the theatre too. With a sinking feeling Lottie realised that she and Sid had spent very little time together over the last month and now it looked like he wouldn't have the time to see her.

The voices in the background came into focus and she took a deep breath. Mrs Andrews was still arguing for being Hero and Sarah looked like she was about to cry. Cecil was stamping his foot having a tantrum and Gregory was waving his copy of *Much Ado* in a rather threatening manner. With a heavy heart she headed back to work.

At least she had her date with Jeremy to look forward to, which, come to think of it, she hadn't told Sid about either. But even though it was Jeremy he'd be pleased for her, wouldn't he?

Chapter 15

'You look wonderful,' said Jeremy when he met her outside the restaurant. It was like he knew she hated walking in on her own and was already there waiting for her. The Courtland was small and intimate with a large glass extension. Rustic tables were covered with plain white tablecloths, and flickering tea lights gave a quiet refined glow.

'Thank you,' replied Lottie. She gazed up at the dim evening sky where a few stars were starting to twinkle against the deep blue, and a dull moon hid behind the greying clouds. She'd purchased a black pencil skirt and chosen a plain black, long-sleeved silk top. It was simple and elegant. She would never think she looked beautiful, not like Selena, but she was at least present-able. The skirt skimmed her rounded stomach and hugged the curves of her hips and the long sleeves of her top hid wobbly upper arms. 'You look very nice too.'

'What this old thing?' Jeremy joked, brushing his hands down his jacket. 'I'm afraid suits are my normal everyday attire. I didn't make it down last night, something came up. Sorry if I'm a little crumpled.' His eyes skimmed up and down her body and knowing he was looking at her sent a heatwave through her.

They went inside and the waiter showed them to a table and

took their drinks order. Lottie, thinking of the bill, ordered a small glass of the second cheapest white wine.

'Shall we make it a bottle?' asked Jeremy as he took off his jacket and hung it on the back of his chair. Lottie admired his toned torso beneath the close-fitting shirt and caught his hopeful smile. 'Yes. Why not?'

The waiter disappeared and Lottie picked up the menu. She'd been so nervous all day she hadn't eaten anything and now, sat in the restaurant, the delicious smells made her absolutely ravenous.

'How are things going with the theatre?' Jeremy asked.

Lottie smiled, thinking of the fun she'd been having – before Selena arrived, that was. 'Not bad, there's a lot to get my head round.'

Jeremy poured them both some water and took a sip. 'Any luck with the council and investors?'

Lottie shook her head. 'I haven't spoken to Roger yet. There's a committee meeting coming up next week. I'll speak to them then.'

The waiter came back with their drinks and poured a small amount of wine in each of their glasses. Jeremy took a sip, swilled it around his mouth and then swallowed. 'Lovely.'

The waiter stared at Lottie who quickly did the same then nodded. Jeremy poured them both quite large glasses and said, 'You really do look very beautiful tonight.'

Lottie felt her cheeks get hot and hoped she wasn't blushing too much.

'So, tell me all about Charlotte Webster.'

'What do you want to know?' she asked nervously, but Jeremy's smile was reassuring and he sounded genuinely interested.

'Tell me everything. Were you born here?'

'Yeah. I got a job on the local paper when I was twenty-one, just after I finished university, and well, I've never left.' Lottie thought how sad and provincial that sounded and took a large gulp of wine. Every time she glanced down she could see her cleavage. It was unnerving.

'What did you study at uni?' Jeremy asked, taking a sip of his wine.

'Photography. Unsurprisingly.' Lottie felt dull and inwardly groaned. If her personality was a Dulux colour chart she'd be various shades of magnolia, or worse, grey. Everything about her was boring. The nerves rolled around in her stomach again and she reached for her wine. Jeremy waited patiently not pushing or rushing her and she relaxed a little more. 'I've been taking photos for as long as I can remember. I'd always planned on getting some exhibitions but there aren't many galleries around here.'

'You should try somewhere bigger,' Jeremy said when she'd finished. 'London, maybe? There are so many galleries, even small ones, who must always be looking for new talent. It's a big place with lots of opportunities.'

'I've thought about it, but not enough to actually do anything about it.' She was definitely going to put all those random photos of abandoned buildings into a portfolio and start showing it around. Why was her glass half empty?

Just as the conversation began to flow and Lottie felt more at ease, the waiter returned to take their order. She ordered a steak and fries, her favourite.

'Don't you want a starter?' asked Jeremy.

A horrible cold shiver ran up the back of her neck. She hadn't thought about a starter. Had it really been so long since she'd been on a date, or even eaten out with anyone other than Sid that she'd forgotten what to do? Idiot. 'Umm, no – no thanks. I get too full otherwise.'

'Me too,' said Jeremy, smiling, refilling their glasses.

She took another large drink, her hands clammy on the cold glass.

'I think I'll have the soy-flavoured salmon with green beans but can I change the new potatoes to a salad?'

The sullen waiter nodded, scribbled on his pad and departed.

'Do your parents live here too?' Jeremy asked. He loosened his tie and Lottie's heart gave a double beat.

She shook her head. There was still a pang of bitterness towards her parents and even after all these years she hadn't got over it. She hadn't forgiven them for missing Nan's funeral either. 'My parents moved away when I was a teenager.' Seeing the same confusion on his face everyone showed when she said this, she added, 'My dad's a diplomat and travels a lot. It was my nan who raised me.'

'I've been meaning to say how sorry I was to hear about your nan,' said Jeremy. His eyes were sparkling even brighter with the concern evident in them. 'It sounds like you were very close.' He placed his large, warm hand over hers, gave it a squeeze then removed it. She liked the feel of his strong but gentle grip as she felt a prick of sadness pierce her buoyant mood. He must have sensed her feelings, or read it on her face as he said, 'So how are the Greenley Players shaping up?'

Unnerved by the softness of his voice and the way her skin was tingling, Lottie took another gulp of her wine. 'Good. We're planning our first production – *Much Ado About Nothing*. We're all very excited.'

'That sounds great. I'm sure it'll be a huge success. I used to be in an am dram group at university.'

'Really?' Lottie smiled at the idea. It was difficult to picture him on a stage, playing a part; he seemed so confident just being himself.

'I loved it,' he replied, meeting her eyes and with a playful smile. 'I was awful though. Dismal. I really can't act.'

'No?'

'No. I got relegated to painting the scenery.'

Lottie laughed. 'Well, if we need a hand I'll know who to ask.' She felt her muscles unwind and she leaned forwards resting her arms on the table. She hadn't meant to flash her cleavage but as

Jeremy's eyes darted down and then back up again, Lottie found she didn't actually mind.

Jeremy stared at Lottie's face as if studying it and her stomach flipped over. The waiter brought their food and the more they talked the more she relaxed. She drained her glass and frowned at the empty bottle sitting on the table. Jeremy ordered another. 'Do you come down every weekend?' Lottie asked.

'I try to.' He ran a hand through his hair. 'I really love it here. The city's great, and I'm so busy I don't have a chance to get lonely during the week but at the weekends, well, it's different, isn't it?'

'I'd have thought you were out every weekend with friends?'

'It may sound silly but most of my friends are either getting married and having kids, or the single ones still behave like students, getting drunk. It's just not my scene anymore. I want something more … more—'

'Stable?' offered Lottie, surprised by how open he was being.

'Yes, exactly.' He smiled. 'I've never felt as settled as I do here. This is where I could see myself getting married, raising a family. Taking the kids on bike rides along the beach, that sort of thing.' His eyes had taken on a far-away quality and Lottie wondered if he was picturing it as clearly as she could and feeling the same rush in her chest.

By the end of the meal, Lottie had told him all about her life with her nan and Jeremy was generous with his compliments but not insincere. After a second bottle of wine between them, Lottie felt intelligent, beautiful and funny, as if the wine had magnified all the tiny, average things about her and placed them centre stage.

'So when's your next committee meeting?' asked Jeremy.

'Thursday,' Lottie said but it took all her concentration to remember the days of the week in the right order. She took a bite of her chocolate torte. It was delicious. The dense dark chocolate swirled in her mouth and she savoured it before replying. 'I don't think we're going to find investors very easily, or anyone to just give us money. I mean, who's going to shell out for our tiny leaky theatre in our boring little town?'

'I would.'

'Sorry?' Lottie held her spoon in mid-air. The wine must have gone to her head because she could have sworn he'd just said he'd like to give some money, but that couldn't be right.

Jeremy set his glass down and smiled. 'I want to donate to the theatre.'

She had heard correctly. Lottie's ribs squeezed around her heart taking her breath away. 'Seriously?'

'Of course.' Jeremy's leg brushed against hers under the table but she didn't move away. 'Listen, Lottie, I love this town more and more every time I come down. I've never felt at home anywhere before. London's great and I'm not giving it up, but I love coming here at weekends and seeing how the community is behind this. It's just … well.' He shrugged. 'I just thought that sort of thing was long dead. I think the theatre will be a huge success and if I can help, I'd like to. I feel like I'm investing in my future, not just the town's.'

Lottie finally raised her spoon to her mouth and swallowed the last piece of torte. 'But what does that mean exactly?'

'It means I'll provide some money to get the place back on track.'

'Oh,' said Lottie, trying to work out if this was a good or bad thing. She didn't know how these things worked and was so worried about making the wrong decision she couldn't say yes or no at the moment.

Jeremy's expression was reassuring. 'Don't worry. I just want to provide enough money for the roof to be fixed and Roger mentioned you had some vacant seats on the committee. I'd love to be involved in that if I could.'

'I — I don't know what to say.'

'Just say you'll let the committee know how much I want to

help. I'm happy to come and present my offer formally if you need me to.'

Lottie again tried to figure out this new situation. Her instinct was to trust him and say yes straight away but her old nervousness was flaring up. 'I guess the mayor will have to ask the council.'

'Great.'

The conversation moved on and by the end of the night Lottie was glowing. She'd been on a real date and so far she hadn't completely embarrassed herself. They'd chatted and laughed and it had felt so easy, almost like being with Sid.

When Jeremy offered to take her home, she had no problem saying yes. They wandered along the quiet roads to her house under a heavy sky streaked with purple and navy. The birds were silent, asleep in their nests, and only the odd car passed them as they walked. Streetlights lit the night and the heavy smell of lavender filled the air. They stopped outside Lottie's house and she turned to face Jeremy. Even in her heels she was at least a foot shorter than him and she raised her head up to see his face.

'Thank you for a lovely evening,' she said, trying to shift from one foot to another without him noticing, her feet aching in her high heels.

'I've had a wonderful time,' Jeremy replied. He'd hooked his jacket on a finger and hung it over his shoulder. The small gap between them felt thick was anticipation.

Lottie brushed her hair behind her ear. 'You didn't have to pay for dinner. I would've happily split the bill.'

'I know,' said Jeremy, putting his free hand in his pocket leaving Lottie disappointed he wasn't taking hers. 'But what sort of a gentleman would I be if I let you pay?'

She looked up wanting to see his face once more before they went their separate ways. She wanted to step into the gap and be closer to him but it felt almost too thick to enter. 'Goodnight then.'

'I'd love to do this again, Lottie. Can I call you sometime?' He finally reached for Lottie's hand and bent his head towards hers. Lottie raised hers upwards and stared at the pale yellow moon as he kissed her cheek.

'I'd love to do this again too,' she said and after saying goodnight, Lottie forgot the pain in her feet and tottered up the steps, and into the house.

Chapter 16

'Do you want to get a bag of chips and sit on the beach?' asked Sid, as they left the office the following Monday. 'It's a nice evening. Or are you dashing off somewhere?'

He couldn't actually remember the last time they'd spent an evening doing some of the things they used to do before all this theatre business started. He missed just watching TV with Lottie and the way they used to laugh at whatever was on. He missed going shopping with her and eating together. Elsie's letter was meant to shake up Lottie's world but had Elsie known she'd be shaking his up as well? He wouldn't have put it past her. She was a mischievous old bugger.

'No, I'm not dashing off anywhere,' Lottie replied, packing her camera away. 'Are you?'

'No.'

'Then if you can bear to be in my company,' she teased, 'yes, please. I would love a bag of chips.'

They headed down to their favourite fish and chip shop and Sid ordered. He took the steaming hot chips wrapped in newspaper and coated them in a little bit of salt, and lots and lots of vinegar, just the way Lottie liked them.

They walked along in companionable silence to one of the old wooden benches on the promenade. Seagulls hung on the breeze above the gently ebbing tide. It was a beautiful evening and the slowly setting sun cast long shadows on the pavement. Lottie, who had brought her camera bag, snapped a shot of a lone seagull hanging in the air and Sid smiled.

Sid stretched out his legs and crossed them at the ankles. 'I can't believe the paper's circulation has gone up so much since the theatre thing started. David's so chuffed.'

'I know,' Lottie replied, happily, putting the lens back on and placing her camera back in the bag. 'I think people are really getting behind us.'

'I guess it makes a change from reading about planning application disputes and the latest large fish to have been caught.'

Lottie giggled. 'Definitely. It's nice to be busy, isn't it? Here.' Lottie took a large brown envelope out of her bag and handed it to Sid.

'What's this?'

'Open it.' Lottie smiled at him.

Sid lifted the flap and pulled out a T-shirt with Chewbacca's face on it. A huge grin spread over his face. 'Thanks, it's great. But why did you get me this?' He suddenly worried he'd forgotten something important.

'Because I've missed you and because I saw it and thought you'd like it.'

Knowing Lottie still thought about him and missed him warmed his soul. Sid handed Lottie the chips, took off the T-shirt he'd been wearing all day and put the new one on. Lottie looked away while he changed. 'There what do you think?'

'I like it,' she said, popping a chip in her mouth and handing back the packet. 'How's Selena?'

Sid heard the tension in her voice. 'She's fine. How's Jeremy?'

Lottie smiled at the mention of his name. 'Fine.'

They fell into an awkward silence. The easy rhythm of their

friendship seemed to flounder whenever one of them mentioned the new people in their lives.

That morning, when Lottie told him she'd been on a date with Jeremy, Sid found himself tensing up so much he nearly dribbled his tea. It wasn't that it was weird someone should find Lottie attractive, it was that Jeremy was too flash, too sophisticated. For goodness' sake, he even clearly whitened his teeth. Not that Lottie wasn't sophisticated, she was just a low maintenance kind of girl, easy going and relaxed, and he'd always thought she'd pick a low maintenance kind of guy. He caught Lottie studying him.

'Why didn't you tell me you had a girlfriend?' she asked and he could sense the hurt even though she kept it from her voice.

Sid shrugged. 'I don't know.' He was surprised she even cared. 'You didn't tell me you had a date with Jeremy until today.'

Gentle creases formed on her brow. 'But that's because you don't like him.'

Sid didn't know what to say so stayed quiet. At least he and Selena were having a really nice time together. After he'd cleaned up and had someone in to professionally clean that weird stain off the carpet he'd let her come to his flat. He still didn't know what the stain was or how it got there. He wasn't going to sniff it and find out. But they'd snuggled on the sofa watching TV and the best thing was she'd loved the flat and the views out over the beach.

'Sid?'

'Hmm?' he replied through a mouthful of delicious potato.

'Did you hear what I said?' Lottie's voice was calm but Sid could always tell when she was acting and the way the intonation lifted at the end he knew he'd missed something important. 'Jeremy wants to donate some money to the theatre.'

He swallowed quickly and the vinegar stung his throat. 'What? Are you joking?'

'No, I'm not joking. Why are you pulling that face?'

'I'm not pulling a face,' Sid replied, hastily rearranging his expression to something more natural.

The gentle lines of her forehead were now deep wrinkles as she scowled at him crossly. 'Yes, you are.'

'I'm just not sure why he wants to. Don't you think it's a bit quick?'

'No.' Lottie's voice rose. 'He's a businessman, he's used to making decisions. He wants to help the theatre and take one of the places on the committee. He sees it as investing in his future and the town's.'

Something about this didn't sit right to Sid. He couldn't put his finger on exactly what and told himself it wasn't jealousy. 'But why?'

'What do you mean "why?" Because he thinks the theatre will be a success, and he likes what it's doing for the town.'

'Really,' replied Sid, scornfully before he could help it.

'Yes, really. Why is that so hard to believe? I wanted to know what you thought about it but I don't know why I asked you now.'

Sid scratched his cheek. If he told her the truth she'd have the hump with him but if he didn't she'd know he was lying. She always knew when he was lying. She had some weird spidey-sense. 'After we met him at the Big Clean, I told you I didn't trust him.'

'But why not?' She turned to him and her large blue eyes held him in a steady gaze. 'You only met him for, like, two minutes.'

'He's just one of those suited and booted London types who comes down here—'

'And steals our homes, yes, I've heard it all before.'

'Well, you asked,' Sid replied, staring at the sea. 'And you used to believe it too.'

Lottie kept her eyes down and her tone was conciliatory. 'I know I did. But maybe I was being a bit judgemental.'

Sid shoved another chip into his mouth and rattled the bag at Lottie. So he was judgemental now? Nice. She took a chip from the bottom, soggy with vinegar. This wasn't going to go down well, but he couldn't pretend it was something else. He wanted

Lottie to be on her guard. If something went wrong, she'd never forgive herself.

'He's a property developer, Lottie. I know what you said about him not doing this type of property but what if he's looking at branching out? Or what if he's checking it out for someone else?'

'That's a bit farfetched,' said Lottie.

'Is it? I don't think so. You can't trust people like that, Lottie.'

'People like what?' He felt her eyes boring into him. 'Better dressed and more successful?'

Sid went to place a chip in his mouth but his heart and hands fell. He'd never known her to be so cruel.

'I didn't mean that the way it sounded. I just meant—'

He knew exactly what she meant. Someone more grown up, more serious, more together. The complete opposite of him.

Lottie took the bag of chips, ate one, then offered them to Sid. It was her peace offering. 'He's offering to fix the theatre roof now, which it desperately needs. And he wants to be on the committee. I don't think that's unreasonable considering he's giving us so much money. He won't be able to just do what he wants if that's what you're worried about. And it would stop the council getting rid of the building. Is it really so bad? I think he's genuinely interested in helping us.'

'But what if he and the mayor are in this together? You could be out your ear if you're not careful and then it won't be a theatre any more, it'll either get knocked down, or the building will suddenly become something else. Offices. Flats. I don't know.'

Lottie's eyes held him as she said, 'Do you honestly think that they're working together to get me out so they can demolish the theatre and sell off the land? Why pay for the repairs if he's going to do that?'

She had him there. 'I'm just saying you should be careful. He could get on the committee then if the money doesn't come through, your time is up as acting chairman and they'll vote you out and tell the council there's no hope for the building and the community doesn't care if it goes. I know you're only a small informal group, Lottie, but you're still the only hope that theatre's got.'

How could she not see there were risks here? Sid bit back his annoyance as his easy-going manner was tested by Lottie's refusal to see things from his point of view.

'This is Greenley-On-Sea, Sid. Not Washington, or New York, or somewhere exciting where things like that actually happen.'

'It happens everywhere, Lottie, you know that, stop being so blind.'

Lottie angrily scrunched up the now empty bag of chips and put it between them. 'I think you're being a bit—'

'Realistic?' Sid tried to diffuse the tension by waggling his eyebrows and though Lottie's tone grew softer he could see she was still annoyed with him for not just agreeing straight away.

'Overzealous.'

Sid repressed a smile. She'd always been more diplomatic than him.

Lottie looked out to sea avoiding his gaze but her voice was full of hurt. 'Do you really think Jeremy is only interested in the theatre and not me?'

Sid's heart lurched trying to punch him for being so tactless. 'No, Lots, that's not what I'm saying. You need to get used to the idea that you're actually worth being with and …' He stumbled over his words. 'And worth looking at.' Sid studied the used-up chip bag and his cheeks flamed. Without thinking he said, 'If he genuinely likes you he won't min—'

'"If he genuinely likes me?"' Lottie parroted. 'So you do think he's only interested in the theatre?'

'I'm only saying "if", Lottie. I hope he's not.' He didn't like saying it but it was truthfully what he was afraid of. He'd never lied to Lottie and he wouldn't start now. He was jealous of Jeremy's relationship with Lottie but the guy could still just be using her.

'Well, I know he's not.' Her voice was rising now. 'And I can't think of anything more hurtful, Sid. You're basically saying the only proper date I've ever had was a business tactic and he's only seeing me because he wants to swipe away a local grotty theatre to make money. Which I could never see happening anyway.'

Sid tried to stay calm. He didn't normally get angry but he could feel it building. She was so determined to defend Jeremy, she wouldn't admit there was even a chance Sid could be right. 'You can't ignore the fact that—'

Lottie turned to him and her face had gone all red. She narrowed her eyes. 'The fact that what? He's a property developer? He's been honest about that from the start. Why would he tell me that if he had some sneaky plan? That's not very sneaky. That's like the worst sneakiness ever.'

All he was trying to do was get her to slow things down. 'Lottie, you're being unreasonable. and you're not listening to what I'm actually—'

'No, I'm not. You are!' she shouted. A couple walking past with their dog looked over. 'You're being so closed minded about him because he's posher than you. I never thought you were like that, Sid. You're being the opposite of a snob, whatever that is.'

Sid felt his lungs constrict as his anger rose further. 'How would you know what I'm like now? We haven't seen each other properly for months. You're always too busy.'

Lottie's mouth fell slightly open then snapped shut. 'I'm too busy? What about you and your secret girlfriend?'

'She wasn't secret. I just didn't tell you until there was something to tell.'

'So the man who hasn't had a date in like, fifteen years, suddenly does and you didn't think I'd care?'

'No, I didn't,' he said snapped and Lottie became still. 'Even now when you're just at home you don't want me interfering and getting under your feet. I can't remember the last time I set foot in your house.'

Lottie turned away. Sid took a deep breath in.

'Listen, Lottie, I—'

'Just forget about it, Sid. I'll figure this out on my own as you're not willing to really listen.'

He leaned forwards and turned to her. 'I am listening, Lottie, you just don't like my opinion of your new boyfriend.'

Lottie stood up. 'I don't know how you, of all people, Sid, can be so unsupportive.' She marched off leaving him alone on the bench, and there he stayed silently watching the sun set wondering what the hell had just happened.

Chapter 17

A couple of nights later, Lottie hurried to the theatre for a meeting of the Greenley Players. She was running late, having forgotten to swap her camera bag for the one with all the theatre stuff in it and had to run back to the office to fetch it.

She wasn't really sure what to expect from tonight's meeting. It wasn't a rehearsal because, according to Gregory, you did a read-through first. But he'd rung Lottie and suggested that while everyone learnt their lines they have a sort of acting lesson together to practise 'the craft'. Lottie agreed but wasn't sure that if she told the rest of them they'd turn up so lied and said it was a rehearsal. After the argument with Sid she'd really not been in the mood to come but these meetings were starting to cheer her up.

The players were all waiting outside for her when she arrived, enjoying some evening sunshine. 'Sorry I'm late,' she said and opened up to let them in. The thought of performing in front of actual people had caused a few more to drop out but Lottie didn't mind. More and more people were showing an interest all the time. It was a hot evening and Lottie hoped it would still be like this when they performed in just a month.

As Lottie walked down towards the stage Sarah caught up with her. 'Are you ready for the committee meeting tomorrow night?'

'I think so.' She was going to tell them about Jeremy's offer and wasn't sure they'd agree it was a good idea – after all, Sid hadn't. The thought of him made her wince. Work had been horrible for the last two days as they'd barely spoken.

'Do you need me to do anything for it?'

'No, but thanks.' Sarah nodded and sat down. 'Right, everyone,' Lottie said to the assembled group. 'I've agreed to Gregory leading this meeting because he's going to take you through some acting lessons. Gregory, if you want to just get on with it, I don't mind.'

'Right you are, dear. Are you okay? You look a bit tired.'

He had such a kind and caring face, she wanted to tell him about her argument with Sid but knew she couldn't. Not yet. Maybe once she knew him better. 'I'm okay,' she replied and he headed to the stage with a grin.

'Okay, then,' Gregory said, clapping his hands together. 'I wanted us all to meet this evening to go through some acting exercises. I don't remember the old group ever doing this and I think it'll really help. We all need to learn and improve our craft and performing *Much Ado* will help a lot, but it's important we shed a lot of our inhibitions before then.' He shook out his arms and legs as he spoke. 'I remember some exercises from my days training at RADA so I'll be leading this evening.'

Mrs Andrews scoffed but Gregory ignored her. 'Let's begin by all of us coming up onto the stage and finding some space to work.'

They did as they were told and nervously shuffled up then stood there staring at each other bemused and terrified.

'I think we should begin by going through the simple exercises I've showed you before,' said Gregory. 'Let's start by pretending to be a young sapling growing into a tree.'

From the front row Lottie and Conner watched on. They were supposed to be talking about staging and directing but Lottie couldn't drag her eyes away. The players looked ridiculous and clearly felt it too.

'That's lovely, Lee. Great work. Well done, Sarah, very floaty.' Gregory wandered around the stage in between the players watching them and making comments. 'Mrs Andrews, you're a bit stiff – can you sway a little more, perhaps? Loosen up those hips?'

Mrs Andrews muttered something under her breath which might have been a swear word, Lottie wasn't a hundred per cent sure. Seeing nervous eyes glance at her, Lottie said, 'Well done, everyone. You're looking great from down here.'

A few moments later after they'd been a piece of rubbish being blown about in the wind and a tiger kept in a zoo, Gregory said, 'Time, everyone. Now, I'd love for us to start working on our imaginations. Let's begin with some mime.'

Oh no, thought Lottie and suddenly wished Sid was there. He would have found this brilliantly funny, but he was out with Selena again and they weren't really talking anyway.

'Now,' said Gregory. 'I'm going to call out some things and each time I do you have to act it out.'

'Excuse me, Lottie,' said Mrs Andrews. 'Why does Gregory get to tell us all what to do? I thought we were a group? A team? Shouldn't we be deciding together?'

'I understand what you're saying, Mrs Andrews,' said Lottie. The woman only ever wanted to be a team when she was in charge of it. 'And we'll decide most things as a group but Gregory has some great expertise and I'm sure this will help in getting ready for the production. If you have any ideas you'd like to share, I'd love to hear them and perhaps we can do those next time?'

Mrs Andrews tossed her bleached hair over her shoulder. 'Well, not at the moment, but I'm sure I shall.'

'Thought not,' Lottie whispered to herself as Gregory carried on.

'So, first off, digging the garden.' The players dutifully began digging and throwing imaginary dirt over their shoulders. Lee was quite good and stopped to pick out a few weeds while Mrs

Andrews appeared completely nonplussed but then, she had people to do that sort of thing.

'Receiving bad news,' said Gregory and Lottie had to bite her tongue at the completely over the top panto reactions. Cecil's hands flew to his face as if his nose was about to drop off, and Mrs Andrews actually laid a hand on her forehead like she was getting a fit of the vapours in some bad Fifties movie.

'You're an angry goat,' said Gregory and everyone paused. Was Gregory actually speaking to Mrs Andrews? He looked around at the confused faces staring back at him. 'Come on, everyone, this is all about inhabiting character and not being embarrassed. Embarrassment will always hold you back.'

No one moved and Lottie was just about to step in when Lee chuckled and knelt onto all fours, snarling and headbutting the leg of the person next to him. Sarah laughed but not everyone joined in and after a few minutes Gregory called time.

Lottie was having a lot of fun and, surprisingly, the players were too. Gregory was very encouraging and she thought he'd missed his vocation as a teacher. The players were beginning to look a little tired and Lottie said, 'Why don't you all take a break for a few minutes, guys.'

'Good idea,' said Gregory. 'We're onto vocal exercises next.'

After the break Gregory said, 'The first thing I want us all to do is to put our hands on our ribs and take a slow breath in through the nose, then blow it out through our mouths making a loud huffing noise. Like this.' He made a long sniffing sound then exhaled saying, 'Herrrrrrrrrr.'

Lottie's laugh nearly got the better of her and she quickly grabbed a tissue and pretended to blow her nose.

'Why are we doing this exactly?' asked Mrs Andrews. 'I can breathe perfectly well already.'

Cecil leaned over to Sarah and whispered, 'She's had so much surgery on that nose I'm surprised it still works.' And Sarah stifled a laugh by chewing her lip.

Lottie rolled her eyes and turned to speak to Conner. 'Have you got any ideas about staging? Where you want people to stand and that sort of thing?'

Conner looked up from under his long fringe which now had bleached white ends and Lottie had to resist the urge to watch his lip ring wiggle as he talked. 'I was thinking we should keep it quite free actually — let them stand where they want and move about naturally. I don't want to give them too much to remember for their first time.'

Lottie nodded. 'Sounds sensible.'

'And I thought we should just have one or two props that show the audience where the setting is, rather than try anything big. People will be sitting all around the bandstand so we don't want to block anyone's view.'

'Great.' Conner was pretty switched on. 'It sounds like you've got it all under control.'

The sound of the players saying 'Yah-yah-yah-yah,' over and over again came into her ears.

'Lovely,' said Gregory, clapping his hands. 'Now, oo-oo-oo-oo.'

'They sound like monkeys,' whispered Conner.

Lottie giggled. 'I'm sure it'll come in handy on opening night. Or if we do a weird interpretation of apes.'

'*Planet of the Apes* meets Shakespeare?' Conner smiled. Gosh, he was young. Lottie remembered being at university, which made her think of the picture of her and Elsie at her graduation sitting on the dresser at home. Lottie's heart gave a little twinge but deep down she knew Elsie would be proud, and that was reassuring. Her mind went back to Sid who had always, always been there and she realised she wanted him there now, on this journey with her. But he was with Selena tonight. For some reason the thought of him with a girlfriend made the hairs on the back of her neck stand on end. Lottie tried to re-focus her mind. 'What sort of props did you need?'

'I don't know yet. I'm still reading it and trying to decide. Is it okay if I email you later?'

'Yeah, that's fine. It's not interfering with your uni work, is it? If it is, we can get someone else to do it.'

Conner's eyes met hers in concern. 'I can do it, it's fine. I have enough free time.'

Lottie thought it an odd response. 'I'd have thought you'd be out with your mates?' Although Lottie's time at university had been spent in the library, she assumed everyone else was out drinking.

'No. I don't go out much.'

'Now everyone,' interrupted Gregory, just as Lottie was about to probe further. He walked to the side of the stage and picked up a football. 'We'll take another break in a minute, but before we do I'd like you all to get into a circle. We're going to explore some of the emotions in *Much Ado*—'

'With a football?' asked Lee.

'Yes. We're going to throw it to each other and when you catch it you have to say an emotion. So think about *Much Ado About Nothing* and what you've read so far. What emotions have you identified? It can be from any of the characters, not just yours. Ready? Go!'

Gregory threw the ball to Cecil who screeched as it came towards him, missed the catch, and ran to get it before it rolled off the stage. By the time he got back to his place in the circle he was red and out of breath but managed to shout, 'Love' before throwing the ball to Lee.

Lottie had to give Gregory credit. Though some of the things were a bit silly he was doing a fabulous job. He was right that they needed to lose their embarrassment if they were going to act properly and the football game was great for getting them to think about the play. Sarah shouted, 'Jealousy,' and Lottie looked up.

Something niggled at the back of her mind but Lottie couldn't figure out what. 'Well done, everyone,' she said. 'This is such a great idea, Gregory.'

Her phone beeped with a message and a smile spread across her face as she saw it was from Sid. She hoped it was an apology for his behaviour before but it wasn't. It was a peace offering, though.

How's the meeting going?

She texted back: Fine. They're playing with a football and shouting emotions at each other.

Sounds weird. Have fun.

It was like there was her old life with Sid and a new life with the theatre and Jeremy. Her nan wanted her to move on but Lottie didn't like the way her old life seemed to be drifting further and further away. She always wanted Sid by her side but so far she didn't know how that could happen. Picking up her phone she tried to think of something funny to say but nothing came to mind. She put it back in her pocket to text him later.

When it beeped again, Lottie was elated to see it was from Jeremy asking her how things were going. She responded straight away and before she knew it rehearsal time was over and they'd been chatting nonstop. Slumping in disappointment that he hadn't asked for a second date Lottie conceded she hadn't had the courage either. As she said goodnight to everyone she took out her phone and wished Jeremy goodnight too. When he signed off with a kiss, Lottie couldn't stop smiling.

It wasn't until later she realised she hadn't texted Sid back but by then it was too late.

Chapter 18

In the living room, hunched on the sofa, Lottie eyed the large glass of wine she had poured herself and took a sip. Savouring the cold fruity liquid, she let her eyes drift back down to her book and tried to concentrate. Her feet ached from a day at the local library where a wasp infestation had taken over the reference section and she'd had to go up and down a ladder trying to get a shot of some of the pesky little things emerging from the nest.

Lottie wiggled her cramping toes. At least it was a Friday night and she could have a lie-in tomorrow. Her eyes drifted to her mobile phone on the seat next to her. The council had approved Jeremy's donation to the theatre and Lottie had offered to tell him the good news but she also wanted, more than anything, to see him again. The trouble was, every time she considered calling him, her nerve failed. She told herself to stop being a great big wimp, took a big gulp of wine for courage and dialled.

'Hello?' came Jeremy's sexy voice.

Lottie launched off the sofa to standing, her grip tightening on the phone. 'Hi, Jeremy, it's umm, it's Lottie. I was, err, I just wanted to let you know that the committee approved your donation to the theatre.'

She could hear the smile in his voice. 'Really? That's fantastic. I can organise the work straight away if they'd like?'

'And umm …' Her brain ran in circles shouting at itself. 'I was wondering if you fancied going out for a drink sometime. Or not. If you're too busy, that's fine, I totally understand—'

There was a chuckle on the other end of the line. 'You're lucky, I'm on my way down to Greenley as we speak. In fact, I'm probably only an hour away.' He hesitated and Lottie wondered what he was going to say. 'If I'm honest, I've been on tenterhooks wondering what the committee said so I left early and was planning on calling you later to find out, but this way, we can celebrate together, if you're free tonight?'

Lottie gave a heavy sigh of relief and did a little dance around the living room. 'That would be great.'

'Okay, I'll meet you at about eight-thirty at the wine bar on the seafront.'

'See you then.'

'Lottie?' He paused. 'I'm really glad you called. See you later.'

Lottie flopped back down on the sofa, grinning, and exhilarated, the tiredness washed from her body. It was time to get ready for another date. Not having run anywhere since the school cross-country, Lottie raced upstairs, arriving in her bedroom hot and out of breath.

In front of her wardrobe, she gazed at the mass of clothes falling from every shelf, slung over every rail and piled on the floor. A box of shoes sat in the corner with unworn high heels and much used comfy flats precariously balanced on top.

'Right,' she said to herself, putting her hands on her hips. 'Operation Sexy has begun.'

As if in some kind of Eighties movie montage, Lottie quickly went through her wardrobe and found a pair of black skinny jeans she'd never worn and a dark blue top with a sequin covered collar. The soft short sleeves of the top would hide the worst of her arms and the length skimmed her tummy – the bit she hated most. She decided on a pair of plain navy ballet pumps to keep it casual, not wanting to look like she'd tried too hard. Plus her feet still hurt and she wasn't that great in high heels. She looked a bit like a baby giraffe learning to walk.

Next was a hot shower and hair and make-up. Having spent time on her appearance, the Lottie that emerged from the bathroom in no way resembled the one that went in. She'd tried the lotions and potions left to gather dust for so long, and the weird hairdryer attachment she'd never used before. Her hair curled delicately and she let it hang loosely around her shoulders rather than tying it up in a boring ponytail as she always did.

Checking the clock on her bedside table she saw she had thirty minutes left. The walk into town would take about ten so she had just enough time to sort out some decent make-up. An internet tutorial taught her how to apply eyeliner without it going all wobbly and the result was a subtle, defined look. A quick swipe of mascara and her usual lip balm and, for once, Lottie felt sexy.

Locking the door behind her, she began to walk to the seafront. As the wine bar came into view, Lottie spotted Jeremy sitting outside in his suit. He'd removed his jacket and rolled up his sleeves to reveal his arms. Jeremy stood up to greet her and she noticed the guys a couple of tables away watching her approach.

'Hi.' He reached an arm around her waist and guided her to the table, placing a kiss on her cheek. 'You look incredible.'

'Hi,' Lottie replied, disappointed her voice sounded the same. She'd hoped it would exude confidence and sexiness.

'What can I get you?'

'I'll have a white wine, please.'

Jeremy disappeared into the bar but glanced behind him before he entered. Was that a good sign? Lottie sat fumbling with her bag as the same guys looked over again. Did she look like a teenager who'd been playing with make-up? She nervously stroked her hair wishing she'd stuck to something more normal.

Jeremy returned and placed a glass in front of her. 'You look amazing, by the way. Really, really stunning.'

'Thanks.' Lottie smiled at the compliment and ran her fingers through a curl. 'I was worried it might be a bit much.'

'No, you look incredible. I mean, you've always looked gorgeous but you just look ... so ... so ...'

'Nice?'

'Yes, nice.' He chuckled. 'Sorry. I'm being an idiot and getting all tongue tied. You seem to have that effect on me, Lottie Webster.'

Lottie looked up. Her whole body tingled at the intensity of his stare. 'I get like that too. It took me a big glass of wine before I rang you.'

'Why?'

She shrugged. 'Just nerves, I guess.'

'Am I that scary?' Jeremy asked and the smile that lit up his face brought a sparkle to his eyes.

'No. I'm just an idiot.'

'I don't think you're an idiot. I've never thought that.' Jeremy leaned in and Lottie copied him. She wanted to be near him, to smell his aftershave again. To be close enough he could put his arm around her if he wanted to. And she really hoped he did.

An hour passed with more drinks and good conversation. Lottie found herself flirting, running her hands through her hair and catching his eye, feeling more and more confident the longer they were together. He was everything a woman could want in a man – funny, smart, successful. The fact that he was completely gorgeous was just a bonus. It was all going very well so far. They talked about his business and the different projects he'd worked on over the years and Lottie talked about her job and even about her parents. She normally only talked to Sid about them. Sat in the late evening sunshine at ease with one anther, it was blissful.

'Shall we get something to eat?' asked Jeremy, looking at his watch. 'It's nine-thirty already.'

'Sure. Where shall we go?'

'How about the new French place by the harbour?'

Lottie nodded and they strolled along the promenade their bodies touching. Jeremy gently took Lottie's hand. His thumb stroked her skin and she leaned in to him as they walked. When they reached the restaurant, Jeremy held open the door for her and they waited to be seated.

Checking her appearance in the mirrors running the length of the wall, Lottie decided she looked good. A little bit round at the middle but the top was doing a good job of hiding it. And it almost disappeared completely when she stopped slouching. But she didn't just look good, she felt good. Taking the time to look nice had made such a difference to how she felt about herself. And it hadn't been that hard. Rather than faking confidence she was actually feeling it.

They followed the waiter to an empty table.

'Lottie?' Her heart lurched at the familiar voice.

'Lottie? Over here!'

In the mirror she saw a long gangly arm waving from the far corner of the room. Sid. Sid was there and so was Selena. Lottie thought her wine might make a guest appearance and swallowed it back down.

'That's your friend, isn't it?' asked Jeremy, as Sid made his way over to them.

'Yes. He's here with his girlfriend.' Lottie tried to hide the disappointment in her voice. She'd wanted it to be just her and Jeremy.

Sid approached the table with a tight smile. 'Hello. What are you doing here?'

'We were going to have dinner,' said Lottie, a bit snippily.

Sid's eyes shot to Jeremy. 'I meant, I didn't know you were going out tonight. Of course you're out for dinner, you're in a restaurant.' He gave a nervous laugh and scratched the back of his head.

'Lottie called me,' said Jeremy, happily, placing an arm around

Lottie's waist. 'We met for a drink and now, here we are.'

Selena tottered over and stared at Jeremy, then flicked her eyes to Lottie, and back again. From the look on her face she obviously couldn't believe Lottie had landed herself such a gorgeous boyfriend.

'Hello, Selena,' said Lottie, placing her hand over Jeremy's, where it lay on her waist. Selena looked amazing in a tight red dress.

'Hi, Lottie,' Selena replied. 'I'd no idea you had a boyfriend. Sid never said, did you?'

Sid didn't reply. The silence spoke volumes and Selena's eyes narrowed.

Jeremy held his hand out for Selena to shake. 'Hi, I'm Jeremy.'

'Umm, why don't you two join us?' asked Sid. His eyes kept glancing towards Jeremy and Lottie sensed he was just being polite.

Selena's hair bounced up and down as she nodded. 'Yes, definitely.'

'No, we can't,' Lottie replied. 'You must be halfway through your dinner by now.'

'No, we're not,' said Selena. 'We've only just finished our starter. You and … Jeremy was it? You should definitely join us.'

'That would be lovely, wouldn't it, darling?' Jeremy replied. Lottie gave a half smile. Would it?

The waiter moved them to a table for four in the corner. Now surrounded by mirrors Lottie would normally have sunk down and avoided her reflection at all costs but even next to Selena, in all her flawless glory, she still felt confident. Lottie sat next to Jeremy and opposite Sid and she was sure Selena kept fluttering her eyelashes at Jeremy. Sid hadn't noticed and Lottie felt her annoyance mounting. She hoped she was reading too much into it.

'You look so nice, Lottie,' said Selena. 'You scrub up really well. But you haven't come to see me for that manicure yet. You really should. I'd so love to do your nails and make them all pretty.'

Lottie looked down at her hands gently holding the stem of her wine glass. She hadn't had time or even thought to paint her nails. From the corner of her eye Lottie saw Jeremy glance over and felt his hand on her thigh under the table. It wasn't a sexual gesture. She could see from his face that he'd heard the bitchy undertone in Selena's voice, even though Sid was oblivious.

Jeremy smiled at Lottie. 'She looks beautiful, doesn't she? As always.'

They ordered their food, Jeremy pronouncing the names of the French dishes with a surprisingly good accent, and as the waiter left Selena said, 'Your French is amazing, Jeremy.' And as she leaned over the table she revealed acres of cleavage.

'It's terrible actually,' he replied, glancing at Lottie. 'I've never been any good at languages.'

Selena continued to praise Jeremy's numerous language skills as Sid fidgeted with his napkin and bent towards Lottie. 'You look nice. Different. But nice. Really, really nice.'

'Thanks,' Lottie said curtly, still cross with him for ruining her dinner with Jeremy. She wondered when the last time was that was Sid had seen her like this and realised he probably never had. She'd tarted up a bit for some of the functions they'd covered but nothing that involved hairdryer attachments or more than one coat of mascara.

'I mean, you look really … good.' A slight redness at the collar of his shirt threatened to reach his cheeks. Poor Sid. He was clearly making an effort and, to be honest, she could never stay mad at him for long. A smile pushed at her cheeks.

'I was looking at your birthday present this week. I've narrowed it down to two options.'

His tense expression relaxed. 'Which are?'

'I'm not telling you!'

Sid made a sad face just as Jeremy leant over. 'What's this?'

As Jeremy wrapped an arm around Lottie's shoulders she could smell the spicy scent of his aftershave and she wondered if all his body smelled the same. She pulled herself back to the conversation. 'It's Sid's birthday in a couple of weeks.'

'Oh, have a happy birthday for then. Listen, Lottie, I've been meaning to ask, did you want to come and see a play with me in London? There's a new interpretation of *Rosencrantz and Guildenstern are Dead*. It's supposed to be amazing.'

'I'd love to,' she replied. Selena asked Jeremy something and as he began to respond Sid leaned over again.

'So do I get a hint about my birthday present?'

Lottie shook her head and smiled. 'Nope. Nothing.'

'Spoilsport.'

Lottie took a sip of her wine and saw Selena giving her the side-eye. The wine warmed her throat and Lottie refused to turn away this time. Sid was her friend and she was allowed to talk to him, whether Selena liked it or not. When their eyes met, Selena's face softened into a wide smile just as Sid looked over.

Jeremy's voice echoed in her ears and he took her hand. 'Isn't that right, darling?'

'Sorry?' asked Lottie.

'I was just saying how amazing you're doing with the theatre.' He gave her hand a squeeze and she laced her fingers through his.

'Oh, right. Well, I'm trying. Luckily, it's going pretty well so far.'

'I can't tell you, Selena, how amazing this girl is. I think she's fantastic. She's won over the town completely and me too. I'm completely smitten.'

'Smitten?' echoed Selena.

Lottie turned her head so fast hair stuck to her lip gloss.

Selena smiled. 'Oh, Sid, isn't that sweet?'

Jeremy looked into Lottie's eyes. 'There's no denying it.' His thumb stroked her hand again. Shocked into stillness Lottie worried he was just saying this for Selena's benefit. Lottie wasn't an expert on flirting, but Selena had certainly been giving Jeremy more attention than Sid, and had been since they first arrived.

Sid stared at Lottie and she had an urge to throw a bit of pasta into his open mouth.

'The more time I spend with this woman the more I realise how amazing she is. Don't you think, Sid?' Jeremy leaned in and kissed Lottie gently on the mouth. Goose bumps rushed over every inch of her skin and she felt herself blush under Sid and Selena's incredulous stare.

Sid nodded and drank some water.

'I'd better stop,' said Jeremy. 'I'm embarrassing her.' The feel of his lips had sent her body into overdrive and soon every nerve was alive and wanting more. Jeremy carried on chatting but a weird tense atmosphere had descended.

After Jeremy's announcement, Selena spent more time and attention on Sid and Lottie wondered if she'd imagined it all. Perhaps Selena was just really friendly and that was more how Lottie should be? And why was Sid finding it so hard that she had a boyfriend? It just didn't make sense to her.

They parted at the door, Selena and Sid heading in one direction, Lottie and Jeremy the other. They walked along the promenade hand in hand. A full moon, perched in a cloudless sky, reflected off the sea, lighting their way.

'You didn't mind that we joined Sid and Selena, did you?' Jeremy asked. 'I just assumed that as they were your friends, you'd want them to. Was I wrong?'

Lottie wanted to tell him, *yes, you were totally wrong, you idiot*, but she appreciated the gesture. 'No, it's fine. It was really nice of you. It's just that Sid and I aren't getting on so well at the moment.'

Jeremy cocked his head. 'Oh? Why not?'

'We're just not seeing as much of each other anymore. I'm really busy with the theatre and he's always busy with Selena. Things are different now.'

'Don't worry,' said Jeremy, wrapping his hand around her waist. 'Life moves on sometimes and friendships do too. Sometimes we outgrow people as our lives go different ways.'

Lottie glanced at him then watched her feet as they moved along. She didn't want their lives to go different ways. Sid was annoying sometimes but he was her best friend and always had been. Surely they would adjust to this new situation?

'I'm sure that won't happen to you two though,' said Jeremy. 'Things will settle down.'

The tide dragged the pebbles backwards and forwards as if telling the world to shush. The ocean asking for quiet as everyone got ready for bed.

'Selena's quite … umm, open, isn't she?' said Jeremy.

Lottie laughed. 'Yes. That's one way of putting it.'

Jeremy glanced at her. 'She has a bit of a snide way of saying things sometimes too.'

'I thought it was just me being defensive.'

'No, she's definitely a bit … snarky.'

Jeremy stopped and turned to Lottie. He stood looking down at her and his hands slid around her waist drawing her towards him. The air between them was thick with tension and Lottie wanted to reach out and put her hand on his chest.

'I meant what I said, Lottie. I've never met anyone like you before. You really are the most remarkable woman and I am falling in love with you.'

Lottie's brain fumbled around trying to remember how to use words. When he next spoke, his voice was quiet and anxious. 'Say something, please?'

Lottie's heart pounded in her chest. Her lungs constricted, pushing the air up so she didn't know whether to breathe in or out. Up until now she'd been too scared to admit to herself that she felt the same way, worried she'd be left embarrassed, heartbroken and disappointed. But he'd said it first. He was falling in love with her.

In the silence, Jeremy's brow creased in concern and his voice was full of nerves. 'Don't you feel the same way?'

'I do,' she said, quickly. 'I do. I—'

In the gentle moonlight he pulled her close so her body was pressed against his. He bent his head down and Lottie's lips tingled in anticipation. As he kissed her again, harder and more passionately, the world paused. Her heart spun, beating faster and faster until she felt it would explode and at last, she let herself go and kissed him back.

Chapter 19

Sid and Selena headed off in the opposite direction to Lottie and Mr Suave. Sid peered over his shoulder, watching as they walked away. Lottie looked so different tonight. Not just grown up, but beautiful, incredible. She'd never dressed like that before.

'Everything okay?' asked Selena, gazing at him from under her long dark lashes.

'Yeah, fine.' Sid tried to smile. He had to get past this. He shook his head to chase the thoughts away. He was so lucky to have met someone like Selena. She was funny and sexy, and he was definitely punching above his weight. As soon as he'd seen their reflection in the gigantic mirrors at the restaurant, he'd seen it again – which reminded him: why would you put mirrors in a restaurant anyway? Who wanted to see themselves chew?

Sid wrapped his arm around Selena's shoulder. There was a slight chill in the air and she'd brought the tiniest cardigan he'd ever seen. Goose bumps lifted the delicate hairs on her skin but she wasn't complaining. He couldn't remember having paid Selena any compliments this evening. He should have. Guys would queue up for her if ever he let her slip through his fingers. He should make more of an effort but there was a hell of a lot to remember in this dating business and there was so much he liked about her.

She enjoyed cuddling on the sofa watching superhero movies or old classics and listening to music. But still, he felt a pain in his chest as he realised again there would never be a Lottie and Sid. Seeing her and Jeremy tonight had shown him the last drop of hope had gone. It was done. Finished. He turned to Selena, determined to start afresh. 'You looked beautiful tonight.'

Selena smiled and pushed her hair behind her shoulders. 'Thank you. Shall we head to yours for one last drink?'

'Okay.' Sid chewed the inside of his cheek hoping it meant what he thought it meant.

'Lottie looked very different tonight, didn't she?' asked Selena. 'The last time I saw her she looked quite, well … never mind. I just hope she's not changing just because she has a man. I hate it when women do that.'

Sid couldn't help the concern that was clouding over him and he knew it showed on his face. Was that what Lottie was doing? God, he hoped not. Normally Lottie went for comfort over style and he hoped she wouldn't change just for Jeremy. She'd looked like an airbrushed photo of herself and as lovely as that was he missed the Lottie who wore grubby jeans and oversized jumpers. 'She doesn't normally look so … polished.'

'Hasn't she had dates before?'

'Not really.' It had always been just the two of them.

Selena glanced at him again. 'I think Jeremy's right though. She's doing a great job with the theatre, isn't she? It's just a shame you guys aren't seeing each other so much anymore. She's making time for Jeremy, if only she could make time to see you too. I know you miss her.' She squeezed his hand and looked at him as if waiting for him to say something but he didn't know what.

'Hey, I know,' she continued. 'Why don't we have a dinner party at your place for your birthday? We could invite Lottie and Jeremy? It could be just the four of us?'

Sid shrugged. That was not how he wanted to spend his birthday, but Selena seemed so excited. 'Maybe. What did you think of the restaurant?' he asked, trying to change the subject.

'It was nice. Bit too posh though. And who wants to eat snails? Yuck.' She cringed then cuddled into him. Sid liked the fact she preferred normal pubs over fancy restaurants, it was another reason they were suited. 'Jeremy's not as handsome as you.'

Sid smiled. 'I'm glad you think so.'

'I do.' She put her arm around him and Sid reached in his jacket pocket for his keys.

As they approached his door, Sid gazed at Selena's beautiful profile. Her full lips had a sexy, natural pout. She licked them and he felt his body burning.

His mind suddenly reminded him that Jeremy had said he was smitten. And that kiss. Sid quickly disregarded it and berated himself for letting it pop into his head in the first place.

Selena stopped and stood on tiptoe, reaching up until her mouth met his. As they kissed she pressed her body against him and his regrets over Lottie faded. After a moment, she pulled back, took Sid's keys from his fingers and opened the door. Without speaking, she took his hand and led him up to his bedroom.

Chapter 20

Lottie was aglow with love. After dinner she and Jeremy had spent an amazing night together. He'd been gentle and kind and she'd lain in his arms feeling attractive and sexy. She hadn't slept with anyone for a long time. In fact, she couldn't remember the last time which was quite embarrassing really. But the weekend had been wonderful. Not only that, since she and Sid had run into each other at dinner, their silly argument was all but forgotten and they were beginning to get on better, like old times.

The Greenley Players were sitting in a circle on the stage beginning their first read-through of *Much Ado About Nothing*. With only three weeks to go they were upping rehearsal time and Lottie was busier than ever. She and Sid had found their way down a rickety wooden staircase at the back of the theatre to the small, dark, basement room that contained the wardrobe department. They were hoping to find some costumes for the play but the cobwebs, enormous spiders and general smell of dust and dirt didn't bode well.

'Watch your step there, Lots,' said Sid, pointing to a broken stair as the steps creaked underfoot.

Lottie held onto the old wooden banister and carefully stepped down two stairs at once as the voices of the Greenley Players echoed above them. She heard Gregory's voice saying rather loudly, 'Don't forget to project, Sarah,' and then a mumbling voice, that was probably Mrs Andrews' reply, before a huge argument began. At first, Lottie had put it down to nerves but the fighting was happening more and more at the moment and she didn't know how to stop it.

'Mrs Andrews and Gregory have got to stop this fighting,' she said, more to herself than Sid. 'They start all the others off and then everyone takes sides. It's like running a nursery sometimes.'

Sid moved another box of rubbish out of the way dodging the bare light bulb swaying from side to side. 'Why do you think they're so bad?'

'Well,' said Lottie, unable to keep the hint of excitement from her voice. She'd been meaning to tell Sid for a while but hadn't had a chance. She perched on an old chair about to begin her story and Sid sat on the edge of a workbench. 'I've been doing some digging in Nan's notes and it turns out that there was a whole casting thing with one of the last productions the old group did. Gregory, Cecil and Mrs Andrews were all part of the group when Nan ran the theatre, though someone else was running the actual players and I've no idea who this Mr Reynolds is. Anyway, there was a big row over Gregory starring in and directing this one show.'

'What show?' asked Sid, smiling. 'It wasn't *Cabaret* was it?'

Lottie giggled. 'Oh, God, could you imagine? Anyway, I can't remember what it was but ...'

'Yeah?' Sid said slowly, staring at her with wide eyes. He loved a bit of gossip.

'Basically, he and Mrs Andrews were the leads and it started out well then Mrs Andrews got all bossy, as she does, and Gregory got all snippy, as he does, and words were said that have clearly never been forgotten. I'm guessing Nan took his side because she always said nice things about Gregory but she never liked Mrs Andrews.'

Sid sat back. 'Blimey. That must have been what ... five years ago? That's quite a long time to hold a grudge. Maybe Gregory threatened to reveal Mrs Andrews' real age or something. What are you going to do about it?'

'I don't know yet.' Lottie got up and began looking around. 'Oh, Sid, look at this place. It's an absolute mess.' She picked up a dirty sock and threw it back onto the concrete floor.

They were surrounded by box upon box of rubbish. Old Christmas decorations, leftover flyers and posters, and old tins of paint spilled out everywhere.

'I'm not sure how much we're going to find,' said Sid.

'Shhh,' said Lottie, holding her fingers to her lips. Her eyes focused on the cracks criss-crossing the ceiling as she listened to the players above reciting their lines. It was terrible. Like hearing a satnav recite Shakespeare. And not even the good Joanna Lumley satnav, it was the weird disjointed one that always mispronounced street names. Hopefully the floorboards were blocking the sound and it wasn't as bad up top.

An hour later they were still rifling through bin bags and cardboard boxes of old smelly costumes, having found nothing at all of any use. 'What about this one?' asked Sid, placing a tricorne hat jauntily on his head. 'Do I look like Napoleon?'

Lottie stopped rummaging and examined him. 'You're too tall for Napoleon. More like a pirate, I'm afraid.'

'What about this one?' He pulled out a clown's bright red wig and swapped it for the hat.

Lottie giggled. 'Now you look like one of those scary murder clowns from a horror film. Don't go near any children or you'll get yourself arrested.'

'I've never been arrested before … it could be fun. Do you remember when we went to that fancy dress party at David's house and we went as Jeeves and Wooster? That was awesome.'

'Oh yeah,' Lottie replied, pausing with her hands on her hips. 'His wife wasn't best pleased when he did those shots of tequila and vomited all over the carpet.'

Sid scratched his head under the wig. 'She went ape, didn't she? I think we left about then. No wonder they're divorced now.'

Lottie paused remembering old times, before life got complicated and messy. 'And we stopped off at the Chinese on the way to mine and then fell asleep on the sofa.'

'Yeah.' Sid laughed. 'In the morning you had a spring roll stuck to your face.'

Lottie smiled. 'I was saving it for breakfast.'

Sid grinned back and Lottie was so pleased to see his cheerful toothy grin she nearly hugged him. She'd missed conversations like this. Sid took off the wig and said, 'Your nan woke us up with a bacon sandwich and a cup of tea, didn't she?'

Lottie remembered the taste. The best bacon sandwich ever. No one made them like her nan, she always used just the right amount of ketchup. Lottie turned to see Sid watching her. 'What?'

'Nothing,' he replied. But he eyed her warily.

'I'm not going to cry, Sid. I promise.'

'Sure?'

'Yes.' Bless him. He'd been there through the days and nights of hysterical sobbing, handing her tissues and bringing her chocolate. She was pleased to know that even with Selena around he still cared.

Sid narrowed his eyes in fake suspicion. 'Alright then. What exactly are we doing here though, Lottie? I feel like I'm at a weird jumble sale.'

Lottie put down the disgusting smelling frock coat she had picked out of a black bag. 'We need to find out what resources we have for *Much Ado* and take stock of any other costumes.'

'You sound like Jeremy,' remarked Sid. 'Take stock. Resources.'

'You know nothing about Jeremy, and I don't sound like him. I just sound like a grown-up,' she replied in pretend petulance, lifting her chin.

Sid examined another box of costumes. He held out a bedsheet, or it might have been a toga then threw it back in the box and

153

cleaned his hands on his shirt. 'Lottie, there's bugger all here of any use to anyone. Apart from this.' He grabbed a fake sword and began fighting an imaginary foe.

'Yep, you're right,' replied Lottie, putting her hands on her hips again. 'We're going to need some money for costumes. And props.'

'And where are we going to get that?' asked Sid, still swash-buckling with thin air.

'Another fundraiser?'

He shook his head. 'No time. Mrs Andrews?'

'I'm sure she'd be more than happy to oblige if you asked her.' Every woman seemed to be finding Sid attractive at the moment. On the way in, Mrs Andrews had been so close behind Sid she'd almost dry humped him.

Sid finished off his opponent with a flourish. 'I'm a bit worried it would be like that film with Demi Moore and Robert Redford.'

'*Indecent Proposal*?' asked Lottie incredulously.

'Yeah.'

'Do you think you're worth a million dollars?'

He put on a silly American accent. 'You know I am, baby.'

Lottie caught his eye and in the tiny wardrobe room with nothing but a harsh, bare lightbulb, he looked almost handsome. Not like Jeremy, who was handsome in a modern, aftershave advert kind of way; Sid was handsome in a classic, Fifties, Humphrey Bogart sort of way. Unconventional and rakish. His hair had ruffled from his exertions in battle and he had a nice smile. She could see how Selena might find him attractive. 'How's Selena?' she asked with fake cheer.

A ruddy tinge crept into his cheeks. 'She's okay. It's my birthday next week—'

'I know. I've already got your present.' Lottie picked up a velvet jacket and began folding it.

'Have you?' Sid looked at her hopefully. He was such a big kid, he loved birthdays as much as he had in their youth.

'Yeah, of course.'

154

Sid gave a wide smile and kept his eyes on Lottie. 'What is it?'

'I'm not telling you,' she teased.

'Go on.'

'No.' Lottie turned away from him, smiling to herself.

Sid huffed, pretending to be cross, as she knew he would. 'Selena was wondering if you and Jeremy wanted to come to mine for dinner? She said a dinner party but it won't be anything that posh. Just dinner with friends, I suppose.'

Lottie didn't know what to say or what was more unnerving, the 'I suppose' or the fact that this was Selena's idea. She wanted to believe that Selena genuinely liked Sid but they just seemed so different. She couldn't imagine her making him happy and Lottie was sure now Selena had been flirting with Jeremy at dinner. Even he'd thought so but been too polite to say it out loud.

Sid continued. 'I gave Selena your number and she's going to text you about it.'

'Oh, okay.' Lottie didn't want Selena to have her number, but it was done now. She'd have to go. Besides, she always saw Sid on his birthday and his being with Selena wasn't going to stop her doing that. Lottie brushed the dust from her jeans. 'Right, we'd better start bagging up the rubbish.'

Lottie watched Sid from her corner of her eye and wondered when their friendship would adjust to their new circumstances. She didn't mind Sid having a girlfriend, she just couldn't warm to Selena, that was all. If it was someone else, she'd be fine.

Every time she and Sid were together, on their own, the weirdness vanished and their friendship became what it had always been. They knew each so well they could finish each other's sentences and tease each other. But as soon as one of them mentioned Jeremy or Selena, things changed. Like a CD that kept jumping, their conversation stopped and started and they forgot how to be together. It was horrible and weird, and Lottie hated it.

Sid put the sword down and picked up a retractable dagger.

He plunged it into his side, groaning and fell to the floor. And just like that, their friendship was back to normal and all was right with the world. Writhing around and screaming in agony Sid said, 'Help me, Lottie. Help me!' and reached out for her with his free hand.

Lottie stepped over him, smirking. 'You're a complete idiot, Sidney Evans.'

He stood up, covered in dust. 'Can I keep this?'

'No. It's the only decent thing here.'

'Spoilsport.'

Lottie threw an old smelly bowler hat into a bin bag. 'Where are we going to get the money for new costumes and props, Sid? Jeremy's offered some funding but that was for the roof. I can't ask him for more money.'

Sid's kept his gaze on the box.

'Have we sold many tickets for *Much Ado* yet?' asked Lottie wondering if that might be the answer.

Sid brightened. 'Yeah, loads. The advert in the paper seems to have worked a treat and people are using the website and following the stories, making comments and things. We haven't seen this much action since that incident at the vegetable show.' He giggled. 'Mr Williams still can't look a cucumber in the eye.'

'Oh yeah.' Lottie sniggered. 'Poor Mr Williams. He was in A and E for hours. Do you think we can use some of the money from the ticket sales?'

Sid looked at her sympathetically. 'I'm not sure it would be enough.'

'Then what are we going to do?' Lottie ran a hand through her ponytail and re-tightened it. 'A public appeal, maybe?'

'There's no time now, Lots. We've only got three weeks till the show.'

She sat down and picked at her fingers. 'I knew there wasn't enough time. I knew it was too soon to put on a show. Everyone's going to be performing Shakespeare in jeans and T-shirts.'

Sid went to her side and put his arm around her shoulder. 'Come on, Lots. We'll find a way and if not, we'll call it a modern interpretation.'

Lottie sniffed and Sid rested his head on hers. 'Maybe I'll pay Adelaide Andrews a visit after all.'

'Really?'

'It's the only way,' he replied, squaring his shoulders and running a hand through his hair.

'Thank you. We don't need a million dollars though, you know? A couple of hundred will do.'

'We'll be lucky if we get two pound fifty,' said Sid. 'But I'll give it a try. For you.' Sid emphasised the 'you' and Lottie couldn't help but blush at the meaning beneath it, reassured that she was still important to him.

Lottie glanced at him again but he kept his eyes on the retractable dagger and she said, 'Maybe you're worth a little bit more than that. But only a little bit.'

After a minute when Sid finally raised his eyes to hers it was like old times, but there was something new there now. Something Lottie couldn't place. They'd both changed since her nan's death and now they'd stopped seeing each other so often a distance had opened up between them – a no man's land of emotions.

Raised voices rang through from above. 'Come on,' said Lottie. 'We'd better get upstairs and see what's going on.'

As she climbed up from the basement and walked onto the stage she couldn't believe what she saw in front of her. Half the Greenley Players were standing up, shouting at one another, waving their scripts in the air, while the others sat slumped in their chairs, some playing on their phones. Conner stood in the middle trying to placate each side but Mrs Andrews and Gregory were almost at each other's throats.

'What's happened here?' Lottie asked, staring.

'Gregory is not our leader,' said Mrs Andrews, jabbing a finger at him. 'If he tells me what to do, or how to recite my lines one more time I'm going to shove this script up his—'

'I'm just trying to help you, dear,' Gregory replied. 'Because you are so bloody awful a child could do it better than you.'

Mrs Andrews took a step towards Gregory. Cecil bravely jumped between them as she continued her onslaught. 'Don't talk to me like that, you drunken old—'

'That's enough, everyone,' shouted Lottie, marching into the middle. She gave them all her best hard stare. 'Everybody please, sit down.' The players did as they were told looking sheepish. 'There's no way we're going to learn this play if we spend all our time fighting. Gregory, I know you're trying to help but you have to let people learn for themselves. Let them practice and decide how they want to deliver their lines. And, Mrs Andrews, I think we all need to learn how to take constructive criticism, otherwise how will we get better?'

Sid was smiling at her and Lottie felt her annoyance subside. 'Come on, everyone, this is just the first read-through, so let's listen to each other's comments, have a think and then work together to make this production the best thing Greenley has ever seen. What do you say?'

She'd hoped for cheers and fist pumps but instead Lottie was greeted by mumbles and dirty looks. She bit the inside of her cheek. It was going to be a long day.

Chapter 21

Selena laid the table in the corner of the living room with four places, each with a placemat (Sid had no idea he even owned placemats) and two glasses. It was like a posh restaurant. She'd even made him clean up, which he'd done, then he had to clean up again when she arrived as it wasn't quite up to scratch. He had to admit that he was a bit lazy when it came to cleaning, though. It was why he and Lottie spent most of their time at Lottie's house.

Selena had dragged Sid around the shops and bought some posh food from one of the delis in town. He'd have been quite happy with a pizza, as Lottie would have too, but they were having a special menu put together by Selena and she didn't want them being shown up, whatever that meant. She was now fussing around the table in an incredibly short, tight black dress.

There was a knock at the door and Sid went to open it. He was wearing the new shirt Selena had bought him. It was blue and had pink flowers on it. He didn't like it but hadn't wanted to say anything.

'Happy birthday,' said Lottie as he stepped aside to let her in. She had a big box under her arm and he felt a bubble of excitement in his stomach. 'Thanks for inviting me.'

Jeremy stood behind her in a striped shirt, jeans and bright white trainers. Did he always have to wear shirts? Sid wondered. He might like him more if he loosened up a bit.

Selena stood at Sid's elbow. 'Hi, Lottie. Lovely to see you.'

'And you,' she replied, sweetly.

'I love your top,' Selena said. 'The colour really suits you – it's really flattering.'

'Umm, thanks. You look nice too.'

'Thanks.' Selena ran her hands down from her waist and over her thighs. 'I like to make an effort. Jeremy,' Selena continued, giving him a wide grin. 'Come in. Welcome to our place.'

Lottie's eyes shot to Sid's at Selena's use of the word 'our' and he felt himself blush. But it was good that she was feeling comfortable here with him.

'I'll get you both a drink,' said Sid, as he shook Jeremy's hand and motioned for him to go through to the living room.

'What a great flat you have, Sid,' said Jeremy, walking ahead of him. 'It's beautiful and has such great views.'

Sid followed to see him standing at the large sash windows looking out to sea. Lottie had placed Sid's present on the armchair in the corner of the room and he wondered what it could be. She always got him amazing presents.

'It's lovely, isn't it? I'm so lucky,' said Selena, joining Jeremy and gently touching his arm 'Would you like a beer?'

'Yes, please. That'd be great.' Selena turned and flashed her eyes at Sid as his cue to go and get one.

Sid went to the kitchen and poured the drinks. He heard Lottie and Selena laugh at something Jeremy had said and felt himself shrink. He didn't like to admit it, but he was a bit intimidated by Jeremy. They must be about the same age but he just seemed so much more together. Sid reminded himself that, if his parents' deaths had taught him anything, it was that the quality of your life, not how much you had, was what was most important. He took the drinks back out.

'Here you go,' he said to Lottie. 'I bought a bottle with a koala on it.'

Lottie laughed and took a sip. Selena stared at Sid as he explained that Lottie always chose wine based on the picture on the label.

'Great idea, Lottie,' Selena said before turning to Jeremy. 'So, Jeremy, have you had an exciting week?'

He took his beer from Sid and went back to the window. 'I wouldn't say exciting. Busy. But not exciting. Lots of meetings and site visits.'

Sid gestured for Jeremy to take a seat and joined him on the sofa. 'Are you working on a lot of projects at the moment?'

'Most of my time is going on a big office block. It's a pretty big job. But I'm not as busy as Lottie. Every spare minute goes on the theatre, doesn't it, honey?'

From the corner of the room, Lottie smiled but didn't join the conversation. Sid wanted to find out more about Jeremy and his business, just to put his mind at rest, so pressed on. 'Do you only do one project at a time then?'

Jeremy shook his head. 'No, I've got some smaller ones on the go too. And my team are always on the lookout for new opportunities.'

Hoping he'd say theatres, or something to prove his suspicions Sid said, 'Anything interesting?'

'Not really.' Jeremy eyed Sid then took a sip of his beer.

'And do you only work in London? That's where your office is, isn't it?'

Jeremy nodded and had another drink. 'That's right. Tell me, Sid, have you covered any interesting stories lately?'

Sid paused as the back of his neck burned. He didn't think 'drunk man tries to ride dog' really qualified and swallowed down his humiliation. 'Not much. It's quiet at the moment.'

Lottie went to sit next to Jeremy but as she lowered herself down, Selena said, 'Take a seat, Lottie, won't you?' Causing her to stop

161

halfway then wobble and flop down in an ungainly manner. Jeremy put his arm around her shoulders. The way they were looking at each other made Sid feel slightly queasy. 'So, let me open my presents then,' he said quickly, before they could start kissing.

Lottie smiled and collected the present from the chair before handing it to him. 'Here you go.'

'Hang on, you've got to open mine first,' said Selena.

'But you got me this shirt,' Sid replied. 'You didn't have to get me anything else.' He certainly hoped it wasn't any more clothing.

'But I wanted to,' she said and leaned down to kiss him. 'Wait here.'

Selena disappeared off to the bedroom and Sid was left with Lottie and Jeremy. Even though she was wearing jeans and a top, she'd done that weird eyeliner thing again and her eyes looked bigger and bluer. A weird silence descended. They'd always been able to talk about anything and everything but it was like being strangers and having to make awkward small talk.

'How are the rehearsals going?' asked Sid.

Lottie rubbed her forehead as if the very thought gave her a headache. 'They've not quite come to blows yet but it's got close. We've upped the number of rehearsals now because we were making so little progress and I'm just praying it gets better once they're practising on the bandstand.'

'I was telling Lottie,' said Jeremy, 'that she's doing a brilliant job and they'll settle down once they get used to working together. Don't you think?'

Sid nodded. 'I'm sure it'll all be alright. They were going to have to perform sometime.'

'Here you go,' said Selena, coming back in with a small flat parcel. Sid slid on to the floor. It was the only place to open presents and it made him feel like a kid again. Selena perched on the arm of the chair on Jeremy's other side, their arms almost touching. She'd bought expensive patterned paper and tied it with a bow.

162

Sid opened it, unsure what it would be. As he peeled back the paper he saw it was an envelope. Why would you wrap up an envelope? When he finally got through the wrapping, he saw it was two cinema tickets.

'There's the new *Batman* movie out soon,' Selena said. 'You said you wanted to see it. I know you and Lottie were going to go but I thought as Lottie's so busy with the theatre, you and I could.'

'Brilliant. Thanks,' Sid replied. He got up and gave her a hug and a kiss on the cheek. It was such a thoughtful gift. Lottie looked at her wine. Selena was probably right, Lottie wouldn't have the time for *Batman* with everything else that was going on.

'What did you get me then, Lots?' he asked. She smiled and handed him the present. It was a fairly big box and it rattled. For some reason he loved a rattly present. She'd also wrapped it in kids pirate paper which made him giggle.

'I thought you'd like that paper after you were swashbuckling the other day.'

He grinned before ripping off the paper. As he read the words on the top of the box he had to swallow down the enormous laugh that was eking out. It was the best present ever, bar none. The new *Star Wars* board game and he couldn't wait to play it. 'This is amazing. Absolutely brilliant. Thank you, Lots.'

He shot up and wrapped her in a hug. He'd wanted this game as soon as they'd said it was coming out. Lottie's arms squeezed him in return as she said, 'I'm glad you like it.'

Sid let her go and resumed his place on the floor to start unpacking all the pieces. Lottie shuffled onto the floor too and together they began reading through the different cards and the enormous rulebook. 'Look, there's a death star!' said Sid and Lottie giggled.

'Wow,' said Jeremy. 'I didn't realise you guys liked *Star Wars* so much.'

Sid studied a tiny TIE fighter and said, 'Lottie and me always

163

go and see the new ones at the midnight showing. It's a tradition.'

'Right,' said Jeremy and Sid saw the smile on his face. As a journalist, Sid prided himself on being able to read people but he couldn't determine what was going on in Jeremy's head right now. 'Well, maybe I could join you two next time? There's a new one next year, isn't there?'

'That'd be lovely,' said Lottie, shooting Jeremy a smile. 'Wouldn't it, Sid?'

He had no choice but to nod. 'Yeah.'

'Do you like *Star Wars*, Selena?' Lottie asked.

'Not really, but I'd go for Sid. It can be a double date.'

Sid pulled out a small model stormtrooper from the box and showed Selena. She didn't look as impressed as he and Lottie did, but *Star Wars* just wasn't her thing. She flicked her hair over her shoulder and said, 'That's so kind of you, Lottie.'

Sid smiled at Selena. She was being so sweet towards Lottie, knowing how shy she normally was.

Selena went off to the kitchen but not before Sid spotted a sullen pout forming on her mouth, and confused, he followed. When he came in she was stood by the sink drinking her wine, her arms crossed over her chest. 'You like Lottie's present more than mine, don't you?'

God, he was such an idiot, making more of a fuss of Lottie's present than his own girlfriend's. He cupped her face and kissed her, then her neck. 'I love your present and Lottie's. And I can't wait to go to the movies with you. We haven't done that yet.' Selena bent her head giving him more of her neck to nuzzle. 'I'm sorry if I was insensitive. I'm an idiot when it comes to all this boyfriend business.'

'You are,' she replied, giving him a playful punch on the chest. 'But you'll get better. You just need some training. Now, help me serve up dinner.'

Sid smiled as he grabbed the plates but he couldn't stop himself glancing through the open doorway to Lottie sat on the sofa.

She'd been watching him and looked away quickly as Jeremy showed her something on his phone. It was Sid's turn to look away as Jeremy kissed her passionately on the mouth, his fingers caught in her hair.

Sid looked at the weird starter Selena was serving up and the large bowl of salad. Tonight was going to be even more painful than the restaurant.

Chapter 22

The sun shone down on the tall white columns of the bandstand and Lottie lifted her head to feel the heat on her face. The weather had turned from a week of summer drizzle and a gusty breeze, to long days full of warmth and light. Hot in her jeans, she uncrossed her legs and studied the width of her thighs, for once not caring how big or small they were. Voices rang out from the bandstand. The first dress rehearsal was underway and so far, it wasn't going terribly well.

Lines were forgotten, if they'd been learnt at all, and Conner was finding it hard to make some of the actors listen to his direction. Lottie sat on the grass bank taking a break before heading back into the fray and sorting them all out, again.

'Working hard, then?' asked Sid, coming to join her.

Lottie ran her hand over the short newly cut grass feeling the spikes on her skin. 'Just having a breather.'

'I might join you. It's been a shocking day on my feet.' He sat down and groaned.

'It's a Saturday, what have you been up to?' Lottie asked, and then, remembering he'd probably been with Selena, wished she hadn't.

'Shopping.'

She spied at him from the corner of her eye. 'Shopping? You hate shopping.'

'Yeah, but Selena doesn't.' He leant forwards. 'My feet are hot.'

'If you take those trainers off I'm leaving.' Lottie held her nose to emphasise her point.

Sid playfully batted her hand down. 'If I take my trainers off it'll be like unleashing a chemical weapon. I'd kill half of Greenley.'

'Only half?' Lottie smiled and watched the cast, admiring their new costumes. Sarah was quite pretty in a white silk dress and something about her seemed different since she joined the group. Even Debbie, clad in grey servant's clothes, appeared very much the part. If only she would speak clearly enough for the crowd to understand her. 'I still can't believe Mrs Andrews said yes.'

'Sometimes, you just have to ask nicely.'

'So you didn't have to sleep with her then?' A part of her worried he actually had as he seemed to be so desirable these days.

'Nah. Just the promise of an announcement in the paper, a mention on the programme and a special thank you on each night of the performance. Not much really, considering.' Sid crossed his hands behind his head and lay back into the grass. Lottie examined the face she had seen a million times. Even with his eyes closed he looked cheeky and she suddenly wanted to lie down next to him.

Lifting her face to the sun Lottie felt the heat renew her failing energy levels. As it began to set in front of them, the sky was painted a deep golden yellow and the breeze from the sea carried its warmth. There was a swell in the voices again.

'Why don't you just—' said Gregory.

'Leave it out,' shouted Lee.

'If you touch me again, Cecil, I swear I'll—' said Mrs Andrews through gritted teeth.

Sid opened his eyes and sat up.

'Listen to them,' said Lottie, crossing her legs and hunching forwards. 'This is going to be an absolute disaster. Half of them can't remember their lines and the other half are too busy arguing to actually recite them.'

'At least they look good.' Sid said, trying to make her laugh.

Lottie wanted to but couldn't. There was nothing funny here. With only a week to go, how could it suddenly all slot into place? 'We've only got two more rehearsals. No one knows where they're meant to stand and Conner hasn't got the bottle to really take charge. He's so young, I knew this would be too much for him. Do you think we should cancel?'

'What? No way,' said Sid. 'You'd lose all the public support you've got so far and then everyone will lose interest.'

'You're right,' Lottie replied, putting her head in her hands. 'It's all a disaster.'

Sid nudged her shoulder. 'It'll be fine, Lots. Just go in there and give them what for.'

Behind her Lottie heard the slap of leather to foot. She glanced over her shoulder to see Selena looking gorgeous in huge sunglasses, a short white sundress and matching sandals. Her flawless skin glistened in the sun and her legs, long and bronze, marched towards her as briskly as anyone can in flapping footwear.

'Hi, honey,' Selena said, kneeling down and kissing Sid. Lottie heard a muffled ringing and Sid pulled his phone from his pocket.

'Are you joining us?' asked Lottie, trying to be friendly but struggling to keep the chill from her voice. She felt herself bristle whenever Selena was around, waiting for the next backhanded compliment.

Selena removed her sunglasses and stared at Lottie, her tone sharper, beating Lottie's for coldness. 'Am I interrupting something?

'Not at all,' Lottie assured her.

Sid put his phone away and lay back down again. 'We were just talking about the play.'

Selena curled her legs underneath her. 'Oh. It's not going very well, is it?' Her voice was all sympathy but something about it riled Lottie. There was definitely a bitchy tone there, another passive aggressive comment very well hidden.

Gregory flounced off stage. 'I need some time to be at peace'.

Sid nudged Lottie again. 'I'm sure it'll be okay.'

'I hope so,' Lottie replied. 'Everyone's working really hard. They just need a bit more time.'

Selena put her sunglasses back on. 'Hmmm. But there's not long to go is there? Isn't the first performance next week? You really don't have much time at all do you? Poor thing. Sid and I are coming though, aren't we, honey?' She gave Sid another kiss. 'Wouldn't miss it, would we?'

Selena smiled but even behind the sunglasses, Lottie could tell it didn't reach her eyes. Lottie had no idea why Selena had such a problem with her and stood up. 'I'd better head back.'

'Good luck,' said Sid and as Lottie turned to him she could see he really meant it.

'Yeah, good luck.' Selena gave Lottie a sweet smile and stretched out her long legs. 'Shall we go now and have a quick drink before we meet my friends?'

'Do you want me to hang on?' Sid asked Lottie, standing up. 'See if I can help?'

'Oh, sweetie, we've only got half an hour,' Selena interjected before Lottie could answer.

Sid threaded his thumbs through the belt loops of his jeans. 'I'm sure your mates wouldn't mind if I missed it. It's you they want to see anyway, I could stay here and help Lottie.'

Lottie really wanted him to stay but wasn't going to get in the middle of this.

'Honey,' said Selena getting up and wrapping her arm through his. 'We really can't. They're dying to meet you. We've cancelled once already when you said you were poorly.'

Lottie wondered if that was like the time he was poorly when he had a root canal appointment? He'd cancelled that with the same excuse until the pain had got so bad, she'd dragged him to the dentist and sat with him through the procedure. Sid looked at Lottie, his eyes imploring her to say yes but Selena looked at her too and her eyes didn't implore anything. Lottie felt a bit scared. 'It's okay, there isn't much you çan do but thanks for the offer.'

Selena smiled triumphantly. 'Come on, honey, or we'll be late. Good luck, Lottie. I'm sure you won't need it.'

'Thanks,' Lottie replied, but she had a sneaking suspicion that Selena didn't mean a single word.

Chapter 23

After the disastrous dress rehearsal, Lottie buried herself in preparations for the play but even so, the first performance came around faster than expected. Lottie's stomach fizzed. She hadn't been able to eat all day.

When she'd finally fallen asleep last night, she'd tossed and turned, the fear in her stomach rolling from side to side as she moved. This morning, though bone tired, nervous energy pumped around Lottie's system. She couldn't sit still but couldn't stop moving either and as the moment of truth came nearer she felt sick. The curtain was up in forty-five minutes and the Greenley Players were dressing in the makeshift backstage area – a white marquee erected a few metres away from the bandstand.

Lottie checked around for Sid. She'd thought he would be here, backstage, supporting her – or if nothing else, to at least capture the action for the newspaper – but he was nowhere to be seen and without him, her nerves intensified. She scanned the crowd assembling in the evening sunshine. Blankets and picnics were spread out as people chatted and laughed. Happy couples and groups of friends giggled, enjoying the anticipation, opening bottles of champagne and cheering at the pops. Even the mayor had arrived in his finery.

If only Jeremy could be here, Lottie thought. She missed him. He'd been delayed in London again and as sorry as he'd been, he wouldn't get there until late, hopefully before the end of the show. Lottie checked the time on her phone; there was no putting it off any longer, she had to go and see the players.

'Where's the blush? I must have the blush,' demanded Mrs Andrews.

'I think you've got enough on, dear,' said Gregory. 'They'd be able to see your cheeks from space.' He turned to Cecil and whispered, 'But at least it'll draw attention away from her squinty little eyes.'

'How's it going, everyone?' asked Lottie, feigning cheerful excitement. 'Everybody ready for opening night? Our first performance! Everyone excited?' The players stared at her as if she'd gone mad. Some were white from too much make-up, others from fright. Sarah looked like she was about to throw up. 'Okay,' continued Lottie, clapping her hands together. 'Good luck, everyone.' She turned to leave just as Sid entered. 'Oh, hello. I wondered where you'd got to.'

'Sorry I'm late, I was just getting Selena settled. Have you brought your camera? We'll need some shots for the newspaper.'

'Yes, I've taken a few already, I just had to get some air. It's a bit tense in here.' Sid smiled and Lottie felt her nerves subside a little. He was always able to make her feel better, just by being there. 'Where've you been? You were supposed to get some quotes from the players and the audience before the performance.'

Mrs Andrews' voice carried over the hum. 'At least I can act without drinking my body weight in gin first.'

'That's what you think, dear,' countered Cecil and Debbie muttered something unintelligible in her thick Scottish accent.

Sid raised his eyebrows at Lottie. 'I'm really sorry. Selena got a bit upset about something and I had to sort it out. I'll get them now.'

Lottie wondered what it could have been but didn't dare ask.

172

'There isn't time now. We'll have to do something else. Oh, Sid, I think I'm going to be sick.'

'Nah, it'll be alright, Lots. Don't worry.' He put his hand on her shoulder and gave a squeeze.

'Curtains up,' shouted Conner from the doorway.

Immediately the chatter stopped. No one moved.

'Come on,' shouted Conner. 'Get going.'

The players leapt into action, making final adjustments to costumes, grabbing props and checking scripts one last time. Lottie could see the terror in their eyes. Sid turned to leave then rushed back and gave her a huge hug. 'Don't worry, Lots. It'll be fine.'

Something stirred inside her – an emotion she couldn't name, something she'd never felt before – and she wanted his strong arms around her one more time. Then the nerves in her stomach flared up and she felt sick again.

The actors left, to the sound of applause and Lottie followed. Her eyes found Sid in the crowd, sitting at the back with Selena snuggled into him. Lottie made herself comfortable on the grass between the marquee and the bandstand, and the play began.

The man playing Leonato came on with Mrs Andrews and Sarah. 'I learn in this letter that Don Peter of Arragon comes this night to Messina.' He delivered the line well but had forgotten the letter and held nothing in his hand. When he realised he went bright red and added, 'But I left it at home.' A chill ran over Lottie as the crowd guffawed and snickered and through the next three hours Lottie's head sank further and further into her hands.

It was awful. Worse than awful. It was embarrassing.

About halfway through Sarah completely forgot her lines and stared at the crowd wide eyed and pale before attempting to make something up. She was supposed to say, 'It were a better death than die with mocks, Which is as bad as die with tickling,' but instead said, 'I'd rather die than be tickled to death,' which left everyone very confused.

173

Mrs Andrews couldn't keep her hands to herself and was flailing around like she did at her audition, so much so that in one scene she turned with her arms outstretched whacking Cecil in the face so hard he nearly fell over. Lottie was sure he said 'Fuck,' but thankfully it was muffled by his hands clasping his cheek.

Gregory made up for everyone else's lack of acting skills by over-acting everything and rather than saying his lines he bellowed them, pointing and motioning with such sharp, jerky movements he looked like he had some sort of medical condition.

No one stood where they were supposed to, and if they were smart enough to realise their mistake, they moved in the most obvious, wooden way to where they should be. It was like watching children recite Shakespeare.

Even the scenery caused problems. One of the plaster columns they had put out kept tipping over so that someone had to lean on it whenever they were on stage and eventually Lee just picked it up and took it away with him.

The crowd hated it too. Most left halfway through, some as early as twenty minutes in. Those that managed to make it to the end gave a slow, unhappy applause as the cast took their final bows.

It was a disaster. An unmitigated, total disaster. Lottie wondered if they had any money for acting lessons, but all the money in the world wouldn't whip this lot into shape.

Lottie had managed to catch Sid's eye once or twice through the evening, at the most embarrassing moments. There had been a glimmer of sympathy in his eyes, but she was sure Selena had been smirking.

Darkness descended on the green as the players took off their make-up, brushed out their hair and changed back into normal clothes. Lottie stared at the marquee. She had to go in and say something, but what? What could she say to make this better? She had no idea but took a deep breath, rolled her shoulders back and walked in.

Sarah was crying on Lee's shoulder. Conner tapped on his phone, an anguished expression on his face, and even Mrs Andrews sat quietly bereft. Gregory and Cecil held hands.

'Well done, everyone,' said Lottie, with fake cheer.

'Are you kidding?' said Gregory, his face pale and ashen. 'Well done? It was a disaster, darling.'

'Shh, now,' said Cecil, stroking his hand. A bruise was forming on his cheek.

The others nodded in agreement.

'It wasn't that bad,' lied Lottie. 'Okay, it wasn't perfect, but we should still be proud of what we've achieved. We need some more practice but a lot of people stayed to the end.'

'And a lot of people left halfway through,' said Sarah, wiping her eyes. 'Someone gave me the finger as they went.'

'Tomorrow will be better, I promise,' said Lottie. 'We've learnt so much tonight.'

'Oh God, we've got one more to go,' sobbed Sarah, her body shaking. Lee held her closely stroking her hair.

'It was horrible, lassie,' said Debbie, throwing her hairbrush onto the table. 'We've made ourselves a laughing stock. Can't we just cancel tomorrow?'

'I can't do it,' said Mrs Andrews standing up, her face a frozen mask and her demeanour exactly like a politician's wife. 'Do you have any idea how embarrassed I am?' She grabbed her things and stormed out followed by the rest of the cast. No one said goodnight. Only Conner was left behind.

'Did you want some help tidying up?' he asked from under his fringe. His shoulders were hunched and he shoved his hands into his pockets.

'Don't you want to get out of here too?'

'I don't mind helping.' He started hanging up the costumes that had been thrown on the floor. 'If I go back now everyone will take the piss. I'll wait till most of them are asleep.'

Lottie wanted to hug him. She felt embarrassed for all of them

175

and picked up a box, tidying the make-up and costumes away. It couldn't be left here overnight – knowing her luck someone would steal it. In hindsight, she should have stuck to her guns that it was too soon.

'I'm sorry,' said Conner, puncturing the silence.

Lottie looked up confused. 'Sorry? You don't have anything to be sorry for.'

'I do. I should have been more professional. I should have told them what to do and not let them boss me around or make suggestions all the time.' He pulled his fringe down over his face. 'I'm sorry I let you down.'

'Conner,' said Lottie, moving towards him. 'You have nothing to apologise for. I'm sorry I wasn't more supportive and encouraging. I'm sorry if your friends will tease you about this.'

'Don't matter. I won't have many left now.'

Lottie's hand flew to her chest. 'Oh, Conner, I'm so sorry. You can blame it all on me. Tell them you didn't get enough support from me. And you never know, we might be better tomorrow?'

He placed another costume on the rail. 'Maybe.'

The door to the marquee opened and Sid walked in. 'Do you want some help?'

Tears stung Lottie's eyes and threatened to roll down her cheeks as she resisted the urge to run to him for a hug. 'Yes, please. Where's Selena?'

'She's gone home.'

Lottie turned to Conner. 'Conner, I'm the one who should be sorry and I'm here if you ever need to talk but it's late. You should go home and get some sleep.'

Conner did as he was told and grabbed his jacket and left.

Sid edged in nervously. 'Lots, I need to talk to you about the review for the paper.'

'Oh, yes. That,' said Lottie. How could they spin this into something positive? If anyone could, Sid could. He had a way with words and his sense of humour jumped off the page like he was there talking to you. Surely he could make it right, or at least soften the blow.

'I … umm …' He reached a long arm up and scratched the back of his head. 'I—I think we need to just be honest about what a disaster tonight was.'

Lottie dropped the box she was holding and stared at him. 'What?'

'We can play it like, "Wow, we know how bad we were, but this is just the beginning and we'll get better."'

She scowled. His voice was so calm, like he didn't see how serious this was. Now was not the time to be laidback.

'You know, kind of, stay with us for the journey type stuff?' he continued.

'No,' said Lottie, shaking her head. 'No. People will think we're a bunch of losers who can't do anything right, and then they'll never come back.'

'But, Lottie, I don't see how we can spin it any other way.'

Lottie's voice hardened. 'Can't you say it wasn't that bad? Play up all the people who were good and—'

'And what, Lottie?' Sid's voice suddenly matched her own. 'And didn't forget their lines, or stand in front of each other, or forget which way they were supposed to be looking, or dropped the prop, or hit someone in the face, or—'

'We might be better tomorrow.' She knew it sounded pathetic but every comment was like a knife being pushed into her skin. Lottie found her sadness turning to anger. 'Can't you just not mention any of that and only put in the nice things people said, or the bits they actually enjoyed?'

'There aren't any bits like that, Lottie,' he said sternly.

'There are.' Lottie hadn't meant for her voice to be that loud but she had to push it up over the lump in her throat. 'There have to be.'

'I don't see any other way to—'

'To humiliate us?'

'You're humiliated already.' He said it so matter-of-factly and without feeling that Lottie felt like she'd been slapped.

How could he say that? This wasn't the Sid she knew, he wouldn't be so harsh. He sounded more like Selena. Why was he being so hurtful? It was only since Selena turned up, all swishing hair and painted toenails that he'd changed. She crossed her arms over her chest. 'How can you say that to me?'

'I'm not trying to embarrass you.'

'Aren't you?' she shouted.

'No, Lottie.' Sid's voice rose to match her own. 'And if that's what you think I'd do then you're not the person I thought you were.'

'And you're not the person I thought you were.' Lottie's breath came in short gulps as if her lungs were in spasm.

'What does that mean?' A redness came into Sid's cheeks and his jaw clenched.

All the nerves, the adrenalin, and months of sadness and loss erupted in a burst of anger. An uncontrollable ball of rage that exploded into life. 'You've not been the same since you met that girlfriend of yours.'

Sid pulled back. 'What do you mean?'

Lottie didn't really know how to describe it. She had nothing tangible. Every nasty comment was wrapped up in a bow or said when Sid wasn't around. 'Sometimes she says really … bitchy things and you don't even notice.'

Sid rolled his eyes. Lottie knew he'd heard her say that before about other people but he had to believe her this time. His voice was resigned as he said, 'No she doesn't, Lottie. That's just you being defensive.'

'It is not.'

She could see a nerve pulse in his neck. 'What has she said then? And when?'

'When I first met her at the theatre and said you didn't like salad. She just looked at me like . . . like—'

'Like what?'

'Like …' Lottie searched for the words. 'Oh, I don't know. I can't explain it. Like she knew you better than me.'

Sid stared, unspeaking, the lines of his forehead deeply etched in confusion. 'Lottie, what are you talking about? That makes no sense at all. Selena likes you. She's always paying you compliments, isn't she?'

'Not real ones.'

'For God's sake, Lottie—'

She stepped forwards, remembering a better example. 'And at the dress rehearsal she said, "Oh, you haven't got much time, have you?"'

He threw his hands in the air. 'But you didn't.'

'But it was the way she said it.'

'Which was?'

She thought of Jeremy's words to describe Selena the night he'd told Lottie he was falling in love with her. 'Snarky.'

'Snarky? That's not even a thing.' Sid put his hands on his hips, his features softening a little. 'I really think you've got the wrong end of the stick, Lottie. I know you get defensive, and it's fine. It's part of who you are and I don't care but just because you're grieving you see the worst in everyone and—'

'Rubbish.' He wasn't going to put this all on her. 'It's not just me,' she said angrily. 'Jeremy's noticed it too.'

'Oh, has he now?' Sid replied, snidely.

'Yes, he has. He says she's passive aggressive.'

'Well, Jeremy can mind his own bloody business. And anyway, she really isn't, Lottie. I wish you could understand.'

Lottie felt the heat rise on the back of her neck. Why was he taking her side? She wanted to say about the flirting with Jeremy but the thought that he wouldn't believe her destroyed her and closed her mouth for her. Besides, if she'd misread Selena's actions, Sid would hate her forever. She blinked, hoping to stave off tears. 'I'm not lying, Sid.'

179

'Well, what about you and Mr Suave?' Sid pointed his finger at her accusingly.

'Jeremy?'

'Yes, Jeremy. You used to be fun, Lottie, and now you do nothing but moon over him when he's not here or work on the theatre.'

Lottie's nose stung as tears formed again, misting her vision. 'I'm only doing what Nan wanted. And anyway, you wanted me to work on the theatre too. You said it'd be fun and just what I need. Or have you changed your mind now?'

They'd never rowed like this before. And he was defending Selena instead of siding with her. Everything had changed and Lottie could see Sid was lost to her now. Utterly and completely lost. She sighed, wiping back the tears from her eyes. She hadn't felt like this since the day her nan had died. The day the doctor had rung and told her to get there soon. Her heart had filled with sadness and despair and that feeling was engulfing her again. Mixed with the physical and emotional exhaustion she now felt, it threatened to overpower her.

A vibration from Lottie's pocket attracted her attention. She pulled out her phone and saw it was Jeremy. She glared at Sid. His jaw was clenched and his eyes were cold but she had to try one last time, for the players, for Conner. 'Will you please change your mind about the article? There must be a way to make it seem good. Don't make us a laughing stock.'

Sid lowered his gaze. 'I'm sorry, Lottie. I can't just lie.'

She bit her lip as tears formed again. She'd always thought his stubbornness a great quality, until now. 'Write what you want, then, Sid. It's all over now anyway.'

'What's all over?'

'Everything,' she shouted, unable to stop the outpouring of emotion. 'Our friendship for one and my place on the committee for another.'

Lottie stared at him and they locked eyes, hers, angry and unwavering, his, stunned. She hoped for a flicker of regret, but there was nothing she could read anymore. Lottie breathed hard, trying to control herself, but it was no use, she'd unleashed her anger and it wouldn't stop.

'Do you think I'll be kept on the committee now? I told you we weren't ready for this, but you kept on saying it would be fine. Well, it's not fine is it? It's a bloody disaster.'

'Oh, so it's all my fault now?'

Her phone was still vibrating. Thank God she had put it on silent. The last thing she needed was 'Jumping Jack Flash' as a soundtrack to this … whatever it was.

'So you blame me for all this?' said Sid, motioning around him.

Another wave of rage built inside her. Her stomach muscles tightened trying to push it down and control it, but it was no use. Her lungs fell into spasm causing her breathing to falter and she gasped. 'It's not all your fault, but some of it is. I'll be kicked off the committee now. I won't get to do what Nan wanted.' Her voice cracked. 'All because we weren't ready for this and because you won't help me now, when I need it most.'

He stepped forwards and reached out for her but she backed away. 'People came to the show, Lottie. They saw it with their own eyes. I can't pretend it was great.'

'But you don't have to say it was shit either.'

He gave an incredulous shrug. 'What else can I say? We'll lose all integrity if we lie.'

'Integrity?' Lottie spat. 'What about my integrity? What about Conner's and Sarah's and Gregory's and Cecil's? Since your parents died all you've ever wanted was an easy life and now you're talking about journalistic integrity? We work on a boring local paper writing stories about opera-singing parrots. You haven't got any journalistic integrity.'

Sid's expression changed instantly and the words stopped gushing from her mouth. She'd gone too far. She'd been callous and cold and knew that she'd hurt him. He turned his gaze away, his eyes full of pain, and Lottie felt ashamed. Her heart split open and she felt every inch of the crack that appeared before it finally snapped and fell apart, shattering into tiny pieces.

They stood not looking at each other in the oppressive silence. Lottie didn't know what to say or how to move on from this moment. They were at a stalemate. And to give in was unthinkable but there was no way back from what they had said to the other.

A muscle twitched in Sid's neck. He threw down his notebook and, without saying a word, walked away. When he'd gone, Lottie stepped forwards, her legs unsteady and shaking beneath her and she picked it up. Underneath the title, '*Much Ado*, First Performance,' were written two simple words in block capitals. Tears blotted the paper as she read them and collapsed dramatically to her knees. 'Oh fuck' indeed, Sid.

Chapter 24

Sid walked for more than an hour after seeing Lottie, hoping that each step would ease the anger in the pit of his stomach and the stabbing in his heart. He'd always been able to control his emotions but this evening they'd got the better of him. In the harbour the boats gently bobbed up and down on the calm quiet sea. The moon reflected off the smooth surface and without the cawing of the gulls everything was eerily silent. Sid caught his foot on the uneven cobbles and stumbled.

How could Lottie say things like that about his career, let alone about Selena? Selena was sweet and kind, and she cared about him more than Lottie did. Lottie had always had such low self-esteem, she took everything the wrong way. He'd learned to live with it over the years but she was clearly doing the same thing with Selena. Well, she'd have to get over that herself. He'd tried to help before but she hadn't changed. He didn't mind her deep insecurities, he'd loved her despite them. They were part of who she was, but Selena had always been sweet and kind to Lottie. She was obviously intimidated by her self-confidence and there was nothing he could do about that. And the thought of Jeremy passing comment on his relationship made him squeeze his fists tightly and want to punch something.

Sid pushed his hands further into his jacket pockets. When he thought of where he wanted to be right now he was surprised that, for the first time, he wanted to be with Selena, not Lottie. He'd finally moved on but at what cost? Their friendship was ruined forever now. It wasn't how he wanted things to be, but what could he do? There was no going back. Lottie had made it clear she blamed him for everything. And he didn't feel he could ever forgive her for mentioning his parents like that.

Now his anger was subsiding, he felt an overwhelming sadness. Grief for the life he and Lottie had had. The one that was gone. He didn't know this version of Lottie. She was a stranger to him. The fierce pain in his chest started again and he clenched his fists willing it to stop.

No matter how hard he tried, Sid couldn't just pretend the play was great and write a glowing review. He'd spent the entire performance trying to phrase things in his mind so they were hopeful, but it was useless. The only thing he could think to do was be honest and hope people understood.

Sid found himself walking home, glad Selena had asked for a key to his flat. He wanted to be in the arms of someone who cared about him, who loved him. It was almost one o'clock in the morning but when he saw the living room light on he was happy she'd waited up for him. As he unlocked the door and walked in, Selena met him in the hallway. She was in a short silky dressing gown, the thin straps of a vest top poked out from the neckline and her legs were bare. A hint of lacy shorts peeked from under her gown. He didn't speak at first as he enjoyed the comfort of being home, and of having Selena wrapped around him.

They walked through to the living room and where she turned around, her smooth forehead wrinkled in concern. 'Honey, what's wrong?'

Sid told her about the argument but didn't mention what Lottie had said about her. Selena sat on the sofa and pulled her legs under her. 'Lottie said what? I can't believe it.'

Sid perched on the edge of the armchair leaning forwards, his shoulders tense. 'And the thing is, I can't lie to the town, can I? I can't just pretend it was all okay. People talk, they know the truth. No one would read the paper again. They'd think we're completely biased and then we'll be a laughing stock. And they'll think I'm a joke too.'

'You're not a joke and I'm sure Lottie will realise you can't lie about the play. I bet she's just embarrassed and lashing out.'

Sid looked into her deep brown eyes. Her long hair was down and without make-up he could really see who she was. Lottie was wrong. What Selena had just said proved it. Lottie was the one with the problem.

'I think that Jeremy is a bad influence,' said Selena, matter-of-factly. 'I mean, think about it, you haven't seen her at all since he came on the scene, have you? I've had friends do that before when they've got new boyfriends and it's really bad. You can't just dump people.'

Selena's words rang in his ears. That was exactly what Lottie had done – dumped him. He'd been a great friend all this time and then as soon as things started to change and a man came along, she chucked him aside. That showed how much he meant to her. Bile rose in his throat and he fought back the sting of tears. He'd been so right to move on with Selena and the relief that thought brought loosened his tight muscles.

Selena ran her hands through her hair. 'And now she's dressing and acting differently too. I have no idea why some women feel the need to do that. To change who they are for the new men in their lives. It's sad.'

Sid looked up to see her worried face watching him. He'd been unfair to Selena, he realised now, never fully committing to their relationship. He'd had one foot in and one foot out, ready to run to Lottie all the while a glimmer of hope remained. He'd been a fool and Selena deserved better.

'And,' Selena continued, 'Jeremy seems the type to think you

185

can just buy everything and everyone. I've never liked him. But money doesn't always get you what you want.' Her voice softened as she said, 'Lottie will learn that eventually.'

She was being sweet taking his side, trying to make him feel better, letting him know he wasn't to blame for this mess. It was just what he needed to hear right now. He'd never have hurt Lottie how she'd hurt him tonight. Not intentionally.

Sid opened his mouth to speak then closed it. He hadn't talked about his parents for years but now he wanted to tell Selena. He wanted her soft voice to soothe over the old wounds that had opened up at Lottie's words. 'Lottie said I've wanted nothing but an easy life since my parents died.' His voice was small and unable to mask the pain. 'But I've always had professional integrity. I've never lied or embellished a story, she—'

'She used your parents against you?' Selena came over and kneeled in front of him, taking his hands in hers. 'I'm sorry, Sid. I know she's your friend but that's completely out of order.'

Sid stayed silent and Selena stroked his face. 'Listen, maybe you and Lottie need some space from each other for a while? She's really caught up in Jeremy and this theatre business, and even though I try and be friendly I don't think she really likes me. I think she just needs a bit of time to get used to us being together?'

He nodded, she was right. The things Lottie said tonight showed that she was struggling with all these changes. Maybe some space would do them both good.

Selena cupped the back of his head, leading him towards her. She put his head on her shoulder and hugged him tightly. 'You have to write the story truthfully and the truth is, it was rubbish. There isn't anything else you can do and you shouldn't feel guilty about it. She shouldn't have even asked you to do something like this. Maybe you need to give her space to realise that?'

Sid breathed in the sweet honey scent of her hair and lifted his head so he was looking straight at her. He kissed her and felt all his troubles slide away in her warm and tender embrace. The only thought that flickered across his brain was, 'goodbye Lottie'.

Chapter 25

Lottie entered the marquee for the second night to see the Greenley Players sitting around doing absolutely nothing. The previous night's fussing and primping had been replaced by a lethargic depression in which nobody raced to get to the make-up stand or fiddled with their costumes. After her row with Sid, Lottie felt the same – tired and depressed.

When Jeremy had picked her up from the marquee the night before and taken her home she'd said goodnight and closed the door, wanting to be left alone to cry. Picking up her nan's old shawl and pulling it tightly around her, Lottie climbed the stairs and got into bed still fully clothed. She reached into the drawer of her bedside table and pulled out her nan's letter. 'I'm so sorry, Nan. I've really let you down this time.' She'd then curled up into the foetal position and cried herself to sleep.

Looking around now, Lottie had no idea what to say. Debbie leaned against a wall and stared into space, toying with the waist-band of her skirt. Lee sat on the floor, his hands resting on his knees, head down, and Sarah was hiding behind the costume rail. Even Mrs Andrews sat with her legs crossed, dejectedly sipping a bottle of water. It was a terrible sight and Lottie felt her heart break for them. It was horrible to think that they had to go through it all again tonight. She put on a smile and adopted a cheerful tone. Perhaps pretending last night didn't matter would help them focus now. 'Hi, everyone.'

Heads turned to her, but no one bothered to speak.

'So, I know last night was—'

'Ghastly?' asked Gregory.

'Embarrassing?' said Mrs Andrews, for once nodding in agreement with Gregory.

'Difficult,' replied Lottie. 'But we need to learn from our mistakes and move on.'

'Has anyone even bothered turning up for tonight's performance?' Debbie asked.

Lottie went to the marquee door and popped her head out. 'There's quite a few people here already.' Lottie feigned excitement. 'And it's still half an hour till we start.'

'Oh God,' said Sarah, raising a hand to her mouth.

'Please, everyone,' began Lottie, knowing she needed to lift their spirits. 'Last night didn't go according to plan, we have to be honest about that. But we've got a lot we can take from it too, and it's all good experience. I really think tonight will be different.'

Amongst the quiet murmurs she could make out the words 'mad' and 'naïve'. 'Conner, did you want to say anything?'

He shook his head and tapped on his phone. Everyone kept their eyes averted and Lottie decided it was probably best to leave them alone. She headed out into the crowd and looked for Sid, but he was yet to arrive, if he even came at all. Surely he would watch the second performance before writing his article? He owed them that much.

'How is everyone?' asked Jeremy when she joined him on the grass. He'd brought a picnic to try and cheer her up but as the champagne bubbles fizzed on her tongue her mood didn't improve.

'Totally depressed. I don't know what we're going to do. They've lost all confidence and I'm really worried they're going to quit after this.'

189

'Don't worry, we won't let that happen.'

Lottie's eyes widened in sudden panic. 'What if they leave halfway through the performance? Just walk out? What will we do then? Or what if they refuse to go on?'

'They won't. Listen.' He took her hand, his voice a calm, reassuring balm. 'We'll sort this out. I promise.'

'But how?'

'I'm a problem solver, Lottie. That's what I do.' He lifted her head and stared into her eyes. 'Trust me.'

'Okay,' she said, and with mounting fear, snuggled into his arm.

The second performance was, in fact, marginally better than the first. The wonky column was left out and Mrs Andrews managed not to hit anyone. Some cast members still forgot their lines, and others forgot where to stand, but the embarrassment of the first night had scared them into trying harder. Scripts had been re-learned, voices were projected with actual feeling, rather than recited like a robot, and gestures were more natural and less awkward. Clearly no one wanted to go through that again.

At the intermission, very few people left and those that stayed, whilst not entirely enjoying themselves, were at least sticking it out in the evening sunshine. The only thing that had gone wrong so far was when a member of the public did such an enormous sneeze it sounded like his face exploded and Sarah and Lee were momentarily thrown off during a tense scene.

As the players left the stage, Lottie took a sip of her drink and turned to Jeremy. His face and the gold flecks in his eyes were illuminated by the deep golden glow of the evening sun. 'Why don't you go and give them some words of encouragement?'

Lottie nodded and headed back to the marquee. Conner was talking to Lee and pointing to the script. Lee nodded and gave Conner a pat on the shoulder.

'Well done, everyone,' said Lottie. 'I think we're doing much better tonight. You're doing really well.'

'We could hardly do any worse, dear, could we?' said Gregory.

Lottie ignored him. 'I just wanted to say keep going, you're doing great.' She gave them a double thumbs-up, then felt like a cheesy TV presenter, so dropped her hands.

'The woman's delusional,' said Gregory to the rest of the players, then turned back to Lottie. 'But thank you, dear.'

Lottie left and found her spot next to Jeremy. He looked like a movie star in his sunglasses. 'I'm not sure it did any good, but I tried.' She checked again for Sid and spied him sat at the back with Selena. When Selena spotted Lottie she looped her arm through Sid's, a smug smile on her perfectly glossed lips, and Lottie flinched. Through the second half Sid gazed adoringly at Selena, and wrote notes in a new notebook – Lottie still had his old one. Lottie's heart ached watching them together.

'Everything alright?' asked Jeremy. He turned and saw Sid. 'I can't believe he's let you down like this.'

It hurt to hear Jeremy say it but he was right. And the mayor had left her several messages telling her an urgent committee meeting had been called for the following night. Lottie feared the worst.

Jeremy's cool, confident demeanour was ruffled. 'Did you want me to talk to him for you, try and find out what he's going to write? He didn't answer my calls this morning.'

'No, it's okay.' Lottie gave Jeremy a half smile. 'He'll write whatever he wants no matter what anyone says. Let's just watch the end and get out of here.'

'Sid can't just go ruining all the hard work you've put into the theatre. I won't let him.'

'There's nothing you can do. Freedom of the press and all that.' Ironic how something she'd always believed in was going to ruin her new life.

Jeremy scoffed. 'There is. It's all because he's jealous.'

'Jealous?' asked Lottie. 'Of what?'

'Of you and me, of course.' He was normally calm but knowing

191

he was upset on her behalf made her feel better. It was good to know someone was on her side. 'Haven't you ever noticed? I saw it that night at dinner. I know you're only friends but he's jealous of how you're making something of your life and he's just treading water as a local reporter.'

Lottie sat in silence. She remembered what she'd said to Sid about working on the paper and her skin prickled with shame.

Jeremy topped up their champagne. 'There is one thing that will cheer you up. I've organised for the roof repairs to start next week.'

'Really?'

'Yeah.' His voice bubbled with excitement. 'We'll soon be getting the theatre back to its former glory.'

Lottie tried to smile but knew that it would be someone else acting as chairman soon. There was no way she could carry on after this. Her head pulled to the side to look at Sid and as he gave Selena another kiss, Lottie turned quickly away.

Jeremy wrapped his arm around her shoulder and moved in closer. It was clear that, as far as Sid was concerned, she didn't exist anymore. And what was worse was that her only hope for staying as chairman was to convince the committee that they could somehow come back from this. But how on earth could they do that?

Chapter 26

A week later, Lottie wandered to the theatre feeling glum. She was on her way to face the Greenley Players for the first time since the shambles that was *Much Ado About Nothing* and she wasn't looking forward to it.

Unable to face Sid, Lottie had taken some last-minute holiday from work. She never took any. Even after the funeral, despite being heartbroken, she'd had a few days off and come back to work as soon as possible. But this time she couldn't bear to see Sid or anyone in the office and have to work on the paper that was going to tear apart everything she'd worked so hard to achieve. Lottie's eyes stung with tears as she relived the same sense of dread and impending loneliness that had consumed her after her nan had died. Now here it was again and without Sid she was totally alone.

The sun had come out for the school holidays and as Lottie walked she watched little red lobster people with sunburnt faces and odd white patches eat ice creams and moan about the weather. Normally it would have made her smile but she couldn't bring her face to form anything other than a frown.

Poor old Shakespeare was probably still spinning in his grave and, as if that wasn't stressful enough, Mrs Andrews had, for some unknown reason, brought a picnic. Mini scones with jam and clotted cream, an array of finger sandwiches and other picnic foods had all been laid out on shiny white platters on the stage, and tall plastic glasses of Pimm's stood beside them.

Lottie's head pounded from the stress of the last few days. She had so much to tell them and no idea how she was going to do it. To make matters worse, the Greenley Players were at full blown war.

How had she managed to put up with their bickering for so long? The din was bouncing off the insides of her skull and battering the backs of her eyes. She began to feel a twitch in her stomach – anger rising up again, or perhaps it hadn't fully evaporated since the last time.

'If you'd have listened to Conner,' shouted Gregory to the poor chap who had played Leonato, 'you would have remembered the letter.'

'Don't blame me. The boy didn't say anything to me about a letter.'

'It's in the script,' said Conner calmly.

Cecil stood in front of Mrs Andrews pushing his finger at her. 'If you'd have spent more time rehearsing and less time getting Botox you wouldn't have walloped me in the face. You nearly broke my cheekbone.'

Mrs Andrews was doing her best to cry. 'I brought a picnic for us all to enjoy in an effort to cheer us up and this is how you thank me?'

Very little air moved through the theatre and in the stilted heat Lottie clenched her fists as she headed onto the stage. Standing back from the edge where the picnic food had been laid out, she gazed at the sea of glum faces. No one had even noticed her arrival. They were too busy shouting at one another, being rude, bitchy and selfish. Lottie felt a surge within her and she held up her hands.

'Right, that is enough, everyone. There's absolutely no way I'm putting up with this anymore. Why do you all think our performance was so bad? Could it have anything to do with the fact that you're always at each other's throats? You don't speak to each other nicely, you don't listen to each other, you don't even seem to really enjoy being here. We might as well just pack up and go home.'

She had their full attention now and the words continued to tumble out.

'Gregory and Mrs Andrews, I really don't give a monkey's bum what happened to make you two hate each other so much. All I know is, you have to get the hell over it. You come in here and you start sniping at each other, and then everyone else joins in. I didn't start this group for you all to come here and act like children. This is not a nursery. You both need to grow up!'

Gregory and Mrs Andrews didn't look embarrassed, they were too busy staring at Lottie in disbelief. She turned her attention to the rest of the group.

'And I don't want to hear any of you blaming Conner. Did any of you actually listen to anything he said, or did you just think "he's young, he clearly knows nothing"?'

Lee and Leonato looked at their shoes, as did a number of the others. They had. How bloody rude. She couldn't stand someone being patronised and especially someone as nice as Conner. 'Don't you think it's ironic that the youngest person here has the most mature attitude? Hmm? Maybe next time you'll show him some respect because he really does know what he's talking about.'

A smile tugged at the corner of Conner's mouth, even though his cheeks were bright red and he was trying to hide behind someone else's back.

Lottie looked at them all, their eyes pinned on her, shame on their faces, and her anger began to ebb. 'I know the play didn't go quite as well as we'd hoped. And looking back, maybe

Shakespeare was a little ambitious for our first ever production, but we need to move forwards and get back on track.'

Lottie cleared some room and sat on the edge of the stage dangling her legs. 'The mayor is putting pressure on for me to stop being chairman.' He'd been less than kind in the meeting when he told her what an embarrassment the theatre and the players were to the council.

'What?' asked Cecil, outraged. 'That's preposterous.'

Tears welled up stinging her nose and she rubbed her temples. She'd normally only have opened up to Sid but he wasn't there anymore and she felt another wall within her fall down. 'I was actually beginning to enjoy myself. I've loved the rehearsals and typing up the scripts and talking about casting and staging. I didn't realise how much until now. And I really don't want it to end.'

'So what can we do about it?' asked Lee, and Lottie looked up, surprised at the support.

'The mayor told me I need to find a way to fix things. He was quite nasty about our performance but because so many people came to see it, and because the town has become so interested in the theatre, I've managed to convince him, at least temporarily, that Greenley does want this. We've also got some funding to get the roof fixed so we've got a little more time. He won't really be able to do anything before the work is finished.'

'What do you think he'd do?' asked Gregory.

Lottie rubbed her forehead. Her neck ached and the throbbing in her temples had been going on all day. 'I honestly think he wants to knock the place down and sell the land for housing. Or just sell the building off for redevelopment.'

The players began talking at once, their voices rising.

'Now come on,' said Lottie. 'I don't know that for sure. All I know is that we need to come back fighting and—'

'How can he do that after that amazing article Sid wrote?' said Gregory.

Lottie's heart jumped against her ribs. 'What?' She pushed herself down off the edge of the stage and moved towards him.

'Haven't you seen it yet?'

'No.' She'd avoided it, knowing his words would hurt even more than they had the first time.

Gregory handed her a copy of the *Greenley Gazette* folded open to the page. 'Here, look. It's not the most glowing review I've ever had, but he encourages everyone to keep supporting us.'

'And he says how much better the second night was,' added Cecil.

Lottie read out loud. '"There is no denying the Greenley Players need to play a bit more before they're ready for their next dose of Shakespeare, but there's also no doubting the enthusiasm and commitment of this amazing group of people who give their time freely for us to enjoy something different. The theatre has brought this town and community together and must be supported so it continues to do so."'

Her throat burned and the pain in her head stabbed again. He hadn't let her down after all and she'd said such terrible things to him. Lottie stared at the page, unseeing.

'So what do we do now?' asked Sarah. 'We can't let the mayor win.'

Lottie couldn't believe Sarah had just said that and came to with everyone staring at her. 'Well, I did have this amazing, bonkers idea that I really think will work, but I wasn't sure you guys would be up for it.'

'What is it?' asked Conner, a little life coming back into his face.

'I told the committee we're going to put on a showcase.'

'A showcase?' asked Mrs Andrews. 'Like one of those ghastly talent shows on television?'

'It won't be quite like that, Mrs Andrews. There won't be any judging.'

197

'Except from all those in the town who hate us and want to see us fail,' said Gregory.

'I don't believe there are many people like that in our town,' Lottie replied and glanced again at the paper. 'I really think people want to see us succeed and they want the theatre to as well. I know some were mean last week but we can't give up because of a few—'

'Idiots?' said Lee, grinning.

'Philistines?' added Gregory.

Lottie nodded. 'Debbie, you have the most sublime voice I've ever heard, and Sarah's is amazing too. Gregory, Mrs Andrews, your monologues were incredible.'

Truth be told, Mrs Andrews' monologue would have been better if someone had tied her arms down by her sides, but still.

'And Cecil,' Lottie continued, 'you were brilliant. I could go on and on about how talented I thought you all were at the auditions and all we need to do is get the town to see that too.'

There was a hushed silence.

Lottie's heart sank but she wouldn't be beaten. 'If we don't think of something, the council will jump on the chance to close the theatre – and how else could we show the different talents you all have?'

'Now hang on a wee minute there,' said Debbie, looking at the rest of the players. 'Lottie's right. We need to pick ourselves up and move forward. I know we're all a wee bit sore, but I believe we can do this and Lottie does too.'

'I couldn't have put it better myself, Debbie,' Lottie replied, smiling for the first time in a week. 'Come on, everyone, all you have to do is prepare a short piece, just like you did for your auditions. It'll be great for everyone to see the variety of talent we have. You can sing, dance, do whatever you like.'

'Well, we're on board, dear,' said Gregory, Cecil nodding by his side.

'Me too,' said Debbie.

'Mrs Andrews?' asked Lottie. Mrs Andrews dramatically strode to the end of the row of chairs and looked away.

'Here we go,' whispered Gregory to Cecil. 'If only she'd acted this well in the production.' Lottie edged over to stand beside Gregory who murmured, 'Sorry, I'll learn to bite my tongue.'

Mrs Andrews placed a hand on her forehead. 'Oh, very well then. I suppose one last shot won't hurt my reputation any more than it has been already. Though my husband is absolutely furious.'

'Excellent,' said Lottie. In the committee meeting it had been a last-minute, madcap idea, but something about it felt right and for once Lottie was truly confident in her decision. But as she looked at her phone, her shoulders sagged, remembering that Sid was now gone.

'When will it be?' asked Conner.

She put her phone away. 'Jeremy has assured me the work will be finished by the start of October. So I was thinking the October half term might be good. It's the end of July now and if we have it during the school's half term, that gives us just about ten weeks to prepare.'

'If I may,' said Gregory, holding up his hand as if he was in school. 'Might I suggest that as well as practising our pieces I lead us in some vocal and trust exercises? I think we could all do with going back to basics a little. Myself included.'

'I think that's a great idea. We need to stop blaming each other for what went wrong, be honest with ourselves about what we can do better and work as a group to make the showcase a success.'

'Well, there's no time like the present,' said Gregory. 'If Lottie doesn't mind, why don't we have some of the picnic Mrs Andrews has kindly provided and then we can have a game or two before we head home?'

Lottie nodded and Mrs Andrews gave the nearest thing she'd ever given to a genuine smile.

Though everyone agreed with her idea, Lottie could tell from their body language they were still depressed. It was going to take a lot of trust exercises to pull them back from this. Picking up the newspaper, she skimmed the article again. And if she and Sid were speaking they could use some too.

Chapter 27

'What do you think of this one?' asked Selena, almost pressing her nose against the glass window.

Sid looked up from the pavement to see her pointing at an extremely short dress and suppressed a sigh. 'Yeah, it's nice.'

'You've said that about all of them,' Selena replied crossly.

'Have I?'

'Yes.' She pursed her lips. 'You are absolutely the worst person to go shopping with.'

Sid took her arm and pulled her towards him, trying to diffuse the rising tension in her voice. 'I'm sorry, I'm rubbish at shopping. I just think you'd look good in anything.'

Selena looked up sulkily then kissed him. 'Okay, I forgive you.'

He managed a smile. 'Good.'

They walked on for another few seconds before Selena stopped again outside another shop, peering at an even shorter dress. Sid checked his phone. Lottie had taken some last-minute holiday so he hadn't seen her for a week. Not since their row. He knew the players were due to meet tonight, and under normal circumstances, he'd have gone to lend Lottie some support, but this time he didn't offer. He still hadn't forgiven her, and Selena said that Lottie should be the one to make the first move, as she was in the wrong. He'd hoped that doing as Selena suggested and giving her space would make her realise how much she'd hurt him.

Before, their silly rows were forgotten within a day or two. Like that time they'd ended up a bit drunk, discussing who was better, Oasis or Blur, and got into a full-blown row over it. They hadn't spoken for a day and when he'd next seen Lottie they were both smiling and laughing within a few minutes. But it didn't look like that was going to happen this time.

'Sid?' asked Selena loudly. She must have said his name a few times before he'd heard.

'Hmm?'

She huffed. 'I said, do you think I should get my hair trimmed?'

Sid's blood iced over. He wasn't equipped to discuss such difficult subjects as hair, or, please, no, not make-up. He stared down at his phone for a moment, hoping it would come to life and give him the answer. It didn't. 'Umm, I think you'd look nice however you want your hair.'

'Oh, you are so useless.' His attention was taken by an email David had just sent. Lottie had taken another week's leave, so he wouldn't see her next week either. He couldn't decide if that was a good or a bad thing.

'Sid?' Selena said, checking in her purse. 'Sid, I really want this dress, but I just don't have enough money. Can you lend me twenty quid, just till pay day, please?'

'Again?'

Selena crossed her arms over her chest and pouted. 'I'm just a bit short, that's all. I had to pay for a present for Toni's birthday. Please? I'll give it you back next week.'

'Okay,' Sid replied taking the cash from his wallet.

'Thank you. You're the best.' Selena kissed him on the cheek. 'I'm just nipping in here.'

Sid leaned against the wall, waiting outside. He looked at his watch wondering how the meeting was going. He pictured Jeremy's smug face and his gut tightened. The roof repairs were due to start soon, using a firm Jeremy had recommended from London. Why they couldn't use local builders he didn't know. Again, there was something not quite right here. His gut had always led him in the right direction before, he had to trust it now. The last time he had he'd uncovered and tracked down a couple of scam artists going round the old people's homes. Lottie had been so proud of him she'd made him a silly trophy with 'Greenley Journalist of the Year' written on it. His heart twinged again thinking about her.

He was positive something was going on. Surely it couldn't hurt to check out Jeremy Bell and his company?

Selena came out of the shop and piled a heavy bag on top of him. He stashed his phone away before all the clothes fell onto the pavement and she started moaning at him again. 'Just one more shop, honey.'

Oh no, thought Sid, please, no more shops.

Chapter 28

Lottie put down her book and stared out of the living room window down towards the sea. In the distance, dense grey waves crashed over the harbour wall and moored boats rocked in the wind. The stifling heat of the last few days had broken and now it rained constantly. She wrapped her nan's shawl around her, breathing in the familiar smell, and settled onto the window seat again. The rain bounced off the roofs and rattled the window panes under a steel grey sky that kept the sun at bay and Lottie traced a raindrop as it slid down the glass.

Work on the theatre roof had started last week, but little progress had been made since the rain began. The scaffolding on the building had signalled to the gods that the heavens should open and not stop till next summer, so everyone had downed tools and gone home.

On any other Sunday afternoon she would be with Jeremy enjoying a few final hours together before he left for the week. But he'd been delayed in London again, and hadn't made it down this weekend. She wrapped her arms over her chest and gazed out of the window.

Jeremy had said the theatre roof needed checking quite often in the rain to make sure it hadn't completely caved in and though she didn't fancy heading out in all that, Lottie grabbed her polka dot wellington boots and left. There was no time like the present. She just hoped he'd been joking.

After climbing out of the car, Lottie took a moment to watch the sea rolling in. The tide was so high it came almost to the promenade, pulling back to form high waves that smashed onto the pebble beach, spraying the passers-by. When she opened the theatre door the strong wind nearly yanked it off its hinges and Lottie slipped through before it was wrenched from her hands. Cold dank air hit her, and the rain was just as audible as it had been outside. It was pitch black and she felt for the light switch, turning it on, but nothing happened. The electrics were out. In the darkness Lottie felt her way along the wall and descended the stairs, heading for the lighting box where they kept a torch.

'Oh no,' she said aloud as ice-cold water washed around her ankles, freezing her toes. She bent down to feel the water was a couple of inches deep. When she reached the lighting box she searched frantically but couldn't find the torch. Keep calm, thought Lottie. Just keep calm. Remembering she had her phone, she took it from her back pocket and turned on the torch app.

Shining it around, it reflected off the water lapping up the walls. Rain ran down from the ceiling pulling off the faded gold wallpaper and shreds of it washed to and fro like flotsam.

Lottie stumbled to the central aisle and the banks of chairs. The seats were sodden and water had gathered at the base of the stage. She shone her torch upwards. There were large holes perforating the ceiling where sheets of rain flew in and onto her face. It was ruined. The whole place was ruined.

Her breath came in short, sharp sobs as she looked around. Her pulse raced and her legs wobbled beneath her. Tears ran down her face and her whole body began to shake. How could this have happened? Lottie desperately wanted Sid there to help. She couldn't call Jeremy. He was all the way back in London and was always difficult to reach during the day anyway.

A tear rolled down her cheek as she tried to calm her mind and sort out her jumbled, panicked thoughts. Her toes felt like icicles in the cold water and Lottie fumbled with her phone, shivering. Eventually, she dialled Sid's number and held the phone to her ear.

It rang. And rang. And rang. Then clicked through to voicemail. She hung up and tried again. After ringing, it went through to voicemail once more. Where was he? What on earth could he be doing? Praying he would pick up this time she tried one last time and was cut off. He must have rejected the call. Her shoulders slumped and her phone nearly fell from her numbing fingers. How could he?

She wanted and needed him here. No matter what had happened between them, she didn't want anyone else right now. Lottie swallowed down a sob as, this time, she was forced to leave a voicemail for Sid. 'Sid, it's me. It's Lottie. The theatre – it's – it's totally flooded.' Her voice broke as tears streamed down her cheeks. 'Can you come? Please. Can you help me? I—'

Her head shot up as a sound like something tearing echoed around her. A piece of plaster fell from the ceiling and landed with a splash beside her, soaking her legs even more. She backed away. 'Please, Sid, I really need your help. It's all falling apart.'

The water-logged carpet sucked her foot down and a loud crash from above rang around the room. Lottie lifted her hair and caught sight of a jagged chunk of plaster as it crashed down and slammed into her skull.

Her knees buckled and gave way. The room spun and swam as she fell backwards into the water. Every part of her head throbbed and blood ran down her forehead into her eyes. The cold water washed up the side of her face into her ear and splashed onto her forehead. Lottie's thoughts raced, and in her mind's eye she saw the sea and waves she had watched only moments ago. Then everything blurred.

A total blackness pulled at her eyes, closing them for her. She tried to open them, but they were too heavy. Her body wouldn't move. She couldn't feel her legs or arms. Her eyelids fluttered open for a second seeing the dull grey sky through the holes in the ceiling. Then everything went dark.

Chapter 29

Sid pulled the duvet over himself still unused to being naked with anyone. Selena had no such qualms and lay exposed, basking in all her post-sex glory.

It had been a great weekend so far. Selena had been sweet and caring, and they'd had a great time together. There was something decadent about lying in a huge bed on a Sunday afternoon without a care in the world. Their clothes were strewn everywhere but he couldn't be bothered with collecting them. Flooded with endorphins, Sid lay back on the fluffy pillows with his hands behind his head. He was glad Selena liked the room, and relieved too, as it had cost a fortune. Their suite in the swanky spa hotel was almost as big as his flat.

Selena's long dark hair, now messed up and falling over her face, cascaded out behind her. Her make-up had been all but removed revealing the flaws in her skin. He preferred her this way. She looked real. Normal.

Sid wondered again what this sexy woman was doing with a geek like him. He wore *Star Wars* pants for heaven's sake. He knew his faults all too well. Even though he was lanky his face had a chubby roundness, his teeth were too big, he couldn't make his hair do anything stylish and his dress sense hadn't changed since he was eighteen. Lottie's hadn't either, come to think of it. Thoughts of her threatened to push in and he squeezed his eyes shut to chase them away.

Selena stretched out like a cat and then gracefully swung her lithe limbs around and walked to the bathroom. Sid closed his eyes to snooze and listened to the rains incessant tapping at the window. He loved the sound of a summer storm. His phone rang from the corner of the room where his jeans were thrown over the back of a chair. He got up to answer it, pulling the gigantic duvet around him.

Selena made her way back into the room in one of the hotel's fluffy bathrobes. 'Who's that?'

Sid looked down and re-read the caller ID, his smile growing wider. 'It's Lottie.'

'Oh.' Selena paused, running her fingers through her hair. 'You're not going to answer it, are you? I thought we were having some special time together?'

'I know but she hasn't really spoken to me since the play.' His conscience tore at him. Selena deserved this break but then again … 'If she's calling me it must be important.'

'If it was that important she'd call Jeremy, wouldn't she? He's her boyfriend after all. It must be something to do with work so you don't need to answer it now.'

Sid looked at his phone again, panicking.

'We've talked about this before, Sid.' Her voice was still soft but there was also a sharpness and he knew he was annoying her. 'You're always on about Lottie bloody Webster. I thought you were giving her some space?'

His hands were sweating.

'Please, Sid, do this for me.'

Before he could answer it went to voicemail. A few seconds later it rang again. He was sure now if she'd called him instead of Jeremy that meant she needed him, not Mr Suave. 'If she's ringing back straight away, it must be important, Selena. I think I'm going to have to answer it.'

'But, baby.' Selena sat down on the edge of the bed letting her robe fall open revealing her cleavage. 'This weekend was supposed to be for us. Jeremy's her boyfriend, she'd call him first over you if it was that important.' Selena walked to him and gently took the hand that gripped his phone. It clicked through to voicemail and Sid's stomach sank at missing it again.

Considering they hadn't spoken in weeks this was big. 'But she's tried me twice now. I really should answer it.'

'That theatre is all you ever talk about. Anyone would think you love her more than me.' As Selena picked lint off the bathrobe there was a whine in her voice he'd never heard before and the sharpness of it pinched the muscles at the back of his neck. Did he? If he did it was only because she moaned about some of the other things he liked to talk about. Sid watched Selena's face.

'Honestly, Sid, I've put up with it for ages but this is too much. She's not ruining my weekend away, she's nothing special.' Selena pulled her robe closed. Her mouth was set in a grim line and her eyes narrowed.

It rang again.

Selena marched over to him and grabbed the phone from his hands and rejected the call. 'I will not let you ruin this weekend, Sid. We've got some massages booked later.' She moved closer to him and lay her hand on his bare chest. 'This was supposed to be for us, our first weekend away.'

Sid remembered he was still wrapped in the duvet and turned to find his jeans. Her hand fell away. 'You've been so obsessed with that theatre, attending everything, working late doing who knows what. She hasn't even thanked you for that really nice article you wrote. I mean, how ungrateful is that? I don't see why you even wrote it, she didn't deserve it. Why are you trying so hard for her?'

It was true Lottie hadn't thanked him yet and he longed to know what she thought. 'Maybe that's why she's calling?'

'Then she can leave a message. Why can't you just let that pathetic woman get on with it?'

Wow. What? Sure, Selena had every right to be mad but if Lottie was calling him out of the blue like this he had to answer. 'Look, Selena, Lottie wouldn't call unless—'

Before Selena would relinquish his phone, a ping told him he had a voicemail. Sid glanced at his phone then Selena. Her face was rigid and her eyes had lost their sparkle. 'Now, listen,' he began in a conciliatory tone, taking his phone back from her tight fingers. 'I'm going to listen to this message, then we'll get dressed and go out for a drink, okay?'

Selena released the phone but didn't move or speak. Sid felt like some kind of hostage negotiator, only he couldn't decide if it was him or the phone being held hostage. His heart sped up as he listened to the message. A nausea rose from his stomach and burned his throat. Lottie sounded weird. Were her teeth chattering? What the hell was happening there? There was a noise. A bang, then … something. He couldn't tell what. All he knew was that something was wrong.

He tried calling her back but there was no reply.

'What is it now then?' asked Selena.

'I have to go,' Sid said, grabbing his clothes from the floor and throwing them on as quickly as possible.

'What do you mean you have to go? Go where? Why?'

'I think there's been an accident. I—I don't know. Lottie went to the theatre and there was a bang. I think something's happened to her.'

'And leave me here?' Selena shouted. Her cheeks were red and her expression was hard and still. He could see her throat twitch with the deep breaths she was taking to try and stay calm. 'I have no idea what she has that I don't to get you and Jeremy fussing around after her.' Sid's heart was beating faster than it ever had before.

'Don't be like that. You—'

211

'Don't be like what? You're running around after that woman, ruining our weekend and I should be pleased?'

Sid couldn't deal with this right now. She had every right to be angry and disappointed that their special weekend was being cut short but he just didn't have time for drama. Lottie needed him. 'You can come with me if you can get dressed in ten seconds.'

'Sid, if you do this, I promise I will dump you. I could get another boyfriend in seconds. You should count yourself lucky. You should …'

Her voice trailed away into background noise as Sid tried to calm himself down. If anything had happened to Lottie he would never forgive himself. He should have been a man and made things right. If they were only ever to be friends, then fine. It was better than not having her in his life at all.

'Oh my God, you're not even listening to me.' Selena threw her arms up in frustration.

Sid finally looked up after pulling on his trainers. 'I'm sorry, Selena, but I have to go and see if Lottie's alright. She was really upset and then something happened. There was a noise – I don't really know.'

'A noise? You're doing all this because of a noise? What sort of noise?' She had her arms crossed over her chest and her head wiggled as she spoke.

Sid clenched his teeth trying to stay calm. 'I don't know what sort of a noise, Selena, that's why I need to go and find out.' He pulled his T-shirt over his head. 'Listen, I get that you're annoyed with me and I'm sorry our weekend's finished like this, but something's happened and I need to find out what. She could be hurt.'

Selena's mouth was pursed tightly and her large brown eyes were cold as she held him in her unwavering gaze. 'It's pathetic. You're both pathetic.'

Sid felt a stab of anger at her response but he had to stay calm and focus on Lottie right now. 'If you want to come, I'll take you home once I've finished, but right now, I have to get going. What do you want to do?'

'I'm staying, Sid, and if you leave, we're through, do you understand?'

Sid put his hands on his hips and stared at the floor. 'I do.' He grabbed his jacket from the chair, slung it over his shoulder and left.

Chapter 30

Lottie's eyes opened slowly and focused on the sun shining through plain blue curtains over a small window. Her hand flew to her face to shield her eyes and swept across a dressing on her head. 'Ouch.' Thinking there would be blood, she checked her fingers, but they were clean. Her brain was pushing against her skull and it pounded worse than the hangover she'd had after last year's Eurovision.

Lottie pushed herself up to sitting and leaned back on the hard, lumpy pillows. Every muscle hurt and her limbs felt heavy. Looking down, her hand had a cannula in it and she studied the rest of the room to see other patients and more medical instruments. How on earth had she ended up in hospital?

A short, incredibly cheerful nurse bustled in. 'Hello, lovey. Nice to see you awake.'

'Hello.' Lottie watched her pick up a chart from the end of the bed and read it, then check her watch and write something down. 'Sorry, who are you? And how did I get here?'

The nurse smiled. She had a kind face full of wrinkles. 'I'm Margaret. I've been looking after you since you were brought in yesterday.'

'Yesterday? What time is it now? How long have I been here?' Lottie looked around for her stuff.

'Calm down, lovey. It's okay.' Margaret sat on the side of Lottie's bed. 'It's about four o'clock now. You were brought in yesterday afternoon at about half past three suffering from a severe concussion and hypothermia. You were unconscious, and we've been waiting for you to wake up. Your body temperature is roughly back to normal now, but you're still quite weak. It's lots of rest for you.'

'I've been here a whole day?' Lottie looked down at the unpleasant hospital gown she was wearing trying to comprehend what was happening. There were quite a few blankets on her bed and the smell of disinfectant stung her nose.

'Yes. Now, let me fetch that nice young man who's been waiting for you. Typical, isn't it? He only nipped out for a cup of tea and as soon as he leaves, you wake up.'

Sid? Lottie's heart quickened. She closed her eyes as the tightness in her head intensified. She remembered now. She'd visited the theatre. There was a leak and the water was everywhere. He hadn't answered her calls. Then the ceiling came down. Lottie shuddered at the memory.

She desperately wanted to see Sid again. She'd missed him so much. When he came in, Lottie would give him the biggest hug of his life. She wondered what awful T-shirt he'd be wearing today and pictured his cheeky, goofy grin. She loved him to bits. How could she ever make up for everything she'd said?

Lottie pushed her hair back from her face. It was lank and greasy, and smelled awful, but Sid wouldn't care. The door opened and Lottie took a deep breath, ready to apologise.

'Lottie,' exclaimed Jeremy as he strode into the room, throwing his suit jacket onto the chair beside her bed, and wrapping her in his arms. 'You scared me so much.' He stood back and held her face. 'I'm so glad you're alright.'

Disappointment hit her like a sucker punch to the stomach and tears came to her eyes. As handsome as he was with a scattering of five o'clock shadow, he wasn't Sid. 'Jeremy,' replied Lottie trying to keep her voice calm.

'Don't cry, sweetheart, I'm here.' He kissed her lips as the tears ran down her face. 'How are you feeling?'

'I'm okay.' She sniffed and placed her hand over his to remove it from her face. She wanted it to be Sid's hand. Jeremy pulled back, concerned. 'Sorry, my head's quite sore,' Lottie lied.

Jeremy stood up straight. 'I'm not surprised. What were you doing at the theatre in weather like that?'

'You told me the place needed checking, so—'

'By experts, Lottie, not people like you.'

'People like me?' She knew what he meant but the comment still stung.

'You know what I mean.'

'I don't think I do, actually.' Lottie sniffed and took a tissue from the box on her bedside. 'I didn't know it was going to be so bad. And I'm the chairman, it's my responsibility.'

He squeezed her hand. 'I'm sorry, it was a bad choice of words. It's just the weather was so bad and you didn't tell anyone where you were going.'

'I didn't expect for there to be great big holes in the roof or to be knocked unconscious.' Lottie saw the shock in Jeremy's face. She hadn't meant to sound quite so cross with him and he was here waiting for her to wake up. Unlike Sid. Her head pounded even more.

Jeremy sat down on the side of her bed looking sheepish. 'We've all been so worried about you,' he said gently.

'We?' asked Lottie, hoping he would tell her Sid had been at her bedside every moment since he heard the news, or at least popped by.

'Well, okay, I've been worried. I came straight back from London when Sarah called.'

'Sarah?' What the hell was going on?

'Yes. The girl from the committee. That's her name, isn't it?'

Lottie nodded and the weight of her head hurt her neck and shoulders. 'How did she know about me? Who found me?'

'Don't worry about all that now,' said Jeremy, caressing the back of her neck and laying her down gently onto the uncomfortable pillows. 'You need to rest. I've got to head back to London tomorrow, I can't put it off any longer, but I'll make sure Sarah gives me regular updates on how you're doing.'

'I can text you myself,' Lottie replied. 'I'm not a child. I'm sure I'll be back to normal tomorrow.' Lottie ran her fingers over the bandage again.

Jeremy took a mobile phone from his pocket and put it on her bedside table. 'Your phone wasn't working after being in the water for so long so I bought you another one.' Lottie looked at the brand new, top of the range phone and berated herself. She shouldn't be so stroppy with Jeremy just because Sid hadn't come to her rescue. It wasn't his fault. 'Thank you,' she replied and lifted her head for a kiss. Jeremy's lips were gentle on hers and it filled her with warmth.

'You look tired, sweetheart,' he said, stroking her cheek. 'Get some rest now and I'll call you later. I love you.' He bent down and kissed her again and Lottie felt her body relax.

'I love you too,' she said, feeling her heart warm up at the words. She hadn't said them to that many people and it still felt new to be saying them to Jeremy. She'd wanted to see Sid because he was her friend, the one she'd called, but she was glad Jeremy was here. And he'd been so sweet and caring replacing her phone. It must have been ruined when he'd found her. She was so lucky to have him in her life and for him to be so caring. 'I'm sorry I've been so awful.'

'That's okay,' he said, chuckling. 'I think you're allowed as you've had such a terrible time.'

Jeremy kissed her again then left and she rolled onto her side,

217

staring out of the window. So that was that. Sid hadn't come. He'd ignored her calls. She'd thought of his article as a sort of apology but it hadn't been, had it? Her eyes burned as she tried to keep more tears from falling. Her pleas for help had gone unanswered. He hadn't forgiven her for what she'd said and wanted nothing more to do with her. Whether she liked it or not things were over between them now. For good.

Chapter 31

Sid unlocked the door to his flat and went through to the kitchen. He chucked the carrier bag onto the counter, retrieved his unappetising looking ready meal and stabbed it repeatedly with a knife. After throwing it into the microwave he rested his hands on the edge of the worktop and closed his eyes, unable to shake the picture of Lottie from his mind.

The drive back to Greenley had been unbearable and he was sure he'd get a speeding ticket. He had no idea his old car could even reach eighty miles an hour let alone keep it up. And when he ran into the theatre that afternoon his throat had closed over and he'd frozen to the spot. His eyes had focused in the inky blackness to make out something slumped on the floor, the water lapping against it. An involuntary noise had escaped from his mouth – a grunt mixed with a sharp intake of breath – and he'd run to her, the water soaking his shoes and feet.

Though he pretended he didn't, he had to admit now that he still loved Lottie. If anything had happened to her he had no idea how he'd live his life without her. Even though they hadn't spoken for weeks, just knowing she was alive had been a comfort. If he didn't have that he didn't know what he'd do.

Sid had turned Lottie's face towards him, her pale white skin lined with the blood that ran down from her head. He'd called an ambulance and they'd taken her off to hospital. The sound of the siren still rang in his ears when he lay down at night and tried to sleep. When they'd said she'd be okay he almost fist pumped the air but he hadn't wanted to let go of her freezing cold hand. Lottie would have been proud of him going into a hospital, she knew how much he hated them.

The microwave pinged just as there was a knock at the door. His eyebrows shot up as he saw Selena stood there. 'Can I come in?' she asked in a quiet subdued voice.

Uncertain as to why she was there he said, 'Sure.'

Apart from some lengthy voicemails berating him again and again, he hadn't seen her since leaving her at the hotel. Selena went through and sat on the sofa, pulling her legs up and cradling them. He, meanwhile, stayed in the doorway of the living room.

'I thought you might call to let me know how Lottie is?' she muttered.

'You didn't seem to care the last time we talked about her.' He tried to keep the anger from his voice but it crept through. He wanted to shout that Lottie could have died and if she hadn't grabbed his phone off him he could have got there sooner. If he'd answered that first call he'd have told her to get out of there and none of this would have happened.

'Sid,' her voice cracked. 'I'm so sorry for how I behaved. I was really out of order and I should never have made you choose between us.'

For a second Sid didn't move, then seeing the tears in Selena's eyes he edged over and sat next to her on the sofa, his heart full of sympathy. She pulled out a tissue and sniffed. 'Sid, I'm so, so sorry. Can you ever forgive me? I was so wrong – so wrong. I didn't used to be like this. It's all because of my last boyfriend. He cheated on me so many times. He would lie to my face that there was nothing going on and then I'd find out from friends that there was. It's made me paranoid and jealous.'

Selena leant against him, sobbing. His feelings for Lottie hadn't really changed and with Selena not calling he'd assumed they'd just stop seeing each other, and that would be that. Now he'd have to end it and he didn't know how.

'You're the best thing that's ever happened to me,' Selena continued, dabbing at her eyes. She lifted his arm and rested it on her shoulders. 'I don't want to lose you. I'm sorry for what I said about Lottie. I didn't mean it. You know how much I like her, and I hoped one day she might learn to like me too. I just got insecure and lashed out. Please say you'll forgive me?'

Sid closed his eyes and ran a hand through his hair. What the hell was he supposed to do now? If he was realistic, Lottie wasn't going to suddenly leave Jeremy and have feelings for him. For Lottie, nothing had changed between them. Was it worth throwing it all away because he'd had a setback? That's what it was after all. He'd been happy with Selena before all this and could learn to be again.

Lottie was still in love with Jeremy. If he told Selena it was over, all that would happen was that he'd be alone. He had as good a chance with her as anyone, more so because they'd already come so far. He could learn to love her as deeply as he had Lottie, given time.

'Sid?' she asked, a single tear running down her face. 'Please say you'll forgive me for being so stupid?'

His heart beat hard sending a vibration through his body. 'Of course I'll forgive you,' he whispered.

'I love you,' she said and buried her head in his chest.

Sid opened his mouth to speak but wasn't sure he could say the words. The thought ran through his mind that he'd always assumed he'd be saying them to Lottie and he felt a shudder in his chest. Selena lifted her head and he looked down into her almost pleading, tear-stained face. He hesitated and her eyes pinned him to the spot, waiting. As if the words were being forcibly pulled out of him, his voice wavered and he said, 'I love you too.'

Chapter 32

Lottie spent the next three days reading books she'd read a dozen times and watching terrible daytime television on the tiny screen by her bed. It was a relief when Margaret told her she was to be discharged the next day and sent home in a taxi.

Jeremy hadn't been able to visit again, and her neighbour had brought her some clothes to travel home in, but Sid had stayed away. Watching the familiar streets go by Lottie shook her head in disbelief. How could things have gone so far between them? She bit her lip, reluctant to let the tears fall again but her heart felt empty without him in her life. She was just happy she had Jeremy to help her patch it back together.

The taxi pulled up outside Lottie's house and she clambered out, careful not to bang her head. Lottie didn't care that the paint still peeled from the front door or that the steep steps made bringing in the shopping such a chore, this was her home. It was where she belonged and she loved it more than anything. Sid had been right when he'd said that sometimes you just had to appreciate what you'd got.

A creeping dread inched into her heart. She missed her nan and didn't want to be surrounded by her things. Maybe it was time to start sorting things out. Touching the plaster on her head as a reminder of what had happened she looked again at the house and with aching legs trudged up the steps.

'Now, remember, lovey,' Margaret had said as she completed the paperwork, 'just because you're being sent home doesn't mean you're one hundred per cent. You've had a head injury and a nasty concussion. And a touch of hypothermia isn't like having a cold. Take care of yourself and get lots of rest.' Lottie liked Margaret's motherly nature and kind but no-nonsense bedside manner. It reminded her of her nan.

Lottie's fingertips traced a patch of bare wood on the front door, then she opened up and made her way through to the kitchen. She'd felt inexplicably cold since being released from hospital and was unsure if it was a reaction to the ridiculously hot temperature they kept the ward, or the after-effects of the hypothermia.

Just as Lottie poured hot water onto a tea bag and was watching it float around in her cup, there was a knock on the door. She considered ignoring it but decided against it in case it was Sid.

'Oh, hello, Sarah,' said Lottie.

'Hello.' She was stood on the step nervously hiding behind a large bunch of flowers and a box of chocolates. 'I bought you a few bits to cheer you up.'

'Oh, thank you.'

The sky threatened more rain, and though Lottie didn't want to see anyone but Sid or Jeremy, she couldn't leave Sarah standing on the doorstep. 'Would you like to come in? I was just making tea.'

Sarah's tense face relaxed into a smile. 'That'd be lovely, thanks.'

Lottie showed Sarah to the living room and came back with two cups of tea.

'How are you feeling?' Sarah asked, taking hers.

'My heads a bit sore, but I'm okay.'

'We're looking forward to having you back. They've all been arguing over who should come to see you first. Mrs Andrews thought it should be her, obviously, and Gregory and Cecil thought it should be them, as they're much more sensitive and just, you know …' She shrugged. 'Nicer, really.'

Lottie laughed. It was nice to be appreciated. Though she was surprised after the telling-off she had given them.

'When do you think you'll be back with us? We're all desperate to talk about the showcase.' Sarah sipped her tea.

'The doctor said I'm not allowed back to work until next week, I still need to rest. But I'm pretty sure I'll get bored before then.' She eyed her nan's figurines in a glass cabinet in the corner. She could start packing those up for the charity shop if she got restless.

'We really have missed you, but you should only come back if you're sure you're up to it. And if I can help at all, I'd be happy too.'

'Thank you,' said Lottie. The warmth of her cup thawed her cold fingers.

Sarah smiled and Lottie saw a kindness in her face she hadn't noticed before. 'It's been a while since your nan passed away, hasn't it?'

Lottie shifted uncomfortably in her chair and pushed her hair behind her ear. 'Yes, it has.'

'I'm sorry,' said Sarah, looking away. 'I always put my foot in it. It's a beautiful house, I can see why you'd never want to leave.'

'I know I need to get things packed up and get rid of some stuff, but I haven't quite got round to it yet, with the theatre and everything.' That wasn't strictly true. She'd used it as an excuse not to touch her nan's possessions and face the final hurdle of losing her.

'I remember when my mum died it took me almost three years to get rid of her stuff.'

Lottie glanced up. 'I'm sorry. I didn't know you'd lost someone.'

Sarah's hair was longer and softer now and she looked her age rather than old and stern. She tapped her cup as she said, 'It was about five years ago but it's taken me quite a while to get back out there, into the world.' She was surprisingly matter of fact. 'You know, if you ever want some support when you go through your nan's things I'd be happy to help. I know how hard it can be. You can't do it till you're ready, but when you do it does help.'

'Thank you. That's really kind of you.'

Sarah gave a shy smile then an uncomfortable silence formed.

'How bad are things with the theatre?' asked Lottie. She didn't really want to talk about it yet but she had to say something and she couldn't think what else they might have in common.

Sarah scowled at her cup. 'The mayor's demanded a full report on your accident. Between you and me I think he's trying to get the place closed down as a health hazard.'

'What?'

'It's okay,' reassured Sarah. 'Don't worry. Jeremy won't let him. The roof's coming along nicely now and the water's been drained out but it's all cost a lot more than we first thought.'

'I suppose it would, wouldn't it?' Lottie hadn't had time to think of all these practicalities. She'd been too busy wondering where Sid was and what he'd been up to. 'Who's footing the bill?'

'Jeremy. He says it'll be fine for the showcase. He's got some extra people in to make sure.'

'Jeremy?' asked Lottie. They'd talked on the phone but he'd never said, probably not wanting to worry her.

'Yes. When your friend told us what had happened to you, I saw Jeremy at the hospital, and he asked me to contact him if Mayor Cunningham started doing anything.'

Lottie looked up and Sarah's face reddened. 'You were at the hospital?'

She blinked then dropped her eyes to her cup. 'Well, you've been very nice to me, and I wanted to make sure you were okay. I didn't realise you and Sid had known each other for such a long time.'

'Sid?' Lottie tilted her head. She didn't understand what Sarah had just said and her brain was beginning to hurt.

'Yes, your partner on the newspaper? That's his name isn't it?'

'Yes, it is. How – how did you get talking to him?'

Sarah looked quizzically at Lottie. 'He was with you nearly all the time at the hospital. He said he'd found you and went with you in the ambulance. Poor chap must have been exhausted. He stayed with you as long as he could that first night until the hospital chucked him out.'

Lottie's unblinking eyes watched Sarah. Her heart was beating erratically and her stomach squeezed so tight Lottie was surprised she hadn't suddenly become a size ten. That was another thing Jeremy hadn't told her.

'He only went home because that tiny, bossy nurse told him to. Apparently he was stinking out the room from the dirty water on his jeans.'

'Oh,' replied Lottie, completely lost for words.

'Are you okay? You seem a little out of it. Maybe I should go?' Sarah put her cup down and picked up her handbag.

'Yes. Maybe,' said Lottie. She shook her head trying to shake her brain into working order but all it did was ricochet off her skull and begin to ache again. 'Sorry. I'm just feeling quite tired.'

'Of course you are. I'll head off and, umm, if you like, I thought, maybe I could drop in again?'

'That'd be nice,' Lottie replied. Having chatted with her, Lottie realised how quiet and vulnerable Sarah was. A bit like her actually.

Lottie showed Sarah out, waving a cheerful goodbye, but once she closed the door she leaned back against it, feeling exhausted.

So Sid had got her message and come to her rescue. A smile crept over her face and she was so happy she wanted to laugh out loud. It didn't mean things were okay between them. She still had a lot of making up to do but at least now there was a chance.

* * *

227

The next evening, Lottie waited nervously for Jeremy to arrive. Having been delayed in London it was now Saturday evening and though she was looking forward to seeing him, she had some questions too.

She'd changed a few times trying to find something both casual and attractive but her overwhelming wardrobe of baggy T-shirts and cardigans weren't quite right. When her head started to ache after pulling off yet another top she gave up, he would just have to take her how she was. After all, she was still recovering from her accident. Well, not quite, but it was a good excuse.

At eight-thirty and with Lottie's stomach rumbling, Jeremy arrived. His knock was always loud and authoritative and she pulled herself off the sofa to let him in.

'Hello, sweetheart.' Jeremy wrapped his hands around her waist and gave her a squeeze.

Lottie eyed the brown paper bag of food. 'How was your journey?'

He planted a kiss on her lips. 'It was good. Straight through this time. And I brought dinner.' He waved the bag at her.

'Great. What it is?' She was praying for fish and chips. Crispy battered haddock and thick salty chips with lots of vinegar, maybe even mushy peas.

'I stopped off at this amazing deli around the corner from my office and I got us two gorgeous asparagus and Gruyère tarts and a big green salad.'

'Oh, lovely.' Lottie tried to hide her disappointment.

Jeremy stepped further into the house and dropped his work bag. 'Well, we don't need to eat chips every day, do we?'

'No, I suppose not,' she replied, but in Lottie's opinion, it was perfectly acceptable to eat chips, or at least potatoes, in some form or another, every day. In fact, it should have been manda-tory.

Jeremy took the tarts from the bag and showed them to Lottie. She gave a resigned smile and he headed off to plate up dinner.

She'd have to sneak down and make some toast later. A tiny posh quiche and fancy lettuce was not going to fill her up.

'So, how are you feeling?' Jeremy asked over his shoulder, dishing out the food. 'Are you looking forward to getting back to work next week?'

'Yeah, it'll be nice to get back to normal. It's school photos coming up for all the little ones who started school this year. It's one of my favourite jobs.'

Jeremy opened the wine and poured them both a large glass. 'You look beautiful, you know. I think the rest has done you good. How do you feel about getting back to working on the theatre plans tomorrow?'

Lottie groaned and leaned back against the kitchen unit. 'I'm not looking forward to seeing what a state the place is in but I'll be happy to start sorting out the showcase and catching up with everybody.' She swallowed a large mouthful of wine and the velvety warmth slid down her throat.

Jeremy wiped his hands on a tea towel and said, 'Well, about that—'

'Oh no, what now?' She couldn't deal with any more bad news at the moment.

He gave a sympathetic smile. 'I don't know if you've been told yet, but the roof and associated works ended up costing a lot more because of the torrential rain and storms. The plastic covering that protects a building when roof work's being done, came flying off and ended up about twenty miles away wrapped around someone's car.'

Lottie's hand covered her mouth.

Jeremy took a sip of wine and waved his hand dismissively. 'Don't worry, it didn't do any damage. But it has meant that because the work needed finishing, I've given more than we first agreed. I've got a contact at the council who let me increase my donation without too much paperwork. And we've had to literally pump water out of the place and rip up the carpets, but the seats have gone off to be refurbished.' He shrugged. 'It's pretty much a shell at the moment, but I'm assured we'll be on track for the showcase. We've still got just over six weeks, after all. And my chaps haven't let me down yet.'

Lottie pinched the bridge of her nose in frustration. 'But a shell with a roof?'

'Yes.' He laughed. 'There's now a fully functioning roof.'

'How much more did it all cost?'

He shook his head, shrugging off her concern. 'About another seven on top of the ten I already quoted.'

'Seven thousand?' She took a large mouthful, finishing her wine in one big gulp and sliding the glass down on the counter top next to Jeremy's and the bottle. 'How do you feel about that?'

'I'm okay. I told you I'm happy to help.' He edged forward and placed his arms around her waist again. 'I was worried how you'd feel. I know how much you stress about the money side of things.'

Lottie looked to her wine glass, empty and now an arm's reach away. 'I just don't want you to feel you have to do it.'

He chuckled. 'Why would I?'

'I don't know, because of me, maybe?' Lottie looked into his eyes, studying the way the green and gold flecks danced in the light.

'Let me tell you something, Lottie Webster.' Jeremy met her gaze. 'I love money, I love making money, I love spending money, and nothing will force me into making a bad investment. But there is one thing I love more than all of that, and that's you.'

Jeremy began kissing her neck but she couldn't enjoy it as much as she normally would. There was something she needed to ask. 'Jeremy, why didn't you tell me Sid was the one who found me?'

'Hmm?' He looked up and she pulled her body away to see his face.

'Why didn't you tell me it was Sid?'

Jeremy sighed and lowered his eyes, backing away to the other side of the kitchen. 'I'm sorry, Lottie. I know that was wrong of me. It was just that…' He ran a hand through his hair. 'To be honest, I was ashamed of myself. I should've been here. If I'd come down like I was supposed to none of this would have happened. And I was embarrassed you didn't feel you could call me.'

'I'm sorry,' said Lottie as her stomach turned over. She should have called him first. He must have felt so betrayed that she'd called Sid.

'I'm the one who should be sorry. Lottie, I want you to feel that you can call me at any time. Day or night. I feel like I've let you down.'

'Oh, Jeremy. You haven't.' Lottie went to him. 'I just thought that with you being in London, there wouldn't be much you could do.' She'd told herself it was just habit that she'd wanted Sid, they'd been best friends for so long. Looking at Jeremy now, she felt disloyal. As if she'd cheated on him.

'I'd have called someone, come down straight away. I love you and I'll always be there for you. No matter what.'

He looked small and vulnerable with his head bowed and shoulders slumped. Lottie slid her arms around his waist.

'I'm sorry, Lottie,' he said again, pulling her close and burying his head in her hair. 'I'll never let you down like that again.'

Lottie put a finger to his lips. 'Shh.' She kissed him, and as their kisses became more passionate and all encompassing, they made their way to Lottie's bedroom.

It was a good thing dinner was a salad … chips would've gone cold.

Chapter 33

With the theatre out of action the Greenley Players were busy moving tables and chairs out of the way in the small village hall Sid had organised for rehearsals. He'd had to report on the damage to the theatre and Lottie's accident even though he hadn't wanted to. Lottie was hot news around town and so was Mr Suave for diving in and saving the day.

Sid wrote the article fairly confirming Jeremy was stepping in and upping his donation. And now the town loved him but during the interview Jeremy had been quietly evasive over some things. Charming, but Sid was sure he'd been hiding something. What, he didn't know. Sid stacked another chair.

It was Lottie's first day back with them all today and she was running late. Lottie never ran late. She was always annoyingly ten minutes early for everything. What if something had gone wrong? What if she'd had a brain haemorrhage? Or what if she'd lost her sight and was flailing around at home trying to call for help? A thousand terrible thoughts ran through Sid's head before Lottie finally walked in.

When her eyes fell on the 'Welcome back!' banner the players had put up with bunches of balloons floating merrily either side, her eyes widened in shock.

'Welcome back, sweetie,' said Gregory, wrapping a speechless Lottie in a hug.

'Are you sure you're okay to be back?' asked Sarah. 'If you need more time, it's no problem.'

Lottie smiled. 'I'm fine, honestly. Raring to go actually.'

'We're so glad to have you back,' said Cecil. 'You've been missed terribly. Here.' He handed her a bunch of flowers.

'Have I?' She was gazing around, wide-eyed and happy.

Cecil squeezed her shoulders. 'Of course.'

'You still look terrible,' said Mrs Andrews, air kissing her on each cheek. 'But we're glad you're back.'

Sid stepped forward and when Lottie's eyes fell on him something flitted across them, but he didn't know what. She did look tired but it was a massive improvement on the last time he'd seen her, lying in a hospital bed, her lips tinged with blue and blankets up to her neck. He'd been so scared then. But now she had a glow about her and even with a couple of stitches in her forehead she was beautiful. A rush of that old deep love filled Sid's heart but he did his best to ignore it for Selena's sake. He was trying to give their relationship one hundred per cent this time. 'Hello,' he said and his voice sounded strange in his ears, distant and tiny.

'Hello,' Lottie replied, softly. 'How are you?'

'Good.' He shoved his hands in his pockets. 'You?'

'Fine.' She gave a weak smile.

Sid wished now that he'd had the guts to go and see her. Selena had warned him not to, saying that Lottie needed rest and he'd listened, worried that if he and Lottie had ended up having another row her head might get worse. But he'd missed her so much. More than ever, in fact.

The dim chatter behind them meant the players had gone back to their rehearsals. Gregory was teaching Sarah another vocal warm-up and Mrs Andrews was walking around in circles muttering her lines like a mad person. Cecil was stretching out his hamstrings which made Sid slightly nervous, and Debbie was reciting tongue twisters as quickly as possible which, with her thick Scottish accent, made her sound completely deranged.

Lottie had kept her eyes on his face but looked around quickly and said, 'They all seem to be working hard.'

'Yeah, they've been nonstop. They were really keen to have somewhere to rehearse so I sorted the village hall. You don't mind, do you?'

'No,' she replied with a smile. 'Of course not. Thank you'

Sid nodded. 'They're taking it really seriously this time.'

'And what about Conner?' asked Lottie.

'He's over there painting scenery. He's roped in some of the players to help with scene changes during the show and made some simple cut-outs to pull on and off stage as people perform. They're looking pretty good actually.'

'Wow.' Lottie smiled and Sid saw her relax. 'I saw the article you wrote about the repairs. It was good.'

'Thanks,' Sid replied, shuffling his feet. 'It would have been better with one of your photos, I'm nowhere near as good.'

Lottie shrugged at the compliment as if shaking it off. She always did that. 'I meant to thank you for the one about *Much Ado* too. You wrote it beautifully. I'm not sure we'd still be here without you.'

'Of course you would,' said Sid. 'You came up with this idea. You made it happen.'

'I suppose,' she replied, fiddling with her hair. Lottie pulled her cardigan sleeves into her hands and crossed her arms over her chest. Her eyes were glassy like she was going to cry. 'Sid I … I kept meaning to call but I just couldn't … couldn't find the words.'

Sid's head shot up and he felt his heart double beat. He worried he was having some sort of heart attack. Lottie looked suddenly tired, and the bright blue of her eyes stood out against the whiteness of her skin. She glanced around as if seeing who was near, speaking quickly like she had to get the words out before they were interrupted. 'Every time we talk at the moment, something seems to go wrong, doesn't it? I don't think we've ever fought like this before.'

Sid nodded once and he forced the words out, trying to keep his tone normal and cheerful. 'Things have changed, haven't they? For both of us. Do you think your nan meant to change our lives so much?'

Lottie gave a mirthful laugh. 'No. But then she didn't always think things through, did she?' Lottie reached out a hand and touched Sid's arm. He felt the hairs lifting under her fingertips. 'And thanks for rescuing me from a cold and lonely death in a watery grave.'

Sid felt himself grow hot. 'Lottie, I wouldn't ignore a message like that from you. You might annoy me sometimes—'

She scowled. 'Cheers.' But Sid was pleased to hear her teasing tone.

'But you're my best friend.' Seeing her bright eyes so full of warmth and tenderness, he wanted to tell her how he felt. How he'd always felt. But his courage waned as quickly as it came and he looked away, annoyed that he still hadn't got over her. 'Did Jeremy tell you it was me?'

She shook her head. 'No, it was Sarah actually.' Was that a hint of disappointment in her voice?

Sid felt anger race through his blood. That figured. Of course he wouldn't admit it was Sid who had gone and saved Lottie, or that he was the one she'd called. He'd felt a strange satisfaction at being the one she chose, though he wished he'd answered straight away. He shook his head as he recalled the hotel incident with Selena and felt a sudden hit of guilt that his feelings for Lottie were a betrayal to her. How had the simple life he'd enjoyed suddenly become so conflicted and messy.

Lottie bit her lip. 'I wished I'd called you as soon as she'd told me,' she said, absentmindedly rubbing her arm. 'I kept thinking you wouldn't want to talk to me again after what I said.'

Sid wanted her to touch his arm again, but he didn't know what to do. His brain hurt with the emotions running through him. He felt guilty over Selena, love for Lottie and anger at Jeremy and everything just seemed one enormous soap-opera style cliché. Lottie was watching him, her eyes soft and comforting, and he knew he had to say something. 'I wasn't trying to attack you that night you know, Lots, after *Much Ado*. I was just trying to figure out how we'd write it.'

'I know. I'm sorry.' She took his hand this time. Again, it was as if someone had set fire to every nerve in his body. 'And I'm sorry I mentioned your parents like that. It was wrong of me. In fact, it was horrible and I'm really ashamed of myself.'

A tear rolled down her cheek and Sid lifted his free hand to wipe it away but she brushed it off herself and he let his hand fall. He wasn't used to Lottie apologising. She was as stubborn as a mule and loved to put her head in the sand like an ostrich – she was a mostrich. Gregory's voice grew louder, saving him from trying to answer.

'Alright if we start, Lottie?'

She turned and nodded.

'Conner, are we ready?' Conner said yes. 'Who wants to go first for practice today then? Mrs Andrews, why don't you take the floor as you didn't have much time last week?'

Mrs Andrews walked onto the tiny stage. 'Thank you, Gregory.'

'What's happened to them all?' asked Lottie, clearly trying to move the conversation on. 'It's like they've been replaced by incredibly polite aliens.'

Sid surveyed them. 'I think the accident made them realise how much they enjoy being part of the group and how much they want it to succeed. Since then they've been a lot nicer to each other.' He turned back to Lottie. 'It was a bit drastic though, Lots. I wouldn't go doing it again. There are actual proper team-building games you can do next time.'

Lottie giggled. 'I'll try not to.'

Feeling the tension ease a little, Sid said, 'I think Sarah quite likes you. I was chatting to her earlier and I don't think she has many friends. She's really nice, actually.'

'I think Lee would like to be her friend.'

'Yeah, I noticed that too.'

Lottie smiled at him and he was seeing a glimpse of the real her again. The Lottie he'd always known.

'You've done a really good thing with the theatre, Lottie.' He didn't know if it meant anything anymore but he added, 'I'm really proud of you.'

Her lower lip trembled as she said, 'Are you?'

And from the smile on her face he could tell that, even after everything, his opinion still mattered.

Chapter 34

Three weeks later and the rehearsals for the showcase were going really rather well as far as Lottie was concerned. Conner had taken charge and instructed everyone where they needed to stand to begin their scenes, and had even advised them on where to move, out on the stage. It would obviously need to be gone through again as soon as they were in the theatre, but the dimensions of the little stage in the village hall weren't too bad, so it should be fine.

Lottie checked her phone to see if Jeremy had texted. Their relationship had developed to that stage where, at the weekends, they were comfortable being apart as long as it was only for short periods of time. She could go off to rehearsals without missing him and when they caught up later it was with all the excitement of a first date. And during the week when he was in London they spoke every day on the phone.

Since her accident he'd also been much happier for her to call and had even called her a number of times checking in and seeing how things were going with the theatre repairs. Lottie sipped her mocha watching one of the players rehearse a scene from *Romeo and Juliet* and smiled. Life was good. Even at work, her and Sid were getting along really well again. There was still an awkwardness when they spoke of their respective partners, so they'd learned to just not ask, except for a basic health enquiry.

Sid sat next to Lottie and sipped from his takeaway cup as Mrs Andrews flounced around on stage reciting her lines.

'I've got something for you,' said Lottie, rifling in her camera bag. Apprehension tensed her neck as she handed it to Sid.

His eyes lit up, then darkened with confusion. 'My old notebook. I'd have thought you'd have burned that with an effigy of me.'

'Ha ha,' said Lottie. She didn't like being reminded of that night, still ashamed of herself, but Sid always tried to make light of things to soften the blow. 'I wanted you to have it back. I bought that for you last Christmas and you said you loved it.'

'I do. Thanks.' He went to tuck it inside his jacket pocket and Lottie held his arm to stop him.

'Wait, I wrote something inside.' She felt her cheeks redden, knowing she was blushing. Sid flicked through the pages to the last one he'd used, the note he had made over *Much Ado*, and his eyes lifted at the corners as he smiled.

'Sorry?' he read out loud.

Lottie nodded. 'Yeah, sorry. And I am really, really sorry.'

'You've already said sorry,' Sid replied. 'You don't need to say it again, Lots. It's all finished now. Forgotten.' He grinned and the tightness in Lottie's lungs vanished, allowing them to expand and for her to take a deep breath. She hadn't realised she'd been so nervous about giving it back to him.

Lottie nudged his arm and rested her head on his shoulder, savouring the familiar smell of his leather jacket. 'Thanks.'

Since they'd made up life was finally adjusting for both of them. Lottie still couldn't bring herself to like Selena, who was staying at Sid's more and more. In their few conversations there'd been some comments Lottie wasn't sure how to take but they'd at least been civil to each other. Sid didn't really run into Jeremy very much because of his being in London, so that made life much easier for her.

The door to the village hall suddenly swung open and a short, rotund woman in a heavy black coat came waddling in shouting, 'No, no, no, no, no!' and waving her finger in the air.

Sid turned to Lottie and raised his eyebrows. Lottie did the same and shrugged. Quiet descended amongst the players as the woman trundled down to where Sid and Lottie were sat. When she reached them her thread-veined cheeks were bright red and her wiry grey hair stood out in all directions, clearly blown by the rising September wind.

Lottie stood up so they were face to face. 'Can I help you?'

'No, you can't, you can just leave.' The woman took off her coat and threw it on a table before starting to lift and stack chairs with surprising strength.

Gregory and Cecil were so shocked by this unexpected interruption they made no comment whatsoever, while Mrs Andrews, as Lottie could see from the look on her face, was preparing for battle.

'Umm,' said Lottie, glancing quickly at Sid as if to check this wasn't one of the crazies they'd come across at work. His face was blank. 'Umm, I'm afraid we've got the hall booked today, Mrs …?'

'North,' the woman replied, harshly. 'Mrs North and no, you haven't. I've got the hall today. I booked it last night with the secretary.'

Lottie shook her head. 'I think there's been some sort of mistake, Mrs North. We've booked the hall for the next two weekends as—'

She was trying to stack the chairs next to Lottie and Sid, almost pulling his out from under him. Mrs North didn't look at her as she spoke. 'You've had the hall enough already and the WI need it.'

'Well, actually—' interrupted Mrs Andrews and Lottie cut her off.

'Thank you, Mrs Andrews, but I've got this.' Over the top of

Mrs North's head, Sid raised his eyebrows. 'Mrs North, are you a member of the WI?'

'Yes. I'm the second in command.'

Lottie edged towards her. 'Only, we know most of the WI – Sid and I – from working on the paper and I don't think we've met before.'

'I haven't got time for all this chit-chat,' said Mrs North, now tugging at the chair in Sarah's hands. To her credit, Sarah didn't let go and Mrs North went to find another one. 'I need to tidy up for the meeting this afternoon.'

'Meeting? Now hang on!' said Gregory and Lottie held up her hand to shush him.

'Mrs North,' Lottie began, calmly, 'I'm afraid your meeting can't go ahead in here today. We booked the village hall weeks ago for quite a long time while the theatre's out of action.'

'I made the booking myself,' said Sid. 'And had it confirmed.'

Lottie nodded at him. 'So you see, Mrs North, the secretary made a mistake telling you that you could have the hall this afternoon. I'm very sorry, but there it is.'

Mrs North stopped lifting chairs and walked to Lottie. Lottie wasn't tall but Mrs North was so tiny she only came up to her chin. The colour in her cheeks had deepened and her eyes had become narrow slits on her face. 'But—'

'Yes?'

'But I made a booking!' Mrs North looked like she might need a doctor if she continued to get herself into such a state. Lottie was surprised she didn't feel intimidated by this small, scary woman, but then Mrs North's jaw slackened and her mouth fell open, and Lottie had to resist the urge to laugh.

'I've explained there's been an error, Mrs North,' Lottie continued, her voice steady but stern, like a schoolteacher. 'Now, if you don't mind, we really need to get on.' She gave Mrs North a kind smile, hoping she would see that the matter was closed.

'Now listen here,' said Mrs Andrews, walking towards them as Mrs North was refusing to move.

Lottie turned. 'Mrs Andrews, everything is under control. Please just go back to your practice. And that goes for all of you,' she called out to the rest of the players.

Mrs North clearly didn't agree that the matter was closed as she said, 'I want to complain.'

'Here you go,' Sid replied, handing her his phone. 'I've just dialled the secretary's number. She'll tell you it's a mistake.' Sid held out his phone for her but Mrs North refused to take it and after harrumphing at Lottie, turned on her heel and stalked off, muttering as she went.

Sid ended the call and he and Lottie silently sat down, then burst into laughter. The players all stopped what they were doing and gave Lottie a round of applause.

'Well done, Lottie,' said Sid, between chuckles. 'She was a bit intense, wasn't she?'

Lottie's cheeks hurt from laughing but her body was filled with joy at the confidence she'd just shown, and what's more, truly felt. 'She was a complete loon! I've never seen her before, have you?'

Sid shook his head. 'No, but if she's the new second in command of the WI, there's no way I'm covering their things on my own from now on. I'm going to need backup.'

'And crash helmets.'

Sid picked up his cup again. 'Full on riot gear, more like.'

She turned to him and they stared into each other's eyes. Suddenly, there it was again – that emotion she couldn't name. His smile wasn't just geeky, she realised now. It was actually quite charming, and the brown of his eyes was so rich and dark. Even the shape of his face seemed different to her. She'd never really noticed how plump the apples of his cheeks were or the sweet cleft in his chin.

Just then, Conner came over carrying a clipboard and she tore her gaze away as he said, 'Sorry to interrupt, Lottie.'

'That's okay,' she replied, quickly taking a mouthful of mocha. 'Everything okay?'

He shifted nervously. 'We've got a bit of a problem with the running order.'

After her run in with Nutty North this morning, Lottie felt like there was nothing in the world she couldn't handle. Sid stood up and went to chat to the players, leaving them alone to talk and she patted the chair beside her. 'Come on then, Conner. Let's sort this out.'

But for some reason her head lifted to take one last glance at Sid before she concentrated.

Chapter 35

Finally, the October half term came around and the players were getting ready for the showcase, their one chance to regain some credibility. In the theatre, Sarah paced back and forth, wringing her hands. Lee sat with his legs splayed looking confident and handsome. Gregory and Cecil preened each other and fiddled with their hair, while Debbie stood near attempting some sort of vocal warm-up involving grunting. Mrs Andrews had edged away from the group and was gazing into a hand mirror moving her mouth in odd circles. Lottie watched them all, stood backstage beside Sid who, from the smile on his face, was thoroughly enjoying himself. 'It's nice to see them taking it so seriously,' he said to Lottie.

'I know. This is our chance to show everyone we're not just a bunch of gibbering idiots. Though I'm glad no one can see them right now.' She took a quick snap with her camera.

'Why do you think Debbie's making that weird noise? It sounds like she has a sinus infection.'

Lottie giggled. 'I'm not quite sure but hopefully it'll help with her performance otherwise it's just weird. My favourite is Mrs Andrews. I don't think her face as been stretched like that since her last face lift.' She watched the others and took in a deep breath as nerves bubbled up once more. Her face must have shown her concern as Sid said, 'I'm sure this time it'll be fine, Lots. They've not stopped rehearsing.'

'I hope so,' Lottie replied, taking another photo to distract herself.

After the flood, and the weeks of work, the theatre renovations had, thanks to Jeremy, finished on time. The stage had survived and been re-waxed, the dense curtains had been cleaned and the seats re-upholstered. There was even a new deep crimson carpet. But the walls were stripped bare and there was still a bit of a smell. Lottie had decided that, instead of selling tickets for the showcase there wouldn't be a charge, but people had to reserve seats and, so far, they had two nearly full nights ahead of them.

Sid checked his watch. 'Is Jeremy coming?'

Lottie checked her phone. 'He's supposed to be. He was going to do the announcements and introduce everyone.'

'Why him?' Lottie glanced at him but could tell from Sid's face that he wasn't being rude, just curious. 'Shouldn't you be doing it, or the mayor?'

'Jeremy wanted to introduce himself to the town after your article and after everything he's done, I couldn't really say no.'

Sid nodded in response. 'He's cutting it fine.'

Lottie checked her phone for the thousandth time, and walked to the door. People were starting to arrive but there was still half an hour till curtain up. Half an hour for him to get there. As if in answer, a text message appeared on her screen.

So sorry, Lottie, caught up in London again. Damn builders. Be back as soon as I can.

Lottie's eyes shot down and disappointment crushed in.

'Isn't he coming?' asked Sid, following behind her.

'No. He's not,' she said, resigning herself to the fact. 'At least not in time.' Lottie slid the phone into her back pocket. She was wearing black trousers and a white shirt. She'd wanted to go for a businesswoman look but feared it was more waitress.

'Sorry.'

'It's not your fault.' Lottie ran her hands through her hair. She'd done it the same way she had for her date with Jeremy. It wasn't that hard once you got used to it.

Sid rocked on his heels. 'Could Mayor Cunningham do the announcements? He's coming, isn't he?'

'I'm not sure I trust what he'd say.'

'Then it's going to have to be you.'

'I was just thinking that but, oh God. Pants.' Lottie groaned and re-tucked her shirt.

'You can do it, Lots,' he said cheerfully. 'It's just standing up and saying people's names and what they're doing.'

'Jeremy was going to give a speech about how important the theatre is to the town. He had little note cards and everything.' She really didn't want to stand in front of everyone. It reminded her of reading out to the class in English. If she got the words wrong people always laughed and jeered. A bolt of nerves shot through from her head to her feet.

'Listen,' said Sid, putting his hands on her shoulders and tuning her towards him. 'When you talk about the theatre your eyes light up and you sound so excited for the town people can't help but listen. They'd much rather hear from you, someone who's lived here all her life, whose nan loved this place, than a stranger from London in a suit.'

Lottie's heart soared. She smiled into Sid's daft face and saw that his eyes had developed gentle crow's feet that reached out from the corners. Funny how she'd never noticed them before. She always thought of him as the teenager she'd grown up with but he was a man now and really was quite attractive in his own way. His face had character and when he smiled at her there was something in his expression Lottie was drawn to.

Clearly thinking Lottie was stuck in panic mode and not examining his face, Sid said, 'If you don't do it, Adelaide Andrews will.'

246

She stood back and folded her arms over her chest. 'Over my dead body.'

Half an hour later the theatre was full. Hopefully people hadn't come just to laugh at them. Backstage, having tucked her camera away, Lottie took a deep breath and brushed her clothes down. She really didn't want to go out in front of all those people. She much preferred being here where the madness and chaos was. It was like being in an exclusive little world. The players had assembled in the wings and were ready to come on. They were grinning and excited and Lottie knew she couldn't put it off any longer. 'Everyone ready?'

The players nodded.

With a final deep breath, she said, 'Come on then. Let's get this show on the road.'

Conner played some introductory music and Lottie walked on to the stage, her legs shaking. Even her feet wobbled. She walked to the centre spot marked with an X and stopped in front of the microphone. As the crowd watched, a cold sweat ran over the back of her neck. She glanced at Sid, standing in the wings and after a reassuring smile from him and one of his cheeky winks, she took a deep breath again and began.

'Good evening, Greenley.'

No one answered, they just stared and Lottie's stomach fell to the floor. The audience's eyes were on her and she tightened her grip on the microphone stand for support.

'Thank you all for coming. My name's Lottie Webster and I'm Chairman of Greenley Theatre.' She'd expected boos but was greeted with more silence. It was difficult to know which was worse. 'We're here today to show you the wealth of talent we have in the Greenley Players, our amateur dramatics group.'

From the sidelines, Sid gave a reassuring nod and a thumbs-up.

'As you know, our first performance wasn't quite up to scratch.'

There were mumbles in the crowd. A stagehand did something

in the lighting box and the spotlights came on illuminating the scenery. Lottie's nerves were replaced with excitement and she found her mouth lifting into a grin. 'We're working hard to get better and today we'd like to show you exactly what everyone can do, because we have such a great team of amazingly talented people and we want to make you all proud. So, without further ado, may I please introduce the first star of the Greenley Players, Deborah McCray.'

A quiet applause circled around the crowd as Lottie left the stage.

'Oh, my goodness,' whispered Debbie, as she passed Lottie in the wings. Her face was ashen making her faded red hair appear brighter.

'You'll be great,' said Lottie, patting her arm. 'You can do this.'

Debbie stepped onto the stage, her flamboyant tie-dye dress wafting behind her. Conner started up her song and she moved back from the microphone. Thanks to Gregory, they'd learned that it didn't do to be too close with a voice as strong as hers. Under the crowd's intent gaze Debbie closed her eyes and began to sing.

She'd sensibly chosen something more popular but still operatic and as the words to 'Time to Say Goodbye' washed over the crowd, Lottie saw mouths drop open. The audience were seeing what she had seen during the auditions.

As Debbie pronounced each word with meaning, that meaning poured out over those listening. Her arms moved freely and her head swayed. There was no fake emotion or bad acting, just genuine feeling, and when she finished the crowd clapped enthusiastically. Some even whistled.

The first act was a success. Lottie bounced up and down and said a silent, 'Yes!'

Next up was Gregory. After *Much Ado*, Lottie worried he would ham it up a bit too much. He'd chosen a piece from *Oedipus Rex*, which Lottie wasn't entirely convinced was appropriate, but despite her best efforts she hadn't been able to dissuade him. It was apparently the piece that got him his big break and, as it meant so much to him, she'd relented. Conner had found some suitable background noises and the sounds of an ancient Greek market played out.

Gregory moved onto the stage wearing a Greek tunic to a mixture of stunned silence and teenage sniggering. Lottie hoped he was wearing something underneath. If he slipped on the newly waxed floor and everyone saw his nether regions it could be the end of the goodwill Debbie had only just garnered. Lottie crossed her fingers behind her back.

"'I care not for thy counsel or thy praise; For with what eyes could I have e'er beheld My honoured father in the shades below, Or my unhappy mother, both destroyed By me?'"

He paced the stage, his movements exaggerated enough for the crowd to see, but still subtle. His face portrayed the emotion of the words so that even those who might struggle to understand could still feel it.

Lottie allowed herself to uncross her fingers as he exited stage left. They had shown the town they could sing and act.

The remaining acts kept up the good work and Lottie couldn't have been more proud. Cecil's rendition of 'Stepping Out with My Baby' was a resounding success. He'd found his forte channelling Fred Astaire with hat and cane in hand.

Mrs Andrews' monologue from *Wuthering Heights* was well received, though Lottie thought she was a bit too old to play Catherine, but nobody was going to tell Mrs Andrews that.

The next one was a gamble and Lottie felt nerves rise up once more. Lee Carter strode onto the stage exuding a confidence that verged on arrogance but in the end the crowd adored him. His speech from *It's a Wonderful Life*, brought some to tears and Lottie felt her lip tremble as he evoked Jimmy Stewart's heart-rending moment of realisation.

The rest of the players performed until, finally, it was Sarah's turn. Lottie introduced her and waited for her to come on. She didn't.

To her left, Lottie could see Sid beckoning. The crowd were waiting and their applause died to silence. 'Sarah Powell, everyone,' said Lottie and legged it from the stage.

'Sarah, are you okay?' she whispered.

Sarah was white and beads of sweat gathered on her forehead. 'I've just been sick.'

Lottie frantically looked around. 'Oh my God. Where?'

'In that bin.'

Lottie peered over and recoiled. 'Can you go on?'

Sarah shook her head. 'I'm so scared. I don't think I can.'

'Of course you can. You're brilliant.'

'You can do it, Sarah,' whispered Gregory. 'We believe in you.'

'They'll laugh at me.'

'They will not, I promise,' said Lottie and took Sarah's hands. 'I couldn't believe it when I heard you sing. You were amazing.'

'They all hate me because of my stupid crush on that idiot, Mayor Cunningham. I was just sad and lonely after mum died and he was strong and—'

Lottie couldn't believe Sarah had chosen this moment to have a breakdown. She had no idea what to do so gave her a hug and hoped she wouldn't be sick on her shoulder. 'I know exactly how you feel,' Lottie said, releasing her. 'I've felt so lost too. But I know you can do this. Your voice is incredible.'

The crowd were waiting and beginning to chatter. This couldn't go wrong. Not now. Lottie told Conner to start the music and using a walkie-talkie he spoke to one of the tech guys and Sarah's song began.

Sarah looked at Lottie and shook her head.

'Come on. You can't put it off. On you go.' Lottie guided her forwards and shoved her onto the stage with a final, 'Just close your eyes and think of Greenley.'

Sarah stumbled on, still visibly shaking as a hushed silence descended. She seemed to be shrinking, getting smaller and smaller in front of the microphone. Sarah closed her eyes and sang the first few lines of 'Someone Like You', by Adele.

Heads lifted as soon as they heard her voice, beautiful even with a slight shake. Eyes widened in amazement as she sang with heartfelt emotion and power. Lottie looked to Sid whose smile signalled success and they high fived.

A volcanic eruption of whoops and thunderous applause reverberated around the theatre as Sarah finished.

Success! Lottie clapped too though Sid had to stop her when it got too loud.

All too quickly it was over, and Sarah hurried backstage straight to the bin to be sick again. Gregory ran to her and started rubbing her back. 'It's your turn now,' said Sid, with a mischievous glint in his eye.

Lottie felt a lump in her throat.

'Speech time!'

'No, no, no, no, no,' Lottie whined.

He blocked her way backstage. 'Do you want me to ask Mrs Andrews?'

She shook her head and sullenly said, 'No.'

'Go on then. People are starting to leave.' He turned her around and sent her out.

Lottie walked onto the stage, panicking. She'd been too busy watching the show to prepare a speech and wiped her sweaty hands down her thighs.

'Umm, thank you, everybody, for coming tonight to see exactly how talented the Greenley Players are. As you can see, we have dancers, singers, actors, everything really to make us successful.'

Those who had started climbing out of their seats stopped and sat down again. Lottie felt the sweat gathering at her temples and glanced at Sid, who motioned for her to keep going.

'We just need some more practice and the continued support of this wonderful town. I don't know if any of you know me, or my nan, Elsie Webster, who was chairman of the theatre before she died, but—'

A round of applause gathered pace as she said her nan's name. They remembered her. Tears threatened her eyes and Lottie tried to hold it together. 'But she believed in this town and felt the theatre could and should be at the heart of our community.'

The Greenley Players shuffled onto the stage to stand behind her. 'We know we're not perfect.' The group nodded and laughed self-deprecatingly. 'But we want to be able to entertain people and as we practise we'll get better and better, but we still need the support of every single one of you. We need you to come and watch our performances, we need you to support us on social media, and we need your help to get the theatre back up and running, because, it doesn't just have to be a theatre, it can be a …'

She was rambling now. Shit. What could it be? Mayor Cunningham's blingy necklace shone in the light. He was looking around at the reaction she had caused.

'It could be a … a bingo hall.' Unable to control her enthusiasm, Lottie loosened her hands from in front of her and gestured as she spoke. 'We could have a youth theatre, or it could be a place for after-school clubs. We could have school visits so the children can learn about the building and acting workshops and—'

'Could the photography club use it?' shouted a man in the crowd.

'Yes,' cried Lottie and the mayor scowled.

'What about playgroups?' asked one mum, bouncing a baby on her lap. 'It'd be great to have somewhere to meet other than coffee shops.'

'Of course.' Lottie beamed. 'The point is the theatre isn't just a building. It can be something that touches every single person young or old, whether you come to a production or just use the space. It can be a living, breathing place again. But it won't be unless we all pull together to make it happen.'

Lottie stepped back to breathe. The Greenley Players were clapping furiously as were the crowd. Even Mayor Cunningham was forced to join in. She looked to the sideline. When Sid's gaze settled on Lottie she saw a light in his eyes again. Conner was standing next to him and she realised there was something else she needed to do.

'There is one more person I need to thank for making tonight happen, and that's our director, because without his hard work, the players wouldn't have any lights on them, or music to sing to, or anything like that. Please give a big round of applause for Conner Shaw.'

Sid pushed Conner onto the stage and he nodded to the crowd as he stumbled his way to the middle, then as soon as possible, hid behind Lee. After Lottie finished the thank yous, the audience left and the players gathered backstage, congratulating and complimenting each other.

Sarah had colour in her cheeks again and approached Cecil. 'I thought your song was brilliant. You're so good.'

'Me? Darling, are you kidding, your voice is in-cre-di-ble! I nearly cried.'

'You did cry,' said Mrs Andrews.

'That's because I have a soul, dear.'

Lottie worried the arguments would start again but the twinkle in Cecil's eye showed that he was teasing and Mrs Andrews responded with a hint of a smile, or as much of one the fillers would allow.

'Well done, mate,' said Lee to Conner, patting him on the back.

'Yes, well done, young man,' said Gregory. 'I think great things are in store for you.'

'You organised it all brilliantly,' Sarah offered.

Lottie wanted to celebrate and as they'd started the performance early enough to attract families it was only nine o'clock. 'Shall we head to the pub?' asked Lottie, on a high from her first real success.

Everyone cheered except Sid who said, 'I'm sorry, Lottie. I'm meeting Selena.'

She opened her mouth to convince him to stay but couldn't form the words. And just like that Lottie was reminded again how different life was for them both now. But at least she had Jeremy. Wherever he was.

Chapter 36

'I'm so sorry, darling,' Jeremy said, planting a kiss on Lottie's forehead. 'Damn builders keep trying to build what they want instead of what I'm paying them for. I had to meet with the foreman and sort it out. But, I heard you did brilliantly without me.'

Lottie smiled but tiredness kept pulling the corners of her mouth down. 'I don't know if it was as good as you'd have done. You're better at public speaking than me.'

Jeremy was less polished today, more rugged, and his eyes were ringed with dark circles. 'I heard you were amazing.'

'I just spoke honestly. People seemed to like it by the end.'

'Well done, you clever girl.' He took her hand and kissed it. 'Shall we find somewhere for dinner? If we're quick we can squeeze in before closing time.'

'Yes, let's,' replied Lottie. 'I'm starving.' After two large glasses of wine with the players her head was swimming.

They left the comfort of the pub and walked onto the seafront, along the promenade. The rough sea had turned brown from the silt brought up by the current and the seagulls had disappeared inland. The cold autumn air helped clear Lottie's head and she looked at Jeremy. He really was very sexy in his suit, his hair ruffled by the wind and a thin spread of stubble over his chiselled jaw. He pulled her closer.

They settled on a quiet restaurant set back from the seafront in the old part of town, nestled amongst the small side alleys. It was still virtually full and Lottie watched delicious meals being brought out of the kitchen as they were led to their table. Lottie sat down, her legs aching from how tense she'd been all day. Jeremy immediately ordered a bottle of red wine which the waiter delivered with frightening efficiency.

'How are you feeling after your victory?' Jeremy smiled before taking a large gulp of wine.

'I wouldn't quite call it a victory, but at least we showed them we're not complete idiots, and proved the Greenley Players have some talent.'

'Are you okay?' asked Jeremy. 'You seem a bit down?'

Lottie wondered where Sid and Selena were. Were they at his flat? No, she didn't want to picture that. She chased the image away but her hackles rose as if she were jealous. Were they out for dinner, gazing into each other's eyes as she and Jeremy should be? And why didn't she want to gaze into Jeremy's eyes tonight? The low candlelight was doing nothing to help her feel romantic. All she wanted to do was eat carbohydrates and go to bed. She looked up to see Jeremy staring at her. 'I think it's just a come-down from all the adrenalin. I'm really tired.'

Jeremy nodded and she went back to reading the menu.

A moment later he said, 'Lottie?' and she looked up. Jeremy nodded towards the waiter stood by their table.

'Oh, I'm so sorry.' She ordered some kind of mushroom pasta thing and told herself to concentrate.

'Well, I'd like the sea bass.' He smiled at the waiter then turned back to Lottie. 'Let's have a drink and a nice dinner then we'll head back to yours, shall we?'

They always seemed to go back to hers. Considering his house was in the posh part of town, it was off they'd never really gone there. Lottie nodded, but deep down she wanted to be on her own tonight. She took a sip of wine. Was that three large glasses or four? No wonder reading the menu had been a challenge.

After a bowl of olives and some small talk, Jeremy took her hand and stroked it. 'I'm so glad things went well today because I've had the best idea. I've been mulling it over for a while, but now I'm positive this is the right thing to do.'

Lottie could hear the excitement in his voice but couldn't match it with her own. For some reason she felt a heavy weight on her mind but she didn't know why. 'Oh yes? What's that?'

Jeremy glanced at her then back at his wine. 'I was thinking that, as there's still a lot of work to do, I'd buy the theatre and make a real investment in the property.'

Lottie paused. The sentences jumbled in her brain, but all with the same question. 'What? I – so – so, you'd own the theatre?'

He grabbed her hand again. 'Yes, well, my company would. But don't you see, Lottie, then we could really invest in the place. You wouldn't have such a shoestring budget, you'd be able to really kit it out. Isn't it a fantastic idea?'

Alarm bells were sounding in her head, or was it just ringing from the amount of booze she'd drunk? She looked around at the laughing, smiling diners. *That should be us*, she thought. After how well today had gone why did she feel so down about everything?

The waiter delivered their food and Jeremy laid his napkin in his lap and picked up his knife and fork. 'I can't wait to take it to the committee, but I'll need your support, Lottie. You're the chairman. We make such a good team.' He gave her a warm smile. 'This just makes sense, don't you think? We can do so much for Greenley with this.'

Lottie's brain felt like someone had put it in a blender, whizzed it up, then poured it back into her head. 'Jeremy, I – I suppose it does, but—'

'I can't see the council objecting especially if I have the full support of the committee. It means there's public support. And you, Lottie. Your nan was such a pillar of the community, your support is invaluable. I mean, the council want it off their hands and I want to buy it, it's a win-win.' He watched her and took a sip of his wine before speaking again, talking quicker and quicker. 'We could get a conservationist in to repaint the ceiling properly and we can find similar wallpaper to what it had before. We can install new lighting and make a decent backstage area. We won't need to cut corners or do things on the cheap. You could really put Greenley on the map with this, Lottie.'

Lottie nodded along, feeling tired and numb. For some reason, Sid's words spoken angrily months ago echoed in her mind. He'd said that they might be a tiny committee but they were all the theatre had.

Jeremy put down his cutlery and took her hand again. 'I know, let's finish dinner and we'll talk some more later.'

Lottie placed a forkful of food in her mouth but couldn't taste anything. Did she want to put Greenley on the map? Despite her fear, in Jeremy's eyes she read only a genuine wish to help. She was just tired and a bit muddled from drinking on an empty stomach, that was all.

There couldn't be anything to worry about, he wanted to keep it as a theatre which meant he wasn't in league with Mayor Cunningham to try and knock it down and build houses. He wanted what she wanted. And saving the theatre for good was exactly what her nan had wanted too. How could she even think of saying no?

No, this was a good idea. How could it be anything else?

258

Chapter 37

On Monday morning, when Lottie climbed into Sid's car, he watched her double take and the way she exaggeratedly checked she was in the right one.

'You've cleaned up,' Lottie said, but she didn't seem that pleased about it.

'I had to,' Sid moaned. 'Selena said she wouldn't get in if I didn't.'

'Oh.' Thankfully, Lottie didn't say anymore. 'Where are we off to today?'

'You won't believe me when I tell you.' Sid grinned.

'Go on.'

He looked at her and wondered why she wasn't smiling. 'I'll tell you the title I'm going to use first.'

The most pathetic smile Sid had ever seen Lottie give crossed her face. 'Okay.'

'Morris Dancer Gangs in Big Bin Bust Up,' he announced proudly. It had taken him ages to come up with it.

'What?' Her tone was flat and Sid hesitated. He'd expected more. Normally she would have been in hysterics.

Sid gave a huge grin trying to cheer her up. 'Okay so, Keith and his gang of Morris dancers from Greenley got into a huge row with Eric and his lot from Denton at the folk festival on Saturday. They'd all had a few too many and decided to have a dance off when Keith fell, or was pushed, into a bin. So he picked it up and threw it at Eric, thinking Eric had put his goons up to it. Then they had a massive bundle on the green.'

Lottie laughed. 'No way?'

'Yes, way.' Sid could see she was finally starting to enjoy this.

'In all their gear?'

'Bells, whistles, and everything. We're off to interview Keith, Eric and some witnesses today.'

'Awesome,' said Lottie, but the smile he'd seen moments before quickly faded.

Sid started the car and drove off. 'I know. I bloody love my job.' Lottie turned away and she stared out of the window, chewing her fingernails. Sid tried to start the conversation again. 'You look nice.'

'Thanks.'

'Selena and I watched Sunday's showcase. It was just as good as the Saturday one.'

'Oh, thanks.'

'And I'm glad you did the speech again that night too.'

Lottie nodded but didn't reply. Something was bothering her. Sid gave a couple of sideways glances but she still didn't speak. 'Are you alright?'

Lottie gave a tight smile and she emphatically nodded yes. Sid feared the distance that had grown between them meant she wouldn't confide in him anymore, but having asked a few times, he didn't know what else to do so chewed the inside of his cheek before turning on the radio to fill the silence.

They interviewed Keith of the Greenley Morris dancers first who assured Sid he hadn't started the fight. But apparently, when you were pushed arse first into a bin, you couldn't take it lying down. Or sitting down, thought Sid. Next, it was a ten-minute trip to Eric, the rival gang leader.

'You were very quiet in there,' said Sid when they were back in the car.

'Was I? Sorry.' Lottie was keeping her eyes down and her voice was small and quiet.

'Are you sure you're alright?'

Lottie nodded and went back to opening and closing the camera lens.

Unsurprisingly Eric of the Denton Morris dancers was adamant the other lot had started it. He'd dressed in full Morris dancer gear for the interview, and had a black eye. But Lottie was still distracted throughout the interview and Sid had to prompt her to take the pictures.

When they were in the car on their way to visit a witness she suddenly took a deep breath and said, 'Jeremy wants to buy the theatre.'

Sid almost stamped on the brake and performed an unscheduled emergency stop. His stomach lurched. 'Hey?'

Lottie pulled her coat tighter around her. 'Jeremy wants to buy the theatre. He said he's already put so much into it because of the roof and – and he wants to buy the land so we can take the theatre to the next level.'

Sid drove on in silence. He didn't feel confident in opening his mouth and having anything other than expletives come out.

'What do you think?' asked Lottie, turning to him.

From the corner of his eye he could see her watching him. He didn't like it. Not one little bit. Jeremy had edged towards this, donating money here and there. Just as Sid had finally begun to believe that maybe Jeremy was genuinely interested in Lottie, this happened and it was a worrying development. One that made him angry. She wasn't going to like what he had to say but he'd been honest with her before and had to be again.

He took a deep breath. 'I don't like it, Lots. He's a property developer. He develops property for a living. He does it up, then sells it off. And now he wants to buy the theatre? How do we know he won't do the same? Just because he says he's never dealt with theatres before doesn't mean he isn't interested.'

'He said he wouldn't,' Lottie replied. 'He said he wants to re-do the ceiling and put Greenley on the map.'

Sid's mind was stuck on a cycle of swear words and insults. 'I don't trust him.'

'But why would he have given us so much money already if his intention was to pull it down and build houses?' From the tightness of her mouth she was getting cross with him again, but she'd seemed bothered by this for some reason, like she wanted his approval or something.

'Maybe he wants to use the building for something else? I just don't believe his reasons are innocent.'

'Well, you don't know him,' said Lottie, heatedly. 'He's taking his idea to the committee and he wants my support.'

'Will you give it?' Sid asked coldly.

'I think so.'

'Then why are you even asking me?'

Lottie gave a half-hearted shrug as if she didn't know herself. 'I just wanted to know what you thought?'

Sid gripped the wheel. 'You know what I think.'

They drove on in silence past the newly built cul-de-sacs and retirement flats. Sid's fingers hurt from holding the wheel so tightly. He couldn't wait anymore. He needed to do something to wake Lottie up. To make her see. He could be wrong about Jeremy, he knew that, but something wasn't quite right here. Even though he was now the hero of the town Sid just couldn't believe his motives were innocent. And what did Lottie expect him to say?

'I can't see how it's not a good idea,' said Lottie.

Sid tutted. 'Well, on your head be it.'

'On your head be it?' Lottie echoed, her voice coming alive with annoyance. 'I'm sorry, did we just take a left into the nine-teenth century?'

'I just mean that—'

'I know what you mean, Sid,' Lottie replied, folding her arms over her chest. 'You mean that if I agree and it all goes wrong and he buys the theatre then sells it, or it gets knocked down, then the whole town will blame me. Isn't that it?'

'Yes,' he answered before he could stop himself, but he was angry. 'You're saying it, Lottie, but have you really thought about it? About what would happen if you're wrong about him?'

'Of course I have.'

'And?'

Lottie's voice rose. 'And I believe him. This could be the solution Nan was always looking for.'

'I don't think it is.' Sid shook his head in disgust. He couldn't think of anything Elsie would want less. She'd want the community to always be involved and there was too big a risk that that wouldn't happen if a corporation took over. Deep down, Lottie knew that too.

'I don't care what you think,' Lottie said huffily. She was acting like an insecure teenager.

'Then why ask me?' Sid focused on the road.

Lottie opened her mouth to speak then closed it again. She was all red and blotchy with anger. 'You're so bloody infuriating.'

The last interview was a tense, hurried nightmare. Lottie clearly hated every minute she had to be in Sid's company and when he spoke to her she ignored everything he said. She answered with a simple 'yes' or 'no' only when she had to and then returned to absolute silence when they were alone.

When Sid pulled up outside her house he said, 'Look, I'm sorry you don't like what I said, Lottie.'

Her mouth dropped open. 'Is that supposed to be an apology?'

'Of sorts.'

'Why of sorts?'

Sid screwed up his brow. 'Because I'm not apologising for what I think. I just don't want it to come between us, again.' Just when they started getting on something happened to drive them even further apart.

Lottie angrily un-clicked her seatbelt and grabbed her camera bag, pulling it onto her lap. 'It already has, Sid. I wasn't sure either at first. But I believe Jeremy wants to help. Do you still think he doesn't actually care about me? It that it? Even after all this time? Why can't you believe someone like Jeremy would be interested in me? I'm not that grotesque.'

'It's not about you, Lottie. It's about him.'

'He's my boyfriend, Sid, and you'd better start getting used to the idea.' Lottie got out and slammed the door shut.

Sid watched her go, then put the car in gear and moved off. Lottie Webster was without doubt the most annoying, clever, stupid person he'd ever met. He opened the window to let the cold air rush in and tried to calm down. He'd tried everything to make it work but Lottie was so wrapped up in Jeremy he was all she could see.

Feeling the anger in his body pulse through to his hands, he hit the wheel. He could really do without this right now. Selena was quite demanding at the moment and being with her was like having another full-time job. Not to mention the fact that his flat was gradually filling up with her things.

He checked his watch. He could easily nip back to the office and really start digging into Jeremy Bell and his company. He hadn't been happy with some of the things Jeremy had said in his interview back in August, after the flood. Like when Jeremy had mentioned his previous experience, Sid had asked if he meant specifically with theatres, Jeremy's left eyebrow had lifted slightly and he'd been thrown momentarily off course. But Sid had been so consumed with getting his relationship with Lottie back on track and giving Selena everything she wanted, he hadn't done anything more with it. But now, things were different.

If he had something tangible, something Lottie could see and read, she might start to realise it wasn't just him being weird and jealous. He'd stalled long enough. Nothing else was getting in the way this time. Sid flicked the indicator on, turned the car around and stepped on the gas.

Chapter 38

The Greenley Players were planning their next move. As it was now late October and people might actually bother coming to another performance, Lottie decided they should start planning the Christmas pantomime, plus she needed to keep her mind occupied and away from Sid. How could they have had another row and why was it always about Jeremy? Sid had Selena now, so why was he so jealous of him? In the theatre, Mrs Andrews had brought another picnic.

'Is she trying to poison us?' asked Gregory, looking over his shoulder to check Mrs Andrews wasn't within earshot. 'What do you think that is?'

'It's chia pudding with fresh strawberries,' said Lottie, peering at the beautifully handwritten label. She didn't like the look of it either. It looked like frogspawn.

'And what in all that's holy is this?' asked Debbie.

'Avocado bruschetta,' replied Lottie.

'Brew-what?'

Lottie patted her shoulder. 'Basically, avocado on toast.'

'Right. That looks safest, I'll have that.' Debbie took one and a glass of cloudy liquid from the side. She took a sip. 'Urgh, what's this? It tastes like the devil's piss.'

'It's coconut water, Debbie,' shouted Mrs Andrews from the other side of the room. 'It'll do wonders for your terribly dry skin.'

'Dry skin my—'

'Can we come to order, please, everyone,' said Lottie quickly, climbing onto the stage. She was getting used to this now. 'First of all, another big well done for the showcase. I think it went really well and we definitely impressed the town.'

'And thanks to you, dear, Lottie,' said Gregory, 'for that rousing speech at the end. You did us proud. Elsie herself couldn't have done better.'

'Thank you,' replied Lottie, smiling at the compliment. 'So, we need to discuss our next performance and I thought, as we're now at the end of October, we'd start work on a Christmas pantomime. What do you all think?'

She was greeted by cheers and hurrahs.

'Don't you think they're for children?' said Mrs Andrews. 'Not to mention lowbrow. I know we used to do them in the old group but, really.'

'Och, I think that would be amazing,' said Debbie. 'What one shall we do?'

When Lottie talked about the shows she couldn't help but feel excited. 'I thought we could do *Aladdin*,' she said, remembering the flyer she'd found in her nan's things, all those months ago.

'Oh, yes,' said Cecil, clapping his hands together. 'Let's do *Aladdin*. I used to love doing the pantos.'

'It could be difficult,' said Conner, receiving disapproving looks from Gregory and Sarah. He held up his hands. 'I'm not being negative. Just, you know, there's flying carpets and stuff.'

'Oh, that's true,' said Lottie, pressing a finger to her lips. She hadn't thought of that.

'Don't worry,' Conner reassured her. 'I'll have a think and come up with something. I liked that film when I was little.'

267

'Film?' said Mrs Andrews. 'It was a fairy tale long before it was a Disney movie.'

'Whatever,' came his mature response, but Lottie let him have that one.

'I'm sure you'll think of something suitable,' said Gregory.

Lottie said, 'I thought we'd do auditions for the roles this time to make it fair. And as you'll be directing it, Conner, I'd like you to be on the panel with me.' She was determined to really support him this time.

'Sure,' said Conner, brightening.

The theatre had finally lost the damp smell and the whole place was brighter. The walls were still bare and Lottie thought of what more she could do if Jeremy bought the theatre. She wasn't bothered about putting Greenley on the map, but she did want it to be the best it could be. If he bought it there'd be money for posters and flyers and things like that. Why couldn't Sid see it was a good idea? She wouldn't even be stood in the theatre now if it wasn't for Jeremy.

Over the last few nights she'd thought long and hard about his offer and about any reservations she'd had but decided to trust her instincts and trust in their relationship. She was going to give it her full support at the committee meeting tomorrow night.

'Are we going to have the same musical numbers as the film?' asked Cecil. He was as excited as a child.

'Oh, I hope so,' said Sarah.

Cecil placed a hand on her knee. 'You could sing "A Whole New World" beautifully, my dear.' Sarah blushed. 'When are we having the auditions, Lottie?'

'Yes, definitely auditions this time,' Gregory cut in. 'We don't want another *Much Ado*, do we? I may be able to act, but I'm not sure casting is my thing.'

The players gave an embarrassed laugh and Lottie smiled at him to let him know it was okay. 'I'll email round an audition piece for everyone tomorrow. I thought we could hold them next week so we have lots and lots of time for rehearsals. Gregory, for now did you want to take us through some more exercises?'

He jumped up out of his seat and stood in front of everyone fidgeting with excitement. 'I've been doing some research and I've found this amazing exercise for building trust. It's called a blind circle. We form a circle and each take it in turns to be blindfolded and walk across to the other side.'

'And how does that build trust?' asked Mrs Andrews, looking genuinely confused rather than snippy.

'Well, you have to trust us to stop you from falling off the edge of the stage and keep you going in the right direction. Come on, let's go.'

Without any moaning and groaning the players got up and went to take part. They were nervous and jumpy but worked together well, enjoying the experience.

Lottie sat back feeling satisfied. She'd made up her mind and soon she would have achieved the goal her nan set for her. The one crusade Elsie never managed to win. The theatre would be saved and Lottie had made it happen. She'd never thought she could actually do it. But as usual when something happened with the theatre, she lost Sid, even if it was only for a while. She should have felt confident they'd make up, like they had before, but each time it happened the gap seemed to widen between them. She hadn't even seen him at work, as he'd been in and out of the office so much on some kind of top-secret job.

'Lottie?' called Gregory from the stage. 'Come on, it's your turn.'

Lottie sighed and gingerly got up and climbed onto the stage. The Greenley Players were really bonding this time. And Lottie reassured herself that they deserved this too. They'd put in so much effort and overcome so much, she'd be letting them down if she didn't accept Jeremy's offer.

She eyed the edge of the stage nervously as Gregory tied a blindfold over her eyes. Trust or no, if they let her walk off the edge and crack her head again, no number of banners or balloons would stop her from killing them.

Chapter 39

It was like the first time all over again as Lottie and Jeremy sat in the town hall meeting room. The butterflies in Lottie's stomach were doing some kind of drunken conga and she tipped her head to one side to wish the nerves away. Jeremy gave her a warm smile exuding confidence and she found herself relaxing a little.

Once everyone had taken out their things Lottie cleared her throat. 'Shall we begin?' Everyone nodded. 'As we have an important matter to discuss I thought we'd move straight to that. After donating a substantial sum of money for repairs Jeremy has offered to buy the theatre.'

Sarah gasped in delight. Trevor seemed unsure, and Mayor Cunningham, judging from the puce colour of his face, was outright mad.

Mayor Cunningham ended the silence that was threatening to descend. 'Well, that is a generous offer.' He narrowed his eyes. If Lottie had been casting for a suspicious pig-faced man he would certainly get the part. 'However, the council needs time to consider it. We need to look at exactly what you're offering and review all our options.'

Jeremy nodded. The mayor's tone hadn't bothered him at all. 'I've prepared a small booklet outlining all that information for you.' He handed around a shiny document with brightly coloured graphs inside. 'All the financial information is at the back.'

They all took one and scanned through it. Lottie frowned, and felt a little cold. He hadn't mentioned this before. Looking down, she saw the cover showed little computer-generated people stood outside the shiny theatre smiling and laughing. The exterior was the same but repainted with a big swanky sign, and there were now flower beds out front with pretty pink and purple dots. Some lights had been added into the ground that shone up at the front. There were no children though which Lottie thought odd. And it occurred to her that all the little people looked quite posh.

'If I may?' Jeremy said to Lottie, who nodded and sat down. Jeremy stood and adjusted his tie. 'Let's be honest here, folks, the theatre was in a terrible state. The costs are huge, more than this small committee can really deal with, and I mean no disrespect by that remark. There's only so much time in the day and this is a full-time project.'

He began slowly pacing around the table and Lottie couldn't take her eyes off him. 'As you can see, I have the capital to purchase the theatre and the land it sits on, and am willing to invest to make it a top-notch venue. If we proceed with this, I'm looking at a two-month timescale with a full-time team of builders and decorators to have the theatre refurbished with new, state of the art equipment and facilities in time for the Christmas pantomime.'

Lottie sat in awe. He made it all sound so simple.

'May I ask why?' said Mayor Cunningham, flicking backwards and forwards through the pages of the glossy booklet.

Lottie opened her mouth to speak, to defend him, when Jeremy continued. 'Why?' Jeremy chuckled and subconsciously fiddled with his tie. 'Because I love this town. It really is that simple. I love the theatre and what it's beginning to mean to the community again. I love seeing people coming together like this.'

He was quoting Lottie's words back at her and it made her heart swell with pride. Coming back round to his seat he stood behind it and rested his hands on the back. 'Don't get me wrong, I'm not a charity. Though you can see on page thirty-four I suggest we register as one as soon as possible. I'm a businessman and I think the theatre will make a very profitable business within the next five years. This is an investment for me and ...' He chuckled. 'I'm a pretty shrewd businessman.'

Lottie watched him speak with wide eyes. There was something attractive about a man with that much self-belief. It really was the only way to explain some women's attraction to Simon Cowell.

'Basically,' Jeremy continued, starting to pace the room again, 'I'm proposing that I purchase the theatre and the surrounding land. We'll keep the committee as it is now, maybe with one or two more people and you'll all still have your places, as would I. We'll continue to work together to make it a success. We can look at new revenue streams, like the clubs I'm told Lottie mentioned in her speech at the showcase, and one or two touring shows. The only difference is that my company would own it and not the council.'

His eyes had shot to her when he said her name and she melted a little more. Not only that, he was taking her ideas seriously.

'As the council needs a substantial sum of money to balance this year's deficit, I felt this was a solution that worked for all parties. The community still get a great local theatre, and I get a great property to add to my company's portfolio. It really is a win-win for all concerned.' He glanced at Lottie again, moved to his chair, and sat down. 'I'm happy to take questions. Or we can go through some of the figures if you'd like, but I'm conscious of the time.'

Lottie tried to focus as her mind whirled about. She'd need to read this booklet in more detail later, though on first glance, it was all very promotional and less business-y than she'd expected. 'Thank you, Jeremy, for your ... presentation.'

'Yes, a good presentation indeed,' said Mayor Cunningham. 'Miss Webster, I think you'll agree there is a lot to take in—'

'I don't want to push,' said Jeremy, leaning over the table and Lottie's eyes shot to him. Was this something new too?

'But I really will need an answer soon. I have another property that I'm looking into and the auction date for that is Monday. If this is a no-go, I'll be moving forward with that, so I really need an answer tomorrow.'

Lottie turned to see Mayor Cunningham whose eyes narrowed. 'I'm afraid that won't be possible, Jeremy. This will need to be voted on by the council.'

Jeremy responded as though he'd known that was exactly what the mayor would say. 'From what I understand we can ask for a special meeting, can't we, Roger?'

'How do you know that?' asked Mayor Cunningham. Jeremy shrugged in response, his face placid. 'We can. If you insist.'

'I'm afraid I'll have to.' Jeremy smiled and nodded. 'I'd also request that this offer isn't made public for reasons of commercial sensitivity. You'll see on page eighty-six of the booklet, there's a letter from our solicitors outlining our reasons for this request.'

Mayor Cunningham immediately turned the multitude of pages, trying to find the letter.

Lottie sat watching the exchange, her throat tightening. He hadn't mentioned any of this before. She felt a giant knot in her stomach pressing down. She'd stupidly presumed it would be simple but looking at the document in front of her it seemed anything but. Worst of all, they didn't have much choice but to make a decision quickly.

Thoughts of Sid's warnings threatened to rise up but Lottie pushed them down. It was just that it was all quicker and more official than she'd expected.

Mayor Cunningham studied the booklet one more time. 'As an official offer has been made I have no choice but to call an emergency meeting of the council for tomorrow evening and we'll examine your proposal in more detail and make a decision.'

'Thank you,' Jeremy replied, confidently. He sat back in his chair, his arms wide. 'I'd just like to reassure everyone that the theatre will remain a theatre. I know that's been a concern for some of you. And to you, Roger, I know the responsibility of balancing the books at times of such austerity is hard, almost impossible, one might say. But this is a great opportunity for Greenley.' He looked at Lottie. 'A great opportunity for the theatre and the council. And for us all to really move things forward.'

With nothing else to discuss, Lottie ended the meeting. She kept her eyes down while she packed up her belongings. Her head was spinning. The alarm bells she'd put down to too much wine the other night were ringing again. This time Sid's voice mingled in with them and she felt queasy. Jeremy hung back and waited for Lottie while everyone else left. Putting on his coat he said, 'That went well, don't you think?'

Lottie didn't feel she could completely agree. The lump in her throat told her something wasn't right. 'Your presentation was … impressive.'

He laughed. 'It was, wasn't it? Shall we go for dinner?'

'Umm, no. No thanks. I need to get home and …' She paused. 'Sort through some of Nan's stuff.' She didn't, but she had to try and figure things out.

'Are you alright?' Jeremy looked down at her.

'I just wasn't expecting all this,' she said, turning the document over in her hands.

'Sorry, force of habit, I do it all the time if I'm looking to buy a property.'

'You've obviously put a lot of thought into it.'

He laughed as he spoke and it sounded slightly patronising to Lottie. 'Of course I have, it's a huge sum of money.'

She supposed he was right. This wasn't a hobby to him, it was business.

Jeremy sat down and motioned for Lottie to join him. 'Listen,' he said, taking her hands. 'It's the way things have to be in business. It's nothing to worry about.'

275

'What was all that about "commercial sensitivity"? Why can't we tell people?'

He shook his head. 'I know it seems overly cautious, Lottie, but as I've already invested some money—'

'Donated,' said Lottie.

Jeremy waved his hand dismissing his last statement. 'Yes, donated. Sorry, just a slip of the tongue. I don't want it all becoming public or snippets of misinformation coming out and people thinking you guys on the committee haven't done things properly.'

'Why would they?'

'They might think that as I made a donation before, then upped it after your accident, this was a done deal. That you, as chairman, were in it with me from the start. Especially as we're kind of an item.'

'Kind of?' Lottie removed her hand from his.

'You know what I mean,' he replied, reaching for her again, but she pulled it away. 'Oh, now, come on, it was a silly remark that's all. I'm sorry. Of course we're an item. We couldn't be more of an item.'

Lottie stared at him, deliberately trying to narrow her eyes like Selena did, to show how annoyed she was with him. 'Then why say "kind of"?'

He shook his head. 'I don't know, I was just trying to be funny I suppose.'

Comedy didn't really suit him, thought Lottie. Not like Sid. 'Well, it didn't work.'

'No, it didn't.' He rubbed that back of his neck. 'I love you, Lottie Webster, and I've told that to anyone who'll listen. So we are definitely an item and I am definitely an idiot for saying stupid things.' He reached for her hand again and she let him take it this time.

'And the presentation?' she asked, hoping he would give the same level of assurance over that. 'It just seemed like there was more to this than you buying the theatre and us all running it.'

His thumb stroked her hand. 'I've done it lots of times, Lottie. It really is pretty standard. Please don't worry.'

Lottie searched his eyes for signs of lies but found nothing. As she looked at them she couldn't help but compare them to Sid's then shook her head to chase the thoughts out. 'Okay.'

'Great. There is something else though that I wanted to talk to you about.'

'Yes?' She lifted her hand to her head, pressing her cold fingers down to ease the rising ache.

Jeremy cupped her cheek. 'If this all goes ahead, will you consider being in charge of the theatre?'

Were her ears blocked and making things sound funny, or was it her headache making her hear things? 'In charge of the theatre?'

'It'll need a general manager once it's all up and running and you've done so much, I obviously thought of you.'

'I – I don't know what to say.' She really didn't. Her nan's picture was in her wallet and she wanted to pull it out and shout at it. She wanted to scream and yell and tell her how much her meddling had ruined everything and thrown her life into total chaos.

'Say yes!' Jeremy replied. 'You're wasted on the paper, Lottie. You're a great photographer but look how you've organised the players and the showcase. You could do so much more. I have a talent for spotting potential and you could achieve so much with me.'

Still shouting at her nan in her head she said, 'I need some time to think about it.' Then added, 'I love my job.'

Jeremy nodded. 'I understand. I just thought with your friendship with Sid being over you might like a change? You've said working together is really difficult at the moment. And Sid and Selena seemed very happy when I saw them the other day.'

Was their friendship over? It'd been a tough few months but surely this wasn't it? Did Sid think so? If it was, why stick around at the paper? Perhaps she did need a change. 'I just need to think it through. I wouldn't want people to think I've only been given the job because of you.'

Lottie felt a niggling in her soul. Her old insecurities were starting to push back through, affecting her ability to make decisions, to think clearly, or trust her own judgement. She didn't want to go back to how she'd been, so scared of life. But the ground was shifting beneath her feet so fast she couldn't get her bearings.

'Okay,' said Jeremy. 'Oh, and one last thing.' He cupped the back of her head and drew her towards him for a kiss. 'I love you,' he said when they separated.

Though not normally snarky, Lottie was still angry about the item thing. 'Do you kind of love me, or really love me?'

'Ouch.' He smiled and his hand moved to her cheek. 'I deserved that though. I really love you. When I saw you in the hospital I realised we don't know what life has in store for us and we can't let people go or waste a single second. That's partly what made me want to help the theatre too.'

Lottie's mind was a sea of crazy thoughts swirling around, knocking into each other.

'Do you love me?' asked Jeremy.

Realising she hadn't said it back, Lottie looked into his eyes. She did love Jeremy, didn't she? What wasn't to love? An image of Sid's face flitted across her brain but she ignored it. Of course she loved him. 'Yes. Yes, I do,' she replied more firmly than she'd intended, as if her brain was trying to convince her it was true.

'Good,' he said, planting another kiss on her lips. 'We're going to do great things with the theatre, Lots, you'll see.' He let go and stepped back, bouncing on his heels.

Lottie kept her eyes on the ground. 'Do you mind not calling me Lots? It's just that Sid calls me Lots and I don't—'

'Oh, you don't like it?' he asked, confusion on his face. 'I always assumed you did. Did you want me to tell Sid not to—'

'No, no it's fine,' said Lottie. How could she tell him she only ever wanted Sid to call her Lots? And she wanted, more than anything, to hear it right now.

Lottie packed the booklet into her bag as the skin on the back of her neck prickled. She couldn't shake off this horrible feeling of dread. A heavy weight in her stomach told her something wasn't right and for once it didn't have anything to do with Sidney Evans or his demon girlfriend.

Chapter 40

Sid beeped the horn to let Lottie know he was there. She was normally out of the door before he'd even put the handbrake on, even in the cold, but he'd waited a few minutes and she still hadn't come out. At this rate they would be late. He was writing an article about the panto to get everyone interested and hopefully get some advance bookings so he was off to watch rehearsals with Lottie. He checked his watch again then turned off the engine and climbed out, mounting the steep steps to her house.

When the door opened Sid almost called a doctor. Lottie's eyes were puffy and rimmed with dark circles. She was pale and tired and looked like she hadn't slept. 'What's wrong?' he asked, knowing concern was written all over his face.

She looked down and in barely more than a whisper said, 'You'd better come in.'

Sid went through to the living room, fear growing with each step. If she was pregnant or something he didn't know what he'd do. He'd have to leave town and live at the arse-end of the world on his own.

'What is it, Lottie? God, what's the matter? Do you need anything? You should sit down. Here.' He moved out of the way and pointed at the sofa but Lottie didn't move.

'I need to tell you something.'

'Oh, God, are you ill?' He felt his throat close over. What if she was dying?

She finally looked at him. 'No, Sid, please.'

'Okay.' He ran a hand through his hair and tried to steady his breathing but his heart was beating too fast. 'What is it?'

Lottie met his eye. 'The council has sold the theatre to Jeremy.'

Sid didn't move as coldness froze all his muscles. He should have felt relief that she wasn't engaged or going to have Jeremy's baby but instead he felt his hands ball into fists. 'What? When did this happen?'

'At a special meeting last night.' Her voice wobbled and she began to speak quickly. 'It's not a bad thing, Sid, please believe me. The theatre will be amazing now. We're guaranteeing its future. The council won't have to cut other things thanks to the money it'll receive from the sale, and we can continue on the committee, so it'll still be the same.'

'You've changed your tune,' said Sid. 'You were dead set against anyone buying it when you thought that was Mayor Cunningham's plan, but now it's your boyfriend you're all for it.' Sid couldn't help his bitter tone. Of course Jeremy would save the day when he couldn't.

'That's not fair, Sid,' said Lottie, folding her arms over her chest.

He couldn't believe she'd actually gone and done it and that Jeremy had managed to keep things quiet. 'It's right though, isn't it?' he replied, pinning her with his eyes. The anger and hurt he'd worked so hard to forget erupted. 'How do you know he's not planning to do the same thing as Roger Cunningham? He could sell it on tomorrow and not even stick around for anyone to shake a fist at. He could be back in London before you can say fish and chips.'

'I trust him,' Lottie shouted. 'And anyway ...' Lottie's words trailed away into silence.

'Anyway, what?' How could anything be worse than this?

'He's asked me to be general manager of the theatre, when we get to that stage.'

'Oh, has he now?' Sid scoffed. 'We'd better not put that in the paper, that'll really make people suspicious. Or have you already written your resignation?'

'How dare you, Sid.' Lottie uncrossed her arms bringing them to her sides, her knuckles white. 'Do you really think that would affect my vote?'

He shrugged. 'It might.'

Lottie shook her head at him. 'Well, it hasn't. And how could you even say that? You know me better than anyone.'

'Do I? I'm not so sure anymore, Lottie.'

'Well you did before—'

'Before what? Before Selena? Before Jeremy?' Sid put his hands on his hips. 'Before you became a completely different person. You say I've changed, Lottie, but have you looked in the mirror lately? Your nan wanted you to get out into the world and you did, only to follow Jeremy around instead.'

Lottie's eyes became glassy with tears. 'This is what Nan wanted, Sid. She wanted me to save the theatre. I've considered all the options. I've thought about what'll happen to it if we don't and—'

'Do you think your nan would have wanted you to sell it to a property developer who doesn't even live here all the time? And why do it privately if he's so upstanding and proud of the community? For God's sake, Lottie, you don't even really know him. He's hardly here these days.' How could she not see this was suspicious?

'I do know him,' she said loudly.

Sid threw a hand out at her. 'So what's his favourite colour? Favourite drink? Favourite movie? I could tell you all those things about you, Lottie and you could tell me all those things about me. I mean, have you even seen a business plan?'

She stood still. 'Not exactly. I didn't go to the meeting – it was confidential. But the document Jeremy gave the committee said that there'd be some renovations to get in more seats and we'd look at hosting a couple of touring shows a year. He said about creating a pricing matrix and meeting spaces and things, but they'd all fit around the needs of the community. I don't know if he presented anything different last night,' she added, but all the confidence had gone from her voice now.

Sid recognised the flicker of doubt that crossed Lottie's features. 'So you've no real idea how he's going to make it successful?'

Lottie shook her head. 'He had a special letter from his solicitor in the pack asking for everything to be confidential. Something about commercial sensitivity.'

Sid rolled his eyes. He wanted to clap his hands in front of her face and wake her up like a magician who'd put someone in a trance. 'I can promise you, Lottie, if he runs it as a business he won't make the theatre profitable through the local am dram's twice-yearly productions. It's one thing to give some money to fix the roof or change the carpet but another to buy it and run it as a business with the aim of making as much money as possible. What else is he going to do?'

'I don't know, exactly,' she shouted, then pressed her hand to her forehead. 'He said one or two touring shows around the am dram programme, but as long as the community still gets to use the theatre it can't be bad.'

'You tell yourself that, Lots, if it helps.' Sid tried to control his voice, but it came out as a croak. 'Tell me one thing, Lottie, if you really believe all this then why do you look so terrible. I can see from your eyes you haven't slept.'

She self-consciously tucked a hair behind her ear. 'I just didn't sleep well. I wasn't sure about it at first but I've been through it all in my head – round and round, again and again – and I know he's telling the truth. I know now this is the right thing to do.'

'So you had some doubts?' Sid asked. 'What were they?'

'Oh, I don't know, Sid.' She reached her hand into her hair and scrunched some into her fist. 'I wondered if this was the best thing for the town, I wondered what would happen if we didn't approve his offer and what would happen to the theatre. I wondered what Nan would want or think or do. I've been through it all a hundred times and I really think this is the right answer. Nan would be happy.'

The waver in her voice told him something different. 'You don't sound like you believe that last part.'

'I do and I love him.' She looked up. 'If I don't trust him, I don't love him, do I?'

Sid felt like Lottie had just plunged a knife into his chest. She couldn't have hurt him more if she'd kicked him square in the goolies. 'You love him this much, do you?'

Lottie couldn't meet his gaze but mumbled, 'Yes.'

Suddenly, Sid couldn't stand to be there anymore. Looking at Lottie was breaking his heart. She'd been all he'd ever wanted and now she was saying those special words about someone else and possibly leaving the paper. If she quit that too he'd never see her. The last thing that had tied them together would be broken and without it they'd completely drift apart. His heart had been bruised and pummelled over the last year and now it was worn out and crushed. He had to leave, had to get out, and pushed past her as he headed for the door.

Lottie reached out and tried to catch his arm but he wrenched it away. 'Sid, please just wait a minute and let me explain better.' As the door swung shut behind him, he could hear her shouting his name.

Outside Sid gulped in the cold, fresh air before he got in his car and drove, not knowing where. The pressure built in his lungs and he wanted to shout and scream. Sid turned the corner and headed for the motorway. He had the address of Jeremy's office in London but his telephone enquiries hadn't given him anything, and he hadn't had the chance to visit in person. He had to figure out what Jeremy's real motive was. He never really seemed interested in Lottie or in making her happy. And now secretly buying the theatre. Sid had to do something. He wouldn't let Jeremy break her heart though it might be too late for that.

There was definitely more to this than just wanting to support the community. It was too much money and had been done too quickly. Jeremy's vague ideas and assurances weren't enough for Sid, and the council wouldn't care – they'd take the money and run. Sid's instincts were shouting it at him. He pressed the accelerator. Maybe he'd been looking in the wrong place and the answers he was searching for were in London, not in Greenley.

Chapter 41

'Oh, Nan,' said Lottie, brushing grass from the base of the head-stone. 'What have I done? What on earth am I going to do?' She stared unseeing at her nan's name and tried in vain to keep the tears welling in her eyes from running down her face.

The sky was dark and rain clouds gathered above. A cold wind cut round the fallen old gravestones and whipped through the churchyard blowing Lottie's hair all over her face. It rustled the falling leaves blowing them to and fro on the ground and the air was heavy with decay. Lottie pulled the collar of her coat closer and hoped once more for some divine intervention. Lost in her own thoughts she could no longer imagine what her nan would have said to help, had she been alive.

From the church, positioned as it was at the top of a hill, she could see the sea, a vast expanse of grey that crashed wildly with the rising wind. She knew she had to leave soon from the pink-ness of her fingers and the numbness of her toes, but couldn't bring herself to go home to an empty house and her mess of a life.

'Come on, Nan,' she said out loud, wiping her tears with the heel of her hand. 'Can't you come down and give me one last piece of advice?' She gathered the dying remains of the last bunch of flowers she'd laid two weeks before. 'I'm sure you're having a lovely time in heaven but I could really use your help right now.'

'The first thing your nan would say, dear, would be to go home and have a nice cup of tea to warm up,' said Gregory from behind her.

Lottie turned to see his kindly face. 'What are you doing here?'

He pulled his collar up against the wind. 'When you didn't show for the rehearsal I thought something must be wrong so I went to your house but there was no answer. Then I thought I'd pop in here. What are you doing sitting on the ground getting a wet bum? And why, my darling girl, have you been crying?' Gregory helped her up and engulfed her in a hug.

Lottie snivelled. 'It's all such a mess.'

'What is, dear?'

She held him tightly overwhelmed by the comfort. 'Everything. Everything's got so muddled and messy, and I've no idea who I am anymore, or what I'm supposed to do, and I miss Nan so much and—'

'Oh, shush, now, sweetheart.' Gregory patted her back.

'What am I going to do about Jeremy?' she asked, moving back and pulling her coat sleeves into her hands.

'You mean handsome, delectable Jeremy? What about him?'

Lottie snivelled and nodded. 'He told me he loves me and he wants me to run the theatre.'

'And how does that make you feel?'

She thought for a moment before erupting again in a huge sob. 'Heartbroken.'

Gregory chuckled. 'Well, it's not supposed to make you feel like that, is it? When a gorgeous man proclaims his love you're supposed to be pleased.'

'I know,' said Lottie, standing back and wiping her eyes. 'I don't know why I'm not.'

'Are you sure you don't?'

'It's because I'd miss Sid, and I like my job. I don't want to run a theatre and—'

'I see,' said Gregory.

'See what?' Lottie wiped her face again, her fingers like ice.

Gregory smiled. 'How long have you and Sid known each other?'

'Forever,' replied Lottie. 'Why?'

'And how long has he been your best friend?'

Lottie had no idea where this was going. 'Ages. Since school.'

'Mm-hmm,' agreed Gregory. 'And how long have you been in love with him?'

'What?' Lottie paused. It was like Gregory had just hit her on the head.

Gregory laughed and pulled a hip flask from his coat pocket and took a sip. 'Come on, darling. It's clear to see that you're jealous as hell of Selena and not because Sid's your friend. I've seen the way you've been looking at him recently, since madam came on the scene. And he's always been in love with you. It happened to me once, I'd been friends with this guy for ages when …'

Gregory kept talking but Lottie had stopped listening. Sid? Love? Like hero–heroine stuff? She opened her mouth but her words were taken on the wind and she stood motionless.

'Don't tell Cecil though, he doesn't know about—'

'I love Sid,' she said, still staring wide eyed at Gregory. The words felt right on her tongue and her heart beat so fast it warmed her soul.

Gregory gave a loud laugh and threw his head back. 'I know, dear. We all do. Try and close your mouth, love, you're looking a bit demented.'

Lottie frowned. 'What do you mean you all know?'

'Oh, for goodness' sake, child. Your nan knew. Everyone in the town knows that you and Sid have been in love with each other for years. You just slipped into the "friendship zone".' He took

288

another sip from his hip flask and offered it to Lottie who had a swig too.

'Friendship zone? Have you been reading *Cosmopolitan* again, Gregory?'

'If one of you had just been brave enough to actually tell the other how you felt you could have been at it years ago.'

'Gregory!' Lottie blushed then wagged her finger as she told him off. 'That's it, you're not reading glossy magazines anymore.'

'The trouble is that you always took it for granted you'd have each other so didn't do anything about it. It was only once one of you got the eye from someone else you realised how you truly felt. You were happy taking the coward's way out and keeping the status quo – a band I rather enjoyed by the way – rather than being brave. It's entirely your own fault.'

'I know,' said Lottie, in a small voice. Gregory was right and now he'd said it all the pieces of Lottie's heart suddenly fitted together perfectly. She felt whole again. The cold autumn rain hit her skin as she stared at the ground. 'But what do I do now?'

'First of all, we go home and get out of this dismal weather, and then you have to pluck up the courage to tell him how you feel.'

'Yes,' agreed Lottie, the strong voice she'd grown accustomed to returning. 'Yes. I have to tell him. And Jeremy. I have to tell Jeremy it's over.'

The self-doubt that had been wrapping itself around her fell away. She'd convinced herself she'd loved Jeremy but she didn't really. It had always been Sid, she just hadn't realised it until now. Gregory watched her, his bright white teeth gleaming at her as he smiled.

'Come on, Lottie Webster. Time for you to be the brave one.'

Chapter 42

It took a week for Sid to find what he was looking for but when it came it lacked any sort of satisfaction. After waiting for what seemed like hours in the pouring rain, Sid watched Lottie come home, trudge up the steps to her house and reach into her bag for the keys. 'Lottie?' he said, coming out from behind a tree.

She turned.

'Listen, I need to talk to you.' He tightened his grip on the papers in his hands, shielding them from the rain running off his head.

'I've been looking for you,' she replied, her voice anxious.

His heart gave a double beat. 'Have you?'

'Yes, I was worried. Where've you been all week?'

He'd thought she'd be too angry to care where he was so her concern surprised him. But if she wasn't angry now, she would be soon. This had to be done. 'I've been working on something. Something I need to talk to you about.'

She kept her eyes on him as she climbed the steps and unlocked the door. 'You'd better come in then.'

Lottie walked into the living room, switched on the light, and dumped her bag down on the sofa. 'Do you want a cup of tea?' she asked, avoiding his gaze.

He brushed his hair down and shook the raindrops from his hand, then took off his jacket and dropped it onto the sofa. 'No, thanks. I need to talk to you about something.'

'Okay.' Lottie sighed. 'Do you want to sit down?'

Lottie moved to the sofa and Sid sat down next to her. His leg pressed against hers and a powerful electric shock ran through him as though someone had wired him up to a battery. Lottie didn't move away and he breathed slowly trying to bring his racing heart back down.

'You're all wet,' she said, and her arm moved slightly as if she wanted to reach out and touch him. For a moment Sid couldn't breathe. He didn't understand what was happening and the possibility that Lottie had forgiven him made what he was about to do all the more painful. 'Is everything okay?' she asked eventually.

'Lottie, I'm sorry to have to do this, but, I've discovered something about Jeremy.'

She raised her eyebrows.

'I've been doing some digging into his company and this whole theatre business and—'

'And let me guess, it's all a money laundering front for the Italian mafia?'

He couldn't tell from her tone if she was joking or not. 'No, Lottie, please, this is serious. I think he's planning on flipping the theatre.'

Lottie's eyes were steady and unmoving on his face but her chin quivered. 'How do you know?'

'I've been looking into his portfolio and I went up to his offices to do some digging.' She looked surprised but not as devastated as he'd expected.

'That's very journalistic of you.' This time she was definitely teasing which was even scarier. He'd been sure she was going to rip his head off.

'I found out that he's done this before,' Sid continued. 'He did the very same thing with a theatre up north.'

Sid unrolled the papers in his hands to reveal proofs of newspaper articles. 'He took over a theatre in Leeds when it was a dilapidated mess but rather than turn it into houses he made it a profitable business and as soon as it was making some money he sold it off to one of the big theatre companies from London. With some extra zeros on the price tag, of course. He made himself a small fortune.'

Lottie took the papers from his hands and read through the articles. '"Stole from the community". "Took the heart of the town".' Lottie's eyes filled with tears. 'But is it still a theatre?'

Sid sighed. Was she still going to try and justify Jeremy's actions, even though she might lose the theatre, the players – everything? 'It is but the community aren't allowed to use it anymore.'

She turned the pages over in her hands and looked up. 'How did you get this?'

'This wasn't easy to find. The articles had been pulled by the papers. They were threatened with legal proceedings if they printed anything. I had to call in some favours to get these proofs but a few old journalist friends of mine had heard whispers. I'm guessing because of the negative reaction he's never made a big deal out of it.'

Lottie shook her head in disbelief.

Sid wondered when the tears would fall. He'd brought tissues with him, determined to help ease the pain and be there for her. 'No one local gets to use the theatre anymore, Lottie. The new company says there isn't capacity. When it was renovated they added in extra seats. Apparently, you have to have a certain number to get the really big touring shows from London. Do you know if he's—'

'He said that after the panto we could reconfigure and get a thousand seats in.'

'That's the magic number,' said Sid.

Lottie was looking between the pages he'd brought and Sid's

face. He was still surprised she wasn't crying or trying to tear his limbs off.

'But what about the community?' she asked eventually.

Sid shook his head. 'It's not one or two touring shows like he said, it's all touring shows with expensive tickets. The locals are priced out of the market. The programme is designed for the rich and well-off. Tickets are so expensive most people can't afford them – not even for the Christmas panto. The am dram group have gone, they weren't allowed to perform there anymore. No youth groups – nothing.'

'I can't believe it,' said Lottie.'

'He's even had some councillors up to his offices in London. Probably schmoozing them to make sure the sale goes through.'

Lottie gasped then dropped her eyes. 'So I guess I was never going to be general manager then?'

Sid placed a hand on her shoulder. 'I don't think so, Lottie. I'm sorry. This must be hard. I know you were in love with him.'

'Was I?' she asked, staring at him and he pulled back at her response. She'd been so sure last week that she was. 'I suppose I was to begin with. But he's used me, hasn't he? And I'm an idiot for believing everything he's said. I kept burying my doubts, pretending everything was fine. And then before I knew it, it was too late to stop it without looking like a fool.'

Sid leaned in to her. 'You're not an idiot, Lottie. Or a fool. He's a complete—'

She turned and her face was so impossibly close to his. He could feel her breath on his cheek. Her mouth had opened slightly to speak and their lips were almost touching. Remembering Selena, Sid pulled back and Lottie looked away. A loud knock on the front door separated them.

'It must be Jeremy,' said Lottie. 'He was late leaving because of another business meeting.'

'What do you want to do?' asked Sid, taking the papers from

her and as their fingers touched he felt the same bolt of shock.

She didn't look scared. She looked determined and Sid realised that Elsie had been right to make Lottie change. He still wasn't sure about himself though. 'Will you stay and speak to him with me?'

Sid smiled. 'Of course I will.'

Lottie stood up and went to the front door. She took a deep breath and opened it.

'Hello, honey,' said Jeremy, sweeping her into his arms. 'Oh, I've missed you so much. Oh, hello Sid. Nice to see you.'

Lottie backed away. 'Jeremy, there's something I'd like to talk to you about.'

'Really, what's that?' He closed the door, took off his long, exquisitely tailored coat and tossed it over the sofa.

Lottie pulled her shoulders back and stood taller. 'It's about the theatre in Leeds you purchased and sold off two years ago.'

Jeremy's shoulders stiffened but his voice remained calm. 'What is it you'd like to know, honey?'

'Please stop calling me "honey".' Lottie's cheeks flamed and there was a fire in her eyes Sid had only ever seen when she was shouting at him. 'I want to know why you sold it off and if you're planning on doing the same to our theatre?'

'Honey, calm down. I'll do everything in my power to make sure that doesn't happen. How did you get this information—'

'Stop calling me "honey",' shouted Lottie. 'It's patronising. Do you think I'm an idiot, Jeremy? Did you think I was so madly in love with you, I'd let you tear the heart out of this town? This is my home. You knew how much this meant to me. To my nan.'

Jeremy gaped like a trapped animal. For a moment his eyes were wide in shock then a glimmer of the cold businessman passed over him. 'It was a business matter, Lottie. Each case has to be dealt with individually. Sometimes the market changes, the value of the pound drops, the cost of materials goes up, and you just have to deal with it. With that property it was the right thing to do.'

'And what about our theatre? What happens if the same situation occurs?'

He shook his head. 'I don't think it will.'

'But what if it does?'

Jeremy shrugged. 'Then I would have to make the right decision for my business.'

Lottie glanced at Sid then back to Jeremy. 'Your business? So you would sell it on?'

'If I had to, yes.' For the first time he was raising his voice and it had a cold hard edge, then it dropped when he saw Lottie's face. 'But I'm going to do everything I can to make sure that doesn't happen.'

Sid stepped forwards. 'Have you got a buyer lined up already?'

Jeremy looked down his nose. 'I have not.'

'I think you're lying there, mate,' said Sid. With Lottie's eyes on him he felt for the first time like Jeremy's equal. 'When I went to your offices I discovered you've been having some meetings with the larger theatre companies. My source said it was about a new property you were bringing into the portfolio, and you'd had lots of shiny presentation documents made up. They wouldn't give me one, told me it was more than their job was worth, but it was in a little seaside town in the back of beyond that was becoming a real commuter spot. Sound familiar?'

Jeremy made no reply, just took a long stride towards Sid. Sid wasn't normally one for fisticuffs but he would to defend Lottie and squared his shoulders.

'It's true, isn't it?' said Lottie.

Jeremy's head dropped and he moved towards her. 'I've made some enquiries, Lottie. That's all. Just in case the situation changes. Nothing is concrete. I have to be prepared for all eventualities.'

Her whole demeanour changed and now, and mixed with her anger was a touch of indignation. 'How could you?'

'I'm a businessman, Lottie, first and foremost. I need to have all the bases covered.'

'First and foremost?' she echoed, derisively. 'And what about Sid's source? They seemed sure it was all go.'

'Well, they're lying.' He looked at Sid. 'Who was it? Rebecca, the silly tart on reception?'

'I'm not saying,' replied Sid, lifting his chin in defiance. 'But they were quite sure your plans were to sell as soon as, and they were quoting you – "as soon as commercially viable".'

'Isn't this all a bit beyond your scope, Sid?' said Jeremy rounding on him. 'You should stick to small local matters. Isn't there a lost toy somewhere you can report on? Lottie, come on. Who are you going to believe? Me or this wannabe reporter who's clearly jealous of how your life's moving on and his isn't?'

Sid was just about to step forward and thump him when Lottie turned to him, then back to Jeremy. The rest of his life hung on this moment, on Lottie's reaction. His heart beat faster than it ever had before and he felt slightly dizzy.

Jeremy stared at her with a confident gaze and a smug smile.

'I think you should leave, Jeremy,' said Lottie, moving to Sid's side.

'Lottie?' he replied. His wide eyes illustrating his shock.

Lottie marched to the front door and opened it, pointing to the cold dark night outside. 'Get out. Or I'll find something from the kitchen to use as a torture device. I think I've got a melon baller somewhere.'

Jeremy gave a derisive snort, grabbed his coat and edged around Sid. 'You'll be hearing from my solicitors. This is slander.'

'It's not if it's true,' shouted Sid as Lottie closed the door and leaned against it, breathing heavily.

Sid scratched his head and exhaled a long deep breath. 'That was pretty cool, Lots. I thought you might need me to step in but that was amazing. You don't really have a melon baller, do you?'

'I don't think so.' Lottie smiled and instantly her mouth dropped open and fear gripped her face. 'Oh, Sid. What the hell do we do now? I've made such a huge mistake. The solicitors have already started the paperwork.'

Sid rushed towards her and put a hand on her shoulder. 'We do whatever we can to stop the sale.' He reached into his pocket for his mobile phone to see seven missed calls from Selena and his mind flew back to the way Lottie had looked at him this evening, and to the bolt of lightning that had hit him. Could Lottie have felt it as well? Inspired by her bravery he realised now that he'd made a huge mistake too.

Chapter 43

Sid waited impatiently for Selena to finish work and come and see him. He walked in circles around his living room, periodically glancing out of the window. He'd never felt so nervous, or to be honest, scared over what he was about to do. Every nerve in his body was prickling and every sensation heightened waiting for what was to come. It was the fight or flight response but he wasn't really prepared for either.

Sid stopped and took a breath trying to keep himself calm. Looking around his flat he suddenly noticed that his stuff was slowly being hidden by Selena's possessions. His video games that had always sat in the fireplace were now in a box in a cupboard. And whereas before his shelves had been loaded with *Star Wars* Lego figures that Lottie had bought him over the years, these were now at the back behind pictures of Selena with her friends, or weird ornaments of cats. He shook his head. How had he not noticed this while it was actually happening?

Nervous energy shouted at him to move and he circled the living room once more. As he passed the window again Sid saw Selena strutting down the street. His breathing quickened and he thought he might be sick. He'd never done this before and he was pretty sure Selena wasn't going to take the news well. She let herself in using the key he'd given her.

'Hi, honey,' she said as she waltzed into the living room. Sid desperately tried to remember the lines he had been rehearsing all day. She dropped her bag onto the floor and flopped down onto the sofa, kicking off her shoes.

'What a day,' she said, lying out and stretching her long legs, encased in tight black trousers. 'I haven't stopped. I'm absolutely starving. Are you doing dinner soon? I've still got to go to the gym so I don't want to eat before that, but I'll need a snack, could you get me some crackers and cheese?'

For the first time, Sid noticed that she wasn't looking at him as she spoke. He hadn't even answered her and she was beginning to speak again. 'So, I had this woman in today for a mani-pedi and you should have seen her feet. I mean, talk about yuck! There's no way I'd let my feet get like that – all gnarly and gross. I told her you have to look after yourself. You can't go letting yourself go. It starts with the feet but then before you know it you've got hairy—'

'Selena,' said Sid, moving towards her. 'We need to talk.'

Still lying on the sofa Selena tilted her head back towards him. 'What's the matter?' she asked, only a hint of concern in her voice.

Sid felt his heart race again and his legs twitch as if his brain was telling him flight was going to be the best option in about three seconds' time. He tried again to remember the little speech he'd prepared to do this nicely, gently, kindly. He'd even searched on the internet for advice on what to say.

'I'm really sorry, Selena,' he said, his body jittery as the words came out. 'But I don't think this is working out anymore. I think we should split up.'

Before he'd finished pronouncing the last word Selena had spun around and jumped up off the sofa. Her hands were on her hips and her jaw was set. Her chest heaved with the effort of taking deep breaths. 'Split up?' she said angrily. 'You're breaking up with me?'

The terror he'd expected to feel once the words were said never arrived and in its place was a strong feeling of relief at having done the right thing. He felt his neck and shoulders relax. It was done. 'I just think it's for the best,' he said calmly.

Selena glanced around the flat and her eyes rested on the Victorian fireplace before her face and tone softened. 'I can't believe you're actually saying this, Sid. Why? I don't understand. Haven't we been having fun? I thought we were getting more serious, not heading towards a break-up.'

Sid watched as, with effort, Selena brought tears to her eyes. She murmured, 'Don't you love me anymore?'

What a fool he'd been. He hadn't realised how manipulative she was and was almost overwhelmed by embarrassment. It was the things he gave her rather than him she was actually afraid of losing and looking back he could see a million and one times that had been demonstrated. 'I'm sorry, Selena. I don't think we're really suited.'

'How can you say that?' She edged towards him but Sid shook his head.

Remembering the words he'd said to Lottie about Jeremy and not knowing his favourite colour, drink or movie, he realised that, though he might know Selena's, there was no way she knew his. He kept his voice strong to show he'd made up his mind. 'I know this is hard and I'm really sorry, but like said, I just don't think we're meant to be together.'

Selena studied his face for a second then the tears magically evaporated and her face hardened. Her hands rested on her hips. She must have realised there was no hesitation in his eyes and that he wouldn't be persuaded otherwise. 'Let me guess your next line. Is it, "It's not you, it's me"? Well guess what, Sid? You're damn right it's you. Do you know how lucky you are to have me? I mean let's face it, you're not exactly Chris Hemsworth, are you?'

Just like on the stage, the curtains had opened, but Sid wasn't seeing an actor now, he was seeing the real Selena. How could he have thought it was Lottie always taking things the wrong way? There was a hard edge to Selena that he'd always been blind to. It was his fault, he knew that. He'd wanted to be blind. He'd needed to feel that someone loved him and was so desperate to get over his feelings for Lottie that when Selena had come into his life he'd wanted to prove to himself. Christ, he was an absolute idiot.

Selena was still watching him, pinned to the spot. Her head was beginning to do the wiggly thing it had done at the hotel. 'You'll regret this, Sid Evans. And when you do, don't come crawling back to me because there's no way I'll be taking you back.'

She spat the words at Sid but the relief in his system acted like a shield keeping him calm against her vitriol. All he wanted now was for her to go. 'I'm really sorry, Selena. I didn't mean to mislead you, I just think this is for the best. If you want I can pack up your things and drop them to your parents' house?'

Selena huffed and shook her head, her long brown hair swishing around her shoulders. 'You'd better,' she said, then reached down to get her bag before she stomped past him to the front door.

After she'd slammed the door with such force the windows almost shook, Sid went and sat down on the sofa. A serene calmness washed over him and every muscle relaxed. It was done now. And as nothing had been smashed or thrown at him as he'd imagined it would, he considered it a success. He'd never broken up with anyone before because he'd never had anyone to break up with, and though tinged with guilt for getting himself into this mess in the first place he couldn't help but feel relief. He genuinely hadn't meant to deceive Selena. He'd given it everything he could and now that flicker of hope of being with Lottie had been rekindled, he knew he had to try just one more time to win her heart.

All he had to do now was pluck up the courage to tell Lottie how he felt.

Someone pushed a flyer through his letter box and Sid almost touched the ceiling as he jumped in panic, thinking it was Selena come back to punch him in the face. He glanced at the kitchen and smiled at what Lottie had said to Jeremy. At least he didn't own a melon baller … Selena wouldn't have hesitated to use it.

Chapter 44

'Gregory, you're supposed to look tanned, not like you've been dunked in creosote,' said Mrs Andrews. Gregory was, at that moment, applying a liberal amount of instant bronzer to become Jafar, the evil advisor.

'Really, darling,' replied Gregory. 'What you don't realise from your limited experience, is that you have to go a little overboard for the stage. The lights demand it. Strong lighting requires strong make-up, it really is the first thing you learn on the West End.'

Mrs Andrews flung her hands in the air and stalked off.

'Right, everyone,' shouted Conner from the centre of the stage. 'Lee, Sarah, can you get ready? You're up first.'

'I have to say,' said Mrs Andrews, sidling up to Lottie and speaking quietly in her ear. 'Conner really seems to have got to grips with things this time.'

Lottie smiled in Conner's direction. 'I knew he had it in him.'

The first dress rehearsal for *Aladdin* was in full swing. Since that night with Sid, Lottie had frantically called the committee and explained everything Sid had learned. Mayor Cunningham had responded with, 'I feared something like this would happen,' but had uncharacteristically spared Lottie any further lecture. Probably because even he couldn't fail to hear the shame and

303

humility in her voice. The sale was stopped pending further investigation and Lottie was confident that, given Sid's evidence, everything would be called off.

And to think she'd planned on breaking up with Jeremy that night. She couldn't – wouldn't do it over the phone. That was cowardly. But then Sid had turned up and he'd saved her again.

A heavy rain battered the roof and the wind whistled round the houses shaking the early hung Christmas lights to and fro. Mrs Andrews had instructed the housekeeper to bring another picnic and the poor tiny woman had gone back and forth in the rain lugging in huge picnic baskets and laying out their contents on the stage, before disappearing off again.

Small white porcelain cups were stacked next to three large, old-fashioned soup tureens full of steaming hot soup. Sprigs of holly decorated the platters of bread rolls with pots of elegantly curled butter alongside. Lottie stared at the stage wondering how many people Mrs Andrews employed to do it all.

'We never got all this in the old group, I can assure you,' said Cecil, before he scurried away when he saw Mrs Andrews approaching.

'Penny for your thoughts,' Mrs Andrews said to Lottie.

'I was just wondering how they manage to get the butter into these little curls,' Lottie replied, pointing to one.

'Oh, for goodness' sake.' Mrs Andrews turned on her heel and walked off.

'I was wondering the same thing,' said Sid. 'What do you think then?' he asked holding up the paper. The headline read, 'Lottie Webster Saves the Day'.

Lottie pretended she was cross. 'You shouldn't have given me all the credit.'

'I mention me a bit. What did I say again? Oh yes, here it is, "the key pieces of evidence uncovered by", blah, blah, blah. But it was you who told him where to get off. That was very brave.'

'Hmmm,' said Lottie, unconvinced. Looking into Sid's face was like looking at a new person. She finally saw the man he'd become rather than the boy she'd always known. His strong hands gripped the paper and she wondered what they'd feel like cupping her face or pulling her close. As her cheeks burned, she turned and stirred a thick dark liquid in one of the tureens that wouldn't have looked out of place in a witch's cauldron. 'What do you think this green one is?'

'It's kale, spinach and courgette,' said Sid.

'Sounds hideous.' Lottie opted for the reddish one, hoping it was tomato.

'I wanted to tell you—' said Sid just as Conner interrupted.

'Shall we begin, Lottie?' he asked. 'We're all ready.'

Lottie smiled at Sid and gave him a wink. She took a deep breath and moved onto the stage. 'Yes, let's start. As you know, the town is now aware of the rather unscrupulous behaviour of Jeremy Bell—'

'Och, he took us all in, dear,' said Debbie. 'Don't you be embarrassed now.'

'I wasn't going to be, Debbie, but I am now, thank you. Anyway, we need to decide how we move forwards. Obviously we need to continue to raise funds for the theatre and we've only got two weeks till we open the show. Any ideas for fundraising activities? A Christmas fair maybe?'

Everyone began to talk and chatter until Mrs Andrews dramatically strode onto the stage next to Lottie. She pushed back her long blonde curls. 'My husband has said he would like to donate five thousand pounds towards the theatre as it has given me such a new lease of life.'

Lottie gasped. 'Wow, Mrs Andrews, that's incredibly generous. Are you sure?'

Everyone stared at Mrs Andrews, who loved the attention. 'Yes, absolutely. Reginald thinks this is the best thing to happen to Greenley for a long time.'

'Well, thank you, Mrs Andrews. We'll be sure to mention it in all of the programmes.'

'And on each night of the performance,' Mrs Andrews added.

Lottie repressed a smile. 'Yes, of course. Well, if any of you have any other ideas, do let me know. Shall we begin the rehearsal?'

The players began to move around taking their spots on the stage or grabbing a seat and reading their scripts. Lottie grabbed a bread roll and sat down in the front row next to Sid. 'That wasn't as bad as I thought it was going to be. I thought everyone would tear me off a strip for being so stupid.'

'You weren't that stupid,' he replied. 'I've seen you be stupider.'

Lottie dug her elbow into his ribs. 'I don't think that's even a word.'

'I think you underestimate how much everyone cares about you, Lottie.'

Lottie didn't respond, she simply nodded at her roll.

Sid shuffled forwards and perched on the edge of his seat. 'Listen, there's something I've been meaning to tell you.'

'Yes?' Lottie gripped her roll. Was he about to tell her how much he loved her? Could this be the moment?

'It's about Selena.'

'What about her?' Lottie tried to stop her voice going all squeaky, but failed. If they were moving in together or getting married she was going to scream.

'We've split up.'

'What?' Lottie spun to look at him and nearly fell out of her chair, spilling soup in her lap.

Sid steadied her and said, 'We split up just after you confronted Jeremy.'

'Oh, right. I'm sorry.' Lottie bit her lip trying to stop a smile forcing its way out.

'No you're not,' he teased. 'You never liked her. And I can see why. I never noticed how she spoke to people. It always sounded different in my ears.'

'Are you okay about it?' She tried to be sympathetic but it was difficult as her heart was about to burst open and spray glitter everywhere.

'Yeah, I am actually.' He shrugged. 'We weren't really suited. She was quite high maintenance.'

'How did she take it?' Lottie asked, scanning his face. 'You don't have any scars, so I'm guessing okay?'

Sid nodded. 'Better than I thought, actually. I dropped all her stuff back to her parents' house yesterday.'

'That must have been awkward.'

'It wasn't too bad. I think they must be used to her. Her dad just took the box and said thanks. I thought he was going to tell me off but he didn't seem bothered.'

Right at that moment, Lottie wanted to tell Sid how she felt. To take his hand and kiss him. But Conner came over and whisked him away to discuss something. He kept looking over his shoulder at her and she had to fight the urge to sing and dance, and grab Cecil's top hat and cane to celebrate. He wasn't with Selena anymore, so all she had to do now was wait for the right moment.

Chapter 45

On opening night, Lottie stood centre stage under the spotlights, ecstatic and happy. She'd grown to love the theatre as much as her nan had and when she looked out at all she had accomplished, at the people she had brought together, and what this theatre now meant to the town, she couldn't believe she'd actually done it.

It had been almost a year since her nan had died and Lottie had feared this time of year most. She was scared of being alone but as she looked around her, she was far from alone. She now had friends and Sid was back in her life. She hadn't known how she'd make it through Christmas before but now she would. It would be painful but she knew she could do it. Gregory and Cecil had invited her, Sarah and Sid to join them on Christmas day and she'd been overwhelmed by their kindness. Had Elsie really known what would happen as a result of her letter? Lottie thought she probably had, the scheming old dear.

'Off the stage now, Miss Webster, please,' shouted one of Conner's friends. 'People will be arriving soon and we need to close the curtains.'

'Of course.' Lottie moved into the wings.

'Ready?' asked Sid, who had been fiddling with the collar of his new shirt. He looked handsome in his suit even though he fidgeted constantly.

'Yep, ready. I think we're going to do much better this time.' Lottie adjusted his wonky tie.

'Well, they couldn't do much worse. Come on, you should be at the front greeting people.'

Lottie smoothed down the skirt of her black prom dress and began to walk away.

'Aren't you going to ask me if you look nice?' Sid called after her. She turned and swished her skirt.

'No, I don't need to. I know I do.' She saw him smile before she carried on.

As the audience arrived she welcomed them with a feeling of warmth and helped them to their seats, listening to their appreciative comments. When the doors closed she joined Sid in the front row for the performance, excited more than nervous.

As the first scene started to a flourish of music, Lottie couldn't help but smile. Conner's smoke and mirrors tricks worked wonders and the magic carpet actually flew. Gregory was indeed a very strange colour up close but under the lights, it seemed to work. Sarah made a beautiful Princess Jasmine, though Lottie noticed the kiss between her and Lee, who was playing Aladdin, was slightly more passionate than originally planned. The risqué jokes necessary to every pantomime drew huge laughs from the audience and everyone joined in the singing and the obligatory booing at the bad guys. At the end, as the curtains closed, the audience gave a standing ovation.

Lottie joined in but was surprised when the claps became chants of 'Lottie, Lottie, Lottie'.

'They want you to give a speech,' said Sid, pulling her out of her seat.

Lottie's heart was about to make a run for it. 'I can't, I haven't prepared anything.'

'Just make it up as you go and make sure you say thank you.'

He pushed her onto the bottom step, and she made her way up to the stage.

Standing under the spotlight was blinding and very hot. A stagehand moved the light so she was properly lit and she pushed her hair back from her face. Children, parents, grandparents, everyone had gathered and enjoyed the production. A sea of happy faces looked back at her.

She took a deep breath. 'Thank you, everybody, for coming to the opening night of our Christmas pantomime. I hope that you've all enjoyed yourselves this evening.'

The audience clapped and whistled in response.

'Firstly, I'd like to thank the Greenley Players for their hard work.' She heard a muffled squawk from backstage. 'And of course, I must thank Mr and Mrs Andrews for their kind contribution. I'm pleased to say that the sale of the theatre to that dishonourable skunk Jeremy Bell has now been stopped.'

In the spirit of the pantomime his name was met with hisses and loud boos.

Lottie smiled. 'But most of all, I want to thank you for the support you've given the theatre.' She felt a tightening in her throat and tears came to her eyes. She clasped her hands in front of her. 'It's thanks to your continued support, through good and bad times, that we were able to keep going. Your encouragement when things got rough, the time and money you've given are what's enabled us to sit here tonight. And I know we have a way to go yet but we will get there, I know we will. Together.'

A tear ran down her cheek and as she paused to wipe it away, a voice from the crowd, that sounded remarkably like Sid's, said, 'Elsie would be proud.' The words carried on the air and soon a new chant echoed around the room.

Lottie's hands flew to her mouth to stifle the sobs as the crowd sang, 'Elsie' over and over again. Tears ran free down her cheeks and she laughed.

The Greenley Players emerged from behind the curtain and joined in the chant, embracing Lottie as they passed.

'Three cheers for our darling, Lottie Webster,' shouted Gregory. 'Hip hip?'

'Hooray!'

'Hip hip?'

This time the crowd joined in. 'Hooray!'

'Hip hip?'

The final response was loudest of all. 'Hooray!'

Lottie wiped her eyes, giggled, and waved before making her way backstage.

'I can't believe it,' said Lottie. 'I can't believe it. Was that your doing?' she asked Sid, who had raced round to meet her. She felt filled to the brim with joy and love.

'I don't know what you're talking about.'

'Yes, you do, liar. Now I'm all blotchy from crying,' said Lottie, taking the tissue Sid offered. He stepped forwards and cupped her face. Her heart raced and every nerve in her body tingled.

'You always look beautiful, whether you're blotchy and wearing a posh dress or that manky old jumper you bring out every winter.'

Lottie looked into the face she had seen a thousand times before, at his grinning, geeky smile, at his fluffy and dishevelled hair and she knew it was the right time. Taking a deep breath, she closed her eyes and said, 'Sidney Evans, I love you.'

The world was suddenly silent and still and all Lottie could hear was the beating of her heart. When she opened her eyes, Sid's face was a mixture of fear and affection then he grinned. 'I love you too, Lottie Webster.'

Lottie's heart felt so light it might float away. 'Really?'

'Really.'

She lifted her face towards his. 'I was hoping you'd say that.' And he leaned in and kissed her.

Acknowledgements

I'm so excited to be writing my first Acknowledgement! I'm making extensive notes to make sure I don't leave anyone out!

I owe a huge thank you to the HQ Digital team for giving me this chance and who have made this exciting journey so wonderful for me. Everyone has been just absolutely brilliant to work with and this book wouldn't be anywhere near as good if it wasn't for their help in shaping my story into the one you'll actually be reading.

Of course I need to thank my online writing group, Scribophile, for helping me grow in confidence as a writer and learn so much.

And finally, I must thank all my friends and family who have been so incredibly supportive of this extraordinary adventure. My dear friends, Jan, Jen and Theresa, my mum, dad, brother and sister-in-law (who built my website!), and my in-laws, have been my biggest cheerleaders. But I owe a very special thank you to my husband Phil and our wonderful children, Ellie and Sam. I love you all so much.

To anyone reading this book, you're absolute super stars for picking it up in the first place and I really hope you'll enjoy it!

Hello!

I'm waving wildly from my computer screen, and yes, I know I look a little bit crazy but don't worry, I'll stop in a minute, it's just the excitement.

Thank you so much for reading *The Little Theatre on the Seafront*. I realise that your time is precious and the fact that you decided to spend it with me is honestly, one of the greatest gifts I could ever be given. I truly appreciate it. Did you like *The Little Theatre*? I'd really love to know what you thought and would be so grateful if you left a review.

This was my first book with HQ Digital but I've another coming out in 2019 if you fancied reading that as well? Until then, we can keep in touch on my social media channels. You can always find me on my website: www.keginger.com; or on Facebook at: www.Facebook.com/KatieGAuthor. I also waste an inordinate amount of time on Twitter so why not stop by for a chat? I'm @KatieGAuthor if you fancy a chinwag!

HQ Digital publish loads of awesome writers, so if you're looking for something else in the meantime, have a shufti on their social media and see what you fancy!

Until we meet again, have a lovely time (you're looking fab by the way!) and I can't wait to see you again soon.

Katie

Dear Reader,

Thank you so much for taking the time to read this book – we hope you enjoyed it! If you did, we'd be so appreciative if you left a review.

Here at HQ Digital we are dedicated to publishing fiction that will keep you turning the pages into the early hours. We publish a variety of genres, from heartwarming romance, to thrilling crime and sweeping historical fiction.

To find out more about our books, enter competitions and discover exclusive content, please join our community of readers by following us at:

🐦 @HQDigitalUK

f facebook.com/HQDigitalUK

Are you a budding writer? We're also looking for authors to join the HQ Digital family! Please submit your manuscript to:

HQDigital@harpercollins.co.uk.

Hope to hear from you soon!

The next book from Katie Ginger is coming in 2019

If you enjoyed *The Little Theatre on the Seafront* then why not try another delightfully uplifting romance from HQ Digital?

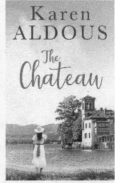